THE TRIAL OF

MISELLA

CROSS

A Novel

Catherine Witek

For Sheila —
I hope you enjoy the story.
Thank you!
Sincerely,
Catherine Witek

Sky Parlour Press
14855 South New Van Dyke Road, #832
Plainfield, Illinois 60544

First Sky Parlour Press paperback edition October 2012

For information about special discounts for bulk purchases, please contact Sky Parlour Press Special Sales at skyparlourpress@charter.net.

Cover Design by Bridget M. Hassan

Author Photo by Walter F. Piper

Manufactured in the United States of America

ISBN-13: 978-0615687971

ISBN 0615687970

The Library of Congress Catalogue No.: 2012915418
CreateSpace Independent Publishing Platform
North Charleston, South Carolina

For Hank

We are all prompted by the same motives, all deceived by the same fallacies, all animated by hope, obstructed by danger, entangled by desire, and seduced by pleasure.

Samuel Johnson
1751

Dark is the sun, and loathsome is the day.

Misella
1751

PROLOGUE

She crouched in the corner on a thin layer of straw, a child's linen shift clutched in her shackled arms. The sudden jangling of keys outside the cell door startled her—a new sound amidst the prisoners' screeching and the heavy footfall of the morning guard flipping open the feeding trap to shove through the daily bowls of porridge.

The heavy door scraped open, and a tall, bony-faced man in a long black jacket stepped inside, a garland of camphor hanging round his neck. In one gloved hand he balanced a wooden box with a Bible resting on top; in the other hand he dangled a ring of keys, the metal loop of a glowing lantern, and a large handkerchief saturated with vinegar. "Misella Cross," he thundered, "I am the Ordinary of Newgate prison. I bring God's comfort to you. I shall help you seek His forgiveness for your crimes."

He set the lantern on the floor away from the straw. Slipping the key ring over his wrist, he removed the Bible, tucking it up between the bars of the tiny window gouged into the thick stone wall above his head. Unlatching the box, he extracted a stack of parchment, a quill, pounce, and a small bottle of ink. He placed the closed box on the damp, filth-encrusted floor in front of her, arranging the writing materials on top.

"Here is the vehicle whereby you shall obtain His mercy. I hear you are a literate woman; thus may you set down your story in your own hand. Confess your sins; tell the story of your perdition so that other young maidens may learn from your woeful example." He pressed the handkerchief to his lips.

The harsh scent of vinegar watered her eyes. Squinting in the unaccustomed light, she stared at him for a few moments before she spoke. "I will need candles and my own lantern," she murmured, "a table and a stool."

He nodded, a thin smile slackening the grim line of his lips. Leaning down, he snatched the doll-size shift from her arms and tossed it, as if it were plague-ridden, onto the dirty straw.

She cried out, twisting away from him and scrabbling her bound hands forward in the straw to clutch the garment, but he kicked it toward the door. He yanked the chain between her wrists, the iron cuffs cutting into her flesh. "Your only hope for salvation," he hissed, "is to seek God's forgiveness whilst you can."

Her anger overcame her fear of him. "I've heard how you sell these confessions at the hangings, to fatten your purse," she blurted. "If you want my story, give the shift back to me now or I will write nothing."

He hesitated, his eyes narrowing to slits. With a sneer, he lifted the shift with the toe of his shoe and flipped it into her lap. "Keep it, to dry your tears on your way to the gibbet at Tyburn."

He leaned down, his pale eyes inches from hers, the pungent handkerchief clasped to his nose. "You will learn," he muttered, his voice muffled, "that those who cooperate with me fare much better here than those who do not." He stood up and drew forth a key from the ring, inserted it into the wrist irons and unlatched them without touching her skin. "You may keep the lantern," he snapped. Swinging the heavy chain, the iron cuffs clanging together, he moved into the passageway. "Guard," he yelled. "Bring me a table and a stool."

The Ordinary waited in silence, his eyes trained on her, until the guard appeared carting a small wooden table and a three-legged stool. "Over there." He signaled the guard to set the table against the wall and ordered him to leave the cell. Only then did he address Misella again. "Read the Word of God," he commanded. "Let Him inspire your confession and lead you to salvation."

Misella glanced at the Bible, then called out as he opened the door to leave. "You offer me hope of salvation. Liar. You have nothing to give but empty promises."

He slammed the cell door and turned the key.

Misella had known far better liars than he, and she no longer believed in hope or foolish pride. They had not served her well in her short life, but she was wiser now, and she could warn other young women.

Blood returning to her lifeless fingers, she picked up the box and the lantern, set them on the table and sat down on the stool. Prying open the vial of ink, she plunged the quill within. Words spilled onto the parchment.

I offer you my story, not a confession nor a plea for forgiveness but an honest and just description of my life. I must begin with the arrival of Lord Maltby's letter when I was a child of twelve, yet untainted and naïve, for that is when the lies, half-truths, tangled desires and fallacies of hope began to change my life.

PART I

CHAPTER 1

I discovered the letter hidden between the pages of the family Bible, a folded slice of parchment crisp as a starched ribbon, my mother's name, MARIETTE CROSS, in bold strokes across the center. Puzzled, I set the book on the candle-lit table and picked up the letter, studying the intricate design of the seal, a swirling letter M embedded deep within a circle of ivy, the leaves melting outward to its edges. Who was "M?" I wondered.

Despite the twinge to my conscience for violating my mother's trust and the sanctity of her hiding place, I read the letter, over and over, the words forever inscribed in my memory.

Hawthorn Manor
April 15, 1748

My Dear Mariette,

 Consider it accomplished. In your dear mother's memory and as your father's grateful heir, it is the least that I can do. With your description of the girls, you have convinced me that Misella is the best choice and can provide needed companionship for our lonely thirteen-year-old daughter Isobel. I pray that the twenty sovereigns and my willingness to take Misella into my home may ease your troubles and help you and your family survive this damnable war that threatens to make paupers of us all. Would that I sat already in Parliament to denounce that swindler Pitt and drive him from office so we can be rid of that war-mongering Whig for good. But Lady Sarah's uncle yet hangs on, refusing to relinquish his seat until his dying breath, it seems. Soon, soon, though, I will have my chance.

I will be traveling through Portsmouth on the first of May, hoping the roads will not be mud soup, and will stop briefly to collect her. As I await our meeting after all these years, I imagine you as lovely as the last time I saw you at the fountain in our gardens.

Your ever humble and obedient servant,
Richard Maltby

Tears flooded my eyes, I, who never cried—almost twelve, too old to cry, ashamed of myself. Anger, thick and hot, gathered in my chest. My mother intended to sell me like a cartload of fish. I wanted to rip the letter to pieces, crush the Maltby seal, throw the spidery writing into the fire, and make it disappear.

"Why me?" I ranted, my heart pounding with fury, my eyes smarting. "Why not bossy Elinor who hates this place and all the work Mother makes her do? Why not slow-witted Annabelle, who could be happy anywhere, with her vacant smile and silly rag doll?"

Wiping my face, I sat down at the scarred table, tracing my fingers along the letters dug with my quill, the twig-like M that had evolved over time into a graceful swirl of soft curves. My mother's initial, too. A demanding tutor, my mother insisted on teaching me from an early age to read and write. Though I resented the hard discipline, I took pride in my accomplishments, and I knew I was her favorite. At least I thought so until that day.

I could not bear the thought of leaving my home, though I hated the musty loft where I slept with my sisters, and complained about having to share my narrow pallet with fidgety Lizzie. I wanted to stay there, where I could tease Elinor and scoff at Annabelle and prod little Lizzie's damp backside away from me at night, and bounce giggling baby Lily on my knee; where I could see the light grow in my mother's eyes and hear her exclaim, "Well done, Misella," when we worked on lessons together; where I could watch my father mending his nets and slitting open the shimmering fish bellies and reading his Psalms at night in the candlelight.

Hope lifted my spirits when I thought of my father. Unmentioned in the letter, he could not have known about the betrayal, and I was certain he would never agree to give me away. How naïve and full of myself I was then.

Careful not to damage the seal, I folded the letter and reinserted it between the pages of the Bible. When the family returned from market at suppertime, I revealed nothing.

"Why so quiet, Misella? You have not finished your supper. Are you pouting, or are you not feeling well?" Mother brushed aside my curls and cupped my forehead in her coarse palm, the scent of fish strong on her fingertips. "Or is Elinor's fish stew not to your liking?"

I drew back and faced my older sister. "Elinor, the stew is good; I'm just not very hungry." Elinor leaned forward, ready to pounce, expecting me to shield my face from our parents and stick out my tongue or mouth the usual insults, "torchy," "bossy." But I only smiled and said, "I'm feeling fine, Mum. And I did not mind staying home today today because I'll be going to market with all of you next month as you promised this morning." I turned to Father hunched over his bowl scraping it clean with a crust of oak cake. "That will be after May Day is over, won't it, Father? Or will we be going on May Day, too?"

He nodded. "Yes, Misella, you'll go next time, on May Day. We won't leave you behind again to slave over your studies. I missed you today."

Tears of joy and relief clouded my eyes. Father never lied. I waited for Mother to mention the hidden letter, but she arose from her chair without a word, her face flushed, her eyes downcast. She scooped up the dirty bowls from the table and dropped them with a clatter on the crudely-hewn plank used as a sideboard. Whirling around, she whisked baby Lily from Annabelle's lap. "We had a long day, young ladies. Time for bed. I will do the cleanup tonight."

I dawdled until well after my sisters disappeared up the ladder, and then, before climbing to the loft, I said to Father mending his fish nets in front of the fire, "Ask her about the letter."

"What letter?" He removed the sacking needle from the torn fishing net in his lap and looked at me.

"The one from Richard Maltby," I whispered as Mother stepped between us, her face tightening into a frown as it did whenever I made mistakes with my lessons.

"Go up to bed, Misella," she ordered.

I stumbled up the ladder, my heart pounding. My hands trembling, I yanked off my shoes and wool stockings, hung my dress on the empty hook, and crept into bed, already shivering in my thin shift. Dry-eyed, I lay quiet on the pallet, my sisters' peaceful breathing whispering around me in the cramped loft. From below, Father's loud voice cut through the darkness. He seldom raised his voice, except when we girls strayed too near the edge of the dock, and he feared we would fall into the sea and be dashed against the rocks.

"We will not," he yelled, "sell Misella to be raised by that scoundrel. We will manage somehow —"

"How?" Mother demanded, her voice harsh. "Tell me just how we shall do that, Johnnie? And Richard is not a scoundrel."

"He's a stiff-rumped sharper who stole your inheritance, and you act like a toad-eater who can't wait to spit-polish his boots."

Mother's voice cooled and tightened. "You do not even know him. You have never met him."

I could tell that Mother was forcing herself to remain calm as she always did to control her anger. If she lost her temper, she might lash out with the truth, that she blamed Father for our hard life. I had noticed the disappointment on her face, the accusing look in her eyes when he trudged off to town with his half-empty fish cart. And though she would never say so, I think she blamed herself for running off in a moment of wild abandon to marry him.

When I asked her once how they met, she told me he had been a groundskeeper on her father's estate. "How could I not fall in love with handsome Johnnie Cross," she said smiling, "with the dark curls overwhelming his cap as he felled trees and tilled the soil, with the shy smile that crinkled his eyes whenever he saw me." She stopped kneading the oat dough for a moment, a faraway look in her eyes. "He was kind," she said softly, "and he adored me." She laughed. "How could I help myself? He beguiled me into

8

loving him, even though he had little fortune and no helpful connections. I did not care at the time."

But she did care now, and Father knew it. "I know how much you have given up, Mariette," he said in a softer voice.

Straining to hear him, I crept from my pallet to crouch on the ladder, the rung cold beneath my feet.

"You thought it was worth it," Father continued. "Love was all that mattered, you said. Or have you forgotten?" In the glow of the fire, he reached out and caressed her hair. "I am trying, Mariette, you know that, but I cannot fight the King's taxes. We can survive until things improve. And we are not going to starve simply because we keep Misella with us."

"With Richard's help," Mother persisted, "Misella will have a chance for a better life, a good marriage, and she can help the rest of us. Her brighter future will be ours as well. Once she marries, she could provide the means to help us withstand our losses and lighten the burden."

Afraid of crying out, I pressed my hand over my mouth, constricting my breath, a chill tingling in my legs and traveling up my spine. I had become a burden, like the clumsy wooden crates that bent the backs of the dock men who unloaded the ships at Portsmouth Bay.

"My daughters are not a burden," Father growled, his voice thick and hoarse. "I'll hear no more of this."

So vast was my relief when I heard his words that I almost flew down to hug him, but Mother snatched the letter from her pocket and thrust it into his roughened hands.

"Richard arrives on May Day," she said. She grabbed the candle sputtering in its lop-sided metal holder and slapped it down on the stone shelf above the fireplace. "Read the letter." From the rigid set of her shoulders as she stood over him and the slump of Father's as he read the letter, I feared that Mother would win the argument.

In tears I could no longer control, I clambered down the ladder, determined to change her mind. "Why can't Elinor go with him instead of me?' I pleaded. "She's the same age as his daughter."

Mother looked up, surprise and annoyance darkening her eyes. "Misella, please go back to bed. We'll talk more about this in the morning."

"Elinor would want to go. I don't," I cried, clutching my arms around the ache in my chest.

Mother's lips tightened, though her voice remained calm. "It has to be you, Misella. I cannot afford to lose Elinor's help with the household, and Annabelle would never do. She is not as smart as you, or as strong-willed. And you know Lizzie and Lily are much too young." She put her arm around my shoulders. "Ah, Misella," she sighed, her eyes dimming with rare tears, "I want more for you than you could ever find here with us. You are our sweet hope for the future."

With a lilt elevating her voice, she described how she first met Richard Maltby at her coming out party in London. "My father rented the entire grounds and the Rotunda at Ranelagh gardens for a Masquerade Ball. Everyone wore decorated masks that glowed as we danced for hours under a canopy of greenery strung with hundreds of small lamps." Her eyes shining, she seemed to forget where she was until Father dropped his net and uttered a rare curse.

She hugged me to her and lowered her voice to a murmur. "Soon, you will have what I once had, Misella. Diamonds will glitter in the curves of your powdered hair, and your jeweled fan will sparkle in the candlelight. You will wear hooped gowns of Parisian silk so wide at the hem you will have to inch sideways through doorways."

Her fairytale description aroused a twinge of excitement in me that I tried to ignore, but for a breathless moment I imagined myself in that silk gown, my hooped skirt dipping and bobbing as I danced around those magical gardens. Shutting my eyes, I pushed away from her, not wanting to see her lined face blooming to life. Confused and frightened, I feared that the radiance in Mother's eyes, the enchantment of her words, might somehow infect me and rob me of my fragile hope of convincing Father to let me stay at home where I felt safe.

"I know you are worried and sad at the thought of leaving us, Misella," Mother crooned, "but Sir Richard will take care with your feelings, and in a short time his daughter Isobel will seem like another sister to you."

Tears erupting again, my voice rising, I confronted Father as he hunched in his chair, the frayed net a tangled heap on the floor. "I don't need another sister," I cried. "Do I, Father? Why should I have to go and leave you? Why?"

Shaking his head in silence, he glanced away from me, trying to hide the guilt and defeat in his eyes. He picked up the damaged fish net, patched

10

and tarred in a useless effort to keep the strands intact. With fear coursing through me, I remembered him telling Mother one night soon after Lily was born, when he thought we were all asleep in the loft, that half of his take had squirmed through the gaps and escaped. "The story of my life," he sighed. "Never enough. The money slipping away while the burden increases."

Hope dissolving, my worry far deeper now than the vague unease those forgotten words had aroused in me at the time, I faced their silent complicity. "Please don't send me away," I begged. "I promise I won't be a burden."

Mother's expression hardened, her eyebrows tightening into a familiar frown. "Please understand, Misella. We no longer have a choice."

CHAPTER 2

After a restless night, I awoke late that May Day morning to the incessant sounds of sea water lapping against the wharf, the bells of Portsmouth's Church tower tolling through the mist, the gulls screaming across the water. Curled tight under the rough blanket on my pallet, I listened to the sounds of the island for the last time, resenting anew Mother's cheery reminders that soon I would awake to the sun climbing the honeysuckled walls of Hawthorn Manor to break through my lace-ruffled bedroom windows.

"Be quick, Misella," she called up to the loft. "We have little time."

I forced myself up and slipped a woolen shawl over my shift, winding it snuggly around me, as if to keep myself there, just as I was. But I had no say in the matter. It would do no good to cry anymore. I had tried that for a fortnight, but the flood of tears and tantrums met with sunny platitudes from Mother, about how much I would love my elegant surroundings and new adventures, and dark, brooding silence from Father. His betrayal cut into my heart more deeply than did my mother's though I still nurtured a shred of hope that he might change his mind.

After days of rain and fog, a patch of sunlight flickered at the open doorway of our smoky kitchen, mocking my low spirits. The smell of the burning bindweed from the fireplace made me gag. I hoped it would sicken Sir Richard, too, and drive him from the cottage, or that Father, when he returned from market, would throw the intruder out.

Despite Mother's urging, I refused to pack my bag. "I want to wait," I insisted. "I can do it later." She gave in to this small rebellion without an argument.

Mother thrust Lily onto Elinor's lap and retrieved a bucket of water warming in the fireplace. "Come Misella, you must dress," she ordered, ushering me behind the rag quilt curtain that hid my parents' makeshift bedroom from view. Like a prisoner about to be incarcerated, I knew I could not escape. I lacked the power to defend myself.

The used pink gown Mother had haggled for on market day shimmered from a wooden peg, its wide lace sleeves and collar gathering like pale sea foam at the wrists and neck. She had stitched a matching ribbon that she stiffened in potato water and shaped into a bow for my hair.

Refusing to speak, my lips clenched, I pulled off my wrinkled shift and washed quickly with a length of torn muslin before slipping into a clean linen shift and a petticoat.

"Now please don't start crying again," Mother pleaded, pulling her horsehair brush through my tangled curls. "You don't want your eyes red and swollen when Sir Richard arrives."

Holding back the tears, I rubbed my eyes hard anyway, trying to redden them as much as I could.

Scooping up a handful of ringlets, Mother gently anchored them back with the stiff bow. "So sensitive and creamy your skin," she murmured, smoothing her thumb across my cheek. I yanked my head away from her touch.

She dressed me for the journey as if I were a porcelain doll that might crack if mishandled. Holding the cloud of pink silk above my head, she let it whisper into place, her fingers looping the rows of tiny pearl buttons. "Ah, Misella, our beautiful, brave girl." She sighed, her eyes filling with tears, and hugged me to her for a moment. "So much like me when I was your age," she murmured, her voice cracking. "Now, please, go sit by the open door away from the fire and watch for the carriage."

Breaking away from her, I kicked the wash bucket on the way out. Soapy water splashed over my polished shoes and stained my white stockings. "I'm not sorry," I muttered, leaving the mess behind for her to clean up.

A lonely sentinel, I slumped onto the low kitchen stool by the open door and waited for Sir Richard's carriage to break through the block of yew trees that twisted along the curved road at the town's edge. To pass the time I counted the snuff-colored puddles strewn along the rutted road

14

until the sun slashed through the clouds, stippling the broken planks that led from the muddy roadway to our cottage door. In that burst of sunlight, four glistening horses whipped around the bend pulling a dark carriage, majestic against the distant shoreline. With a frightening inner confusion of excitement and dread, I watched as the coach drew near, my breath aching in my throat. The horses pulled to a stop in the roadway, their frenzied hooves kicking up clots of mud, the driver arching his back over the taut reins and shouting "Hoa! Hoa!"

Mother hurried through the open doorway to stand in waiting on the mud-spattered planks. "Richard, Richard," she sang, her voice soft, so perhaps only I could hear it, her face glowing with color. She had rouged her cheeks and lips and piled her hair in pale swirls atop her head. Her best mended shawl was bunched at the neckline, held together by her reddened hands. Her apronless skirt flapped in the stiff sea breeze.

The carriage door opened and Sir Richard emerged wearing a scarlet cloak and knee-length leather boots. Stepping down onto a small fringed stool his driver had placed for him in the mud, he balanced himself there before stepping onto the plank.

For a moment, surprise and curiosity overcame my trepidation. He wore no hat or wig, though his fair brown hair was arranged to look like a wig, with rolled side curls brushing his ears. The rest of his hair rippled into a thick tail gathered in the back with a narrow ribbon. His face was youthful and smooth, free of whiskers and pock marks. *He's not old, and he's more handsome than Father.* The guilty thought flashed through my mind.

The wind whipped his cloak against the buckled tops of his boots. I thought of the drawing I had seen in one of Mother's books of the highwayman Dick Turpin, resplendent in cape and boots, swirling with musket in hand to face his adversaries.

Mother floated forward to meet him, calling his name. He stared at her for a moment, and then grinning, sang, "Mariette, Mariette, won't you marry me."

She laughed. "Oh, Richard, not that old, worn out tune."

He grasped her in his arms and drew her close, trying not to lose his footing on the wobbly plank.

I slid back from the doorway as she led him up the walkway, apologizing for the rundown appearance of the cottage.

"I hope my letters prepared you for this desolate place, Richard. I call it our little shack at the end of the world." She sighed. "I do what I can for the girls."

I wanted to burst through the doorway and confront them, order Sir Richard to leave, but I sat in silent misery staring at the two accomplices trying to trick me and Father into believing that being wealthy was more important than being happy.

Sir Richard leaned close and brushed the back of his hand along Mother's cheek. "And my dear I want to do what I can for you. I had no idea where you had gone, and your father ignored my inquiries." He seemed about to kiss her but stepped back still holding her hand. "I had no say in the matter of the Will, you know. I hope you did not, do not, hold me responsible."

She leaned away, her head down, her voice low. "You had announced your betrothal to Sarah Wentworth. How could I compete with the daughter of an Earl?

He placed his fingers on her lips as if to silence her. "I was but a boy, Mariette, only twenty-two. She meant nothing to me. She was my father's choice, not mine. You disappeared before I could explain. You were a goddess to me. I loved you. I did not want to lose you, and I have regretted my marriage all these years."

She hesitated for a moment. "Too late to dwell on the past, Richard," she murmured. "I made my choice, too. Against my father's wishes."

My face grew hot. I wanted to yell at her to hush, to hurry inside before Father came home and saw her like that with Sir Richard.

Mother led him into the kitchen. He stooped as he came through the doorway, for he was taller than Father. I moved back nearer the fireplace and waited. She bustled forward and pulled Eliza to her, brushing a lock of her hair away from her face. "This is our little Lizzie, six years old and all better now, though we almost lost her to the pox." To my surprise, Lizzie, never shy with strangers, hung back, clutching Mother's skirt in one hand. With the other she drew a string of brown hair into her mouth and chewed, refusing to look at Sir Richard. I thought perhaps his fancy clothes and deep voice frightened her.

Sir Richard tried to take Lizzie's hand. "I am happy to meet you, lovely Eliza." But she pulled her hand away and buried her face in Mother's skirts.

In the background, Elinor tucked her damp curls, coiling like fish guts as I called them, under her sagging linen cap and pulled down the sleeves of her brown dimity to cover her freckled forearms. She came forward, curtsied, and murmured, "Welcome, Sir Richard," but he didn't seem to notice her. Her face flamed bright red as he focused his attention on Annabelle.

I almost felt sorry for Elinor, but my own worries hardened my heart and triggered my usual mockery toward her. I stuck out my tongue and mouthed, "Torchy," behind Mother's back. Elinor hated the nickname I gave her in honor of her wildfire red hair and the way her face flushed crimson whenever I provoked her. She raised her fist at me, her curled lips forming the word, "Brat."

"You are Lady Annabelle, I presume. And you are, let me see, ten years old." Annabelle giggled and reached out to shake the ungloved hand he held out to her. "Ah, my Lady, those copper curls could make a sunset jealous." He smiled at her and turned to me.

"And Misella," his hand warm and smooth in mine. "I would know you anywhere. You are your Mother in miniature, the same radiant blue eyes and sassy blonde curls." I wanted to slap his hand away, stamp my foot, shout at him, "I am not my mother," but I lowered my head and said nothing. He squeezed my limp fingers, and, withdrawing his hand, unbuttoned his heavy cloak.

Mother took the cloak from him and hung it carefully by the door. "Please sit, Richard." She drew him to Father's chair, and, her hands on his wide shoulders, pushed him gently into it. "Elinor will bring you some of her special tea and biscuits." Elinor withdrew to the sideboard to prepare the tea and to set out the oat flour biscuits she baked earlier that morning.

"And while you have your tea, Richard, Misella will read a brief passage for you from the Book of Psalms." She motioned me to come forward and handed me the Book she had ready on the table. "We may be poor, Richard," she said, seating herself next to him, "but Misella can read and write as if she had attended the finest London boarding school."

"Well, Misella." Sir Richard lifted a sugared biscuit to his lips and took a small bite. "I am listening." He took a slow sip of tea.

Turning to Psalm 45, I read the lines Mother had selected. *"Hearken, O daughter, and consider, and incline thine ear; forget also thine own people and thy father's house: So shall the king greatly desire thy beauty: for he is thy Lord: and worship thou him."*

Sir Richard laughed and raised his cup to Mother.

Snapping the Book shut, I began to recite the first of Mother's two favorite Shakespearean sonnets from her youthful days. *"No more be griev'd at that which thou hast done: / Roses have thorns, and silver fountains mud:/Clouds and eclipses stain both moon and sun:/ And loathsome canker lives in sweetest bud."*

Sir Richard stared at Mother throughout my sing-song recitation, his eyes never leaving her face as she raised her trembling cup to her lips. She told me to keep going, so I did. *"Since brass, nor stone, nor earth, nor boundless sea. /But sad mortality o'er-sways their power. / How with this rage shall beauty hold a plea. / Whose action is no stronger than a flower?"*

The sound of Father's cart banging along the planks outside interrupted me. We heard a thud as he propped it against the side of the hut before he entered bringing in the briny smell of fish. Scowling, he removed his cap and tossed it in the corner along with one of his fishing nets.

Sir Richard settled his cup into the saucer and stood, smoothing the creases and brushing the crumbs from his garnet jacket. "Brava, Misella," he said. "You are learning the power of the written word, and the pleasure it can bestow. Thank you." He hesitated for a moment before stepping forward and holding out his hand. "Mr. Cross," he said, "Richard Maltby."

Mother rose from her chair and put her arm around me. Father glanced at us and my sisters. He rubbed his hand along the front of his woolen vest and returned the handshake without a word.

Mother dropped her arm from my shoulders and began twisting the fringe of her shawl between her fingers. "Elinor, get your father a cup of tea. Isn't it wonderful for all of us, Johnnie, that Misella will have a chance to travel and to learn?"

Father remained standing, motioning Elinor to set his tea on the table. I held my breath, waiting for the storm to break, for him to holler, "No," at Mother, to tell Sir Richard to leave our home and never come back, but it was Sir Richard who spoke.

"Johnnie, I would be most happy to accept Misella into my home, to welcome her into our family."

"No."

The word escaped into the room, from me, not from Father. When Sir Richard looked at me, I turned away, leaning down to pick up Lily who tottered over and clung to my skirt.

Father spoke, his voice firm. "She cannot go, Mariette. She has cried for weeks, more upset than I have ever seen her. She does not want to part with us." He reproached Sir Richard without looking at him. "This, Sir, is a mistake. We will survive without your charity."

My heart soaring, I hugged Lily so hard she began to whimper. "I'm sorry, Lilylu," I whispered, nuzzling her ear.

Sir Richard leaned toward Father, his face flushed. "I do understand, Johnnie. I am here only because Mariette has asked for my help which, as her father's heir, I feel obligated to provide. But this arrangement is only temporary, until things improve for you—and believe me, they will. Once the King comes to his senses, he'll end this bloody war, and trade will balloon not only on the Continent, but with the Indies and America as well."

Mother broke in. "Go and pack your things, Misella," she said quietly. "I will be up to help you in a moment."

"Do you wish this, Misella?" Father asked, his voice low and somber as if he were reading a psalm to me as he often did.

Mother's hope-filled eyes implored me to do this for her and for our family, as if their very survival depended on me. I stared at her worn face and glanced at Father's fishing net waiting to be mended. In a small voice, my throat barely squeezing out the words, I answered. "I–I would like to see Surrey, and the rolling hills and gardens and all the things I have never seen."

Mother smiled, taking Lily from my arms and handing her to Elinor. "It is settled," she said, putting her arm around me. She led me to the loft ladder, my chest as tight as if I had the croup, stealing my breath and silencing my voice. As I mounted the ladder alone, I glanced back at Father, but he had already gone outside, leaving his tea untouched on the table.

I had little to pack in my small woolen bag: a nightshirt Mother had mended, an extra linen shift, a clean but faded muslin day dress, a few hair ribbons and darned stockings.

Mother climbed the ladder, her face aglow, one arm cradling a small wicker basket from her bedroom. She took out a covered jar. "Goose grease, Misella, to rub on your face and hands each night, though I'm sure Lady

19

Sarah will soon replace this for you with better creams." Next, she presented me with a fine linen handkerchief embroidered with delicate forget-me-nots. "I have kept this," she murmured, her voice catching, "since I left my home fifteen long years ago." She tucked it inside the pocket of my gown.

Hesitating for a moment, she drew forth her silver-backed hair brush, tracing her fingers along the lines of her family crest hammered into the silver. "The most valued possession from my past, Misella. I want you to have it and to remember that I love you whenever you use it." After she slipped the brush and the jar of goose grease into my bag, she hugged me to her. "You take my heart with you," she whispered into my curls.

I stood rigid as a statue in her arms, silent and unmoved by her words, wanting to punish her for sending me away.

When we descended to the kitchen, Sir Richard was waiting at the door. "We must hurry, Misella," he said. "We want to reach Aldworth by nightfall, and Surrey by tomorrow evening."

"Hug your sisters good-bye," Mother urged. "Your father is waiting outside."

I hugged each of my younger sisters, but Elinor avoided me. I knew how jealous and angry she was. She had always resented me for being Mother's favorite. Even when I was too little to defend myself, she would pinch my leg under the table or mess my hair after Mother brushed it. When I grew older, Elinor sneered at my ability to read and write because she never had the time or the patience herself to learn.

Yet now, I wanted to whisper in her ear that I was sorry, that I would gladly change places with her, but when I reached out to hug her, she pushed me away. "Little strumpet," she whispered. "Mother's little pet."

Outside, Father waited next to the carriage, his shoulders slumped, hands clutching the worn copy of the Psalms. He thrust the little book into my hands. "I know you'll be back with us soon," he said. "Until that day, read from these each night."

"But Father," I protested, "this is yours. What will you do when you want to read your psalms?"

"I know them all by heart, my girl. When you learn them too, you can return the book to me." He embraced me and kissed me on the forehead.

I slipped the book into my pocket. Blinking back tears, I thought of him empty-handed in front of the fire, missing me. Mother came forward and kissed me. She hugged Sir Richard and made way for the coachman who helped me onto the stool and into the carriage.

I almost forgot my sorrows as I settled into the plush cushion and stared at the amber silk-lined walls, the green velvet curtains drawn back to expose the shining windows. *A glass coach*, I thought, *like the drawing I saw in one of Mother's books.* The inside smelled of lavender and honeysuckle.

When Sir Richard entered, the coach tilted. I felt the plunge as he heaved himself inside, smiling wide. He sat opposite me, his cloak fanning out to cover the seat. The coachman closed the door. Sir Richard lounged against the seatback, his fingers stroking the soft-looking leather gloves he held in his lap. "You may miss your family at first, Misella," he said, "but you will make new friends and have such adventures that soon you will forget the sadness of leaving your little home."

I did not reply. I leaned my cheek against the glass as the carriage drew away from the cottage. Sitting upright, I waved at Mother standing at the edge of the plank, her skirt flapping, and at Father, who stood shoe-deep in the mud, without his cap. I waved until I could no longer see them, until the carriage rounded the bend and lurched toward Hawthorn Manor.

CHAPTER 3

Alone with Sir Richard in the coach, I clutched the rope handle of my bag and stared out of the window at the ragged shoreline as we made our way across Portsbridge over the canal that united the island to Portsmouth Harbour. Against the horizon, the azure hills of Wight melted into the cloudless sky, and on the left, boats of every size left the harbor, their white sails gradually diminishing until they were lost in the distance. *Like me*, I thought.

Sir Richard leaned forward to capture my attention. "Will you miss the sea, Misella? The roar of the waves?"

I shook my head without looking at him. "Father calls it music," I said, "the constant rustling of the waves against the shore. The heart beat of the sea, he says. But I dislike the dark, dirty water." Sir Richard laughed. I felt his gaze on me and blushed.

"No need to be embarrassed when I look at you, Misella, and admire you. You have the face of a young Boticelli Madonna." He set his gloves aside and reached out as if to take my free hand, but I clasped it in my lap. "You will soon find many men staring at you, fighting for your company." He patted my knee instead and smiled when I looked at him. The shine and color of his dark eyes reminded me of a print Father once showed us of the amazing cuttlefish, he said, with its human-like eyes and ink brown secretions. I tried to smile back. To this day in my dreams, I often encounter those luminous eyes devouring me.

We entered Portsmouth's High Street and passed by the stone slaughter house squatting at the end of the street. I remembered Father telling us one night at supper that this huge, decaying structure used to be the old government house. "See how things can degrade," he had said. "What used to be a suitable home for persons of the most exalted rank is now converted to the lowest and most ignoble purposes." In front of that historic building, he added, shone a brass bust of Charles I with an inscription describing the dangers the hunted King encountered by sea and land before arriving in Portsmouth in 1623, and the joy felt throughout the kingdom that he was safe. The thought that I might not visit Portsmouth again for a long time or hear Father's stories at the supper table increased the pressure in my chest and dampened my eyes.

The coach began to move with great speed when we left Portsmouth, flying over the bumpy road so fast my ears rang, and I bounced up and down like Father's tethered fishing boat fighting the waves in a wind storm. I grasped the seat cushion with both hands and held on tight.

Sir Richard patted my clenched fist. "Don't worry, Misella, Jack Finn is the best driver in England, and he knows these roads like no other coachman. No highwayman will catch him."

"Highwayman? Could we be robbed or even killed?"

Sir Richard shook his head. "Jack can shoot a musket with the accuracy of an eagle eye. But just in case. . . " He swung his leg up and rested his leather boot on his knee. He pushed a tiny lever on the inside of the heel, and the bottom popped open. A blue velvet bag tied round the top with a thin leather string clinked into his hand. He untied the string, opened the bag and showed me a stack of gold coins. "And even if they managed to overtake us, they won't find the money. We outwit the robbers," he boasted, returning the bag to its hiding place. "Jack and I are a team."

Soon we pulled onto a smoother road. Sir Richard lifted the window next to me, sliding its wooden pegs into place to hold it open. I leaned out, the stiff breeze whipping my collar across my mouth and nose. I tried to catch a glimpse of Jack on his high seat, wondering if he brandished a musket at the ready in his hand. But I could not see him. I drew my head back inside and asked Sir Richard, "Does Jack carry the whip-cord in his mouth? Are his front teeth filed down so he can hold it? Does he strike the horses?"

Sir Richard smiled. "He never strikes them, I would never allow it. They are well-trained and so is Jack. Though he is but a lad of twenty-three, he knows how to handle horses. He has no need to carry the whipcord. It

24

rests against his seat. He only strikes it against the fore wheel to signal the horses to set off."

The coach slowed to a stop, and I caught my breath in fear of a highwayman, but it was only a toll gate up ahead. Jack's shout rang out into the early evening's fading light, "Pike. Gate. Hallo. Lord Maltby here, open 'er up." The high white gates swung open and a gnarled-looking man in a tri-cornered hat waved us through, a speaking trumpet swinging from his belt, to warn of robbers, Sir Richard told me.

When we gained speed again, I watched the rows of wooden posts fly by on the side of the high road, their whitewashed tops chasing the coach through the deepening twilight like a band of ghostly outlaws on its trail. The coach slowed again when we came to a crossroad where three roads splayed out before us. Ahead stood a tall cross, painted white like the fence posts, rising up where the roads joined together. A dark figure clung to it as if to keep from being blown away by the wind.

As the coach drew closer, I heard its dark cape snapping against the post and saw its white wig twisted sideways, the hair lifting and spreading and glowing like floss in the rising moonlight. I thought it a strange place to hang a scarecrow, but as the coach pulled alongside it and Jack veered to the road on the left, I saw its face. Greenish-black skin like the head of a fly pulled away from the black cave of its gaping mouth; protruding white eyeballs glittered like huge polished pearls; a thick rope bundled round the scrawny neck pulled the head up so that the colorless eyes stared at me as it dangled in the wind.

When I screamed, Sir Richard leaned forward and squeezed my hand. "A dead highwayman, Misella. I guess you have never seen one."

I shook my head, unable to speak.

"You will see more of them, especially when you travel to London. Wherever a robbery has taken place on the King's Highway. Highwaymen are hanged where captured."

Swaying with the coach as it moved faster and faster, I shut my eyes, but I could still see that blackened body. I bit my bottom lip to keep from crying, remembering a gull I had seen once trapped on the shore, a broken fishing line tangled round its lifeless wings. I reached into my pocket for the worn book of psalms, gripping it tightly as if holding on to Father's hand. I thought of him murmuring the psalms as he sat by the fire, and I felt sorry about teasing Elinor so often. I wished I had tried harder to be kind like him and sweet like Annabelle.

I kept my eyes closed for a long time until Sir Richard spoke. "Did your mother tell you that you are to be a companion to my thirteen-year-old daughter, Isobel? She is lonely and needs companionship. She spends too much time in the company of Lady Sarah, her mother."

"Why didn't you take Elinor?" I blurted out. "She is the same age as your daughter, and she would be a much better friend for her."

He laughed, his generous mouth opening wide to show his grinders, as Father would call them, tinged slightly gray against the pure white of his ruffled neckline. "Ah, Misella, Isobel doesn't need a cook maid, she needs a smart girl like you who can read and write and recite with ease. Isobel struggles with her studies. She does not like to learn, so you can inspire her to try harder."

He began to describe the lush landscape of Surrey, more beautiful, he said, than the drab countryside we now passed through. "In Surrey," he exclaimed, "as far as you can see, the hills unfold like bolts of emerald velvet covered with multi-colored wildflowers."

I sat up. "Like a rainbow?"

Sir Richard nodded and leaned forward, his face close enough that I could smell the faint scent of mint tea on his breath. "Our house, enclosed behind miles of matching stone walls, nestles between softly rising hills." He reached out, brushing my neck with the back of his fingers. "At sunset, the house glows like a ruby pendant on the necklace of a goddess."

"Oh," I marveled, forgetting my fears, "I cannot wait to see it!"

He leaned even closer. "Have you ever seen a maze, Misella?" he purred. "Behind the house lies a maze, a puzzle not easy to solve. Yew trees, taller than me, zig zag from its entrance to a marble fountain and a domed hermitage hidden in its center like a Garden of Eden."

I clasped my hands together, my breath quickening. "I've never seen a maze, but I am good at solving puzzles. Much better than my sisters. I always won when we played games."

Sir Richard leaned back and sighed. "Poor Isobel has tried to reach the hermitage many times, but has always had to be rescued by the gardener or me." He raised one eyebrow and stared at me. I could not look away from his probing eyes that seemed to challenge me to do better than Isobel, and I knew I would.

The clatter of horses' hooves striking stone broke the spell of his gaze. The coach had entered the brick courtyard of the Maid's Head Inn, Sir Richard explained, where we would spend the night and head for Surrey early the next morning.

When Jack Finn opened the coach door, I studied him. A mass of black curls bounced around his head as he bent down to place the stool. As he stood back up, he noticed my stare. With a grin, he winked one blue eye at me, and I could see that his fine white teeth were not filed down at all. Sir Richard stepped down and reached to help me, his smooth hand curling around my fingers. How different from Father's hard, bumpy hand, I thought, and Mother's rough red ones.

"You won't need your bag, Misella," Sir Richard said. "Travelers sleep in their clothes." We made our way together to the open front door of the noisy inn.

A large shiny-faced woman in a lace cap stumbled forward with a big smile. "Ah, welcome back, Sir. Do we need a room again? One room for you and your lovely, ahh, daughter? A little beauty she is, Sir." She winked at Sir Richard. I thought her very rude to treat Sir Richard as if he were her equal.

Several men, many dressed like Sir Richard, sat at small tables scattered around a smoke-filled room drinking from tankards or goblets and smoking cigars. One gentleman wore spectacles that flashed and seemed to wink at me in the bright candlelight. Rows of reddish-brown curls thicker than my own framed his face and tumbled down his fat cheeks to rest in a tangled clump on his heavy shoulders. He waved his cigar at Sir Richard. "Hi-ho, Maltsy, come have a bumper with us. Bring your pretty little Miss with you. Has the old Fumbler died off yet? We've your Parliament seat all dusted and waiting for you."

His companion at the table half stood, his face flushed and damp above his crumpled neck piece. Wobbling from side to side, he thumped his goblet on the table and hollered, "Come rescue me, Maltsy, from this tiresome Lord Booby, this gentleman of three outs—without money, without wit, and without manners."

At another table a man with a broad gray mustache raised a silver tankard and grinned when he saw me staring at him. I looked away, not liking his attention. Where are the women or other children, I wondered. They must have all retired for the night.

Sir Richard ignored the gentlemen and in a stern voice told the grinning woman in the lacy cap that we would need two private rooms, each with a fireplace. "Be sure there are clean sheets on the beds," he ordered, "and locks on the doors. And bring a tray to the young lady's room with the day's special and a pot of tea. We will be up as soon as the rooms are ready."

The woman shrugged her wide shoulders and headed to the kitchen, calling to one of the maids to hurry up and finish serving because she had rooms to prepare.

Sir Richard steered me away from the noise into a smaller room with a fireplace. He took a silver case from his pocket, pressed a tiny lever to open it and drew out a slim cigar which he lit from a taper on the mantle. He stood in front of me as if to shield me from the other room and smoked without saying a word. I leaned against a chair back, warmed by the fire and sleepy enough to forget any fears about what lay ahead.

When a maid with a lantern came to get us, we followed her up wide carpeted stairs to a door at the end of a long, shadowed hallway. "Here we go, Miss." She opened the door and motioned me into a large bedroom. A huge four-post bed piled high with feather mattresses stood against a crimson silk-lined wall; a wooden stepstool rested on the rose-carpeted floor beneath the bed. A breeze from the tall, open window across from the bed rippled the pink velvet draperies and stirred the filmy lace curtain surrounding the bed. Wax candles burned on a mahogany table, set for dinner in front of a glowing fireplace. I thought perhaps I had fallen asleep and dreamed.

Sir Richard called softly from the doorway, "Sleep well, Misella, and be sure to lock your door. You'll need a good night's rest. We will be leaving at sunrise. We have a long way to go tomorrow."

The maid told me to step outside and ring the bell sitting on the landing table if I needed anything more, and the door whispered shut behind her. I locked the door and sat down in awe to the finest meal I had ever seen—a juicy beef steak bigger than my fist, fat potatoes with salt butter,

Cheshire cheese, and a plum pudding crusted with sugar. A silver knife and fork, with the letters M & H intertwined with flowers on the handles, lay next to a gold-trimmed china plate. A matching tea set steamed on an embossed napkin. Like the fine lady of a manor house, I dined until I could no longer keep my eyes from closing.

Unbuttoning my dress as far as I could reach, I tugged it over my head, not wanting to crush it while I slept, and laid it carefully on an overstuffed chair in front of the fireplace. I untied and dropped my petticoat, climbed the little staircase, and flopped onto the deep foamy sea of the mattress. Pulling the embroidered counterpane up to my chin, I stared at the shadowy canopy over my head, the firelight skipping there like bright stones across dark water. *If Mother and Father could see me now, and Elinor and Annabelle. Father would want to pick me up and carry me back home.* Without permission, my throat began to close, and tears threatened to tumble from my eyes, but I held them back, settling down in the wide, empty bed.

Faint laughter and a voice that sounded like Sir Richard's seeped through the wall and kept me from sleep. A man cried out as if in pain, and a woman screamed. *No, it cannot be him. He would not hurt anyone.* Frightened, I sat up, wondering if I should ring the bell to call the maid. I held my breath and waited, but all remained quiet.

Sinking back among the pillows, I drifted into sleep until a clicking noise awoke me. The doorknob circled back and forth, followed by a persistent knocking and whispering. *Sir Richard checking to see if I am all right,* I thought. Climbing down from the bed, I hastened to the door and drew back the lock.

The heavy door flew open, the hall lantern illuminating the outline of the fat man with the red curls. He lunged forward and grabbed my bare shoulders. Stumbling into the room, he fell against me, pushing me to the floor. I screamed and tried to roll away from his mountainous stomach. Thick, grease-scented fingers slapped across my nose and mouth. "Shhh, shhh. No need to wake the house, little lady. I'll be done with my business in a minute." His other hand fumbled with the buttons of his breeches.

Kicking hard, the way I did when Elinor would pin me to the floor for calling her names, I tried to claw his hand away from my mouth, but could not pull free. Unable to breathe, an old childhood nightmare returned as

I began to lose consciousness. I felt myself sinking slowly into the dark, dirty water near the dock, dragged down to the bottom of the sea.

Grunting, the attacker rolled off of me, and his hand fell away from my mouth. I gasped with shuddering breaths.

"What the bloody hell do you think you are doing? Get up you cork-brained fumbler ...." Sir Richard stood above us, his shirt hanging loose over his breeches, a red smear across his cheek, his face and eyes aflame with fury in the light of the taper that shook in his hand.

The man rose up on to his hands and knees coughing, a thread of dark spittle dangling from his lips. He tried to pick himself up. Sir Richard stepped around him and leaned down to me, his free hand outstretched. "Hush, now, Misella. You're all right now." He grabbed my wrist and lifted me to my feet, holding the taper away from the tangled mass of my hair. "You're not hurt, are you?"

I shook my head, trying to stop the tears.

"This was all a mistake. Lord Banfry has had too much to drink. Thought he was at home looking for his wife. Isn't that right, Banfry?"

Lord Banfry mumbled something, swaying and clutching his side with one meaty fist and wiping the slobber from his lips with the other.

"Hold this." Sir Richard handed me the taper and gave his attention to Banfry. Grabbing his arm and the back of his wide collar, he dragged Banfry to his feet. Breathless from the effort, he gasped, "You owe Misella an apology, Sir."

Lord Banfry groped inside the crushed lapels of his jacket and pulled out a pair of wire-framed glasses, shoving them half-hazardly onto his nose. He gaped at me through the twisted frames, but I looked away, frightened and shivering in my damaged shift.

"Sorry there, little Miss, for the mistake. No harm meant."

He mumbled to Sir Richard, "Didn't know she was your nug, Maltsy. Just trying to avoid getting peppered with the clap, you know. You should have warned me earlier."

Sir Richard ushered him to the doorway and pushed him through without another word. With a stern face, he asked, "Did you forget to lock your door, Misella?"

The taper wobbling in my hand, I shook my head, sorry to have caused trouble and displease him. "I—I did lock it, but I thought it was you meaning to tell me something. I'm very sorry."

His face relaxed. He reached for the taper and patted me on the head. "You have much to learn, Misella. Quick now, lock the door after me and get to bed. We have only a few hours until morning. You're safe now. I'm here."

Still shaking, I locked the door and climbed into bed, but I could not sleep, unable to erase the image of Lord Banfry groping at the buttons on his britches, his rancid smell, the sound of his panting, the feel of him crushing me against the floor. I jumped up in the darkness and stumbled to the chair in front of the dying fire. Plunging my hand into the deep pocket of my gown, I grasped the forgotten book of psalms. I carried it back to bed, holding it tight as I fell asleep.

In the morning, we had a quick breakfast of biscuits and sausages, though I ate little before climbing into the coach. Sir Richard did not mention the late-night incident, and I stayed very quiet, huddled in a corner of the coach, looking out the window at the bleak, overcast sky until my eyes closed. Exhausted, I slept most of the way to Surrey until Sir Richard shook me awake to say we would soon arrive at Hawthorn Manor. Through the rain-speckled glass I glimpsed a massive brick wall that seemed to be holding the land in, or keeping the world out. The coach rolled to a stop in front of a grand set of filigreed iron gates, the gold Maltby crest centered within each side.

Jack Finn swung down from his high seat, his green coat swirling open to reveal his breeches tied at each knee with multi-colored strings. He opened the gate and clicked the horses through. After slamming the gate shut, he climbed back up and set the horses moving again.

We trotted down a curved roadway loosely defined on each side by sprawling hawthorn trees, a surprising contrast to the orderly brick wall, their twisted branches alive with white-edged buds about to spring open. Shimmering lawns, stained yellow-green by the rain, arched into gentle slopes that drew my gaze forward to the mansion poised like a giant bird, its stone wings clutching the landscape.

"Home," Sir Richard murmured.

The coach stopped alongside a stone portico flanked by polished white columns. A wide set of granite stairs led up to broad double doors, a pattern of leafy vines carved into the wood, the stained glass windows alight with color despite the gloomy skies. The doors swung open, and a trio of servants scurried down the steps. A tall black-coated man assisted Sir Richard from the carriage first, mumbling a welcome. Stiff-faced and silent, he lifted me down. Another reached in and grabbed my bag and whisked it up the stairs. A plain-faced woman waddled forward. "Hallo, hallo, Sir. And this is the little lady, is it? How do, Miss."

"This is Misella, Maggie." Sir Richard laid an ungloved hand on my shoulder. "Maggie will show you where to go." He nudged me forward. "Are her rooms ready, Maggie?"

Maggie's face reddened. "Well, Sir, Lady Sarah arranged that before she left. I'm to take the miss to her room and get her settled in."

"Before she left?" Sir Richard's hand clenched my shoulder, his fingers pinching the skin. "Where did she go?"

Maggie glanced at the black-dressed man standing next to Sir Richard and cleared her throat. "Uh, she and Isobel left yesterday for London. They'll be gone a fortnight, she said. She wanted to see Doctor Russell, the one with the seawater cure for weak hearts and fainting spells."

Sir Richard's mouth tightened. He snatched his hand away, snagging the collar of my gown. He drew a deep breath and uttered what sounded to me like the name Elinor had called me when I left home. He seemed to forget about me as he stomped up the steps, his cloak falling from his shoulders into the waiting arms of Black Coat.

Maggie huffed up behind them, seeming to forget about me and grumbling loud enough so I could hear her comments about "the blackguard," the "traitor" who made her Lady so miserable. "What does he care?" she mumbled. "He'd better be careful. She's warned him for the last time."

At the doorway she hesitated, twisted around and snarled, "Well, come along, little princess. I'll show you to your quarters. They've been vacant for a while now——since the last girl left."

At the time, I did not understand Maggie's anger or Sir Richard's. I trailed behind Maggie's swaying backside into the marbled hallway of the manor house, my confusion and worry increasing when I realized Sir Richard had vanished.

An enormous stairway filled the right side of the hall, its carved banister curving upward to a vaulted ceiling painted with billowing clouds and angels with trumpets floating in the air—like a vision from the Bible. Maggie bustled down a tiled hallway as wide as one of the inlets near Portsmouth harbor. Polished mahogany doors shone like dark mirrors along each side.

At the end of the hall loomed a large set of double doors. Maggie pulled them open and barged down the few steps into a huge sunken kitchen. A fireplace that could hold me and all of my sisters together covered half of one wall. Long tables cluttered with dishes lined the opposite wall. Several maids, dressed identically in gray cotton gowns with white starchy aprons and caps, bustled back and forth from the fireplace with pots and platters.

The maids looked up as we entered the room, but continued working without saying anything. Maggie led me to a small door on the far side of the room. She pulled it open to reveal a narrow bank of stairs. "Up there," she growled, pointing a knobby finger. "Keep going 'til you run out of stairs. The room at the top is yours. Miss Isobel left you a present, a doll she made for you." My bag lay in a heap on the bottom step. "Take your baggage." She kicked it with the toe of her scuffed boot and swung around to swat at one of the young maids struggling to carry a steaming cauldron to the table. "Move your arse, Peggy Slow Motion, or I'll move it for ya."

I hung the bag over my shoulder and began climbing as the door slammed shut behind me. The stairway was dusty and dark though a faint light descended from above. I tried not to brush against the grimy walls to avoid soiling my dress. Reaching a small landing with a closed door, I peeked behind me before opening the door a crack. An unlatched window at the end of a long narrow hallway provided light and a breath of cool air. Four doors were strung out along the hall, the maids' quarters, I guessed.

Easing the door closed I resumed climbing the winding stairs which became much narrower. I had to feel my way in the growing darkness to a cramped landing at the top where a strip of light outlined a warped wooden door. The door opened inward to a room not half the size of the loft at home. An uncurtained window beneath the roofline provided the glimmer of light. A small cot crouched in one corner under cobwebbed eaves. A three-legged stool held an unlit candle stub in a saucer of greasy tallow.

I dropped my bag on the bare planked floor and approached the bed where a rag doll sprawled face down atop the thin quilt. I picked it up and moved closer to the window. The doll had yellow yarn hair, tangled into curls, and chipped black button eyes. My name *MISELLA* was scrawled across the bodice in black ink, a sacking needle thrust between the letters, red dye staining the cloth around it.

Flinging the rag doll to the floor, I sank down on the cot, bewildered and scared by Maggie's anger and Isobel's cruel gift. The two of them, it seemed, had joined forces against me. I could not understand why they hated me so much without even knowing me. I had hoped to find a friend in Isobel, but now it seemed I must be wary, on my guard against both her and Maggie.

Seeking some distraction from my worries and curious to see what lay outside the gloomy room, I set the candle on the floor, pushed the stool against the wall beneath the window, and climbed up. Though streaked with soot, the glass offered me a sparrow's eye view of the back lawn of the estate with its geometric gardens: an enthralling array of squares and circles and triangles of flowerbeds etched with hedges, snaked with walking paths, and dotted with statues emerging from water fountains.

At the far end of the sloping lawn lay the maze Sir Richard had described on our journey, a dominating image in the fading light of late afternoon. From my vantage point, the sculptured maze enclosed a dizzying swirl of sea green circles within a widening series of carved squares. An opaque dome, like an unwelcome blister, marred the perfect center.

A shiver of foreboding passed through me, the same feeling I had standing on our dock whenever a sudden storm arose. In fear that the roiling waves would entrap me and drag me out to sea, I would flee, panic-stricken, to the safety of our cottage.

I jumped down from the stool. The excitement I felt earlier during Sir Richard's description of the maze disappeared leaving me anxious and homesick.

I curled up in the sunken center of the cot, like a fish caught in a net, missing Mother and Father, wishing Lizzie slept next to me, an out-flung leg or arm pressing against my chest. In my sorrow and loneliness, I must have fallen asleep until a persistent knocking once again startled me awake. I sat up, not knowing where I was.

CHAPTER 4

The door opened, and Peggy, holding a lantern, peered inside. "Are you all right, Miss?" she inquired, a tinge of a brogue in her voice. "'Tis time for supper. Maggie says ye are to eat with us in the kitchen."

Squinting in the sudden brightness, I jumped up, my dress rumpled. "Should I change my dress first?"

"If you can hurry, I'll wait for you." She glanced at the doll twisted up on the floor. "We don't want to keep them waiting. Maggie wouldn't like it."

I grabbed the muslin dress from my bag. Peggy stepped in and set the lantern on the floor nearby. Turning her back, she waited while I fumbled with the pearl buttons, the tiny loops slipping through my fingers. Two of the buttons bounced to the floor when I yanked the dress over my head and tossed it onto the cot. I pulled on the muslin and smoothed my snarled curls before picking up the lantern and handing it to Peggy. "Thank you," I whispered, reassured by her kindness, and traipsed down the stairs after her.

The long table in the center of the room was crowded with servants, the men sitting on the right side and the women on the left. Fourteen in all, with two places left open for Peggy and me. Maggie sat at the head of the table, and a scrawny, red-faced man sat at the other end. Peggy set the lantern on the side table and motioned me to the empty stool next to her seat at the end of the women's bench.

35

I slid onto the stool and eyed the steaming bowl of stew in front of me. The talking ceased. When I glanced up, everyone was staring at me. A maid in a dingy lace cap giggled and whispered something to Maggie.

"Ladies and gents." Maggie smirked and lifted her glass. "A toast to the little miss, the Master's new guest. May she last longer than the last one." She drained her glass, spilling some of the reddish liquid onto her bodice. The rest of them laughed and raised their glasses too. I blushed and stared at my hands clasped in my lap. Peggy reached over and patted my arm.

"What's your name, Miss?" The scrawny-necked man's deep voice sounded kinder than Maggie's.

"M-Misella Cross," I answered.

"Well, I'm Joseph, the gardener, and this here is Pecky, my son and helper." He gestured to the broad-chested young man sitting nearest him. "And this is Martin, the Master's groomsman." He nudged the black-coated man who had greeted Sir Richard earlier. Joseph continued around the table, introducing each of the staff.

When he got to the pudgy young maid sitting next to Maggie, he said, "And this is Lindy, Maggie's daughter and Miss Isobel's personal maid." Lindy squinted her piggish-looking eyes and grinned.

I wondered why Lindy had not gone to London with Isobel, but I remained silent. Pressing my crossed arms against my empty stomach, I was embarrassed that all might hear it rumbling. I stared at the stew, the hunk of buttered bread on my plate, and the mug of true milk, not the thin bluish stuff my family purchased from the milk vendor at home. A slice of raisin cake waited beside my mug. At least, I would eat well here, though I was disappointed that I had not been asked to dine with Sir Richard.

After the meal, when the maids began clearing the table, Sir Richard's groomsman informed Maggie, his voice clipped, "The Master will want his breakfast at dawn tomorrow. He leaves for London at sun-up."

Maggie started, her face ruddier than usual. "London? Whatever for? We thought him home to stay for awhile."

"To escort her Ladyship and Miss Isobel home. Miss Isobel cannot abandon her studies on a whim such as this." The groomsman peered at Maggie, his nostrils pinched, his head thrown back as if to pull away from her. "They will return in three days." He whirled around, his coat tails snapping, and left the room.

Maggie snorted, wiping her shiny brow with the crisp end of her apron, and said to Lindy, "Better prepare Mr. Fothering. His Mopsey returns to her lessons on Friday." She frowned when she saw me watching her and plucked the straw hearth broom from Peggy's hands. She shoved it against my chest. "Get busy, you. If you eat, you work. You sweep and scrub. The whole floor better shine like a baby's bottom when you finish. Peggy can show you what to do."

The scorn in Maggie's eyes and voice burned through me. I had never felt so reviled and helpless.

When I finished the sweeping, Peggy helped me wash the floor. "Sprinkle the ashes like this, Miss," Peggy cautioned, "more sparsely so as to use just enough to scour the slate without adding more grime to it. And widen the circles you make with the scrub brush to cover more tiles." She took the brush from me and swirled it in a wide arc, moving swiftly, sprinkling, dipping, and scrubbing her way toward the hearth.

I followed along on sore knees, my dress dripping with dark splotches. "Thank you, Peggy, for helping me. But when Sir Richard returns from London, I will not be spending my time in the kitchen, or in that attic room."

Peggy stopped scrubbing for a moment, a frown tightening her bristly eyebrows. "You'll get used to it, Miss," she said, beginning to scour again without looking at me. "It's hard at first. It was for me when I came two years ago. Oh, how I wanted to go right back to Galway."

My voice trembled. "I wish Sir Richard could see me right now. If I knew where to find him, I would run to him."

"Sir Richard is generous to his hired help," Peggy persisted, ignoring my distress. "Did you not see that at dinner, Miss? We get plenty of good food and wine. And fair compensation for our work."

Determined not to cry, I tried to control my wavering voice. "I'm going to wait down here early tomorrow. When I hear him readying to leave, I can tell him how I have been mistreated."

Peggy stopped scrubbing and leaned back on her heels, a concerned look on her plain, ruddy face. "Better not try to do that, Miss. Maggie will be working here when Sir Richard descends from his quarters. It wouldn't do, Miss. You best hold your tongue for awhile." She hesitated for a moment. "You should know, Miss, that Lady Sarah is the one who decides what jobs we are to have in the household, not Sir Richard. And Maggie will always side with the Mistress and with Isobel. She worked for the Wentworth family when Lady Sarah was naught but a babe in arms and came here with her when she married Sir Richard."

Peggy inspected the floor with approval. "We are almost done. I'll show you where to clean up and how to remove those stains from your dress."

"Thank you. But I think you are wrong about Sir Richard and me," I blurted out, though I smiled at her, not wanting to offend her. "You remind me of my sister Annabelle," I said, "who is as kind and gentle as you." I did not add that simple-minded Annabelle, like Peggy, was easily fooled and cowed by anyone with authority.

But I would be different, I thought, smarter and stronger and able to fight for myself.

CHAPTER 5

Until Sir Richard's return from London, I did my chores, without complaining. Maggie forced me to scrub pots and floors, grind spices and nuts in the mortar, and beat batter for cakes and breads until my fingers curled with cramps and the skin on my palms burned raw. Inside I seethed and daydreamed about how Sir Richard would rescue me, would curse Maggie when he discovered how I had been treated, his voice hard, his brown eyes icy.

When word came that the carriage had arrived from London, I worked quietly in the scullery away from the bustle and scurrying, biding my time. Hours passed before Maggie banged through the scullery door and waddled up to the table where I separated eggs for the dinner's *blanc mange.* "Scrub up and get into your fancy dress. The Master wants you in the drawing room, to meet her Ladyship and Miss Isobel." Her lips twisted into a grin as she smoothed her hair and snapped her linen cap as if to mimic the sudden fluttering of my hands to my disheveled curls.

I whipped off my grimy apron and raced up the stairs gloating to myself, "Oh, now you will see how things will change, Old Magpie."

Washing my face and hands with the cold water in the basin, I wished Mother were here to do me up right. I slipped on the pink dress, hung from the peg since the night of my arrival, wrapping my old shawl around my shoulders to cover the gap from the missing buttons. Looking into the round eye of my little hand mirror, I tried to fix my curls as best I could, my fingers shaking with excitement.

I floated down to the kitchen where the butler James waited to escort me. Maggie was nowhere in sight. James led the way down the marbled hallway with me in his wake stepping only in the white squares for luck and avoiding the black ones. When we reached the largest door on the left, James rapped twice and swung the door open into what seemed the quarters of a queen.

Sir Richard stood to the left of a vast marble fireplace, a fire roaring high between two enormous flowered vases glistening on each side, their design reflected in the polished oak floor. Floor to ceiling windows flanked each vase. The heavy garnet curtains, drawn back with thick gold beading, matched the color and texture of Sir Richard's velvet jacket and tawny breeches. Brown leather boots encased his legs to the knee. A white carpet, thick as new snow, drifted across the center of the room.

To the right of the fireplace a wispy, childlike woman languished on a pale yellow sofa sprinkled with embroidered flowers. Her mauve silk gown billowed around her engulfing her slender torso. A white gauze scarf, draped in folds, embraced her delicate neck. Her head rested against the stiff back of the sofa, as if exhausted by the swirled mass of whey-colored hair. She held a silk handkerchief to her lips with one pale hand. The other clutched the edge of the lacy pillow tucked behind her back.

"Come here, Misella." Sir Richard beckoned me forward. "This is Lady Sarah who is most happy to make your acquaintance."

I curtsied to her, but Lady Sarah covered her eyes with the handkerchief and refused to look at me. A snort erupted from behind me. I turned and saw a larger, healthier-looking version of Lady Sarah leaning over the back of a flowered, wing-tipped chair, one hand clutching its scrolled wooden top, the other stroking a fat, cream-colored cat spread across the chair cushion.

"And here is Isobel," Sir Richard continued, "and her haughty friend, Cleo, who thinks herself the reigning Queen of the Nile. Isobel, your new companion, Misella."

"How do you do, Miss Isobel." My voice trembled, against my wishes.

Isobel screwed up her face and twitched her lips as if she had bitten into something rotten. Ignoring me, she asked her father, "May I go now? Mr. Fothering will be looking for me. I have missed my morning lesson already."

Sir Richard leaned against the mantle. "Yes, you may go. But take Misella with you and introduce her to Fothering. I want her to sit in on your lessons, too. You both can learn together and help one another."

Isobel grimaced and beseeched her mother, "Must I, Mother? Please. I do not need help." She sneered at me. "And I do not need a companion." She spat each word at me as if peppering me with well-aimed birdshot.

Lady Sarah lifted a wan hand in Isobel's direction, her closed eyelids fluttering. "Do as your father says for now, Isobel. Please. I cannot handle any more arguments at the moment."

Sir Richard smiled at me as if to reassure me and calmly stated, "Misella, you will be moving to a new room today, one just down the hall from Isobel's. I want you two to be closer to one another."

My heart swelled with gratitude, and I felt a warm, comforting sense of peace. The worry of the last three days and nights, the nagging questions about what would happen to me, the fear of meeting Isobel, the insults from Maggie, all dissolved in the glow of Sir Richard's kindness.

Isobel scowled at her mother and whipped around so quickly a prong of the chair caught her sleeve tearing through the lace. "Bloody Balls," she muttered. Lady Sarah gasped. Scooping the cat into her arms, Isobel turned to me with a murderous look that chilled my heart. "Follow me," she growled. I trailed after her as she stomped from the room.

She waited on the first landing of the winding staircase, her dark face and Cleo's light one looming together over the carved banister. "Go away, little bitch," she muttered, "You will not be joining me now or in the future. Mother will put an end to this. She always gets her way. Most of the time, he's gone anyway."

Ignoring her, I climbed a few stairs, refusing to be intimidated and determined to carry out Sir Richard's orders.

Isobel looked straight into my eyes, her face twisted, her thick waist straining the seams of her gown. "He has tried this in the past, you know, bringing a little charity case into our home. She was supposed to be a companion for me as well—hah! Mother made him pay dearly for that violation."

She leaned down, her hot breath grazing my forehead. "You can now find that other companion of mine walking the night streets of Dublin."

41

I backed away, certain that Isobel was lying. She had the same jealous glint in her eye as Elinor did whenever Mother favored me. I clenched my fists and glared at her. "I'm not afraid of you or your lies or your mean, ugly gift. I know what you are. You're just a miserable bully like my sister Elinor."

I did not fear Isobel then. Instinctively, I recognized her self-loathing and believed I could handle her as I had Elinor, with cool disdain and sly manipulation. I tossed my head back, my blonde curls bouncing, and smirked at mousy-haired Isobel.

As she choked with speechless fury, I said sweetly, "Well, I guess I'll just go back and ask your father if I heard him correctly when he told me that you need extra help with your lessons, and I am to provide it." I swirled around and marched down the stairs, heading back toward the drawing room, hoping Isobel would not suspect that I was bluffing.

The drawing room door stood slightly ajar, and Lady Sarah's voice, surprisingly loud, echoed from the room. "I have only to tell Uncle that you are up to your old tricks again, and he will cut you off like that."

I heard the snapping of fingers, and Sir Richard's calm response. "As you have done for years, my dear, from your chaste little sanctuary?"

Lady Sarah's voice rose. "You never cared that Isobel's birth almost destroyed me. Left me an invalid."

"Only in your mind, my dear. You knew I wanted a legitimate heir, a son, just one, and I would have gladly left you alone."

"And you knew I could not risk giving birth again." Lady Sarah's voice hardened. "And you have Isobel," she snarled, "if you would take the time to notice her. She adores you."

Sir Richard snorted, his voice curling with sarcasm. "Wrong, my dear. Isobel takes her cues from you. Since you cannot hide the disgust in your eyes when you look at me, neither can she. She detests me."

"With good reason," Lady Sarah shouted, "after Annie. I was never unreasonable about your baser needs as long as you were discreet. But you violated my trust. And now here you are, humiliating us once again, taking in another little ragamuffin to feed your warped fantasies."

Sir Richard's voice tightened, his words clipped and cold. "I was honor bound as the heir of Mariette's family to help out, and this is what she wanted. I am simply doing my duty."

Lady Sarah laughed, a crude, guttural sound that belied the delicate creature I had just met. "Ah, of course, your duty!" Her voice choked with rage. "That's what you claimed at first about Annie, wasn't it? Foolishly, we believed you. Now Isobel fears that will happen again, that another little mewling waif will take her place."

Mortified, I fled to the safety of my attic room, not wanting to hear Lady Sarah's spiteful voice any longer, feeling sorry for Sir Richard that he must live with such a cold, heartless woman, and her vicious daughter. Sorry for myself, too, and angry at their cruelty to us both, I felt bound to Sir Richard by a new sense of loyalty. The idea of him as my protector, my only advocate, grew stronger in my mind. It was easy for me to ignore the implicit warning about him in Lady Sarah's and Isobel's hateful words.

The doll lay face down in the corner where I had kicked it. With a renewed sense of outrage, I wanted to rip it apart, find Isobel and throw the pieces in her face, and stab her with the thick needle. But instead I picked the doll up and shook it. "I hate you, Isobel," I cried. "I'll get even with you. You'll see. Someday, I'll show this creature to Sir Richard."

I tucked the doll away in the bottom of the makeshift wooden box that held my few belongings.

CHAPTER 6

My lessons with Isobel and her tutor never took place. That very afternoon Lady Maltby called me to her rooms. Wrapped in a richly embroidered flower quilt, she reclined on a chaise lounge in front of a roaring fire, a china tea set and a collection of dark vials resting on a little table next to her. Maggie hovered behind her, a smirk distorting her reddened face.

Curtsying, I murmured, "Good afternoon, Lady Sarah."

She stared at me, her pale eyes as colorless as the eyes of mackerel dragged up in Father's net, the life draining from them as he hauled them from his boat.

"You will not be joining Isobel for lessons," Lady Sarah sniffed. "You are kitchen help here, nothing more, ragamuffin. Sir Richard has made a mistake. You will continue to work for Maggie." Her voice was as cold and lifeless as her eyes. "If it were up to me, you would be sent scurrying back to your little fishing shack. You will remain here, however, since Sir Richard has let it be known that you are related to him. But you will not be allowed to take advantage of that flimsy relationship or upset this household. The first sign of trouble or distress, and you will be sent packing. Do you understand?"

I mumbled, "Yes, ma'am."

"Yes, my Lady," she said sharply. "You will address me by my title."

"Yes, my Lady," I muttered, my eyes cast down, not wanting the grinning Maggie to see the angry tears gathering.

"You are dismissed. Maggie will show you to your new bedroom. Be grateful that I have agreed to this move—for the moment."

45

Minutes later Maggie opened the door to my new room. "Don't get too comfy," she snapped. "You're back in the kitchen starting tomorrow." She laughed and strutted from the room, holding the corner of her apron aloft in her fingers.

Throwing myself down on the wide, quilt-covered bed, I wept in despair, despite the big, lace-draped windows, the scarf-covered tables, the gay round rugs, and the log-rich fireplace. *I hate them*, I sobbed. *I hate them all. I need Sir Richard.*

A knock on the door aroused me from my misery. Drying my eyes on my sleeve, I hurried to open the door, thinking Sir Richard might have come to check on me in my new quarters. But it was Maggie's daughter Lindy who leaned against the door frame. "You are wanted in the Library, Missy," she said with a sneer. "Right away."

Despite Lindy's insolence, my spirits soared. I silently thanked Sir Richard for reversing Lady Sarah's decision and allowing me to join Isobel and Mr. Fothering. I followed Lindy down to the Library, smiling all the way, my heart racing.

Glass-fronted cases lined one wall of the Library from floor to high ceiling. The opposite wall held more books in open shelves that receded into an alcove at the far end of the room where Isobel sat at a heavy-looking table, her back to the doorway. Across from her a white-haired gentleman in wire-framed glasses rested his chin in one hand while drumming the fingers of the other on the table. A fireplace glowed behind them. On each side of the table, fat candles in silver holders provided additional light. I inhaled the intoxicating scent of hundreds of books waiting to be read.

As I moved further into the room, Maggie emerged from the corner behind the door. Swinging a wooden pail, she grabbed my arm, hooking the rope handle over my wrist. Her usual raspy voice muted, she said, "You'll work in here every afternoon, Missy, but not with Fothering." She pulled out some rags and a bottle of cloudy liquid. "You're gonna dust every book in the place, and polish the shelves with this cloth as you go along." She shoved the bottle and the rags into my hands. "And you better be careful. Don't you dare splash a drop on the books or on the glass. Understood?" She beckoned to Lindy slouching in the doorway.

Lindy shuffled behind the door and reappeared lugging a wooden ladder which she rested gently against the carved framework of the open book case. Hands on her wide hips, she faced me, a big grin closing her eyes to slits.

"You'll need this," Maggie muttered, with a grin at Lindy. "You can't reach that high without help." They both chuckled. "From now on this is your job after you're done in the kitchen. Get busy."

Maggie and Lindy left, easing the door closed behind them. I stood in the room, bereft, listening to the monotonous sound of Isobel's voice.

"No, that's wrong, Isobel. Try reading the passage one more time." When Mr. Fothering admonished her, I felt a little better.

Isobel tried again. "*O, let my books be then the elo-eloq-eloqution.*"

Mr. Fothering sighed. "eloquence, el-o-quence."

"Eloquence," Isobel mumbled. As she stumbled on, I recognized the passage from one of Shakespeare's sonnets. "*And dumb pres-pressures——*"

Mr. Fothering's voice rose. "Presagers——*And dumb presagers of my speaking breast.* All right, enough of this. Read the section from Carte's *History* you were asked to prepare."

I yearned to join them. I had never read that history of England. Setting the pail on the floor without making a sound, I crouched down out of sight and began easing books from the lowest shelf, running the rag carefully across the embossed spines with their intriguing titles. *I will find a way*, I promised myself. *I will show them.*

Each day, I listened to Fothering's lessons as I worked—to Isobel's halting answers to his questions, to her painful sounding out of words, all the while wondering whether it was lack of intelligence or lack of interest that made Isobel such a careless pupil.

As my jealousy and frustration increased, I became a sneak, spying on Isobel whenever I could and stealing down to the Library late at night to practice writing and to read Isobel's books. I'd bring with me the goose feather quill I had stolen from her lesson box and cream-colored paper from the thick stack that she hardly used. I had filled an empty laudanum vial Lady Sarah had discarded with ink from Isobel's bottle.

One night Isobel must have heard me creeping down the stairs, or perhaps she saw the glow of my candle as I passed by her room.

She found me hunched over the table reading Carte's *History of England*. She rushed toward me, her frothy nightgown bloating out behind her, a brass lantern swinging wildly in her hand. She snatched the book from me, her nails leaving angry red trails along my arm.

"You little thief." Her face flamed. "How dare you prowl around at night and take what doesn't belong to you." A limp rope of her hair swung into her face as she leaned over and swept the writing paper off the table.

I remained calm. "I am only using what you don't need, Isobel. I have already finished the first three books. Since you are only on Book One, you won't need this one for at least a month. I will be done with the whole set by then." Though I knew I was only fueling her anger, I peered into her flashing eyes and smiled.

She grabbed a fistful of my hair and dragged me from the chair. "These books are mine. Do you hear? Don't you dare come near them again. Don't you ever come into this room again." She seized the ink vial, tossing the ink down the front of my shift. A dark spidery stain spread across my chest. "Mother will want to see what you have stolen from her," she screamed, shaking the medicine vial in my face.

"I did not steal it. She threw it away, and I found it." I tried to unlock her fingers from my hair. A head taller and heavier than me, Isobel was not as easy to overpower as Elinor had been.

"We will see what mother has to say. We knew you couldn't be trusted, you ungrateful little bitch. You will receive no more charity from us. Do you understand? Do you?" Her voice grew shriller, her grasp tighter as she yanked me up on the very tips of my bare toes. I feared she would pull some of the hair right out of my head, or scalp me as the Indians in the Americas did to their victims. My scalp burned, but I would not give Isobel the satisfaction of crying out from the pain.

I heard the door fling open. Sir Richard appeared in the shadowed doorway, a crimson robe wrapped around him, a lighted taper in his hand. His leather slippers scuffed along the polished floor, the candle illuminating the gleam in his eyes. "That's enough, Isobel," he announced, his voice firm.

Isobel's hands dropped to her sides. "Fa-father. I didn't know you had come back from London."

But he only said, "Come here, Misella."

I brushed my curls back into place, my sassy curls Sir Richard had called them, and ran to him, angry blood pounding through my veins.

With his back to Isobel, he leaned forward and whispered in my ear, "Plain-faced Isobel is jealous, Misella, because you shine like a goddess."

His honey-rich voice soothed my blood. Sweet and warm, his words filled my empty heart. He never called me Missy as Lady Sarah and Isobel did, curling their thin lips into hard lines. He called me Misella, spinning the soft "s" sound slowly across his tongue, almost singing my name.

He glared at Isobel, who stood quivering with rage, her face blotched and perspiring from exertion. "Please make an effort to act more like a lady, Isobel. Your lowly behavior is most unbecoming. But you will have the opportunity to do better, to show a little kindness to Misella when she accompanies us on our outing to Southhampton."

Isobel gasped. "You're taking her with us? That little thief, that puny bag of fish bones with her frizzled hair and moon-eyed stares? If she goes, I am *not* going!" Isobel's voice cracked.

His voice stern, Sir Richard ordered, "You will go. And never mind whining or complaining to your mother about this. She has already agreed. From now on you will treat Misella with respect, as a member of our family."

Isobel took a deep, rasping breath and yelled, "No, I won't. I won't. And you can't make me."

"Do not fight me on this, Isobel," he said, his voice deathly quiet. "You will not win." He handed me the taper. "Go back to your room now, Misella," he said gently.

As I fled from the room, I took great comfort in these signs that Sir Richard cared about me, that he didn't approve of Isobel and Lady Sarah treating me like a scullery maid, that he considered me an equal member of the family.

CHAPTER 7

The next morning when Peggy entered the kitchen after serving in the breakfast room, she told Maggie, "Misella's wanted, ma'am. The master said to send her in."

I stopped scrubbing the grease-stained front of the box stove and, with a triumphant toss of my head, dropped the brush into the bucket.

Maggie scowled at me. "Get moving," she snapped, "and get right back here when he's finished with you."

I nodded, wiping my blackened hands on my soiled apron, soggy curls hanging in my face. I wanted Sir Richard to see me dirty and disheveled, proof that I was being misused.

Hurrying to the breakfast room, I knocked on the door and entered. Sir Richard sat in the same scarlet dressing gown he had worn the previous night, but with a silken scarf now flouncing at the neck. He leaned back in his chair and smiled. Isobel hunched over her plate shoveling spoons of egg into her mouth. Lady Sarah was not in the room.

"Well, Misella. We have planned an excursion to the sea at Southhampton and you will accompany us. Isn't that so, Isobel?"

Isobel muttered something I could not hear.

Sir Richard beckoned me to come closer. "Lady Sarah's physician has ordered the bathing cure for her. Dr. Russell sends many of his patients to dip themselves in the sea at Southhampton. So we will all go and partake of his medicinal expertise." He laughed at Isobel's red, scowling face. "It will invigorate us, Isobel, and we'll return purged and ready for the holiday season." With a warm smile he told me, "We leave early in the morning.

51

We'll be gone for four days. And don't worry about bathing clothes. We don't need any, do we, Issy?" Isobel swallowed a mouthful of bread and shook her head, her face flaming.

After Sir Richard dismissed me, I danced into the kitchen, catching Maggie off guard. "I'll be leaving in the morning. Going bathing in Southhampton—with the family. And I don't know when I'll be back," I announced. "I probably won't be working in the kitchen anymore either."

Maggie just smirked. "Oh, you'll be back scrubbing pots sooner than you think, Missy. This trip is just for show—the Master showing the other wealthy hypocrites how charitable he is, how kind to take in a poor, destitute ragamuffin like you and make you a part of his family." She pranced back and forth with the edge of her apron held up daintily between her thumb and fore-finger. "Trying to improve his image. To show he deserves to inherit Lord Wentworth's seat and can hold his own against the benevolent Whigs. At least, that's the rubbish he uses to convince Lady Sarah."

She picked up the scouring brush from the floor and slapped it into my hand. "But he won't get that seat unless she says so, and she won't say so unless he behaves himself. And when Isobel has the chance to confront her mother about this trip without him around, believe me, Lady Sarah will change her mind about taking you with them. Now, get back to scrubbing the stove. Oh, wait, do you need to wear silk gloves to keep your hands soft for the Master? Anybody here have an extra pair of elbow gloves that the little lady can slip on before she dips her hands into that scummy bucket?" She threw back her head and laughed, her bull's neck stretching and vibrating against her sweat-stained collar.

I plunged the brush into the bucket. *You are wrong, old Magpie,*" I muttered under my breath. *"I'm part of the family now."*

Worried, however, that Isobel might convince her mother to change her mind, I escaped later without Maggie's knowledge and hid in the shadowed alcove opposite Lady Sarah's quarters. Because Lady Sarah stayed abed until late morning, I knew Isobel would not disturb her before then. I did not have to wait long before Isobel stormed down the hallway and barreled into her mother's rooms, slamming the door behind her. I crept forward in the deserted hallway and eased the door open a few inches.

"I won't do it," Isobel screamed at her mother. "I'll scratch her eyes out first and fling myself down the stairs, and you'll be sorry. It's not fair," she panted. "You have to stop him from bringing her to Southhampton with us."

"Isobel, please, dearest. Control yourself and listen to me." Lady Sarah stumbled a bit when she arose from the chaise, her morning gown catching beneath her slippered foot. Her laudanum bottle and her tea cup sat on the bedside table. Though she had not yet applied her day make-up, the ashen skin of her cheekbones flamed with color.

"This time will be different. He knows what's at stake." She grasped Isobel's hand and reached up to tuck a loose strand of hair behind her daughter's ear and trailed her fingers down her cheek. "When your father inherits Uncle's estate, my Bel, think how much your prospects will improve. You will be pursued by every unattached nobleman in the country."

Isobel wrenched her hand free. "I don't care about any stupid suitors," she shouted. "Just tell him *No*. Do what I ask for a change. If he wants all of that as much as you say, you could just refuse to take her with us. You could send her back where she belongs. Why won't you do that? Why?"

Lady Sarah sighed and sank down on the chaise, her breathing ragged. "I will explain in a moment, Isobel. I need some lemon water first. Please bring my glass and my pill box. This is all very distressing and exhausting for me."

With a loud sigh, Isobel did as her mother asked and handed her the box without a word.

"Thank you, dear." Lady Sarah opened the lid with shaky fingers and extracted two pills. Isobel took the box and gave her the glass. Grimacing, her mother took each pill with a few sips of water and handed back the quivering glass. She leaned against the embroidered pillows, throwing a lap quilt over her legs as she raised them to rest on the chaise. "You know perfectly well that he promised to help her penniless family who could no longer afford to keep her."

She sighed and retrieved a handkerchief from her sleeve, touching it to her lips, her voice weakening. "Everybody in London knows the story now about him inheriting the mother's estate. The gossip has spread like a pestilence. She made sure of that by sending letters not only to your father but also to Uncle and some of your father's colleagues in Parliament asking them to intervene with him on her behalf."

My breath caught in my throat. I was stunned to discover how far my mother had gone to get what she wanted. She had painted us as beggars in the eyes of the world. My sense of shame and my anger at her deepened.

"I don't care," Isobel wailed, "What about me?"

Lady Sarah sat up straight, her voice stronger. "That's enough, Isobel. She is a blood relative; your father had no choice. He had to do what the mother asked in order to preserve his reputation and not appear a churl. Taking Misella with us on this trip will improve his image and show that he is caring for her as he promised to do. You need have nothing to do with this creature as I promised you before she arrived. I will see to that."

"Just like Annie?" Isobel cried. "Did you forget about that?"

"Not like Annie at all. He knows better, and so do we. That will not happen again. In a few years, when Uncle is gone, when your father is installed in Parliament, and we are rich beyond our dreams, you will make your triumphal entry into the London social scene. Trust me on this, Isobel."

She pushed aside the lap quilt and stood up to embrace her fuming daughter, but Isobel recoiled and would not look at her. "Isobel, you are all that matters to me." She reached for her daughter's hand. "I want you to be happy, to marry someone who will love you or at least respect you—not some unloving, unprincipled libertine who will make you miserable. And, no matter what, I promise that you will never be forced to marry against your will." She slipped her arm around Isobel's waist. "Cheer up, dearest. When we return from Southhampton in a few days, Misella will be under Maggie's thumb. That brat will know her place. Nothing will change."

She smiled at Isobel and patted her on the cheek. "Oh yes, dear one, I know how to handle your father, and you and I both know how to handle Misella. Now go and lay out the things you wish to take on our little trip."

Easing the door closed, I escaped down the hall, my face hot with anger and embarrassment. Had I been older and less consumed with my own misery, I might have wondered about Annie and tried to find out more about her. I might have felt some sympathy for Isobel, realizing that we shared a common curse——mothers who try to relive their lives through their daughters. I might have recognized that Isobel needed and deserved Sir Richard's affection and attention. And I might have been wise enough to reject him when he offered them to me instead.

CHAPTER 8

We left just after sunrise in Lady Sarah's carriage. Lady Sarah rested her head against a small pillow, the sharp bones of her face pale as ivory, her eyes closed. She did not open them when I entered the carriage. Sir Richard sat next to her, a book in his lap, his green velvet coat mounded into a small hill on the seat between them. I slid onto the seat next to Isobel.

Sitting opposite her mother, Isobel scrunched against the side and stared out the window. She snapped the edge of her skirt from the seat into her lap and tried to move further away from me.

The journey all the way to Southhampton was made in silence, the only sounds the whack of the horses' hooves against the hard packed road and Jack's occasional whistles or shouts to keep them flying.

We did not stop to dine. Instead, Isobel and I each had a wrapped slice of bread and plum jam. Isobel also ate a stack of little cakes that she munched one after the other without offering me a single one. Lady Sarah went without nourishment, never lifting her head from her pillow. She seemed hardly to be breathing, though she grimaced whenever the carriage bounced hard over a rut. Sir Richard drank every so often from a silver flask that rested on the seat next to his coat.

When we stopped to relieve ourselves, Jack jumped down and carried the chamber pot into a secluded bank of trees. Lady Sarah and Isobel followed, with me trailing behind them. Jack placed the porcelain bowl on a smooth carpet of leaves. "I'm after leavin' you here, ladies. Holler me back when ye finish." He plunged further into the woods.

Lady Sarah extracted a small bundle of folded rags from a canvas bag. With an icy stare and a wave of her gloved hand, she dismissed me. "Go and find your own spot away from us."

My chin in the air, I marched across the road and headed downhill toward a weeping willow I had noticed from the carriage. I returned before the others and sat prim and silent. With Jack's help, Lady Sarah and Isobel climbed into the carriage in a flurry of huffing and rustling. Sir Richard mumbled something to Jack, perhaps a joke, and swung into the carriage. Jack laughed, touching one hand to his cap in a kind of salute. Lady Sarah shuffled inside her bag, extracting her pill box and her bottle of liquid. Sir Richard shook his head as if disgusted with her. When Isobel asked him how much longer our journey would take, he picked up his book and muttered, "As long as it takes."

We arrived at Southhampton in late afternoon. Jack pulled up to a row of tall brick houses lining the shoreline, a string of carriages spread along their backside. At the end house, he restrained the horses and jumped down, step stool in hand to help us disembark. Sir Richard grabbed his coat and alighted. Lady Sarah sat up, her watery eyes fluttering open with a look of bewilderment and pain. She sighed and accepted Jack's outstretched hand with gloved fingers. Isobel followed. When I climbed down after her, the stool was out of place. I lost my balance and would have fallen, but Jack grabbed me.

"Careful, Miss," he said, standing me upright and flipping a few black curls out of his eyes. He frowned at Isobel. "That magic stool seems to have a mind of its own. Best to look before you leap next time." He grinned and tipped his hat to me, its scarlet ribbon flapping in the wind.

"Bed the horses, Jack," Sir Richard said, "and head to the inn. We'll need you back and ready to go at dawn."

"Right to do, Sir." Jack closed the door of the coach, picked up the stool and climbed up to his perch. Grabbing up the reins, he clicked the horses forward.

We entered a fishy-smelling foyer. A maid in rumpled clothing came forward to greet us and show us into the main room with a cavernous fireplace glowing and spewing smoke. Encircling the room was an open loft displaying a series of doors, each leading, she told us, to sleeping quarters. "You'll want the first one, Sir," she said, motioning to a set of double doors at the top of the stairway, "and perhaps your daughters can take the other double suite."

Isobel spoke up hotly. "I'll have my own room. She's just a maid, so she can sleep off the kitchen." She flipped a hand in my direction and moved closer to her mother.

Sir Richard told the maidservant, "One of the smaller rooms for each of the girls," he said. "We'll have our dinner here by the fire, and retire immediately after. Just tea in the morning early as we'll be setting out to bathe at dawn."

After dinner, at which Lady Sarah ate only a few bites of her pigeon pie, Sir Richard reminded her with a smirk, "Be sure to take the rest of Dr. Russell's pills to pave the way for your seawater cocktail in the morning, my dear." She gave him a venomous look but did not reply.

When the maid woke me before sunup, she brought a tray with a pot of tea and a mug. "Ten minutes, Miss, the Master says."

"Wait, please," I asked as she was about to leave the room. She paused, a bit annoyed it seemed. "Must everyone who goes to the bathing hall swim in the waters?"

"Course, Miss. Why else would you bother to come?" and she closed the door behind her.

The air was frosty, the emerging sky a roof of slate-colored clouds in the dim morning light when we prepared to depart. Jack Finn blew into a steaming mug as he waited beside the carriage. As we emerged from the house, he set the mug aside and stood at attention. While Jack helped the family board and settle in to the carriage, I hung back shivering.

"Are ye cold, Miss?" Jack asked.

I shook my head. "I'm—I'm afraid of the water," I squeaked, my voice so faint Jack had to bend close to hear me, the flowers in his lapel brushing my cheek. "I don't know how to swim."

"Ah, ye won't be havin' to swim," he said, his voice kind, a softness in his eyes. "Two minutes in the water for the dip, with a tether to hang on to if you need it. That's all. Don't you be worryin' about it. 'Chin up, eyes to Heaven' we say in Ireland to remind us not to be afraid." He slipped a finger under his chin, tilting his head back for a moment. Smiling he said, "I'll keep an eye on ye."

Sir Richard leaned out of the carriage, a frown drawing his arched eyebrows together. "Get in, Misella. Let's be off, Jack. We're late."

Jack squeezed my hand as he helped me up into the carriage, as if to remind me that I could count on him, and I relaxed for the first time since our journey began.

We traveled along a wide dirt path that swerved onto a sand-covered roadway stretching along the shore in front of a few tumble-down fishing cottages. In the distance a line of horses stood like statues with what appeared to be little wooden houses shafted to them, like a little horse-drawn village poised at the brink of the sea.

We followed a string of carriages to a white pillared building where ladies and gentlemen and children of various sizes descended from their carriages and waited in line on the broad stone porch. After Jack Finn dropped us off, Sir Richard drew us to the front of the line, telling the restless crowd that Dr. Russell awaited us inside. He received several resentful looks and surly comments of "Wait your turn," and "We're cold out here, too," but he pushed ahead.

Several ladies gathered around a large slate hung on the entrance wall, writing down their names and paying the attendant, but Sir Richard brushed past them stating, "Dr. Russell awaits us." We entered a large seating area where brightly clothed ladies and a few gentlemen sat drinking from pewter mugs and chatting or reading papers.

Sir Richard escorted us to a closed door off of an attached hallway. He knocked briskly. A woman in a long flowing robe tied tightly around her neck opened the door.

"Good morning, Betty," Sir Richard said. "Here we are: Lady Sarah, Isobel, and our new daughter, Misella." He grinned when Isobel muttered something under her breath and said, "Betty will be your dipper this morning. She is the finest dipper in the Bay."

Without smiling she ushered us into a large circular room with a domed skylight. Centered beneath it sat a black-suited man curved over a stack of papers, a cluster of jars and bottles strewn across the long table in front of him. He straightened up when we entered, looking over the tops of his half-moon glasses. Tufts of steely gray hair sprang in disarray from his head, his cheeks, and his chin. He limped around to shake Sir Richard's hand and to hug Lady Sarah to him.

"I have your drinks all ready for you," he said. "A cup for each, but we will do a little bloodletting first for you, Lady Sarah." He lifted a large decanter from the table.

"Ah, none for me, Doctor," Sir Richard said, "just the ladies. I do not need pickling at the moment."

The Doctor did not seem amused. He frowned but said nothing as he poured cups of greenish water and solemnly handed one to Isobel and one to me. "Drink slowly," he warned, taking Lady Sarah by the hand to a curtained area of the room. He pulled back the curtain to reveal an alcove with a wooden armchair, a footstool, and a small desk with some metal instruments. After seating her in the chair, he closed the curtain. Sir Richard motioned us to a long wooden bench against one wall, and we sat down with the drinks.

I took a sip of the thick salty slime and tried to swallow but spit it back in the cup. "What is it?" I croaked.

Isobel laughed and Sir Richard smiled. "Seawater doctored with a bit of Russell's special tincture. Good for you," he said. "You don't have to sip it, just take it down in one gulp, if that's easier."

Isobel looked right at me and raised her cup. Drinking slowly without a flinch, she finished it, turning the cup upside down. Resolving to match her performance, I closed my eyes, tried not to breathe through my nose, and gulped it down, swallowing furiously. I flipped my cup over, too.

We heard a soft moan from Lady Sarah, and Dr. Russell's low murmur. He reappeared to pour a cup of seawater for her. "She'll be ready soon," he said to Sir Richard, and retreated once again behind the curtain.

I kept swallowing, the seawater fighting to find its way back to the sea. I craved a cup of tea, but none was offered.

Soon Dr. Russell reappeared, his arm supporting Lady Sarah, who leaned her pale face against his dark coat. He eased her into a cushioned chair. "Give the elixir a minute or two, and you'll be strong enough for the plunge." She closed her eyes and nodded, still holding on to his hand.

Dr. Russell extracted his hand and opened his door. "Betty's ready for you now."

Betty swirled into the room and hustled us out through the growing crowd milling around in the great hall. She led us outside and down the teeming stairway, pushing past richly dressed ladies in wide brocades and gentlemen clad in velvet. Jack Finn leaned with another coachman against a pillar, smoking a pipe and watching the display. As we passed nearby, I heard him say to his companion, "Nothing but silken folly and bloated disease." When Jack noticed me, he smiled and raised his hand, tipping his chin up with his forefinger and lifting his eyes to heaven.

Dodging oncoming carriages we made our way across the road and through the sand to a bathing machine, its horse submerged to its forelocks. Lady Sarah clung to Betty who seemed to almost carry her along.

Sir Richard headed to a small boat resting on the shore, one end of it covered over with a barrel-shaped till, the oarsman sitting in the center waiting for him. He climbed in and disappeared into the till as the boat began to move forward.

Isobel and I climbed into the bathing machine after Betty had half-lifted Lady Sarah up and through the doorway. Daylight disappeared. I could see nothing inside the dark room until Betty lit a lantern hanging from a hook near the back door. Wooden benches lined the small room with a row of hooks jutting out above them. Sand gritted the floor, and the room smelled of fish and dampness. Betty threw open the seaside door and the chilly air gushed in. She picked up a switch lying on the bench, reached out to the left and slapped the horse's backside.

We creaked forward into the water. The waves lapped against the walls, rocking the machine from side to side like a cradle. Betty retrieved a long, flannel cloak from one of the hooks and began helping Lady Sarah disrobe.

Isobel kicked off her shoes and removed her stockings. Untying her petticoat from around her waist, she said to me, "You better start getting undressed. You're going in first. Missy wants to be first," she called to Betty who told me to hasten. Lady Sarah sat huddled on the bench wrapped in the heavy cloak.

Isobel had already undressed down to her shift. "D-d-on't we have cloaks, too?" I asked her.

"We go in naked, stupid." Isobel smirked. "Everybody does." Her sneering expression challenged me to back out like a baby.

Facing the wall I slipped out of my clothes, my flesh shrinking from the cold. Bent over, arms and hands covering as much as I could, I let Betty position me in the doorway and stared in horror at the roiling waves.

Ahead I saw Sir Richard's boat. He stood up, the profile of his naked body outlined against the emerging horizon, a troubling image I had never witnessed before, not even of Father in our cramped hut. Yet, I did not look away. Clasping his hands together, he raised and lowered his arms, the muscles rippling across his wide shoulders. He stretched his arms straight out, poised for a moment at the edge of the boat, his backside tensing in the chill air, a light breeze stirring his unbound hair. He looked over his shoulder and smiled, right at me I thought, then plunged head first into the swelling sea.

I stepped back, the seawater in my stomach crawling upward into my throat.

"I'm going to be sick," I gasped to Betty, "I can't go in." I pushed away from her and slid onto the bench across from Lady Sarah, my hands across my mouth.

Betty clucked and spoke to Lady Sarah. "Let's go, my Lady."

Lady Sarah stood up. Betty led her to the opening, guiding her down onto the metal stair. She slipped forward into the water, holding up her hands and grasping Lady Sarah's outstretched fingers. Gently, Betty drew her down into the water.

Lady Sarah gasped. Her cloak fanned out around her, slowly darkening and dipping into the waves. Still holding her hands, Betty plunged her under the water. Lady Sarah emerged, her braided hair askew on the top of her head, her eyes squeezed shut, her mouth open in a silent scream as she tried to catch her breath. Betty waited a few moments and dragged her under again. This time Lady Sarah sputtered and cried out as she surfaced, twisting away from Betty and clutching toward the rope tethered to the shaft to pull herself up. Betty came up behind her and hoisted her up into the doorway. Lady Sarah sprawled forward, trapped in her soggy cocoon, her teeth chattering, her lips and fingertips blue.

Betty lunged in, dripping cold water onto my legs. Grunting, she leaned sideways to flip up the bench top and snatched a blanket from within. She grabbed the bundled Lady Sarah, lifting her to her feet and moving her away from the door. Betty untied the cloak, whipped it from Lady Sarah's trembling body, and swaddled her in the blanket. "Go, go, Miss," she motioned to Isobel.

Isobel lumbered to the doorway, the skin on her puffy backside pimpled from the cold. She sneered at me before she jumped in and vanished under the lapping waves. She shot out of the water, foam milking her torso, and dipped down again. She popped up and grabbed the rope, shaking her hair and finding the iron step to haul herself up. She shivered through the doorway and clutched the blanket Betty held out to her.

Betty seized my arms. "Just sit on the edge for a moment, Miss, and at least dangle your legs in the water. It will help you feel better." Her iron grip forced me to do what she said. Hunkering down onto the wet, gritty floor, I closed my eyes and slipped my quivering legs over the side into the icy water. My feet hugged the narrow step, my hands gripping the bottom edge of the doorway.

A blunt shove against my back threw me forward into the churning sea, and as I thrashed my arms in panic to keep from going under, I glimpsed Isobel's stolid body blocking the doorway. Her eyes glittering, she shouted, "Missy decided to go in, after all. She wants to swim a bit."

The waves twisted me away from the bathing machine, moving me further out so I could not touch the bottom. I struggled to stay on the surface. When I screamed, thick, acrid water filled my nose and mouth. I went under. When I came up, I tried to push my arms and legs against the strength of the waves, but only managed to draw myself sideways, further from the machine and the shore. I swallowed more water. The sky darkened around me.

As I sank once more into the swirl, an iron fist gripped my hair, and I thought, *this time Isobel will finish me.* My head was tugged up out of the water; a headlock imprisoned my neck. I was pulled with giant strokes through the water until I landed on the sand. Strong hands grasped my shoulders and rolled me over, pushing on my back until streams of steamy water spewed from my mouth. A heavy cloth wrapped around me, and I opened my stinging eyes to see Jack Finn dripping over me.

"You're all right, now, Miss. Just rest here a wee minute, take some deep breaths." Several faces gathered over me, staring and murmuring, as if I were some aqueous creature on exhibit.

"She's fine, fine now," Jack said. "Let's be givin' her some privacy, if ye don't mind." He shielded me from their stares and urged them to go ahead to their respective bathing apparatuses.

"Can you sit up, Miss?" He wrapped one arm underneath my shoulders and leaned me up against his soggy vest. My lips quivered, and I tried hard to keep the tears from showing. He tightened his arm around me. "Chin up, eyes to Heaven. Ye'll be all right."

He had encased me in his surtout, the crushed flowers in the lapel hanging their heads, like me. "You're still shakin' like a baby's rattle." He put both arms around me. "So you didn't get enough seawater to drink from Dr. Russell? So tasty, you just wanted more, eh?" Jack leaned back and grinned. "Maybe ye want to tell all these crazy people ye could save them the trouble of seein' the famous Doctor and payin' him for what they can have free right out here like ye did. I can't stand the sea, myself. In all me twenty-three years, I've niver gone near it if I can help it, except, of course, to rescue a damsel in distress."

He released me and stood up to give a sweeping bow, dark, wet curls falling into his dancing eyes, water dripping from his saturated breeches, their colorful strings dangling around his ankles like Maypole ribbons. He looked so silly, I had to smile.

He sat back down beside me. "All of these people here dash to the coast not because they love the water, but because 'tis the fashion. For a Connemarra lad like me, I find no home here. I would exchange all these seagulls for sheep and that salty foam for a heather-grass meadow."

"Oh, I, too," I told him, my throat hurting, my voice raspy, "though I was born near the sea and Father loves it so and my sisters do, but not Mother and me. I hate it."

He held out his hand. "Well, shake me hand on it. We both swear niver to go near deep waters again."

When I clutched his hand, I noticed a black letter "F" imprinted on the bottom half of his thumb. I wondered if a "J" was inscribed on the other one, but had no chance to look because Sir Richard appeared suddenly, with Betty and Isobel running after him. He reached us first, sand spraying from his bare feet, his shirttail flapping against his breeches.

"Good heavens, what happened, Misella? Why didn't you say you didn't know how to swim? Are you all right?" He grasped one of my numb hands in his. He brushed the wet curls from my face and began briskly rubbing my fingers between his hands.

Isobel stood back, not saying a word, her face impassive, but her eyes smoldered. Betty came forward, my clothes across her arm. "I don't know what happened, Sir. She must have fallen in off the edge. She was just to sit and dangle her legs a bit. This young man rescued her before I realized she couldn't swim."

Shaken and weak, I said nothing. I did not want to look at Isobel or say her name or think about what she had done.

Sir Richard slid his arm around me, helping me to stand. "Assist Lady Sarah to the carriage," he said to Jack. "I'll handle Misella from here." Stumbling on the long coat, I clutched it around me as we traipsed through the sand toward the line of parked carriages.

"I had forgotten how you felt about the sea, Misella," Sir Richard murmured so only I could hear him, his arm tightening around me. "I am certain, in all of your twelve years, you have never had a more dangerous adventure than today's. Such an experience, though, helps you to grow, makes you less of a child and more of a woman."

Shivering despite the heavy coat, my hair dripping in my eyes, I tried not to burst into tears. I swallowed the lump rising up in my throat and took a deep breath.

"You mustn't fear to tell me when you don't want to do things," Sir Richard crooned. "You're not afraid of displeasing me, are you?"

"N-no."

We arrived at the carriage, and Sir Richard lifted me inside, bundling Jack's coat around me. Isobel climbed in and sat silently beside me.

Lady Sarah made her way slowly with Jack holding her up on one side and Betty supporting her from the other side. When they reached the carriage, Sir Richard and Jack hoisted her up and onto the opposite seat where she collapsed against the cushion, shuddering, her breathing shallow. Like me, she spoke not a word.

Sir Richard climbed up next to his wife. He patted my hand, disregarding Isobel. Jack signaled the horses, and the carriage lurched forward towards our lodgings.

"I had thought," Sir Richard said to me, "to surprise you with a brief side trip to Portsmouth to visit your family while we were here since it is less than a morning's journey. But I think after all that has happened we had best head for home today. Lady Sarah is unwell, and you need to recover, too. I hope you will not develop chills or a fever."

I tucked my chin deep inside the rough collar of Jack's coat and closed my eyes. How I yearned now to see Mother and Father, to play "Hinch-Pinch" again with my sisters and find the best places, as I always did, to hide the wooden key Father had carved for our game. I thought of the silly song we always sang—*Vesy vasy vum, Buck aboo has come; Find it if you can*—the words in my head matching the rhythm of the carriage wheels.

We arrived home in the early evening, spent from the day's events. I rushed to my room, to avoid Isobel and Sir Richard. I threw Jack's coat on the bed, and with my hand shaking, I poured water from the pitcher on my night stand into the washing bowl. Grabbing the folded rag next to it and the piece of lye soap Peggy had given me, I scrubbed my salt-coated body and face and ears until they burned. With mother's silver-backed brush, I raked through my wet curls. Wrapped in my woolen nightdress, I hung Jack's coat on a hook, intending to give it back early in the morning.

Disturbed by a dark feeling of threat that still hung over me, I relived the day's confusion and terror in my mind, blaming Isobel, hating her. Filled with fury, I yanked the wooden box from under the bed, tossing its contents onto the floor until I found the doll crushed at the bottom.

I tore the yarn from its head, pulled out the sacking needle and stabbed at the cloth body. I ripped the seams until dirty straw bulged from its sides and legs and arms, transforming the doll into a pathetic scarecrow. From the pile of clothing beside me I took the ink-stained shift from my late-night battle with Isobel in the Library. I threw the doll's remains in the center and tied the ends together like a beggar's bundle.

Slipping out of my room, I tiptoed down the dark hallway and leaned my ear against Isobel's closed door. A drawer slammed shut, and Isobel screeched, "Get down, Cleo. You'll smear this. Leave me alone until I'm finished." Her voice rose higher. "Now look what you've done," she bellowed. "Ink stains on my new diary. You stupid cat." A thud and a yelp from Cleo.

Without making a sound, I eased the knotted end of the bundle over the door knob and drew back into the shadows when Isobel trilled, "What is it, Cleo? Did you hear something?" The knob twisted and the door creaked open.

Cleo leaped up to attack the bundle swinging back and forth. Isobel picked her up in one arm and freed the bundle from the doorknob. "I think we know the drowned rat this came from, don't we, Cleo?" she snarled, slamming the door and locking it.

A new plan formed in my mind. While Isobel worked with Fothering, I would find a way to steal into her room. I had to read her diary.

CHAPTER 9

Determined to find the diary, I tried for months to sneak into Isobel's room, but she always locked her door, taking the key with her whenever she departed, until the day Lady Sarah became desperately ill. Distraught when Maggie summoned her with the news, Isobel left the door to her room wide open. I slipped inside and closed it.

Suspecting that Isobel would use an obvious hiding place for her diary, I searched her desk first, familiar with a similar one I once explored in the Library. Removing the quills and pot of ink from the top drawer, I ran my fingers along the edge of the bottom panel to find a slight rise in the smooth wood. When I pressed it, the catch that held the panel in place released, and the bottom sprang open to reveal Isobel's red leather diary spotted with Cleo's inky paw prints.

The first entry was written on the night we returned from the bathing trip to Southampton when Isobel, it seems, had tried to unburden her troubled mind onto the pages of her diary.

Father will hate me more than ever now, she wrote in a surprisingly neat script, *if M. tells him what I did. I don't care. Mother understands. I didn't mean to drown M., just scare her, and teach her a lesson so she knows — she may fool him, but not Mother and me. Or Maggie. Or Cleo who hisses whenever M. comes near me.........*

Cleo must have sensed it was me skulking outside the room that night and alerted Isobel. And it seemed that after Isobel had retrieved and opened the bundle, she resumed writing in her diary, describing the torn doll as *a naked threat, a declaration of war, like the Pretender to the throne of King George,* as if I were threatening to take what she possessed away from her.

I read on as Isobel recounted how she retied the bundle and shoved the broken doll under her bed as a reminder to increase her vigilance and find a way to drive me from their home. She had slashed in bold, black letters, *I will crush her!* The exclamation point punctured the heavy parchment. The next entry was dated three days after our return from the Bath.

<u>15 September 1748</u> *Father has been nice to me since our return from the Bath. Maybe he doesn't know because the mewler hasn't had a chance to tattle to him. Mother fixed it. He has had no contact with M. since our return.*

He has complimented me twice on the neatness of my dress and hair. I've asked Fothering to tell him how much I am improving with my studies, and I have ordered Maggie to keep M. out of the Library from now on. Lindy can do the dusting. I make Fothering lock the Library every time we leave it.
Father has gone to London for a while. He left without telling M. I saw the surprise and the scared look on her face when Maggie told her he would not be back for weeks. She knows what she's in for when he isn't around.

He did say goodbye to me, and touched my hair.

<u>26 November</u> *Father is back today bearing gifts—a morning gown for Mother, a set of inlaid pearl combs for me, and a little silver crown for Cleo though she refuses to wear it. I laughed with him when she flicked it off. "She was probably expecting rubies," Father joked.*

He tells Mother that Uncle is stronger but cannot leave his bed. Father spent the days attending Parliament sessions in his place, though he could not cast votes. At night he wrote up the sessions' notes and composed letters in Uncle's name. M. seemed so forlorn when I showed Maggie the combs in my hair. I watched carefully all day and evening, but he ignored her, did not speak to her, and never mentioned her!

<u>3 December</u> *He is spending more time alone with Mother in her chambers. I even heard them laughing together. When I joined her for tea today, she was better,*

more color in her face than I have seen in a long time. And smiling! She tells me we will all spend Christmas together with Uncle in London. Not M. But Cleo can come. Hooray!

Our worries about M. are over. She knows her place now. Father pays no attention to her. Not to me either, but I know he is busy. He does love me. He and I have dinner together in silence most nights because he has so much work to do. He eats with a sheaf of papers in front of him, and I try not to distract him. I did think he would say something when I wore my pearl-seeded blue gown with the pearl combs he had bought for me in London, but he didn't. When I mentioned them, he nodded, looking annoyed, and resumed reading.

<u>8 December</u> I have seen Jack Finn talking to M. when she works in the kitchen garden, cutting away the dead plants or whatever she does scurrying around out there on her knees and scrabbling in the dirt. She probably reminds him of Annie and the potato farmers back home, one of his own kind. I have spied M. hanging around him whenever she can, fluttering her eyelashes at him, laughing at his jokes. He never talks to me anymore. I'm sure M. has told him lies about me. Father needs to know what the two of them are up to.

Leaving for London tomorrow, and Jack Finn will drive us. M. will have only Maggie and the servants for an audience now.

<u>12 February 1749</u> Home without Father who must stay longer with Uncle to handle the Parliament business for him. We were delayed in leaving London because of the weather. Too much snow and wind to risk traveling, though Jack insisted he could make it despite the roads. He will go back tomorrow as Father needs him there.

Cleo is glad to be home. She didn't like all of the rules she had to follow at Uncle's townhouse. Neither did I. He is grumpy and old and crippled. But Father did take Mother and me to a few parties and shopping. He bought us lots of gifts. He wanted me to look my best.

M. looking hideous and miserable had the nerve to ask me when Father would return. I flashed my new fan under her nose and told her that was none of her business and she'd better not ask again. Of truth be known, I don't know when he will be back and neither does Mother.

<u>8 April</u> I wish Father were here. Mother has done poorly ever since we came back from London and grows worse each day. Dr. Russell comes every few days bringing

that hawk-nosed Dr. Pritchard with him. O detest them both. They ban me from her rooms, telling me she must rest, so O don't know what they do during all their time with her. Yesterday, as O crouched in tears outside her door, O heard them say they will have to begin the blistering if she does not improve soon.

I was shocked to see this written evidence of Isobel's hatred and jealousy of me, though I was too immature and angry at the time to understand or appreciate the extent of her own misery. When I read that she made Fothering lock the Library every time they left it, destroying the little happiness I had found since my arrival, I was not surprised. Though I had assumed Maggie or Lindy was responsible, I should have suspected Isobel.

She captured my feelings well in her diary— my despair when Sir Richard departed for London without telling me though he said goodbye to Isobel and touched her hair; my fear and insecurity when left unprotected without him or Jack Finn to help dispel the harsh monotony and cruelty of my days; my misery and jealousy when he came back without a gift or a word for me; my anguish when he continued to ignore me. Isobel's words enraged me, and the desire for revenge mounted within me.

I restored the diary to its hiding place and carefully replaced the other items in the drawer. Leaving the door open, I left the room to resume my kitchen chores, relieved by Maggie's absence, though she bustled through the doorway soon after. A frown darkened her face, and she glared at me with reddened eyes.

"You're needed in Lady Sarah's chamber," she barked. "You've a mess to clean up. Pour some eucalyptus oil in a bucket of water and take some rags. Go at once and do what the doctors tell you."

I opened the door to Lady Sarah's bedroom and stepped inside, mindful not to slop any water onto the carpet. Isobel was not there. The sour smell of vomit permeated the room. At first the Doctors were too busy to notice me as they restrained Lady Sarah who struggled to free her arms from their clutches. "No more," she begged. Her voice diminished to a strangled whimper. "No more, please."

She lay in bed on her stomach with her bare back exposed. Blisters erupted from a range of fiery red patches on her skin. Dr. Russell leaned over and murmured something to her. He straightened up holding a clear glass cup, the size of a plum, in one hand. He inserted the cup into a set of pincers and held it over the flame of a fat candle resting on the nightstand.

70

After awhile, he handed the pincers to Dr. Pritchard who slid the cup onto Lady Sarah's left shoulder. Dr. Russell imprisoned her arms while Dr. Pritchard held the cup in place with the pincers. She writhed and screamed out.

When Dr. Pritchard saw me, he snapped his fingers and pointed to the floor at his feet where a yellowish puddle invaded the carpet and stained his shoes. I shuddered and moved toward him, setting the bucket next to the bed, and knelt down. With Lady Sarah moaning pitifully above my head, I wiped the film of vomit from his shoes and mopped the carpet.

"Now, now, just relax, madam," Dr. Pritchard ordered. "We'll finish soon."

As he began to affix another cup to Lady Sarah's ravaged back, I grabbed the bucket and escaped from the room.

Three days later, Maggie and Isobel sent a messenger to Sir Richard telling him he must come home immediately. Lady Sarah had to lie on her stomach day and night because of the ugly blisters across her back and shoulders. She moaned whenever we touched her or tried to force her to eat.

Maggie stood guard over me while I bathed Lady Sarah's back day and night with cool chamomile water and applied one of Maggie's herbal concoctions. She had taken charge and would no longer let the doctors in to see their tortured patient. Exhaustion and pity for Lady Sarah, despite her cruel treatment of me, often brought tears to my eyes. Isobel never came to her mother's rooms because, as Maggie explained to Lady Sarah, Isobel could not bear to see her mother in such distress.

Within a week, Sir Richard appeared, and Lady Sarah began to mend. Her spirits and appetite improved. She sat up in bed and even allowed Cleo to jump up and sit with her. The best news of all—Sir Richard would remain at home until he was needed in London.

CHAPTER 10

Maggie kept me slaving from sunup until late at night, many of those hours tending to Lady Sarah with her bouts of vomiting and diarrhea. After her health improved, she no longer left her chamber, so Maggie and Isobel spent most of the morning hours with her.

For the first time since my arrival at Hawthorn Manor, I had the chance to visit the maze, to show Sir Richard that I could do what Isobel had never done: reach the center. But as I stood at the ornate stone entrance, I hesitated on its soundless threshold, afraid to go any further, staring at the green walls that threatened to entrap me like the waves of the sea.

Two paths of equal length curved away from each side of the entrance. Rising above the shaved tops of the yew trees, the glass dome of the hermitage marked the center of the maze.

As I wavered at the entrance, someone approached behind me. I whirled around, startled to see Joseph standing with the rose clippers in his hand, his straw hat shading half of his wrinkled face.

"Sir Richard wants you in his study, Miss. He says be quick; it's important."

"He's asked for me?" I cried. "I thought he had returned to London. That Lady Sarah's Uncle is dying."

"Lord Wentworth is close to death, but Sir Richard has remained at home to attend to Lady Sarah's needs." Joseph removed his hat and fanned himself in the unusual early June heat. "Hurry, now. He waits in his study."

I had never been summoned to Sir Richard's study and felt reluctant to go. *Have I done something wrong?* I wondered. *Or perhaps Lady Sarah has expired.* My heart racing with that dark shadow of hope, I dashed across the sloping lawn and through the geometric gardens, trying not to trip on the discarded dress of Isobel's I was forced to wear, a brown muslin she disliked. It drooped from my shoulders and hung too loosely from my uncorseted midsection despite the folds the seamstress had stitched into the bosom and waist line. Isobel made sure I received her ugliest castoffs. Her lace-trimmed silk gowns in her favorite shades of magenta and blue she donated to the parish minister's daughter when tired of them. I dared not complain though and had seen little of Isobel for months.

The door to Sir Richard's study was open, but I waited on the threshold. He leaned against his desk reading a letter, wearing spectacles I had never seen. When he noticed me, he quickly removed them, setting them down on the desk and coming toward me, the letter still in his hand.

"Come in, Misella. We have received some shocking, sad news from your father. Your mother—poor Mariette—has died of the fever." He put his arm around me and led me closer to the fire blazing in the fireplace. "She was ill such a short time, your father writes, otherwise he would have notified you sooner so you could have gone home to see her. She talked about you often, he says. She missed you very much."

I could not at that moment accept the terrible truth that Mother could no longer love me or miss me or remember me. Instead I thought of Lily and Lizzie.

"Whatever will Lily do?" I blurted out. "She will die without mother; she's only three, and sickly Lizzie, how will she manage? Father can't take care of them, nor can Elinor."

Sir Richard hugged me to his chest, his warm breath stirring the ruffled edge of my cap. "Lily and Eliza have died of the fever, too, a day after your mother. They will all be buried together. Your father asked that you not attend the funeral because the fever still rages throughout the town and your house. Annabelle has it now, but she appears to be mending. Your father and Elinor were sick as well, but have recovered."

My cheek resting against the smooth brocade of Sir Richard's vest, I thought, *I will not cry.* I stared dry-eyed at his smooth, tapered fingers, so close to my face, holding the letter. Father's awkward, printed words spilled across the paper, arousing in me, despite the awful message, a momentary selfish resentment because he had never written to me, nor had Mother. In my hurt and anger I had chosen not to write to them unless I heard from them first. They were the ones who abandoned me, who sent me away.

Sir Richard pressed his lips to my forehead. "I am so sorry, my dear. Don't worry, we will take care of you. I have told Isobel and Lady Sarah, 'We must be kind and gentle with Misella, for losing a Mother is a terrible thing.'" Still embracing me, he eased me back gracefully so he could look into my eyes. "I will always take care of you," he said, and in my troubled mind and aching heart, I believed him.

As he held me at arm's length, his firm hands gripping my shoulders, his eyes gleamed with tears. "I'll leave the letter on my desk. When you are ready, please make use of my stationery to reply to your father."

I broke away from him and escaped to my room, trying to remember Mother's face and voice. Tormented by guilt, ashamed of my foolish pride that had prevented me from writing to her and to Father, I wanted to cry, but could shed no tears. In truth, I had not wanted her to know how I was being treated, how drab my clothes, how miserable I felt. I wanted to write to her, when I grew older, about balls and journeys to London, of evenings spent at the theatre or in elegant drawing rooms.

It frightened me to think of Mother and my little sisters gone forever from our home. Though away from my family for so long, I could not imagine our home without them. Lizzie had almost died from the pox when she was four, but she survived, and I had forgotten the anguish and fear that invaded our home while she was ill. I tried to picture their faces, how they had looked the last time I saw them, but all I could think about was my anger at Mother then and how I had blamed her for my misery ever since. *I never want to see her again,* I would often tell myself. *She sent me away. It's her fault that I have been so miserable here.* But in my heart, I knew that she loved me, and I grieved for all that I had lost.

In the late afternoon, I slipped into the quiet study, a fire burning small. I lit one of the sconces and the thick candle resting on Sir Richard's desk. Seated in his chair, I picked up his quill, and from a stack of embossed writing paper, I drew a single sheet, its gold crest gleaming in the candlelight.

Struggling for words, my sentences stiff and awkward, I composed a sympathy letter to a man who seemed a stranger to me now. "I read from your Book of Psalms each day," I wrote, "and whenever I am lonely or sad or discouraged I say the first words from one of them that you taught me: *'The Lord is on my side; I will not fear.'* The psalms comfort me now at this desolate time." I signed the letter, Your Loving Daughter.

As I inserted the ivory-handled quill back into the ink pot, the study door flew wide open. Isobel stood glowering in the doorway holding a spray of white roses wrapped in a cloth.

"See these?" she snarled, shaking the roses so that petals drifted to the floor. "These were for you. I was sorry about your mother. I searched every-where for you. And here you are." Her voice rose higher, shrill with rage. "Here, where I have never been allowed. Here, sitting at his desk. Holding his quill. The candle shining on your precious curls. I wish you were dead, too."

In my own grief and anger, I struck back. "Stop acting like a spoiled, jealous child, Isobel. I no longer care what you say or do. Since the day you tried to drown me, I have hated you. You are already dead to me."

With a strangled screech, she flung the flowers at me, knocking over the candle, which I managed to rescue before it damaged my letter. Cursing me, she fled.

Trembling with anger, I folded the letter, broke off a plug from a cyl-inder of wax, and held it in the tongs over the candle flame until it gave way to my touch. I pushed it in place over the folded flap of my letter and pressed Sir Richard's stamp deeply into its center. Writing Father's name on the outside in my best penmanship, I left the letter on the desk for Sir Richard to give to Jack Finn for the mail coach. I left the roses there, too, hoping Sir Richard would ask me about them so I could tell him about his wicked daughter. But he never did.

A month later I received a return letter from Father. They had all recovered from the illness, he and Elinor and Annabelle, but not yet from the deaths. He had found work on a merchant ship and the promise of a job on a fishing trawler in America. He would be crossing the Atlantic soon and would arrange passages for my sisters, and find a suitable house for them in a town called Boston.

"I have confidence in Elinor's ability," he wrote, "to keep the house-hold going in my absence. I pray for you and am happy that you found comfort in the psalms as I have." He would write when he could, though he wondered why I never answered any of his or Mother's previous letters. "Though I know you were angry with us, Misella, and I am sorry for that." He hoped to see me sometime in the future when his finances improved and he could afford to visit or to send for me if I wished to join them in their new home. My sisters sent their love along with his.

Shocked and puzzled, I showed his letter to Sir Richard asking what might have happened to the other letters. Though I didn't say so, I suspected that Isobel may have somehow gotten her hands on them and hid them from me or even destroyed them. I thought he would investigate for me.

"This is strange, Misella," he said with what I assumed was sincerity that such a thing had happened in his household. "I will question Jack Finn about this. He handles the mail for us."

I asked Jack about the mystery myself when I saw him. A frown narrowed his eyes, and he shook his head. "I'm sorry, Misella, I'd niver know. I bring the bundled letters, but I'm ordered not to look through them." He hesitated for a moment. "But sure and I will check the mail from now on. If I see any that belongs to ye, I'll give them only to ye."

For months I waited for another letter from Father, watching each week for Jack when he brought the mail from town. "Anything for me?" I'd cry from the porch as soon as the carriage drew up to the portico. Each time, when he offered a sad, half smile and shook his head, I would hasten inside, not wanting him to see my disappointment, not wanting to hear his cheerful, "Give it more time, Miss. It will come."

But I never heard from Father again.

CHAPTER 11

During the next three years, little changed at Hawthorn Manor in spite of Sir Richard's promise to take care of me. How naïve I had been to believe that Lady Sarah and Isobel would feel sympathy for me now that I was almost an orphan. Though I depended more upon Sir Richard for kindness and affection, they resented me even more and treated me worse than ever.

With a smile, Jack explained why. "Isobel envies your looks, Misella, especially now that ye've reached your sixteenth year. Your clear skin, your golden curls, and your lovely figure make her more jealous than ever. 'Tis why she gives ye her ugliest castoff dresses."

Isobel had grown thick, her skin more blemished as she neared her eighteenth birthday. With her fattened cheeks and squinty hazel eyes, she reminded me of her cat. Even her pallid yellow hair resembled Cleo's. To puff up her pompadours, Isobel had her hair ratted daily and passed her time lounging with her mother in her stuffy chambers or reading theatrical novels.

Sir Richard was absent most of the time, and that meant Jack Finn was gone as well. I missed Jack: his smiles, his stories, his listening ear, his questions about Portsmouth and the family I once had. Not that I saw much of him when he did return from the frequent trips to London. If he came into the kitchen garden while I worked there, Maggie's sharp voice ordered me inside. If he slipped into the scullery while I scrubbed pots or separated herbs, Maggie, alerted by one of the maids, barreled in with a summons for him from Sir Richard.

When Lady Sarah's uncle finally expired, she and Isobel left for London to join Sir Richard and to attend the funeral. They were back in a fortnight, but not Sir Richard. He stayed in London deeply worried about keeping his newly inherited seat in Parliament. Within the year, he would have to defend his appointed position against a Whig opponent, Jonathan Proctor.

Lady Sarah and Isobel were to return to London in six months for Isobel's introduction into society and to support Sir Richard's campaign in the upcoming election.

They made it cruelly clear to me that I would not accompany them and made sure that I participated in their frenzied preparations. For months, they demanded my help with the dressmaking, that I hold the cloth as it was being cut, measure hems, trim laces, string seed pearls and wind lengths of thread. Isobel would attack me as I worked, pinching my arm or pushing me. "Can't you do anything right?" she'd snap, the seamstresses watching, embarrassed for me. Lady Sarah would cluck her tongue from her chaise lounge and lift her laudanum-laced tea to her thin lips.

My only comfort came from participating in Isobel's fittings. Her corset strings would be strained to the breaking point by her thick breasts and bulging waist, and the laced and jeweled bodices appeared dull against her mottled skin. How I longed to wear such gowns, to remove my worn leather shoes and slip on the rose silk pumps with diamond-edged buckles, or the gold-threaded brocades with filmy silk ribbons.

After weeks of constant badgering and ridicule from Isobel and Lady Sarah, I grew more and more depressed though I concealed my feelings, swallowed my pride, and remained congenial.

Sir Richard tried to soothe my wounded feelings when he returned. The day before the family left for London, he called me to his study and apologized for leaving me behind. "Once I have secured my seat in Parliament, I promise, Misella, that things will change. And I guarantee that on your eighteenth birthday you will have your introduction to London society, and you will mesmerize them. You will have your chance to shine in a way that Isobel never can." He drew a small velvet bag from his waistcoat pocket and pressed it into my hand. "Something to comfort you, my dear."

I untied the taut strings and removed a thin gold chain with a shiny heart-shaped locket attached. Sir Richard urged me to open it. When I pressed the tiny latch, the heart sprang open. On one side a small cut diamond was centered upon a bed of mother of pearl, on the other the Maltby crest finely etched in ebony and gold. I caught my breath.

Sir Richard pulled me to him. "I want you to know that you belong here, Misella," he said. He lifted the locket from my hands, snapped it closed, and undid the delicate latch. He encircled my neck, brushing the curls aside, and clasped the necklace in place. His fingers touched the bare skin below the hollow of my neck as he centered the locket in place.

"Let this be our secret for now," he said. "Don't let Isobel or Lady Maltby see it for they would be jealous and want one, too. But this is just for you. Your life will change, I promise."

The recent pain and humiliation, the frustration and anger I had felt for years, vanished with his loving touch, the richness of his gift, and the promise that began, for the first time, to seem attainable. I felt the change in him; he spoke with a resolve in his voice I had not heard before. I was humbled by his confidence in me—elated that he thought me worthy, that he would in time introduce me in society as his daughter, and fulfill my mother's dream and mine. My heart swelled to bursting with happiness.

The next morning the coach stood at the portico awaiting the family's departure, the trunks of gowns and shoes having been sent ahead, along with Lady Sarah's medicine boxes and pillows. Unable to hold back a few tears of envy, I watched the preparations from the marble bench in the garden gazebo.

Jack Finn spotted me there. He jumped down from the coach and crossed the lawn. "You look so sad, Misella. I suppose ye wish ye were going, too," he said as he approached. "Niver been to London, have ye?"

I wiped away the tears and smiled. I always had to smile whenever I saw him—he appeared so outlandish with his ribboned breeches and his bright plaid vests. A bunch of red and purple posies sprang from his lapel and a garland of matching flowers ringed his tri-cornered hat cocked at a jaunty angle, a red ribbon tying back his mass of dark, jumbled curls.

With a serious face, he removed his hat and held it like a book in his hands. "I'll miss seeing ye while I'm gone. I niver like staying so long in London, though even here he keeps me so busy I've no time for our talks. I'm sorely troubled about that."

He twirled his hat through his fingers a few times. "Believe me, you're not missing anything important in London. A pack of pretty fools on the prowl in expensive clothes hoping to gig a rich spouse. You should see them dance. They shake their silly fans in gentlemen's faces and cover their grinning mouths as if they were too shy to say a word. And the gentlemen peacocks prance about on their toes, their powdered wigs askew from their tipsy dancing and from stopping after each minuet to pinch a wad of snuff."

Jack rose up on his booted toes like a dancer using his hat as a fan, stopping in mid-step to become a bowing dandy, whipping out his linen handkerchief and flaunting it in the air. I laughed and clapped my hands.

Extending a limp-wristed hand and snapping his fingers, he said, "Come, come, Miss, the music calls."

I gave him my hand. He pulled me up and spun me around, singing in his fine baritone, *He can move you fast or slow/Touch your heart or stir your toe/ Piping Tom of Galway.* Giggling, I twirled with him around the grass until he danced me back to the bench, swiped his handkerchief across the marble seat and sat me down. He extracted the bunch of posies from his lapel and presented them to me.

"Thank you, kind Sir," I cried. "Never have I seen such exquisite flowers."

Jack leaned down and with mock seriousness kissed my hand.

"Jack." Sir Richard's voice startled us as he emerged from behind the gazebo's rose-covered trellis, his face as red as the flowers. "I am waiting," he snapped. I had never heard Sir Richard speak so to Jack, but Jack seemed undisturbed as he tipped his hat to me and, with deep strides, headed for the waiting carriage.

I feared Sir Richard might be angry with me or think that I called Jack to me, but he smiled at me, the dark color receding from his face. "Don't worry, Misella. I won't punish Jack for not staying with the carriage as he should have. Sometimes, however, Jack forgets his place. He mustn't mingle with the rest of us. You'll remember that, won't you, and let me know if he tries to entertain you with his antics in the future?"

Not waiting for an answer, he walked back to the coach, Jack standing in his usual post by the open door. After Sir Richard entered, Jack closed the door and bounded up to his seat, still unfazed it seemed, by Sir Richard's stern demeanor. When Jack saw me watching, he tipped his chin up with his index finger and gazed skyward before he took up the reins. I decided at that moment that I would disobey Sir Richard's orders about

Jack. I could not bear the thought of losing his companionship, and I realized as the coach pulled away that I would miss him more than I would Sir Richard.

During their absence my chores increased. Maggie kept me running errands, airing pillows and feather mattresses, cooking and scrubbing and tending the kitchen garden. The hidden locket cooled the skin beneath the bodice of my muslin gown as I worked with renewed energy and a meekness that surprised Maggie. My time would come soon.

I was sweeping the portico when the family came home. Sir Richard carried Lady Sarah to the door, her pale face pinched with pain and exhaustion. "A serious flare-up of her nervous condition," he told Maggie in the doorway. "Dr. Russell has ordered complete bed rest for her. Indefinitely."

Isobel hovered behind as the servants struggled to remove the trunks and boxes from the carriage hold, her reddened face limned with moisture, her eyes darting after Lady Sarah. When she noticed me, she yelled, "You! Carry these to my rooms." When I approached, she scowled at me and pointed at two stuffed brocade bags. I hoisted them up without saying a word, the weight almost knocking me over. After Isobel vanished through the open front door, I waited awhile before lugging the bags up to her rooms.

Isobel didn't answer when I banged on her door, so I let myself in, tossing the bags, one by one, onto her rose-patterned rug. One of them split open, spewing its contents across the rug: a mass of wrinkled scarves, a large scrolled make-up box, a novel titled *The Reform'd Coquette*, a smudged box of Swiss chocolates, and a brown bottle labeled "Laudanum" that I assumed belonged to Lady Sarah.

Before I could return the items, Isobel burst through the doorway. "You little sneak," she screamed. "How dare you spy on me, rummaging through my things." She stumbled toward me, eyes blazing, her hand raised as if to slap my face, but I stepped backwards. "Wait until Father hears about this violation," she spat. "Pick them up, now, and put them back where you found them."

My anger at Isobel, suppressed within me for years, erupted. I kicked the box of chocolates and the laudanum bottle, sending them spinning across the gaudy rug. "Pick them up yourself," I cried, grinding a few of the scattered chocolates under my shoe. "They fell out of your fat bag when it split open because you stuffed it, like you stuff yourself, with your mindless trash."

Scarlet-faced, Isobel lunged for me, but I slipped past her to the door, slamming it on my way out. Though I knew Isobel would make me pay for my insolence, I felt a newfound sense of satisfaction and a firm resolve to fight for myself, confident that Sir Richard would not side against me. I headed happily to Lady Sarah's quarters where Maggie had ordered me to spend the remainder of the day unpacking. Worried about her mother's condition, Isobel, I knew, would not create a scene there.

Late that evening, after a flurry of unpacking the family's trunks, scrubbing down and rearranging Lady Sarah's quarters to her liking, fluffing her pillows, replacing her old medicine bottles with a daunting display of new tinctures and "female strengthening" elixirs, crushing a mad array of herbs and bulky pills together in a mortar until my fingers curled with cramps, and dumping the powders in equal amounts into little enameled boxes, I finally finished, blurry-eyed with exhaustion.

When I left the room, Sir Richard appeared in the dim hallway outside Lady Sarah's chambers. "Misella," he whispered, his face inscrutable, "I need you to come to my study for a moment. We have something to discuss." Half asleep, I followed him uneasily down the stairs and into the well-lit study, afraid of what Isobel might have told him. He closed the door.

"Dear one," he said softly. "This is a difficult time. The Doctors believe Lady Sarah will be an invalid from now on." He dabbed at his eyes with his handkerchief, though I had not noticed any tears. "She may have only a short time to live."

He grasped one of my hands. "It is time for you to assume the place which I always intended you to hold in the family. I can assure you that Lady Sarah and Isobel will not hurt you again." He took a small drawstringed bag from his pocket. "I want you to buy a rich suit at the mercers. I have arranged for the phaeton to take you to Mr. Ellinson's shop early tomorrow."

I gasped with surprise and pleasure, my weariness and worries forgotten.

"Oh, and, Misella," he added, a frown disrupting his smooth expression, "I fear I must warn you about Jack. I never disclosed this because I did not want to cause alarm, but I watch him closely for good reason." He tossed the bag back and forth in his hands, as if weighing whether or not he should continue, the clinking of the coins seeming to mimic the progression of his thoughts.

With a troubled look on his face, he set the purse down behind him on his desk and took my hand back in both of his. "Jack is not to be trusted so easily." He released my hand, closing his eyes for a moment and rubbing his temples as if to relieve some tightness there.

"You need to know this," he sighed. "Jack once rode as a highwayman, first in Ireland and then here after he arrived in England. He was a scoundrel, very clever, always in disguise, caught twice. The first time he escaped the noose by claiming benefit of clergy. Because he attended Trinity College for a time, he knew his Bible verses and so only received the branding on his thumb as a felon. Foolishly, however, he resumed his trade. I first made his acquaintance some years ago when he tried to rob me on the road to London."

He picked up the bag of coins and bounced it in his palm. "At gunpoint, I bargained with the notorious thief, offered him the pay and security my title would afford him if he would protect me from other highwaymen. I promised to keep his past a secret. Which I have done until this very moment."

Stunned into silence, I remembered the "F" tattooed on Jack's thumb, his initial I had thought. How naive I was. His friendship, the charm and humor I had come to enjoy, what if that, too, was just a disguise meant to disarm me? I knew highwaymen terrorized their victims, often beating them, and even slaughtering them if necessary to escape capture. I thought of the corpse I saw on our journey to Hawthorn Manor. A familiar feeling of dread and betrayal coursed through me reminding me of the day I left home.

Sir Richard handed me the heavy purse, his hands closing around mine. "I want you to apply privately to me for money whenever you need it, my dear. Let it be known for now that your well-to-do father in America has sent it to you."

"B-but that would be telling a lie, Sir, about Father. I cannot do that. I am—"

"No, no, not a lie," he interrupted, "just a temporary falsehood—until Isobel learns to accept you as her equal. She would be inconsolable if she knew I provided you your wardrobe, and we cannot have her upsetting Lady Sarah right now. Anyway, I'm sure your father would send you the money if he could. Don't worry. I will take care to confirm the falsehood."

His reasoning convinced me, and his generosity and kindness helped to relieve my fearful thoughts about Jack. My tenderness and gratitude toward Sir Richard increased, along with my dependence upon him as my only ally.

Any uneasiness that still troubled my conscience departed at the mercer's where I selected a bolt of silk in a rich shade of azure, material for a matching petticoat quilted with strands of gold, a pure linen shift, a whale bone corset of the finest quality, and a pair of satin pumps in a darker shade of blue.

The following week when the outfit was delivered, Sir Richard invited me to accompany him on an outing to visit the estate of a colleague in Parliament who lived close by. The maids gawked when they saw me so richly attired, my hair dressed for the occasion.

Jack Finn stared, too, as I descended from the front portico to meet Sir Richard waiting by the carriage. "A beautiful gown," Sir Richard said, his eyes shining. He reached out to touch one silken sleeve. "You do it justice," he murmured.

He had to remind Jack to open the door for us and set the step stool. I had never seen Jack look or act so serious. No grin, no twinkle in his eye, no wink or greeting. I thought perhaps Sir Richard had warned him as well. When Jack reached out to assist me, I brushed his hand away and climbed inside the carriage on my own.

Sir Richard introduced me to his acquaintance and his startled wife as his adopted daughter, whom he had taken into his care. The wife, who urged me to call her Margaret instead of Lady Hawkins, ushered me into their drawing room where we chatted while the men conducted their business. *This is what my future will be.* I thought, the gold locket glittering between my breasts as I delicately sipped strong tea from a china cup as thin as a butterfly's wing.

Jack was just as solemn on our journey home. I hesitated when I left the coach wondering if he would dare to say something to me, but he did not. He only grimaced as if in pain and would not look at me.

When I thanked Sir Richard for the outing, he smiled and straightened the locket which had twisted backwards. His fingers lingered for a moment against my skin. *He wants me to know*, I thought, *how pleased he is that I have worn it today.*

"We will do this again, Misella, many times," he said. "You are an exquisite companion. I think it is time that you join Isobel and me for dinner—I'll see you in the dining room this evening at 8:00."

In a daze of happiness, I strutted inside, swirling my sky-blue skirt around as I had seen Lady Sarah and Margaret do, hoping to encounter Isobel. But sadly she was nowhere in sight. My disappointment quickly diminished, though, when I remembered that she would come upon me at dinner. I could not wait to see her reaction.

CHAPTER 12

As I relaxed in my room before dinner, one of the new maidservants knocked on my door and handed me a note, folded twice over. Without a word of explanation, she curtsied (how elated that made me), and took her leave. From Sir Richard, I assumed, but the brief note came from Jack.

Misella,

> *Take care with yore heart. Beware of rogues offering ye*
> *flattery and finery. Remember yore own dear Pa who I know*
> *from our discussions would warn ye to be careful and to look*
> *to yore book of Psalms. He would tell ye to find strength and*
> *wisdom in those Words.*

> *Jack Finn*

Jack's audacity, his fake concern, angered me. He was a low-class thief and a cheat, jealous of my good fortune and Sir Richard's kindness to me.

Wanting to confront him, I dashed from my room, the letter clutched in my hand. I found him in the mews behind the house where he lounged against one of the horse stalls, laughing and teasing Joseph's son as he brushed down Sir Richard's mare.

"Jack!" I waved the note in his face. "Who made you my guardian?"

Jack grabbed my arm and steered me away from the stable, his blue eyes flashing. "Watch what ye say, Misella. Whom ye trust. That note was meant to be private, just for ye to ponder. Not the servants, or any one else."

A large shadow fell across the lawn behind Jack. Facing me, Jack could not see behind him. Isobel, I thought, but with the sun in my eyes, I could not see clearly. My hand shielding my eyes, I squinted for a better look.

Sir Richard lunged forward, startling me, his brocade coat shiny in the late afternoon sunlight. Jack had no time to drop his hand from my arm or to grab the note from me. Instead, Sir Richard whisked the note from my fingers. "What have we here, Jack," he asked, his voice like a blade cutting the air around us. "A love note? Setting up a rendezvous with our young maiden without her guardian's knowledge?" Jack stepped back, his face a mask.

Sir Richard told me firmly, "Go inside, Misella. And be prompt at dinner."

Upset and confused by Sir Richard's unfounded accusations, I felt a faint resurgence of loyalty toward Jack. My anger at him began to dissolve, and I regretted my childish outburst and the trouble caused him. "Please, Sir," I reached out to take the note from Sir Richard, but he pulled it away. "Jack meant me no harm. He always treats me kindly and with respect."

Sir Richard kept his eyes on the note. "Go back to the house, now, Misella," he ordered, his voice cold. Ashamed, I ran, the wrangling of their raised voices following me. I heard Sir Richard yell, "I warned you with Annie," and Jack's voice even louder shouting, "Annie was like a sister to me," and Sir Richard responding, "And you expect me to believe that is how you feel about Misella, too?"

I escaped through the kitchen doorway, my head pounding with confusion, not wanting to think or to hear any more.

Later, when I came early to the dining room, I heard the servants chattering in the kitchen. Peggy came in to set up the table and arrange the sideboard. Wordless and frowning, she refused to face me.

I had to ask her. "Peggy, please, can you tell me about Annie? Who was she?"

She stood perfectly still, her broad back rigid. Finally, she turned around, avoiding my eyes, her face flushed, her voice clipped. "She was a servant from Galway, like me. She left soon after I arrived." Biting her lips together, she seemed reluctant to say anything more, but as she escaped from the room, she said, "Jack Finn is a good man."

Silence met me when I followed her into the kitchen hoping for more information. None of the servants would look at me, and even mild-mannered Joseph wore a look of disgust on his face. I knew they must have heard about the confrontation with Jack and the argument between him and Sir Richard. With a heavy heart I entered the dining room to wait for Sir Richard and Isobel to come to dinner.

When Sir Richard arrived, dressed elaborately in a slate-colored velvet jacket with a froth of lace at his neck and sleeves, he smiled, took my hand and led me to the chair where Isobel always sat. With great formality he said, "You may sit here, Misella. Isobel will not be joining us this evening."

The servant came forward and pulled out the chair for me. Relieved that Sir Richard was in good spirits, I took my place. He seated himself and motioned for the servant to pour wine for us both. "A toast to you, Misella, my second daughter," he said raising his glass. He waited for me to raise my own and, looking into my eyes, drained his glass.

I had never tasted wine, and I relished the sweet, sharp bite of it, though it made my eyes water. Sir Richard laughed and refilled his glass. "Drink up, Misella." And I did, so happy that he seemed not at all upset about the misunderstanding with Jack.

He refilled my glass several times throughout dinner. I laughed at everything he said, lapping up his fond gazes and preening under the warm approval in his eyes. When we finished dinner, he said, his voice low, "We'll move into the study, my dear, for I have something to tell you."

I wobbled behind him into the warm and shadowy study, the fire burning low, only a few candles lighting our way. He turned to me, his eyes glittering, his voice subdued. "I have a challenge for you, Misella, to reach the center of the maze. I know you can, if you trust your instincts and your mind. And when you do, I will reward your intelligence and persistence." Picking up a teakwood box from his desk, he opened it to reveal, curled on a velvet bed, a gold necklace sprinkled with tiny diamonds, its yew-shaped emerald pendant set afire by the candle's glow.

He leaned in and kissed my cheek. "And when you wear this at your coming out celebration next year, I will be the envy of fathers everywhere because no other man in the world could have a daughter as beautiful as you."

I felt myself blush. My cheek burned, perhaps from the heat of his lips, and my heart soared.

"Now, good night, my dear." He poured himself some claret.

Before I left him, I asked if he was angry at Jack.

He raised his head, the stem of his glass suspended between his fingers, its carved bowl cupped in his palm as if he were holding a crystal ball. "Jack no longer works in my employ," he said. "He's gone. Let's not mention him again."

A sense of loss and desolation gripped me, destroying my previous elation. A feeling of homesickness, which I thought I had outgrown, overwhelmed me. Suddenly, I longed to go home—a foolish desire since that home no longer existed. Before Sir Richard could see the tears slipping from my eyes, I hastened from the study.

CHAPTER 13

I resolved to accept Sir Richard's challenge, to trust my instincts and my mind, not because of the necklace, but because in my loneliness and isolation, I wanted to see the flash of admiration in his eyes, to hear his voice soften with praise when I succeeded.

For weeks I prepared for my solitary journey to the heart of the maze, slipping into Sir Richard's study and raiding his private library unseen, scouring his books on ancient labyrinths until I came up with a plan to conquer the maze.

That day floats unchanged, ever present in my memory.

I step through the shaded opening into the maze, the hem of my gown catching on a lowly branch, the air sharp with the scent of evergreen. A shimmering dragonfly spins its way ahead of me, an iridescent flash of wings in the shards of sunlight that dart across the tops of the towering yews. The grass path is smooth under my feet; no sound breaches the silence of this narrow, verdant womb. A muslin bag swings from my wrist weighed down by a thick ball of twine and heavy scissors.

The little wooden whistle Sir Richard gave me is tucked into my bodice. Its shrill blast will summon Joseph if I should lose my way as Isobel did, he said, whenever she tried to reach the center. Then Joseph will have to haul the tall wooden ladder to the outer edge of the maze and climb to the top so he can locate me and coach me back to the opening. But I am determined not to use the whistle.

I turn left. I knot the end of the twine to the base of a tree branch and begin to unravel it, like Ariadne's thread, along a much narrower path as I proceed, my lifeline to the outside world.

As a child I excelled at solving puzzles. On market day, my sisters and I played games of hide and seek, sneaking through the market stalls that meandered like a maze. They were afraid to venture very far from Mother. Not I. I would disappear for hours, but I was never lost. I always counted my steps from one row to the next, marking each turn with a symbol to help me find my way back—a crooked brick, a discarded urn lying sideways against a stool, a colored bead glinting in a cobblestone crevice, a stall keeper's bodice stained in the shape of a fish head.

The twine snaking behind me, I run my hand along the stiff leaves on the left side until I reach the first hairpin twist. I look for some identifying marker to help me decide which way to go, but the trees on each side are precisely symmetrical, the path smooth and unblemished. I will have to rely on the twine each time I encounter a dead end, though it will take me longer to rewind, retrace my steps, and begin again.

Turning more corners, surrounded by the stillness, a cloud-filled sky overhead, I strip leaves from one branch in each section as I move along. I count my footsteps, eliminating each dead end until, at last victorious, I reach the center and the glass-enclosed hermitage, its dome gleaming in the sun.

I step through the open doorway and find myself within a circle of shoulder-high brick walls, exotic plants spilling from curved stone shelves set at random along the bricks, a broad stone bench centered under the dome. The heat from the sun releases a powerful fragrance from the trapped plants and flowers of brilliant reds and oranges and yellows.

A tall, dusky statue, set into a wide niche in the far wall, commands my attention, a goddess of some kind. A small fountain gurgles at her feet dispensing water into a slim trough that supplies the plants spread all around it. I feel drunk with the quiet beauty of this place, sequestered from the world. At this moment, finding this place seems reward enough for me, though I cannot wait to tell

Sir Richard of my discovery. I pluck a red hibiscus to take with me, an emblem of my victory.

"Congratulations, my dear. You have done it."

I whirl around, dropping the flower. Sir Richard lounges jacketless, blocking the doorway, a large wicker basket in his hands, a richly woven blanket over his arm. His fine linen shirt gapes open, its lace tie dangling to his waist. He moves toward me, sets the basket and blanket on the bench, reaches for my hand and brings it gently to his lips.

"How do you like my little paradise?" he asks. "Worth the struggle to reach it, don't you agree? Come sit while I lay out our lunch. We must celebrate your victory and mine. My re-election is assured. I have won the seat in Parliament this time through my own efforts without Lady Sarah's family influence."

He smiles at me, his eyes aglow, the sunlight from above gilding his hair, his face shining in the humid air. Moving the basket to the stone floor, he spreads the blanket onto the bench, takes my hand again and sits me down. He opens the basket and lifts out a goatskin bag, beads of moisture clinging to it. Drawing forth two goblets, his fingers smudging their outline onto the silver, he sets the goblets upright on the blanket. He withdraws the bag's jeweled stopper and pours amber liquid into each goblet. "Mead," he tells me. "Made from the honey of South American bees, infused with rare spices and fermented for years in caves in the Andes Mountains. So rare is it, that no English woman has ever tasted it. You will be the first."

He hands me a goblet and takes the other. "You must close your eyes," he whispers, "as you taste and keep them closed until you finish it all. That was the rule of the ancient Goddess. . . . .to any who dared to drink her elixir."

My breath catches when the cold metal touches my fingers. Sir Richard returns the wine bag to the basket and sits down next to me. "Sip slowly, Misella, and experience the nectar of life." He touches the rim of his glass to mine, closes his eyes, and raises the glass to his lips, his garnet ring glowing in the light like the eye of some ancient centaur.

I close my eyes and lift the heavy goblet to my lips, inhaling the scent of ancient spices, the taste on my tongue sweet and thick, cool as a spring mist but with a fire to it, too. It burns at first and then cools my throat. The fumes engulf me. I imagine myself at the feet of the Goddess, her hypnotic eyes, gold-flecked granite, holding me captive.

I drain my goblet, and feel myself weaving to some ancient chant, its music moving through me almost against my will.

"Misella," the goddess whispers, her warm lips against my ear. I open my eyes, and Sir Richard brushes his lips across my cheek. He takes my hand, caressing it, circling his fingers across my palm, creating a vortex that seems to spin deep inside me. I am confused, not sure where I am. His shirt is gone. He lifts my palm to his lips, his tongue tracing the circle his fingers had made. "No," I whisper, my hand limp and helpless in his grasp, my heart beating with fear, or excitement. I am not sure.

He leans into me and presses his lips to mine, gently, at first. I hesitate, inhaling the sweet warmth of his breath. He touches my lips with his tongue, nudging them open, stopping my breath, his arm crushing me to his bare chest. Panting with a terrifying inner confusion, I try to pull away, but I am trapped. His hand unhooks the front of my gown, releasing my petticoat. "No, please," I whimper.

"Misella, my sweet," he whispers, "I have loved you for so long."

I think I am drowning, my gown billowing out around me and then lifted over my head with a powerful force. He rips open my shift, tears at my stays. My bared arms thrash against him; I rake his chest with my fingers as I struggle to free myself, to save myself from the tide sweeping me further out to sea, but his arms tighten around me.

He moans against my naked breast, his mouth opening to draw me in. He thrusts me down upon the stone bench, hard and unforgiving against my arching back. He pushes into me. Searing pain rips through me. I gasp for air. Half-conscious, I imagine I have fallen from our dock and am dashed against the rocks with Father crying out my name in his hoarse voice.

The heat of the room presses against me, threatening to dissolve me. He sighs, his lips against my neck. "Misella, you have hypnotized me," he murmurs. "For so long, I have needed you. You belong to me now."

I shiver with disgust against the clammy, slackened weight of his body. I cannot look at him or speak. I stare at the dark statue of the goddess, overwhelmed with shame and guilt at the bitter irony of his words and the twisted sense of victory they offer. My foolish vanity has led me to this tortured ending and the agonizing question that lingers in my mind—*Am I to blame?*

I lie passive as he arises and prepares himself to leave me. "Wait for a time before you follow," he cautions, his voice no longer softened with desire. "This shall be our secret meeting place." He drapes my gown across me, then takes the basket with its tumbled contents and departs.

I know not how long I lay motionless, some of the words from my father's favorite psalm running through my brain. *The Lord is on my side: I will not fear: what can man do unto me?* I feel betrayed by the sweet promise of those words. They do not comfort me.

The sun had set and a damp chill had begun to creep into the hermitage when I arose and cleansed my aching body with water from the trough, scrubbing away as best I could the remnants of my sin and the tears I could no longer contain. I dressed quickly, my stays half unlatched, my clothes wrinkled, and fled into the shadowed pathway leaving the twisted blanket where it lay.

* * *

That evening I feigned a headache, ignoring the maid's summons from Sir Richard to join him for supper. I lay in bed, the feather quilt encasing my aching body, Father's book of psalms, retrieved from its hiding place, resting unopened beside my clenched hands.

Sir Richard left the next morning for a few days in London. I spent much of the time in my room, avoiding Isobel and her probing eyes, afraid she might detect some outward sign of my transgression. Though I tried not to blame myself for what happened, I had to face the guilty truth that, however innocent my intentions, I had sought Sir Richard's attention whenever I could and encouraged his affection. I accepted his gifts with joy and rejoiced in vain triumph whenever he preferred my presence to that of his wife and daughter.

The next day I opened the little book, my hands caressing the frayed pages, longing to see Father's care-worn face again, remembering his coarse hands encasing mine as he taught me to carve my own quills from the sleek goose feathers he saved for me: soaking the tubes overnight in water, then immersing them in heated sand to give them resilience and toughness. With a gentle touch, he showed me how to use his small fishing knife to scrape the bits of plume away until the shafts were smooth and the tips could be shaped and sharpened.

Thinking of him and how much he lived his life within the boundaries of his beloved psalms, I cried in despair and loneliness. My memories of him, and the readings, forced me to confront my conscience. Over the next several days, I began to dwell on the words of Psalm 32. *I acknowledged my sin unto thee, and mine iniquity have I not hid. I said, "I will confess my transgressions unto the Lord;" and thou forgavest the iniquity of my sin.* I found some comfort in those words, and I prayed for forgiveness.

When Sir Richard returned, he insisted that I meet him in his study. "He'll not have you refuse him," Peggy warned when she barged into my room without knocking. "He says I am to drag you down the stairs, if necessary." She would not look at me, but cast her eyes toward the shuttered window, her arms crossed in front of her chest. I missed Peggy's friendship, her warm smile and bright eyes, lost to me since Jack Finn's departure. I yearned to confide in Peggy, but her cold voice and stiff posture discouraged any attempt at intimacy.

"All right, Peggy," I sighed. "Please tell him I will come down in a few minutes. I must dress. You needn't wait for me."

Peggy nodded and snapped the door shut. I did not change out of my daytime muslin, nor did I brush my hair or even glance in my looking glass.

Isobel hovered in the shadows outside Sir Richard's study, waiting for me. "Good evening, little strumpet," she said, thrusting herself in front of me and blocking my way. When I tried to step around her, she grabbed my arm. "I know what you're up to," she whispered. "You think my father will take care of you, treat you like a lady. You fool. You're nothing but a fancy toy he will throw away when he grows tired of your shiny newness. We have been through this before, Mother and I."

I pulled away from her, choosing to ignore the insults. I understood that Isobel's anger and jealousy fueled her shameless lies. With the lessons from the psalms ringing in my mind and heart, for the first time I felt sympathy for Isobel. Hesitating for a moment, I whispered, "I am sorry, Isobel."

"Too late for that," she hissed as I slipped past her into the study.

Sir Richard arose from his chair and came toward me, closing the door and taking me in his arms. I stiffened as he hugged me to him, kissing me on one cheek and then the other. "My beautiful Misella, how I have missed you."

I began to cry. "I cannot do this, Sir," I sobbed. "I cannot sin this way again."

He released me, a look of concern on his face. "Misella, have you forgotten how much I love you? I would never want to hurt you." He drew his linen handkerchief from his pocket and gently wiped my tears. "Love cannot be a sin, my dear. It would only be a sin if we hurt others with the love we share. And we have hurt no one. Lady Sarah has never loved or respected me. Nor has she wished to share my bed for years. That is her choice. Why should she be hurt if I choose to share my love with another? I still honor our marriage vow, but that is not a promise of love, it is merely a legal arrangement."

"But what of Isobel?" I sniveled. "She hates me because you love me."

"I love Isobel as a daughter," he continued, "and have given her everything she needs. If she is hurt because I share my love with you in a different way, not as a father, she must learn to accept that. She should not be greedy. My love for you takes nothing away from her." He dashed some remaining tears away with his fingers, and kissed me again on the cheek.

"B-but it cannot be right," I persisted.

"All of that is simply further evidence of my love for you, dear one. Protecting you, protecting your reputation. If I didn't love you, I wouldn't care what others thought; I wouldn't care about society's silly rules or the nonsensical restrictions imposed on us by foolish men acting in God's name. I would flaunt our love openly if I could do so without hurting you or embarrassing Lady Sarah."

His arguments dazzled me with their novelty, filled me with doubt, undermined the repentance I had achieved in the lonely silence of my room, and weakened my resolve to avoid any future encounter with him. I wanted to believe that he loved me, and I welcomed the warm glow of comfort his words gave me, for no one else cared about me. I had to depend upon him. I had nowhere else to go. He pulled me to him once again, and brushing back my tumbled curls, he held me against his ruffled chest. "I-I do love you, too," I admitted.

Come, my pet," he breathed into my ear, "I have something for you."

He drew me to the fire, stood me firmly in front of the mantle, and lifted from the teakwood box the sparkling necklace. When he held it aloft, a prism of diamonds flashed in the firelight. I hardly dared to breathe as he undid the clasp and looped the shimmering stones around my neck.

He took a small jeweled mirror from his pocket, holding it in front of me so I could witness the transformation——fire ringed my bare neck. He handed me the pearl-studded mirror. "This, too," he whispered. "A companion for the diamonds, like your radiant skin." His voice caught. He took my chin in his hand; his lips brushed mine again and again, waiting, I knew, for me to respond. And I did.

From that night on, I met him in the hermitage whenever he left his signal, a small cluster of violets tossed outside my bedroom door, or thrust into the small china vase in the Library, or laid inconspicuously on one of the side tables in the unused ballroom. I searched each day when he was at home, a scavenger hunt for violets and for the rewards that came with them: his indulgence, his reassurances that he loved me, needed me, and would protect me.

I worried that Isobel and Lady Sarah might find out about my changed relationship with Sir Richard, though both I and Sir Richard were careful to conceal the meetings and our feelings for one another. In an agony of guilt I watched Lady Sarah's health decline as the doctor visits and pills and her addiction to laudanum increased. When Sir Richard hinted that soon he might be free to wed again, the last of my misgivings disappeared and my hopes for the future soared. His authority softened my qualms and subdued my conscience.

I quit reading the psalms and returned the book to its resting place, until I found myself with child.

CHAPTER 14

"Sir Richard, I need to meet with you."

With a quill in his hand, he looked up at me standing in the doorway of his study, surprise and annoyance evident in his face. "Not today, Misella. No flowers today. I have business to conduct."

"Yes, I know. But you have been gone so long, and I thought to hear from you upon your return." I tried to keep my voice calm, knowing from his comments to me about Lady Sarah that he detested whining.

"Please, my dear. You must be patient. Perhaps I will have time tomorrow." He focused his attention on his papers, dipping his quill into the inkpot resting on a folded linen cloth in front of him.

Desperate, I walked into the room, closing the door behind me. "Please, Sir. It is imperative that we speak." I pressed one hand against my pounding heart, gaining confidence from the outline of the busc bone thrust into the pocket of my stays—the whalebone shaft he had given me, his crest carved upon it in delicate swirls, his name entwined with mine, underneath a profusion of tiny violets drifting down to the tip. He had pushed it in place between my breasts, inserting it with love, he said. "Now you can feel me always next to your heart."

Alarmed perhaps at the urgency in my voice, he laid down his pen and pushed back his chair. "Well, what is it, Misella? What is it you need so immediately that you must take me away from my important correspondence?"

My face burned, and I struggled to remain calm. "I-I fear, Sir, that our, our relationship has had the usual consequences."

He jumped up. His chair thundered backwards whacking against the globe behind his desk, almost knocking it from its mahogany stand. He came around to stand in front of me, frowning, the fine lines around his eyes deepening. "What are you saying, Misella?"

I could not stop the tears. "I think I am with child," I sobbed. "More than two months past my time. And sickness in the morning."

He looked sick himself, his color waning, moisture gathering along his wrinkled brow. "A sorry mistake," he muttered, more to himself than to me. "Leave me alone, Misella, while I decide what to do." When I tried to leave, he grabbed my arm. "You must keep this to yourself if you expect to remain here with your reputation intact."

"Of course I will, Sir." I was insulted that he thought so little of my judgment. "You needn't worry." I brushed away the last of my tears and departed, my fear somewhat diminished, trusting that Sir Richard would know what to do.

He left the next day and did not return for a fortnight. In his absence Lady Sarah commanded me to her quarters one morning, the first time in several weeks. Though frightened and worried, I tried to remain calm and pleasant. I had rouged my pale cheeks and hoped to control my usual morning nausea when I knocked on the door to Lady Sarah's quarters.

"Yes, enter," came a weakened voice I hardly recognized. The dying woman lay half prone upon a bank of white pillows, a shocking contrast to her yellowed skin. I was surprised to see her all alone without Isobel or Maggie. Her cold eyes, encircled with bruised-looking skin, peered at me with sharp awareness.

"Come closer, Miss Rosy Gills," she rasped. When I approached the bed, Lady Sarah reached out and grabbed my wrist, locking it within her skeletal fingers. "I know what you are up to. You think you can steal him away, a bird-witted Bunter like you? He'll tire of you very soon, and you'll be out on the street with all of the other stray Cats who forgot where they came from and where they belong."

I pulled away from her grasp, familiar bile rising in my throat. Stumbling back, I clamped my hand in vain across my lips. While Lady Sarah stared in horror, I grabbed a linen coverlet from the foot of the bed and retched into its folds.

"You filthy swine," Lady Sarah screeched, the strength of her voice belying her weakened condition. She struggled to sit up, an ugly flush transforming her face, strands of colorless hair springing loose from their side combs. "Get out of here," she screamed, pointing to the stained coverlet bunched in my arms. "Get out. And take your sickness with you."

Shivering with embarrassment, I staggered backwards to the door, unable to look away from her venomous eyes. I managed to reach my room unseen and stuffed the foul coverlet out of sight under my bed. The questions I had long ignored rang in my mind: *What have I done? What will become of me?* This time I knew I deserved Lady Sarah's hatred. I loathed myself and my willing complicity in this crime that transformed me into such a reviled creature. How vain and weak and foolish I had been.

The day Sir Richard came back, I found a small sheaf of violets lying just inside my bedroom door. I rushed to the maze, running through it now without touching a leaf, my feet familiar with the twists and turns. He was waiting inside the hermitage, smoking a thin cigar. Its heavy stench mingling with the cloying scent of jasmine made my stomach curl. I covered my nose and mouth and rushed outside, afraid I might be sick in front of him.

He followed me and said, his voice not unkind, "I'm sorry, my dear, of course you need fresh air. We must take good care of you." He placed his hand on my back and rubbed with firm downward strokes, as if he were quieting his skittish mare.

"Put your worries to rest, Misella. I have a plan. You will receive a letter from your long lost sister Annabelle who will be visiting Portsmouth with her sea captain husband from America. I will urge you to go and will arrange passage for you to Portsmouth. You will stay until your sister returns to Boston." He threw down the cigar and ground it into the gravel with his boot. "When your time is finished, you will return to your home here with us. In the meantime you will live in London, in lodgings arranged by my good friend Lady Marian Bentley."

"You've told someone?" I gasped in horror. "What of my reputation? How can I face her or anyone? And I don't have a sister anymore. I don't know what has happened to Annabelle or Elinor or Father, if they are even alive."

"Don't worry, my pet. It is all taken care of. The fake letter, the journey. And you will never have to meet Lady Marian. She has retired to her country estate for the next six months. Your landlady will know nothing. Lady Marian has told her you are my married daughter awaiting the return to London of your Navy captain." He cupped my face in his hands, caressing the worry from my brow with his smooth fingers. His gentle touch soothed my nerves and somewhat reassured me.

"I'll visit you often," he said. "Our own private nest until my little dove is ready to fly back home."

"But what about the child?" I cried.

"Sh-sh." He placed his finger against my lips. "Don't worry. Don't worry." He traced the outline of my lips, leaning down and kissing the path his fingers had made. "Think how free and happy we will be when you are safe and warm in your own little nest in London. I will take care of everything."

Yearning for privacy, for safety from the prying eyes of Isobel and Lady Sarah and the servants, I squeezed his hand in a frenzy of urgency and relief. "When shall I leave? Oh, soon I hope."

He laughed and twirled me around in his arms, my cloak swinging out to brush the tops of the white irises that framed the hermitage doorstep. "Be ready by tomorrow," he said and raised his voice. "You'll leave for Portsmouth at noon."

* * *

I packed my best gowns and shifts, jewelry, the fancy shoes and shawls, all the fine gifts from Sir Richard, and tried not to think about the trouble ahead. I put my trust in him, deciding not to worry or let any dark thoughts interrupt the happy ones.

Joseph loaded the boxes and chests without a word or even a glance in my direction, his wrinkled face passive and unsmiling as he heaved each carton into the luggage hold under the seats. When he finished, he opened the door and waited for me to climb in without his help. I tried to act as calm and disengaged as Lady Sarah did whenever she prepared for a long journey.

Sir Richard was nowhere to be seen, and no one else from the house appeared to see me off, except for Isobel. She stood in the alcove at the end of the veranda, staring at me without saying a word, biting her lip as if to keep from blurting out one of her obscenities.

The journey was long. I stopped Joseph twice along the way so that I could stumble from the coach to be sick in the brush. I tried to sleep after dark, for he told me he would drive until we reached London late Saturday evening. "I don't drive on the Sabbath," he said curtly. The coach rattled from side to side, and I began to think that perhaps my problem would be shaken from me before we arrived.

I dozed off and on, but sat up wide awake when we crossed Westminster Bridge, lamps flickering all along its narrow walkways. Dark hulks of all sizes bobbed on the water near the banks of the Thames. Some watermen wrapped in tarpaulins lay sleeping in their boats. We proceeded onto a paved street running parallel to the river, well lit with flickering lanthorns, the street no smoother than the country roads. Elevated stone causeways connected the footpaths on either side of the road, raising the level of the street so that each jolt wrenched me up from the seat. Nevertheless, I leaned from the window to witness London for the first time despite the occasional bump to my head.

Several coaches hampered our progress despite the late hour. Bells fastened to the ears and collars of cart horses rang incessantly as farmers brought goods for the city markets. Porters shut up gates for the night. Ballad singers performed on street corners, and noisy revelers walked the streets from alehouse to alehouse.

We paused beside a narrow passageway. Several minutes passed and still we did not move. I peered into the darkness to see what kept us. A splendid coach, its lanterns dimmed, sat motionless in front of us commanding so much of the roadway that we could not go around it. Movement coming from the dark passageway drew my attention.

Two dark figures huddled together, to keep warm. *Poor wretches*, I thought. I had heard that many such vagrants prowled the London streets at night because they lacked a place to sleep. A hunched figure appeared in the distance, progressing slowly toward us carrying a lighted torch in one hand and a long pole in the other.

When he reached the unlit lantern directly in front of our carriage, he attached the torch to the pole's tip. With a grunt, he struggled to reach the dead lantern and, with a final thrust of his torch, he set it afire. "Eleven o'clock," he called out, his voice cracking. "All's well." A coughing fit bent him double as if the effort of speaking had damaged his throat. He spat into the road. Wiping his hand across his mouth, he drew a flask from his pocket and drank, all the while holding the torch aloft in one hand. His attack under control, he proceeded on, staggering a bit, the light wafting back and forth.

The lantern cast its glow into the alleyway. A maid, dark hair frizzing from under the lace cap skewed to one side of her head, leant back against the brick wall, her skirt hiked up around her waist, the front of her dress gaping open. Her hands grabbed the bared backside of her frenzied partner, breeches heaped around his ankles, his head bobbing inside her torn bodice.

I drew back against the cushions, my face burning. Had Joseph seen, I wondered. I dared not close the window and call attention to myself. Joseph climbed down from his seat. His grizzled face appeared in the window. "We'll be on our way soon, Miss, soon as our young dandy is finished. Don't mind the trembler against the wall. You'll see a lot of that in London." His wrinkled mouth stretched into a smirk. He shuffled away and clambered back up to his post.

I felt sick, exhausted, ready to burst into tears, needing Sir Richard—to hold my hand, and kiss my brow, and convince me once again that everything would be all right, that Joseph would be punished for disrespecting me, even let go so he would no longer be around to torment me with his searing gaze and veiled threat to my reputation.

The slap of the reins and whack of the crop against wood indicated that Joseph was urging the horses forward. When we finally stopped again, he had pulled into a square surrounded by rows of stately three-story brick houses fronted by wrought iron fences. Two iron pillars adorned the rail in front of each house supporting lamps enclosed in crystal globes, their flickering lights outlining carved front doors with glass windows. Joseph parked the carriage in front of a house with a narrow front porch flanked by a set of marble planters, roses tumbling from them and climbing up the wall. Its tasteful appearance lifted my spirits.

Joseph opened the door and pulled the foot stool into the road but did not offer to help me alight. I climbed down and waited without saying a word. He pointed at the door and motioned me to go ahead. "I'll follow with the baggage," he muttered.

I walked up to the gate and lifted the latch, climbed the steps, and tapped the heavy brass knocker lightly against the wood. I could hear Joseph grunting and dropping boxes onto the paving stones.

A cough erupted from inside, and the door opened. A maid, with a heavy robe clutched around her, squinted at me. "Are ye the Captain's wife?" she hollered, as if she were hard of hearing.

Disoriented, I blurted out, "No."

She eyed me with suspicion. "You ain't Lord Maltby's daughter?

"Yes, yes, of course," I murmured quickly, for Joseph was lumbering up behind me. "Captain Barry's wife," I whispered, so he wouldn't hear my lie.

The maid opened the door wide and waited for me to enter the dimly lit foyer. Behind me, Joseph dropped a large box onto the slate floor.

"This way," she said. "I'll show you your quarters. You are on the third floor, I'm afraid. I hope in your condition you'll be able to handle the climb. The Mistress needs the rest of the house." Traipsing after her up a winding staircase, I prayed that Joseph had not lingered below to gossip with the maid when she returned downstairs, perhaps to disclose the truth about me.

CHAPTER 15

The rooms were well furnished. In the parlor, two brown Moroccan leather chairs rested on either side of a black walnut table in front of the fireplace. A matching rocking chair nestled in the corner, a fuzzy blanket folded over its back.

The bedroom held a large four poster with a flowered chintz canopy and a mound of feather pillows and quilts. A writing desk perched across from the bed in front of a large window which overlooked a small rose garden. A gold velvet chaise lounge stretched invitingly next to a tiled fireplace.

The Mistress of the house, Mrs. Barron, hovered over me, sending the maid Ella to take care of whatever I needed. Ella brought tea and meals, arranging them elegantly on beautiful Wedgwood dishes. Yet I waited in anguish for Sir Richard to arrive, hiding inside my rooms, ashamed and alone.

In unpacking my bags, I had discovered the copy of the psalms stuffed inside the silken folds of a gown. Surprised and puzzled, I did not remember packing it and could not imagine how it came to be there.

Plagued with fear and guilt, I began reading the psalms again that very day in front of the fire as my father used to do. When Mrs. Barron came to check on me one day, she found me in tears. "Ah, you poor little thing. Missing your husband, all by yourself at a time like this. Will he return soon?" she inquired, her little eyes shining with pity.

I felt a flush inflaming my cheeks. "I-I am not sure when his ship will arrive. But I believe Lord Maltby, my f-father will visit me soon." I busied myself pouring our tea for us.

Mrs. Barron's kind concern and my own bold lies heightened my abhorrence of myself, for I could not conceal from my own mind the enormity of my crime. Over and over again I read psalm 32, the words of repentance burning into my brain, compelling me to acknowledge its warning that I must no longer follow the counsel of the wicked. I began to think very carefully about how I might gain restitution and yet preserve my reputation.

Sir Richard finally arrived on the eighth day. I knew it was he by the sharp rap on the door, more insistent than Mrs. Barron's timid tap, or the thump of Ella's hip when she brought a tray. I flung open the door. He stood before me dressed in a dark green velvet coat and satin breeches, his thumbs stuck in the sides of his brocade vest, its gold threads glittering.

He whisked his hat from his head, its plume waving merrily, and bowed to me. "The quarters of my darling daughter, I presume." He thrust me backwards, closing the door behind him with the heel of his boot. He laughed, grabbing me around the waist with his free hand and pulling me close. "I'm here, sweetheart. Dry your tears."

He drew a silk handkerchief from his pocket and wiped my eyes, dabbed at my nose. He began to kiss and caress me. I tried to resist. With new-found courage I started to tell him about my decision, but with tears welling up again, I could only whimper, "Mrs. Barron and Ella, they may come up."

Shaking his head, he began to unlatch my gown. "I told them not to disturb our reunion," he murmured against my throat. "That I have bad news to deliver. Your husband will be delayed for some time, and I will need to comfort and reassure you."

I let him lead me into the bedroom, though I did object as he undressed me, his hands quick, his desire mounting. Finally, undone by his passion and afraid of displeasing him, I gave in for the last time.

Later as Sir Richard lounged sated against the pillows, he agreed to listen to my plan. "I will stay here alone," I told him, "until the baby comes and I recover. With a modest inheritance from you, I could stay on here as a widow with a child, or move to other lodging and pretend that the child is my sister's, who died in childbirth and willed me to—to raise the child for her." I faltered under the weight of his wintry stare, but, though breathless with dread, I continued. "We would not have to see each other again," I whispered. "You would be free of me, of any scandal."

He bolted up to a sitting position and grabbed my naked arm, ripping aside the quilt tucked around me with his other hand, leaving me exposed and shivering. "Look at me, Misella," he ordered, his voice icy.

My eyes drifted upward to stare into the hard glare of his.

"You belong with me," he said. "I am your guardian and your benefactor. You would be lost here on your own, unable to survive in this city with its swarms of shysters and crooks who would cheat you, destroy you. You will return to Hawthorn Manor as planned—with your reputation secure, and without a child."

He slipped into his breeches, leaving them untied, and sat down next to me. Tucking the quilt around me, he took my hand and kissed my chilled fingers one by one. I averted my eyes and asked in a small voice, "What is to become of the child?"

He arose from the bed, retrieved his jacket hanging from the bedpost, and fished a bag from a pocket. He dropped the white leather bag onto the bed, slipped his arm around me under the quilt, and drew me to him, kissing my cheek. "I need your love, Misella. I need you with me."

He opened the bag and withdrew a small vial half filled with brown liquid and a pearl-glazed pill box. "This will take care of the problem. I want you to take this at bedtime tonight." He opened the box to reveal a mound of whitish powder. "Mix the powder with the treacle and swallow it down. By early morning, you will begin to feel some cramping. Soon after, you will expel the fetus. Call Mrs. Barron to help you. She will believe that your grief and anxiety over the disappearance of Captain Barry's ship has precipitated the event. Have her send Ella to fetch me at my lodgings. In a few days, after your recovery, we will return to Hawthorn Manor."

I stared at him in horror. "I cannot do it, Sir," I croaked. "It would kill me like it did the wife of Father's fishing partner." The story tumbled out of me, in a high-pitched, breathless voice I didn't recognize as my own. "I heard Father talking of it with Mother late one night after Lily was born. How Mrs. Flaherty took powders because they didn't want another child. How she writhed for days before she died, in agony, Father said, much worse than childbirth." I forced myself to take a breath. "Her husband was afraid to summon help for fear her condition would arouse suspicion that he had given her abortive powders, and he would be charged with a capital crime."

111

Sir Richard placed the items carefully on the table next to the bed. He took my trembling hand and stroked it as if I were still a small, frightened child. "My dear, my dear," he said with exaggerated patience, "I would never let that happen to you. Your Mrs. Flaherty was poor and ignorant. No doubt she consumed some kind of cheap poison sold to her from the cart of some witless tinker. This treatment is safe, and quite expensive. The powders have been secured from reliable sources, carefully examined and secretly mixed by one of London's most renowned chemists. You have nothing to fear."

He kissed the top of my head. "You and your reputation are more precious to me than that little thimble of tissue you carry within. We must think first and foremost of you, of protecting you. It is no crime to eliminate this problem now in order to save you from the trauma of childbirth and the pain and the retribution that would follow. I'll await your summons." He left me sitting speechless on the edge of the bed.

I spent the night in an agony of indecision, my Father's psalms no comfort to me now. Wanting to be free of this fear that tore at my heart, this fear that I would be damned no matter which option I chose. Fearing childbirth and scandal, but fearing death even more—especially in my present state of sin. If I disobeyed him, would he refuse to help me any further?

At the end of the night, as dawn arose, I tossed the powder from my window into the wind and the rain of early morning. Not because I had decided to defy Sir Richard, but because I could no longer bear to see it there, the milky calfskin bag like a caul covering a sightless eye, an emblem of my crimes.

For two long days, I refused to answer the knocks on my door, ignoring the trays set down with a bang outside it, telling Mrs. Barron and Ella over and over again to leave me alone, until Sir Richard's stern voice got through to me.

I arose from the rocking chair in front of the dark fireplace and let him in. Appearing concerned, he ordered Mrs. Barron to leave us alone. He thought I was in pain or in mourning for what I had lost. He could not know that I had crossed a great divide.

He held me in his arms, my body rigid and lifeless. He tried to soothe me, crooning into my ear, "There, my dear, I'm here now. I'll take care of you. As soon as you can gather your things, dress yourself in clean clothes, we'll leave for home. Ella will help you pack." He brushed my tangled hair from my eyes, and rubbed my back, one hand along my neck lifting the mass of my hair.

"I did not take it," I blurted out. "I threw it away."

He dropped his hands from me and stared. His face changed, hardened, a flush crawling up from his neck into his cheeks, the same look I had seen when he read the letter from Jack Finn. His lip curled and his voice when he spoke was strangled, as if he were straining to control it. "You have made your choice, Misella. I can do no more."

He swung the door open. Hesitating on the threshold, he swerved around to face me. "Those letters from home that mysteriously disappeared years ago? I intercepted them, and burned them. To put an end to your mewling homesickness. What a lot of trouble you were for so little in return." He slammed the door behind him.

I heard him say to Mrs. Barron, "We must talk." The sound of their voices diminished as they proceeded down the hallway.

I don't know how long I stood rooted to that place, until the sourness in my stomach entered my throat, and I rushed to the chamber pot and wretched, the burning liquid making me cough and choke, the tears streaming from my eyes.

The violent action of my body seemed to wake me from my stupor. I poured water into a deep porcelain bowl, dipped a chunk of rose-scented soap and a cloth into the water and scrubbed the tears from my face. I tore off my clothes and cleansed my soiled body, running the cloth over my head and soaking my hair, rubbing the stench of my illness from me. I dressed in clean linen and slipped on one of my plainer gowns, leaving my stays where they lay. Yanking my silver-backed brush through my snarled curls, I welcomed the stinging pain, for it reminded me that I was still alive.

When Mrs. Barron banged on my door, I was ready to tell her the truth. She pushed into the room, her face a dark mask of anger. "You'll be out of here by noon," she barked, her normally soft voice a growl. "If not, I'll have the justice of the peace with me when we break down this door. You're lucky Lord Maltby decided not to press charges. All that he tried to do for you. Taking you in. Treating you like his own daughter."

Her lips curled with disgust, spittle collecting in the corners of her mouth. "You little tramp. Taking up with that crook Jack Finn, trying to extort money from your own guardian, betraying his trust in you. And him willing to see you through the birth of your bastard. Willing to help you avoid scandal. Willing to take you and the babe into his home as if to raise your sister's child."

Stunned beyond words, I could only stare at her twisted face and listen to the poison spewing forth from her wrinkled lips.

"Where did you get the killing powders, eh? From Finn? Lord Maltby thinks you must have met Finn somewhere. I said a wench like you could have arranged it, scurrying out late at night without our knowledge. Getting rid of the evidence, too. Probably dumped it in the Thames, I told him. I've half a mind to report your crime, but Lord Maltby convinced me not to. It is enough, he said, if we throw you out on your own, let you lead a life of crime with that crook. You'll pay in time for what you have done."

The impact of her venomous tirade, of Sir Richard's cruel betrayal, his nonchalant dismissal of me and his utter destruction of my reputation, left me breathless with shock. I knew it was useless to try and defend myself against her wall of lies. Why would she ever believe me instead of the charming, dashing, Lord Maltby? She had, however, spoken one truth—I would continue to pay for my sins.

Lost and alone, I headed into the bedroom as she slammed out of the parlor, not knowing if the money I possessed would be enough to hire a coach, to rent rooms somewhere else or even how to arrange such things.

I packed all my belongings, throwing them into boxes, stuffing my best gowns into the large chest, slipping my jewelry into a small, velvet bag and into my pocket. Throwing a shawl around my shoulders and taking several deep breaths to calm myself, I eased the door open, relieved to find the hallway vacant. Skulking in the shadows of the unlit hall, I peered over the banister like a punished child running away from home. I descended the deserted stairway and escaped into the street, hoping to find a rental coach.

CHAPTER 16

Parked on the side of the road a few doors down from Mrs. Barron's, a coach driver sprawled upon the seat of a dilapidated coach, drinking from a tankard. He seemed to be waiting for someone. I swallowed my fear and approached him.

"Ex-excuse me, sir. Is your coach for hire, to move my things to different lodgings? Can you help me?"

He sat up straight on the cracked leather seat, his legs, clad in soiled leather britches, swinging back and forth. He grinned, his front teeth blackened stubs, filed almost to the gums. "Mr. Swallow, at your service. Where ye headed, Miss?" He set his tankard down on the seat next to him.

"I-I don't know," I stuttered. "Would you know of any place available to rent?"

"Well, certainly," he drawled. "It depends, Miss, on what section of the city you want to live in, and, a'course, how much ye can afford to pay."

"Not anywhere near here," I said. "As far from here as possible."

He stroked his whiskered chin. "Well, I know a woman who has two rooms for rent on the other side of the river, in the center of town." He squinted at me as if measuring my worth. "A guinea a month, she charges."

I gasped at the high cost, realizing I had little more than three months rent in my pocket.

"But that includes your coal for the fireplace, and tea, and your breakfast," he added quickly.

"How much for the trip and the move?" I asked. "I have several small crates." I gestured toward Mrs. Barron's.

115

"How many boxes?" He appeared skeptical.

"Six, and a large trunk."

He stroked his chin and thought for a moment. I held my breath.

"I'll have to get somebody to help me. I suppose yer not on the first floor?" He looked pained.

"Third floor," I added. "But it's not a high third, and the stairway is wide."

"Cost you a crown," he figured, "for the move, the trip, our labor. I'll have to see if I can find a helping hand."

"Can you hurry," I begged. "I must be gone within the hour."

"Whew!" he breathed. "Kind of close, Miss. I have to scour up a man I know by the name of Pistol first."

"Maybe you could manage with my help," I urged. "We could move the boxes, and you and Pistol could come back for the trunk later."

He thought for a minute longer, looking me over as if he doubted I was strong enough to carry much. "Okay. Let's see what we can do."

"Please, if we could hurry." He set his tankard on the floor, swung his legs over the side and jumped down. He stripped off his upper coat and tossed it up on the seat. He was much shorter and scrawnier than I expected. I headed back to the house with him wheezing behind me.

The door to Mrs. Barron's was locked, forcing me to use the knocker. Ella opened the door and sneered when she saw me. "What do you want?" she snapped. "Is that your lover boy you got with you?" She smirked at the coachman behind me.

I pushed past her. "I'm moving my things," I said. I signalled the coachman. "This way." And I marched into the foyer and up the stairs.

We struggled with the larger boxes, I carrying more of the weight than he. He stopped to catch his breath after handling each one, mopping his brow with the dirty handkerchief he whipped from the waistband of his britches. "Hurry," I urged. "We must be quick."

When he saw the trunk that he and Pistol would have to move later, he sighed and shook his head. "That's a big one, Miss. I'll have to hire another mover. It'll cost you more. Mmm, another half crown."

Disgusted, I told him yes even though old Joseph and Ella had carried it up to the room. I left a note attached to the door for Mrs. Barron explaining that the men would be back shortly to remove the trunk, and I returned to the coach, the driver already in place.

Scrambling inside, I tried to latch the door, but its twisted hinge prevented it from closing snugly. I slid to the far side not wanting to be flung through the opening as we traveled over the bumpy roads. The interior reeked of onions and unwashed bodies; the scrolled paper covering the walls was filthy, its design hardly visible; the leather cushions were torn in places, their edges split and curling. After the elegant coach rides with Sir Richard, I despised the contrast.

We rattled past the courtyards lined with brick homes, over the bridge and into the heart of the city where black smoke and fog thickened the air. We slowed almost to a crawl, the road thronged with wagons and carts carrying every kind of building material. They slopped through the muddy street, their heavy wheels splashing walkers on the paths, their clothes bedaubed with mud and soot from the blackened air.

The noise deafened me: the slap of the wheels, the grinding of metal on stone, hawkers crying out their wares, milk carts and bread carts, laborers working in the streets, chairmen plying their trade or scooping passengers into their chairs. Carts were piled with pewter pots, their drivers throwing the pots into open doorways or at the foot of closed doors, ignoring those that rolled dangerously to the edge of the streets.

Longing for the peace of Hawthorn Manor, the wide, clear fields of green, the stillness of morning, the quiet afternoons alone in the gardens, I felt lost, still stunned by Sir Richard's betrayal. I yearned to return to my yesterdays at Portsmouth Bay, to hear father loading his fish cart at dawn, to feel Lizzie curled against me, her hand seeking mine in the dark.

In the midst of the din, Mr. Swallow stopped and jumped down. He nudged the door open. "Well, here we are, Miss."

A dirty, wooden building sat hunched at the edge of a dark passageway choked with rundown shops. Its front door hung open, pushed back with a three-legged stool; a fat woman slouched on it, fanning herself with a sheaf of paper. "That's my friend Poll," Mr. Swallow said. He yelled to her, "Hey there, Poll, I've brung you another boarder."

"Hi hoo, Swalley," she yelped. "I've rooms ready." She hauled herself up, teetering a bit on the balls of her slippered feet, stuffing the papers into her pocket. A tankard tipped over next to the stool. She waddled over to us, giving Swalley a slap on the shoulder. "A real bargain, Miss. Two fine rooms. Swalley knows. He wishes he could afford 'em hisself." She laughed, revealing a gapped row of stained teeth. "I'll have Prue, my maid, show you to the rooms on the third floor. Have ya any bags?"

I nodded, unable to speak.

"Swalley and me'll get 'em for ya and bring 'em on up." I wondered how she could even climb three flights of stairs much less carry boxes while she did so.

She led me into the dim hallway of the house. A veneer of black soot covered the floor and dusted the top of a small, sagging desk propped against the wall, a vase of drooping flowers in its center. She swiped at the desk top with the end of her soiled apron. "Ah, this coal dust," she said, "covers everything. Hard to keep things shiny around here, but you'll appreciate the coal fires, Miss. They'll keep you warm and comfy on frosty nights and crisp mornings. The rent includes as much sea coal as you need.

"Prue, get in here!" she bellowed. With a gaping smile, she said to me, "Oh, and yes, deary, that will be two guineas, for two months. I don't rent out for less than that."

Digging into my pocket, I pulled out a handful of coins. She stared greedily at the coins as I picked out two guineas and held them out to her. She snatched them from me, dropping them down the front of her tight bodice as a slovenly looking young woman sauntered into the room from what I imagined to be the kitchen quarters.

"Here you go, Prue. Take this young lady—what did you say your name was, Miss?"

"Misella," I murmured.

"Take Misella up to her quarters. You better have cleaned them spic and span this morning like I warned ya. Then come down for her things."

Prue gave me a bored look, her broad face smudged with coal dust, her dirty linen cap drooping around her greasy hair. She shuffled ahead of me without saying a word and began to climb the stairs. Poll grabbed my arm and whispered loudly, "She can't talk; something wrong with her tongue. But she can hear just fine, so you tell her whatever you need and she'll get it for ya. If she don't, you tell me and I'll whup her good."

118

I followed Prue up the dim winding staircase, the air growing chillier as we ascended. We crossed a small landing in front of a scarred door, shut tight, with a large brass key tilted in the lock, and trudged up another long flight of stairs to the top. We came upon another door. Prue creaked it open, leading me into a chilly, dark room, the air thick with the smell of burned coal and mildew, the scent taking me back to our hut in Portsmouth.

Two bare windows crusted with coal dust blocked much of the outside light. I squinted, trying to make out the room's furnishings. Prue stood in front of a tiny fireplace, a mere hole in the wall, with a cheap iron grate coated with sludge. She bent down, picked up a flat metal horn and scooped up some chunks of coal from a bin next to the fireplace. A cloud of black dust billowed up around her. She dumped the coal onto the grate and took a flint from the narrow mantel and a strip of ragged cloth from a wooden box. She struck the flint several times until it caught, lighting the cloth, which she tossed onto the coals. She struck the flint again and lit a tallow dish resting on the mantel.

The meager light at least allowed a better view of the room. A wooden armchair sat to one side of the fireplace, no cushion softening it. A table, no bigger than the one in the hallway downstairs but in worse shape, sat in the center of the tiny room. A cabinet with only one door sagging on a broken hinge yawned at me from the corner. The room held no other furniture.

Prue lit a candle stub from the dish and led me toward a dirty length of woolen cloth tacked to a ceiling beam, its blackened hem resting on the floor. She pushed it aside to show me not a second room, but merely an alcove that contained a narrow cot, a wooden stool, and a wall lined with a shelf and a row of wooden pegs. On the shelf a cracked pitcher, its handle missing, rested inside a large bowl; a stained chamber pot squatted nearby.

She approached the fireplace, picked up a length of iron pipe leaning on the side, and poked at the coals, smoking now but without a glow. She shrugged, replaced the poker and trudged out of the room without looking at me.

I stood in that stinking room, choked by the dust, the street noises battering my ears despite the closed windows, knowing I had been robbed. Like Prue, I could not protest, I had lost my voice. At that moment, I wished I held that smooth leather bag in my hand, Sir Richard's voice whispering words of salvation into my ear.

119

Instead, I heard wheezing and thumping outside the door. "Open up, Miss. I'm about to have me a spasm." Swalley rested against the wall, coughing into his kerchief, one of my boxes lying on the landing, its lid off, my linen shifts sprawling around him.

That was the last I saw of Swalley. Poll told me that when he went back with his friends to collect the chest from Mrs. Barron's, it was gone. Mrs. Barron claimed she never saw it. My chest with all of my expensive gowns, not that I could wear them now, but I could have pawned them along with my jewels to give me more time and better food than I was able to purchase from Poll.

During the next four months, I stayed in my rooms, too ashamed to go out and face the turmoil of the dark streets and Poll's grinning, know-it-all looks. The child grew within me, every jab of foot or elbow a reminder of my hopelessness. I grew listless with bloat and worry, no longer bothering to dress, loose morning gowns my only apparel, their sleeves and hems grimed with coal dust, the bodices tight against my unbound breasts.

I had to rely on Prue, sending her off, mute, to the pawn shops with pieces of my jewelry, one by one, receiving far less than they were worth, not knowing if the pawnbroker or Prue had robbed me, perhaps both.

Desperate for help, I wrote a letter to Sir Richard, begging him to send me money so I could secure better lodgings, hire a skilled midwife, support myself until after the child came and I could find work. Weeks later, Prue brought me the response one frigid morning. I had slept little the previous night, a nagging backache keeping me awake. She handed me my letter smudged and unopened, a message scrawled across the back in a hand I did not recognize——THE MALTBY FAMILY HAS RETIRED, PENDING FURTHER NOTICE, TO THEIR ESTATE IN IRELAND.

Stabbed by a sudden shooting pain, I flung the letter to the floor. Prue handed me another, a folded note from Poll, a notice of eviction if I did not pay the month's past-due rent by the end of the week. Four days left. "Prue, I am going to need help soon. Can you find a midwife for me?"

She shrugged her shoulders, her face passive, and turned to leave. I grabbed her skirt, the coarse wool rough in my fingers. She stared at me with dull eyes. "Find someone!" I ordered, my voice guttural, the timbre of Poll's. She pulled away and swept out of the room, slamming the door behind her.

I stumbled to my cot and sank down upon the rough sheet, another pain ripping across my back and digging its spiked fingers into my midsection. My stomach tightened, stone-hard beneath my hands. Slowly, the pain receded, the muscles eased, and I could catch my breath.

I thought of Mother, giving birth to Lily, shrouded behind the quilt screen of her bedroom wall, her screams and curses biting the air. Father's voice as he escorted us outside, ordering us all, except Elinor, to "run and spend the day at the Flahertys."

The slow beat of pain began again, gently at first. I braced myself as the pounding waves crashed against me, struggling to withstand the crushing pressure.

I know not how long I lay clutching the soiled coverlet, the room darkening as night came on. I tried not to cry out, but I lost control, panting, my body bucking and thrashing, simulating the dance of passion that had brought me here, a mockery of my foolish desire.

Prue appeared, drawing back the curtain, a wooden bucket and some folded rags in her hands. I gasped when I saw she was alone. "The midwife," I screamed. She shook her head and plopped the bucket on the chair. She dipped a rag into the bucket, wrung it out, and handed it to me. I clutched it and tried to wipe my dripping brow, but she took it from me and pressed it to my lips, forcing the rag between my teeth. I bit down, the stinging taste of vinegar in my mouth. I tried to spit it out, but she pushed it back.

I rose up again, gnashing the rag between my teeth. Prue sat down in the chair and crossed her arms, waiting. At least I was not alone. I did not care that she could hear my shameless whimpering.

My screams became grunts. Hot liquid spilled through the folds of my gown, scalding the sheet which slowly absorbed the cold from the room. "No fire in the grate," I moaned, my teeth rattling despite their grip on the cloth, my knees drawn up, as if I could spring away and save myself.

The raging pain tore through me once more as this creature battered me without relief to reach its opening into the world. The ball of its head finally crashed through. Prue hooked its head in her powerful grip, like a fish monger reaching into her net to pull up her catch, squirming as it hits the air, slippery in her wet hands, its crimson scales flashing in the light.

A knife flashed in Prue's hand, to gut the fish, I thought, but she only meant to cut it loose. She laid the squirming thing upon my chest. I could not look at it. She dipped more rags and washed it. Then she took a large, dry rag and wrapped the bundle up as if for market, laying it next to me. She washed me, her rough hands pressing and prodding, slapping the wet rags around me, slipping a pile of dry ones underneath me.

She went into the other room and reappeared with a large mug of warm tea, its taste strange, spiked with some spice I did not recognize. She dipped a thin strip of cloth into the mug, and dribbled it into the mouth of the fish, its lips sucking, its eyes squeezed shut. She handed me the cloth, picked up the bucket and the bundle of soiled rags, and left us. Alone.

The knife still lay on the chair where she had dropped it when she picked up the bucket. I could reach out and pick it up in my hand, free myself, escape as Sir Richard had done, and regain my damaged reputation when I regained my health. Or, a cleaner option—slip my pillow over its tiny face, leaving no mark of violence, until the bundle no longer moved, a simple accident, like its creation. Not a crime, not an act of passion, but a conscious choice in the clear light of reason, which I should have made earlier. I had suffered enough. I had to save myself.

In the midst of my dilemma, I lost consciousness, my hands still clutching the grimy pillow to my chest. *Father struggled on the dock, black fish line in the water, his hawthorn pole bending in his hands. Tears streaming down his cheeks, he called to me as I stood on the shore watching him. "Help me, Misella," he pleaded. "I cannot do this alone. It is too heavy. You will starve if it gets away."*

Unable to speak, I began to weep, too afraid to walk out to him.

I awoke, my cheeks wet with tears. The child stirred next to me and began to whimper. It opened its eyes, its tiny fists poking the air. I lay for a long time watching it flail. When its whimpers became a strident wail, I set down the pillow and began to unwrap its binding cloth, not knowing if its puckered red face belonged to a boy or girl.

"Poor child," I thought, "lost little girl, my own little Lily, like the sister I lost." I picked her up in my arms, untied my soiled bodice and pressed her wailing mouth to my breast. Her tiny lips like little inch worms found what they needed, and she began to suckle.

She slept peacefully that night, nestled in my arm, as I decided what to do. I could throw myself on Sir Richard's mercy, appeal to his sense of decency and duty. With Prue's help, with the money from the last of my possessions, my mother's silver-backed brush, I would find Lady Marian Bentley, his London friend, and ask her to contact him for me. She was a woman of the world, Sir Richard had told me, who understands the devious logic of love, the delicious turmoil of desire, and never asks questions.

Prue promised to deliver my letter into Lady Marian's hands.

Dear Lady Bentley:

    Please forgive my forwardness in writing to you, a trusted friend of Sir Richard Maltby, as I have been unable to reach him at his estate in Ireland. I would be much obliged if you could contact him on my behalf to inform him that my newborn child and I are stranded, penniless, here in London. If you could convince Sir Richard to contribute a small sum for our subsistence until I am able to survive on my own, I would be most grateful. I may be reached, for a few days only, at 18 Pye Street, Westminster.

    Your Most Obliged and Humble Servant,
    Misella Cross, (late of Hawthorn Manor)

CHAPTER 17

"So you are Misella. Yes, yes, I can understand Richard's obsession." Lady Marian eyed me up and down, ignoring the baby bundled in my arms, as I stood in her elegant sitting room. Her amber eyes, enlarged and shining, peered at me through her jeweled eye glasses, the lace sleeve of her morning gown hanging almost to her waist.

She was quite portly, her bosom full and straining at the embroidered bodice of her gown, her gray-laced brown hair unpowdered and piled haphazardly on her head. She wore no cap, her appearance a stark contrast to the perfection of the room with its rich rosewood writing table, brocade chairs scrolled with gold, a thick Persian carpet in shades of deep rose and amber. A pink-veined marble fireplace supported an ebony mantel strewn with crystal birds, their bodies reflecting the light from a massive chandelier, its candles aflame despite the morning light.

"You are fortunate, my dear, that I have just recently returned to town. Otherwise, I might have missed your letter. I have not yet contacted Richard, but I will this very day. In the meantime, we must find you a better place to live. The area you are in is not safe." She dropped the eye glasses on the writing desk and picked up a parchment envelope, its wax seal the size of a guinea, and handed it to me.

"My driver will take you right now to your new quarters in New London. Give this to the landlord. Three months rent." She drew a cloth bag, fattened with coins, from the pocket of her gown and gave it to me. "For a visit to the mercer's, my dear. You must have some new clothes, and anything else you need for yourself and the little one." She patted Lily's head. "A tiny sweet thing she is."

Overwhelmed, I grabbed her hand. "You are so kind, Lady Bentley. I cannot thank you enough. You have saved me, and, whatever Sir Richard's response, I will repay you no matter how long it may take me."

She smiled. "Well, you must take these three months to recover your spirits and your strength, my dear, without a single worry about the future. I will see to it that Richard assumes his rightful responsibilities. And you needn't worry about any gossip. Your reputation will remain intact as long as I have any say in the matter."

I could not stop myself. I kissed her rough cheek. She drew back, and I feared that perhaps I had been too forward. But she recovered, smiled at me, and said, "Godspeed, my dear."

My rooms, on the second floor of the King George Arms, were luxurious and elegantly furnished. A large sitting room and a bedroom, both with expansive fireplaces, and an alcove in the bedroom perfect for Lily with a cradle swathed in pink muslin. Lady Marian's generosity and kindness brought tears of gratitude to my eyes. A measure of tranquility entered my life, though Lily demanded much of my time.

Lady Marian waited a month before sending a letter telling me that she had sent an emissary to Sir Richard, discreetly, and was awaiting his response. I prayed that he would honor her request.

Lily grew plump with my milk, enriched by my healthy diet of hearty meals delivered to my rooms by a courteous staff of crisply uniformed maids. She smiled now and gurgled at me. She bore no resemblance to Sir Richard that I could see, or perhaps I did not want to see. I saw my mother in her wide blue eyes, her flaxen hair, her curved lips.

After our second month in this lavish setting, Lady Marian came to see me one day, clothed in garnet silk, her hair piled high and powdered, jeweled birds perched around the velvet rim of her hat. Her rouged face serious, her voice sharp, she told me that she had heard nothing from Sir Richard. "I don't understand it," she stated. "I know he has received my letters. My man has personally handed them to him. We are running out of time. Your lease will need to be renewed in a few weeks, and the cost of your upkeep has been quite high." She frowned, her eyes sweeping the room as if to admonish me for the extravagant setting she had chosen. "What do you propose we do?"

She glared at me, her eyes steely, a gloved hand stroking the gold-chained ruby pendant resting between the pillows of her powdered breasts.

"I—I don't know, Lady Bentley," I stuttered. I did not know how much money she had already spent taking care of me. "I am strong enough now to find employment, and certainly cheaper lodgings. I don't really know where to look, or, or what kind of work I could do—or what I would do with Lily." My voiced trailed off in a whisper of desperation and embarrassment.

She waited for a long moment as I stared at the tips of my brocaded slippers, unwilling to look at her.

"Well," she asserted, "we will hope for the best, that Sir Richard will come through. If not, you better start planning your future." She opened the door to leave, her hat angled on the side of her forehead, the birds' feathered wings flapping as she shook her head. "I am not a charity, you know." She swept through the door, pulling it shut with a firm snap.

Not knowing where to turn or what to do, I swallowed my pride and asked the maids, one by one, if they knew of any work in the area. With closed faces, they refused to offer any suggestions. Perhaps they feared I was after their jobs. Even the meekest one of the group refused to watch Lily for me for an hour or so while I searched for work. She had her own babes at home, she told me, and could not be responsible for any more.

Lily came with me, bundled in my arms, while I bought penny broadsheets off the street, looking through them to find employment, walking for miles from job listing to job listing. Most employers would not even speak to me when they saw a child in my arms. When I hid Lily in my canvas bag, covering her sleeping face carefully with a thin blanket, one mistress did speak to me, while I stood in her foyer.

"I don't train my maids," she sniffed. "I expect my girls to be skilled when they come here, with good references."

"I have plenty of experience in kitchen work and in house cleaning, Ma'am," I stated, my head held high. "and I am a hard worker. You will see if you but give me a chance."

"Where are your references? Whom have you worked for?" She stared at me with suspicion in her eyes. "Come back when you have proper references."

My shoulder aching from the weight of my bag, my head spinning with exhaustion and worry, my eyes brimming with defeat, I gave up on seeking work as a maid, the only job experience I possessed. How could I give the Maltby household as my only reference and hope to preserve any shred of my reputation much less expect a good report from Maggie?

A mercer in the area of Covent Garden was willing to give me a chance as a trimmer, but I would have to buy the bolts of lace and bags of sequins and glass beads myself and be reimbursed later after the gowns were finished. I had no money.

Hopeless, I came home that afternoon to find Lady Marian waiting in my sitting room. Her back rigid, her russet gown draped around her, she filled the leather chair next to the empty fireplace, her hands grasping the curved ends of its carved arms. Like Deborah from the Old Testament, I thought, ready to sit in judgment of my fate.

"You better put the child in bed," she stated. "We have some business to discuss."

I walked into the bedroom and laid Lily in her cradle, careful not to wake her, for I feared Lady Marian would not accept any distraction. I peeled off my gloves and laid them on the bed, along with my straw hat. I wanted to wash my face and hands, but I was afraid to keep her waiting.

When I returned to the sitting room and sat down in the matching chair across from her, I grasped its arms and held on tightly.

"Sir Richard," she uttered, "has refused to have anything to do with you or the child, which he claims belongs to his ex-coachman, Jack Finn."

"He is lying," I cried out, thrusting myself forward to the edge of my chair. "I have known no other man but Sir Richard. He is Lily's father. I swear it on her life. You should know that already. You arranged my lodging for him when I first arrived in London."

She shook her head, a half smile on her painted lips. "I never questioned him at the time about the details. I simply did what he asked. And now I find out from him that he was trying to protect you, but you conspired with Finn to extort money from him."

She waited for me to speak, but I was struck dumb by his continued lies and cruel abandonment of us. How could I, a lowly scullery maid, a fishmonger's orphan, expect Lady Marian to believe me and not the Lord of Hawthorn Manor? The utter hopelessness of my situation drained what little fighting spirit I had left.

"So I fear, Miss Misella, that you have not been honest with me." She lifted a long parchment sheet from her lap. "I have a bill here from this establishment in the amount of three hundred pounds. Can you pay it?"

I gasped in shock, could only shake my head.

"Then my dear, I am afraid that you and your highwayman's bastard are headed to debtor's prison."

She waited for me to respond, but I feared I was going to be sick. I pulled my handkerchief from my sleeve and pressed it hard against my lips.

"Unless——," she waited for a moment, "you work for me until you pay off the full amount."

I caught my breath with relief. "Oh, yes, yes I can, I mean I will, Lady Marian." I wiped the moisture from my lips, from my brow, beseeching her to offer me my pardon.

"Anything, whatever you shall want me to do, I will."

She bent forward in her chair, her eyes glittering, the bill slipping to the floor unnoticed. "I have an establishment in Covent Garden, the Swan Court, where a select group of young women, beautiful and literate like you, live in elegant quarters and entertain Dukes, and Lords, and even Princes, each evening. You will have the opportunity to live in luxury under the adoring eyes of great men of power and influence." She bent down, grunting, as she retrieved the bill and folded it on her lap. "Having lived under the tutelage of Sir Richard, you certainly have the experience to qualify for such a position." Her piercing stare challenged me to disagree.

I pushed against the hard wood of the chair, digging my back into its scrolls, as if to avoid breathing the air she had poisoned. I shook my head over and over, no words forming on my lips. Accepting her obscene proposition would send me to the depths of hell from which I could never hope to return."

"As for the child," she said, disregarding my state of shock, "I have a country nurse who will take her while you complete your service."

Words burst from me, tumbling almost incoherently, "No, no, she would die. She would die at the hand of such a woman. I know about these nurses who take their pay and starve the children. I would never do that to my child. Never," I shouted.

She flinched, her face closing like a fist, eyes narrowing, coral lips tightening like the puckered drawing of a stringed purse. She struggled up from the chair, staggering a bit, the bill wrinkled in her hand.

Her voice when she spoke cut through me. "You will take nothing but the clothes on your backs when you and your bastard leave here. I have the warrant with me from the Justice of the Peace. The wagon outside will carry you to your hell hole on Fleet Street. You will never earn enough money walking the streets outside the prison to pay what you owe me. Never!"

Rage at her and Sir Richard for duping me and at myself for being duped by the likes of them fueled my pride and hardened my voice. "Being poor no longer frightens me, Madam. I have lived my life in poverty, an honest poverty in my family home; in Sir Richard's care, a poverty of decency and moral courage, qualities I hope, however, to restore no matter how long it takes."

"Silly little fool." Lady Marian sneered at me as she prepared to leave. "You'll come begging for my help again. I guarantee it."

I maintained my steely posture until she slammed the door behind her, and then I collapsed into my chair in tears, shivering with dread at the thought of what lay ahead for Lily and me. After a few minutes of self-pity, I dried my eyes and went to get Lily. Lifting her from her bed, I cradled her in my arms and kissed her sleepy eyes until she opened them and yawned. "Time to leave, my love," I murmured into the warm fringe of hair above her ear. I laid her on my bed and began pulling all of her little garments from the armoire and throwing them on the bed next to her. She watched me with curious eyes.

"We'll put on all these pretty things," I babbled. "You'll keep nice and warm." I removed her soiled napkin and bound her tightly in a clean one, piling extras into my bag. I slipped shift after little shift over her head. I cocooned her in three of her sweaters, tied two little knit caps under her chin, and wrapped her tightly in several of her blankets. If she was uncomfortable, she didn't complain but peeked out at me wide-eyed with wonder. Grabbing two of my own shawls, I flung them around me, hoisted Lily into my arms, picked up my woolen bag, and hurried out the door.

When I reached the street, the debtor's cart stood waiting, the back of it unlatched and hanging down, the driver scowling next to it. "Get in," he barked.

I threw my bag in first and clambered up, tripping over the bag and almost dropping Lily. The driver slammed the back closed. Before I could obtain my footing, he whipped the horse forward, and I fell against the side of the cart. I sat down hard on the dirty floor. Clutching Lily to me, I stared in disbelief at the sorry-looking occupants crammed into the small space.

CHAPTER 18

Swaddled in the layers of clothing and blankets, Lily slept throughout the journey, hugged tightly against me so that the jolting of the cart would not awaken her, though I feared she might roast in her cloth oven before we arrived at the debtor's prison.

Crammed into that small cart with another destitute family, I stared around me in despair. I tried to keep Lily away from the disheveled child scrunched next to me, and the scrawny one sitting listlessly in a torn blanket on her mother's lap. Both children looked feverish, their gaunt cheeks aflame with bright red circles, hoarse coughs shaking their bodies every time the cart jolted going over the ruts in the road. Their father, a grimy peaked cap in his hands, rested his head upon his drawn up knees. Not once did he look up. I wondered if he were sick as well.

Our driver beat at the lone horse with his crop, even when the clogged roadway made it impossible for the tired horse to move. At least, the day was mild for fall, though as we travelled closer to the center of the city and nearer the river, thick, blackened smoke, mixed with a blanket of fog, obliterated the sun.

We threaded through the narrowing streets, bypassing dilapidated houses no more than shacks, wooden huts with broken doors, gaping holes for windows, some covered with faded cloth, others with sheets of tattered parchment. Children, barely clothed, rummaged in the streets, picking through garbage heaped on the rough boards that served as sidewalks. Others sat begging; one child no older than five, stared sightlessly from scarred empty sockets, her hand rattling a cup at every person that passed by, an old woman standing guard nearby. Some of the little ones were missing limbs, or fingers, or had suffered other wounds that distorted their bodies.

I shuddered and looked away, imagining Lily growing up in such conditions. Each block we passed revealed a pub, with peeling wooden doors and swinging signs that dangled from chains or, broken from their moorings, were propped upon window ledges. With the help of dented pewter kegs or bosomy barmaids, their doors stood open, luring passers-by to enter and join the rowdiness within.

Our progress stalled to a crawl inhibited by the dray wagons and run-down carriages clogging the lane. I held a perfumed kerchief to my nose to obscure the stench of rotting garbage, the contents of chamber pots dumped from upstairs windows, and the leavings from horses and other animals that littered the streets.

We lumbered to a stop in front of a massive stone building, a wide archway cleaving the center of its high walls. A crowd, some of them richly dressed, milled around outside a set of open grated windows that flanked each side of the yawning entranceway. I read with shame the words carved into the stone above each caged window that welcomed us to our new home: "Remember the Poor Debtors, Having No Allowance." The frowzy capless head of an old woman was visible through the grate of one of the windows, her claw-like hand clutching at the alms some women in the crowd passed to her from their gloved fingers. In her other hand she rang a bell, its mournful clang accompanying her anthem, "Help a poor woman feed her children. Keep us from starvation." I averted my eyes unable to watch her anguished pleading, fear clutching my heart that I would soon find myself in the same situation.

Our driver lurched down from his perch. Waving a sheaf of papers at us, he unhitched the backboard of the cart. "Get out," he yelled. "I ain't got all day."

He stood guard as we tried to exit the cart. The children's father raised his head and looked around with bloodshot eyes. He didn't seem to notice me. He staggered a bit as he rose to his feet and picked up the child sitting next to me. "Hang on to me, Jemmy," he muttered as he stumbled out of the cart. His wife trailed after him, the sleeping child in her arms. Clutching my bag in one hand and Lily to my breast in the other, I climbed down into the street, trying to avoid the muddy ruts that had almost caused the woman ahead of me to fall. I wished I had thought to take my patens with me to at least protect my shoes from being swallowed in the muck. Having no free hand to hold my skirt up, its hem blackened with the foul soup that filled the roadway.

Trying to avoid the stares and the jostling of the crowd which surrounded the entranceway, we traipsed after our driver through the archway into a gloomy chamber empty but for a scarred wooden bench shoved against the brick wall. He pounded a fist on the small wooden door that seemed to be the only access to the main cellblock inside.

A guard dressed in unclean muslin breeches and soiled shirt opened the door and peered at us with rheumy eyes, his mouth widening into a toothless grin. "Welcome to the prince of prisons," he smirked. I swallowed hard and tightened my lips in an effort not to cry. Lily began to whimper as if she, too, dreaded this place. The other two children clung to their parents in silence.

"Wait here," the guard rasped. He snatched the papers from our driver, squinted at them in the poor light, and nodded to the driver who fled into the street without uttering a word. "After me," he said, and led us through a small hallway into an inner court which seemed to span the entire length of the building.

Several prisoners milled about, some playing rackets and other games of amusement. It shocked me to see revelers laughing and playing against the backdrop of the solid brick wall surmounted by a formidable row of iron spikes. A clutch of ravens flitted about feeding on rubbish piled in one corner of the square.

The guard inspected me and said, "You wait here while I show the others to their quarters on the common side." He led the poor scraggly family away, the mother by this time unable to hold back her tears.

My heart pounded so fiercely I feared the other prisoners would hear it as I hovered against a small tree in the corner, jostling Lily back to sleep and avoiding the looks of some of the other residents. In a short time, the guard returned. "I can show ya a decent room for you and the babe. Only 1 pound, 2 shillings for the week."

"I can't afford that," I mumbled so the other inmates wouldn't hear. "Have...have you anything decent for a smaller fee?" I hated the pleading sound of my voice.

He sneered. "You look pretty well dressed, Miss. You'll find it best to pay for decent lodging, specially with that babe to care for. Or there are ways a comely lass like you can earn your keep." He leered at me, his toothless grin and lust-filled eyes sickening me.

"Just show me what you have for half that amount," I snapped.

"Oh, you won't like it, Miss. Believe me." He laughed and motioned for me to follow him.

He steered me to a bank of dirty stone steps. "This way, madam," he said, "to your suite on the common side." He paused at the bottom of the steps and held out his callused hand. "That'll be eight shillings for the first week."

I set my bag down on the step and fumbled in my pocket for my suede purse, trying not to jostle Lily as I struggled to open the strings. I extracted a pound and handed it over. "I'll need some food, too." I tried to sound firm.

He flipped the coin over in his fingers. "A few penny loaves and some weak tea is all you'll get with this."

I tried to maintain my composure despite the bolt of fear his words sent through me. I had only enough food money to last a few days. We proceeded to climb to the third level of the prison. We entered a huge room cluttered with people, stretched out in clusters on the tilted wooden floor, or huddled against the stone walls like bands of gypsies, little mounds of clothing piled around them. Ragged blankets draped on clotheslines tacked into the wall's crumbling mortar reminded me of my childhood home and mother's makeshift bedroom in our little hut.

We crept around listless children and dull-eyed parents to a sectioned-off area towards the end of the room where small carrels of thin plywood provided a modicum of privacy. He motioned me into the only empty one, hardly room enough for the two of us to stand side-by-side. A naked straw pallet, no bigger than a child's trundle, festered against the wall, the straw mottled with the stains of previous residents. No other adornment marred the dim, cavelike dwelling, the trapped air a thick presence that made the open, seething common room smell fresh by comparison.

"Make yourselves at home," he said. "Ye'll get your bread delivered later. And no cooking or candles in here—fire hazard. Ye'll have to use the common room for that. And to make connections. Just ask some of the

136

ladies how you might earn enough to move to more elegant quarters." He winked, covering one rheumy eye, and left us.

I laid Lily on the stained and crusted floor, spreading her blanket out around her. She whimpered, overheated from her many layers of clothing, her little face red and contorted with misery. When I loosened the wrappings imprisoning her legs and arms, she flailed them about, kicking her lambs-wool-covered feet in the air and waving her arms.

As she cooed with contentment, I set about seeing what I could do to protect us on the pallet. If only I'd realized what we would face, I could have managed to bring more with us. As it was, I had only a small cotton coverlet in my bag, intended for a child's bed, but it would fit this miserable crust of straw.

With my cherished bottle of perfume, I doused the straw as best I could. How I wished for the jars of herbs from Hawthorn Manor's kitchen, the sprigs of rosemary and crushed sage, ropes of camphor and jugs of vinegar, the dried lavender and crushed rose petals from my dressing table. I padded the dismal heap with my shawl and my extra petticoat. The room was very warm; we wouldn't need blankets yet. I refused to consider that we might still be here when winter came.

I slept fitfully, grateful that Lily, tucked snuggly against my side, my scented handkerchief draped lightly across her face, seemed oblivious to the night sounds around us. When a lumbering shadow blocked my doorway, I sat up startled.

"Well, Miss, how's about a quiver for a bit of beer and a kidney pie?" the guard muttered lunging towards me, a jug swinging from a strap around his wrist. "I always like to welcome our newcomers," he whispered, his fetid breath fluttering the handkerchief. "Make your first night easier. You and me can set up a partnership. I can take care of you and your wee one, protect you. You'll need it here, believe me."

I struggled away from him, thrusting Lily deeper into the covers. I crawled to the corner and grabbed my pewter candle holder. I raised it, ready to strike. "Leave us alone," I panted, "and don't come back."

He hovered over me. "I could tear you to bits," he whispered, "and your babe, too, if I wanted. Stick you like pigs on a spit, and who do you think would care? But I'm a god-fearin' man, I am. I don't force my ladies, and I don't do to young uns like some around here." He bent closer, his forehead almost touching mine, his devil's breath burning my eyes. "There's those who look for the nice, virgin flesh of babes, to rid themselves of the disease or to protect themselves from it. You'll know at night when you hear the young uns' piercing screams."

I stared at him, limp with horror. Lily began to whimper, raising her head to look for me.

"Just remember," he growled in my ear, "she's not too young for the likes of some." He straightened up, and hesitated, waiting for me to cry out for his help, but I remained speechless, shivering with disgust. He lifted the jug and guzzled, some of the liquid drizzling down his grimy throat onto his leather vest. Then he left us.

For the remainder of the night I watched over Lily in horror, the candle holder my only weapon, struggling with my grizzly dilemma—to thrust myself into the claws of Lady Marian and try to save Lily, or remain here and expose her to this hellhole.

In the morning, I bribed the bread delivery boy to find Lady Marian and to give her my message—three easy words for him to remember, "Misella will comply." When he left, I gathered Lily into my arms, one hand cupping her head against my shoulder, and rocked her back and forth, back and forth. "I'll always protect you," I cried into the soft fold of her neck. "I promise."

CHAPTER 19

Lady Marian's carriage pulled into the side entrance of a lavish three-story brick building. A golden domed canopy, like the much larger one over the front door, shaded a polished wooden door with a small oval window in the center. The footman lifted the ivory-handled knocker and let it fall discretely. The door swung open and a crisply dressed maid, her dark face impassive, ushered me inside.

"I'll take you to Lady Marian," she said in a foreign-sounding voice, her soft brown eyes matching the color of her skin. She motioned me to follow her up a narrow, winding staircase to the second floor. I prayed that Lily would remain quiet, her shiny eyes peeping out of the coverlet I had wrapped around her.

The air was cool, spice-scented, the broad, carpeted hallway silencing our footsteps. The windowless walls lined in pale green silk gave way at measured intervals on either side to polished, black walnut doors. A rash of gold-framed garden landscapes, some glistening with artfully posed nude goddesses, drew the eye to a massive set of doors at the end of the hall. The maid led us to them and rapped lightly. She held out her arms. "I'll take the child for now, while you finish your meeting."

She saw that I wanted to refuse, hugging Lily to me. "She's only three months," I said. "She's never been separated from me."

"I'll wait right here with her," she whispered, not unkindly, reaching to take Lily from my arms. She tucked the bundle gently into the crook of her arm, opened one side of the double doors and waited. After I entered, she closed the door behind me.

Lady Marian sat queen-like behind a sprawling mahogany desk, a sheaf of papers strewn about, a large pot of ink open in front of her, its cork stopper resting on a stained linen rag. She whipped off her glasses and laid down her quill. "Well, Misella, I'm glad you have come to your senses." She frowned as her eyes traveled over me, assessing my unkempt appearance, my soiled face and gown. Unable to wash at the prison or to dress my hair, I welcomed her disapproval, my outer appearance a reflection of how I felt inside.

"Your rooms await you," she said, "where you'll find suitable clothing and a small box of jewels. A closed-off chamber adjacent to yours will house the child for a few months, in case Sir Richard should change his mind about supporting her. And Sachi, the wet nurse who brought you to me, will tend to her needs. But hear this, my dear. If the child causes so much as a ripple of noise or distraction for my guests, she will be sent to the country. Do you understand?"

I dared not speak, only nodded my head.

"You will appear early evening tomorrow for my inspection before you entertain your first guest, Lord Whittingham, whose interest in you has been aroused by the stories he has heard–from others, not from me–about your liaison with Sir Richard. He feeds on gossip; he'll want all of the prurient details." Her heartless gaze checked any protest I might have made. "And you will provide them to his satisfaction." Her words sent me deeper into a hell I now realized I could no longer escape.

She raised her arm, her lace cuff swaying as she flicked her wrist at me and lifted the quill to continue her record-keeping. "Sachi will take you to your rooms." She dismissed me as if I were the lowliest of servants. And I knew in my heart that was what I would become, something far worse than a scullery maid.

Sachi showed me to my third-floor rooms, her dark face smooth and expressionless. The upper floor was laid out like the one below, my quarters at the end of the hall, behind heavy double doors, a room the size of Lady Marian's large office, but lavishly decorated. A large canopied bed loomed in one corner. A crimson, silk-embroidered settee with a matching chaise adorned a richly scrolled Persian rug set at an angle in front of a white marble fireplace. A heavy French armoire stood against a far wall; a Queen Anne writing table and chair was positioned in front of a wide set of floor to ceiling windows, rose velvet draperies pulled back to allow rare muted sunlight to filter through sheer curtains.

She drew a key from her pocket and unlocked a small door next to the armoire, leaving the key in place. We entered a tiny, windowless room that housed a narrow cot covered with a bright quilt, a trundle bed with slatted sides next to it, a chintz-covered rocking chair in the corner, and a small chest of drawers nestled behind the door. A rag rug provided a dot of color before a little fireplace barely wide enough to hold a single half-log.

"Your baby and I will reside here," she murmured. "We will never disturb you in the evening unless you unlock the door and call to us. Your daughter seems placid and content. She will not be a problem for me." She laid Lily carefully in the trundle and straightened up. "You needn't worry, Miss. I'll take good care of her."

A flash of anguish crossed her face. "My own baby died at birth a few days ago," she murmured. "I worked here as a kitchen maid before the birth. Lady Marian offered me this job today when I returned." Lily began to fuss. "She is hungry?" Sachi asked. "I can feed her now."

With a pang of jealousy, I cried out, "No, no. She needs me."

Sachi shook her head. "I am sorry, Miss, but my rules are that I am to begin immediately to feed and care for her." She bowed her head, seeming embarrassed. "Lady Marian gave me strict orders. She–she–says she wants your milk to dry up right away."

* * *

With scented soaps I bathed in the porcelain tub of heated water brought in large buckets by the maids, lathering my hair and rinsing away the odor of Fleet Street. I dried myself gently with towels of Egyptian cotton, wincing at the pressure against my engorged breasts. I bound them carefully with the long silk scarf Sachi provided and slipped into a shift made of finest lawn. I would not need stays this evening, she told me.

While Lily slept peacefully in her little bed, Sachi had me lean close to the fire as she rubbed and brushed my hair until it crackled. Afterwards, she oiled and powdered it, sweeping it up in a ratted pompadour, tucking diamond-studded pins randomly through the curls. She applied white powder sparingly to my face. "Your skin is so fine," she cooed, "you need little paint. Perhaps just a touch of rouge to your cheeks and lips." She daubed a bit of scarlet paste on my lips and cheeks, applying a small, fashionable patch of black-dyed mouse skin next to one dimple, and brushing a paste of coal dust onto my lashes.

"Perfect," she sighed. She steered me to the bed where a satin embroidered petticoat lay shimmering in the light from the fireplace. She tied it around my waist. "You won't need pockets this evening," she stated as she eased the matching stomacher over my tender breasts, and slipped the heavy, gold-threaded gown in place.

As Sachi finished tying the gown, Lady Marian entered the room. She eyed me through her wire-rimmed eye glasses held in place with one satin gloved hand. She frowned and motioned me to turn around. I did as she wished, but with my head held high.

"Lord Whittingham waits below," she huffed. "He'll be up in a moment. You will serve him brandy from the decanter on your table, but you will drink nothing yourself. Whatever he wishes, you will provide. He may stay an hour, or he may want to spend the night. Be prepared to do whatever he asks of you." Sachi vanished into Lily's room as Lady Marian swept out my mine.

Closing the door behind her, I stood in the darkening room, the candles in the wall sconces offering a shadowy light. I waited, hardly daring to breathe until a sharp knock on the door propelled me forward. Composed and smiling, I opened the door.

A slender gentleman, no taller than I, leaned with one velvet clad shoulder pressed against the door frame. His ruffled cravat, advancing upward from his lapel, threatened to overtake his receding chin. Flecks of powder from his wig dusted his collar, like dry snow sprinkled across the purple cloth. He stared at me, unblinking, his pale eyes alight against the dark circles underneath, the shelves of his unruly eyebrows commanding my notice, more prominent than the pock marks that marred his face. Smoke from his cigar, held upright as if to puncture the air around it, drifted into my face. His thin lips twitched as he muttered more to himself than to me, "Well, well. The Mistress Misella, at last we meet."

I bowed my head. "Lord Whittingham," I said stepping back to allow him entrance. He straightened and entered the room, trying to mask a limp that tipped his body slightly sideways, as if he were leaning away from an unwelcome wind.

His eyes swept over the room and came to rest on me, staring rudely at my mounded breasts struggling to break free from their uncomfortable confinement. I tried not to flinch when he touched my skin trailing his fingers across the edge of my bodice.

"Why don't you remove these impediments to your freedom and my vision," he commanded. "But first bring me a brandy and a tray for my cigar." He held it upright in one hand while he unbuttoned his jacket and slipped it off of his shoulders, leaving it where it landed. He pulled one of the brocaded chairs around to face me and sat down almost daintily as if attending a play at the Palace.

Retreating to the side table, I poured a large brandy and grabbed a porcelain saucer. Wordless, I placed both items on the side table next to him. With shaking fingers I began to unhook my stomacher and free my gown from the heavy petticoat encircling my waist. Without looking at him, I removed my stomacher and tossed it on the chaise lounge, shrugged off my gown and dropped it onto the floor. My petticoat followed, landing in a heap. His eyes glowed. "I am comfortable now," I said.

He laughed, a short high giggle, sat forward in his chair and said in a deliberately husky whisper. "Keep going, my dear. Pretend I am Richard."

Shuddering, I forced myself to pull the fine shift over my head, turning away from him and struggling with the knotted scarf that held my breasts in place. He arose from the chair, putting his drink on the table, intending to assist me. I cringed, unable to face him. He tugged gently at the knot, not touching me, and finally loosening it, he returned to his chair. I unwrapped the scarf slowly, letting the ends drape to the floor but held the final expanse of cloth in place over my breasts.

I decided to be bold and truthful. "I will need this cover for a while, Sir. Until I no longer show signs of child birthing. Perhaps another week, if you don't mind."

He stared at me with what I feared was disgust. He took a long drink of the brandy. "I can wait. The anticipation will sweeten the moment. Put your shift on, then come here and sit next to me." He pulled the other chair closer. "Tell me about Sir Richard and his daughter, Isobel. I want to know them, inside and out."

That began our long involvement. He would come at least three days a week, paying Lady Marian dearly to keep me for himself. He never touched me. He didn't even bother to pretend an interest in me or in my body. Our first encounter was meant to intimidate and frighten me into submission. I heard from the other girls that Lady Marian supplied him regularly with young boys. From me, he wanted information; he only cared about the Maltbys, their estates, their money, and especially Isobel, a spinster soon to be an enormously wealthy heiress.

Sir Richard, he told me, was confined to a wheelchair by a sudden and virulent stroke, a drooling mute, his wife dead. His only heir was Isobel. I gasped in shock to learn how much had altered in the ten months since I left Hawthorn Manor. I had to stop myself from blurting out the bitter truth. *He has another heir, my Lily.*

Lady Sarah's death did not surprise me, but the news about Sir Richard emboldened me. I felt vindicated, elated by the supreme irony that a stroke had silenced the voice and disabled the reptile who had betrayed and corrupted me—and now to be given this opportunity to take revenge against Isobel. Oh, sweet justice!

"I want Isobel's money," Whittingham declared bluntly. "My own inheritance has been severely depleted, thanks to a profligate father and grandfather. I will do whatever I can to gain control of her fortune. I must use you, my dear, in my pursuit of Isobel, wooing her with help from you about how to do it since I am sure you know her well. You and I have a pact. I expect my investment in you to come back to me a hundred fold."

"Well, first of all," I advised Lord Whittingham, "you must not let Isobel know anything about me. If she knew you were seeing me, her revulsion, her hatred of me would not work in your favor. But I know where her vulnerabilities lie and the ways to flatter her."

We spent our time together outlining the methods he would use. He would prey on her sympathy, tell her how isolated he has always felt because of his physical disability. How he despised the intellectuals at the schools he attended who flaunted their intelligence and made him feel like a dunderhead. How he never seemed to have a flair for fashion no matter how much money he spent, so had given up and decided to adopt his own eccentric style to please himself and no one else. How he despised beautiful women who snubbed him or made him feel inferior.

He should study the wit and cruel satire of poet Alexander Pope, I told him, and learn how to use it against the social class, her own, that Isobel hates. "You cannot woo her with jewels or expensive trinkets," I told him. "She loves sweets–Belgian or French or Swiss chocolates in decorative boxes, and fanciful novels. But what she needs most from you is to feel that she is loved and worthy of your love. She has never received that from her father. She is not stupid, though, so it will not be easy to trick her."

With glee, I watched Lord Whittingham change before my eyes at our sessions. He eliminated the satin waistcoats, the velvet jackets, and began to wear sturdy wools and heavy cottons lined with sharp, no nonsense edges, excellently cut to reveal his slender body. Fine lawn shirts minus the frothy lace suggested a prudent temperament, as did silk stockings of a heavier weave and more sensible footwear without buckles or rosettes, higher heeled to make him appear taller. He carried a gold-headed cane that he thumped decisively upon the ground as he walked, accentuating the limp. Discarding his arrogant gestures, his cigars, and his clipped tone of voice, he adopted a more hesitant manner of speaking.

Soon after achieving this transformation, he learned that Lord Maltby and Isobel had arrived from Ireland. Within a few days, he called at their London home, taking it boldly upon himself, he told them, though his approach was meek and tender, to welcome them back to England and to express his condolences on the terrible loss of Lady Maltby.

That initial visit proved successful. He offered to escort Isobel to several upcoming social events if she should desire to attend, perhaps to help her readjust to the mad whirl of London at this time of year. Or if she thought such goings-on too strenuous at this time, and frankly, they did not appeal that much to him, perhaps just a carriage ride to see how London had changed since their last visit. He understood, of course, that any such activity would be too much of an ordeal for Sir Richard. But he would be delighted to accompany both of them in his larger carriage which could accommodate Sir Richard's wheelchair most comfortably.

With some fawning from Isobel, which surprised him, they both accepted his offer, and he was to return the next morning to pick them up. "I believe she was most flattered by my obsequious attention," Lord Whittingham puffed. "And why wouldn't she be? She knows my family's background and thinks, as everyone in town does, that I am richer than most. And that poor sot Sir Richard, spittle oozing from his lopsided mouth, managed to scratch *"Yes!"* with chalk on his slate, his hand shaking with palsy."

Lord Whittingham began courting Isobel in earnest, so Sir Richard and his love-stricken daughter delayed their return to Hawthorn Manor. Unwittingly, Isobel cooperated beautifully with the plan—indeed, with so much enthusiasm did she welcome Whittingham's attentions that he had trouble, he told me, keeping Isobel at bay. She kept finding ways for them to be alone and thrusting herself upon him, panting with desire. Poor Whittingham pretended that his desperation equaled hers, but his stern values about wanting an untainted woman as a bride kept him from indulging his needs. She believed him and became ridiculously coquettish in order to tempt him: batting her eyelashes, leaning against him suggestively, kissing his cheeks and devouring his lips, heaving her large bosom, and dabbing her inflamed face with the linen handkerchief he so readily provided from the pocket of his securely buttoned jacket. I enoyed his colorful descriptions.

Two months later, when he asked Isobel to marry him, she all but swooned against him and, righting herself, called out, "Father." She dashed to the study to tell Sir Richard and wheeled him into the sunroom. Sir Richard raised his right arm, saluting Whittingham, and stretched his frozen lips into a grimace intended to pass for a smile. He gurgled something unrecognizable and with his other hand drew out the slate board from under the wool blanket covering his legs. Taking a piece of chalk from his coat pocket, he scrawled upon the slate and held up the sign he created. *Hurrah. Happy.*

Isobel began planning immediately, Whittingham said, for the wedding—when it would be, where they would marry, what they would do to celebrate. "I want to invite everyone you know in London," she bellowed, "and all of Father's friends. I want it to be the fanciest wedding London has ever seen."

"I was astounded," Whittingham admitted to me, "by her reaction, all out of proportion to what I expected. I thought we could have a quiet little ceremony with just a few of my friends—I don't believe she really has any. She wants a circus and Lord Maltby is willing to pay for it."

He laughed, his eyes alight with merriment. "We make a good pair, you and I," he chortled. As I refilled his brandy goblet, he grabbed my wrist. "I want you to come to the celebration. Surprise Sir Richard and Isobel. It will be great fun to see their faces when you walk in."

I pulled away and set the brandy decanter back on the side table, my mind reeling at the thought of surprising and confronting the Maltbys. "I'm afraid Lady Marian would never allow it," I said. "She will put me to work when you no longer need me."

Whittingham flicked his hand as if to brush aside my concern. "I can arrange everything. You're my private property until after the wedding. I will secure you a formal invitation, without letting Isobel know, and inform Lady Marian at the last minute. She won't be coming. Isobel will never agree to invite her."

I smiled, delighted with his plan and hoping that I could somehow force Sir Richard to acknowledge his obligation to Lily.

"You, of course, will play along until after the wedding is over," he warned me. "I don't want you throwing anything up in Isobel's face before the die is cast. Nor must you suffer a guilty conscience and suddenly feel sorry for her."

I picked up his brandy glass and took a sip. "And what will you do for me in return for my silence, and for my help in coaching you about Isobel's eccentricities?"

He narrowed his eyes and snatched the glass from me. "Have I not done enough for you already, protecting you from the other animals here waiting to pounce?"

"No. I want more. Your guarantee to protect Lily and me, to pay for our lodging away from here and a stipend to support us if Sir Richard refuses. After all, thanks to my help, you gain control of Isobel's inheritance after the marriage."

Tilting his head, Whittingham studied me for a moment, then lifted the glass to his lips and drained it. "You have my word on it," he said with a crooked smile, reaching out to shake my hand. "My solemn promise to take care of you and the little one."

CHAPTER 20

Sir Richard had rented the Rotunda at Ranelagh Gardens for what was scheduled to be the wedding event of the decade, Isobel defying the convention of a small, intimate reception. She wanted a glorious celebration to announce her victory. I planned to make my entrance after all of the guests had arrived.

Crowds of onlookers clogged the lawns surrounding the gates and pushed against the heavy wooden barriers blocking the sides of the road leading to Ranelagh. My hired carriage proceeded to the main gate where the head guard waved us through after checking my invitation.

We traveled along the tree-lined roads fronting the gardens to the wide circular driveway of the Rotunda building. A few carriages of other late-comers were parked at the entrance when we approached. While we waited for them to pull away, the view to the far right of the building—a narrow man-made lake with the new Chinese pavilion rising majestically from its center—calmed my nerves. By the time I exited the carriage, I was ready to face Sir Richard.

I edged sideways through the main archway to protect the beaded skirt of my hooped gown from rubbing against the scrolled sides of the entrance. Whittingham paid a great deal for this Parisian gown, the scarlet silk shimmering with crystal and diamond beads, the embroidered stomacher cut so low, I had to hold my shoulders straight, for the merest slouch would expose my breasts.

My hair, studded with diamond pins, swirled upward to a golden plateau, supporting a small diamond and pearl tiara perched on top. I carried a fan decorated in gold leaf and sheer strips of Mother of Pearl to flash open when I met Sir Richard.

One of the velvet-clad couriers standing at attention beyond the archway took my invitation, murmuring, "Good Evening, Miss Cross. Please follow me. You are rather late. I'm afraid the receiving line has disbanded, but I will escort you to the bride and groom."

I glided after him, our footsteps soundless on the tightly woven matting which protected the plaster floor. Delighted to be the final guest, I welcomed the admiring glances and smiles I received from the other couriers. This would be my supreme moment of revenge, my chance to face Sir Richard and dispel his influence over me for good. How long I had waited for this moment.

The courier led me to the middle of the Rotunda, where a huge ornate centerpiece, containing a chimney and fireplaces, heated the frosty, early-April air. I stood tall as the courier rang the small bell he carried and announced, "Lord and Lady Whittingham, Ladies and Gentlemen, Miss Misella Cross."

Gasps of shock and a swell of voices accompanied me as I approached Lord Whittingham and Isobel, toasting with glasses of champagne, Isobel holding her cup to Sir Richard's lips, his slackened body bent sideways in a flower-decorated wheel chair. A few of his close friends stood by also raising their glasses. Whittingham smiled at me, a look of exquisite pleasure lighting his eyes.

Isobel stared, motionless, her silver goblet frozen halfway to her lips. A snowy lace veil fine as spider webs floated from her coiffed hair and spread across her broad bare shoulders. Her silver threaded satin gown stretched across her hips, accentuated by the hoop of her ivory colored skirt.

I smiled and stopped before her. "Congratulations, Isobel. I could not let this opportunity pass without wishing you a world of happiness with your fine groom." I tapped Whittingham on the arm with my fan.

Then I faced Sir Richard, his fine muscular body shriveled, his rich gold velvet coat emphasizing the yellowish cast of his skin. He wore a wig, its brown curls mocking the abundant head of hair he never in his prime sullied by artificial means. He held a silk handkerchief to his lips to catch dribblings or perhaps to hold in the cry of horror which, from the look on his face, threatened to burst from him.

I hesitated, overcome by an unexpected feeling of pity for the depleted man he had become, so unlike the virile, charming Lord I once loved. My long-held anger dwindled; the scathing greeting I had rehearsed died on my lips. I simply said, "Greetings, Sir Richard."

He gaped at me, his eyes burning with rage. He dropped the kerchief onto his lap and with a shaking hand, struggled to pull forth from a side pocket of his chair a small slate board which he cradled in his arm. His other hand crawled inside the pocket of his jacket and withdrew a small cylinder of chalk. With desperate strokes, the chalk squeaking in the dead silence that surrounded us, he eked out some letters. He threw down the chalk which bounced against his chair and fell to the floor. He clutched the slate with both hands and held it up facing me. The bold letters, visible to all those around us, screamed at me, "WHORE!"

My mouth dry, I struggled to speak, all of my suppressed anger welling up inside me. Taking a deep breath, I snapped open my fan and raised my voice. "Yes, Sir Richard. Of course you should take credit for naming me, for what I have become. You branded me from the day you took me into your home. You created me." I picked up the handkerchief hanging from his lap and wiped it across the slate, erasing his scrawled judgment of me. "You poor, pathetic creature," I whispered to his face. "All that I feel for you now is pity."

Isobel stood close to me, her voice low and guttural so that only I could hear her. "You meant nothing to my father."

Stepping back, she managed a tight smile. More loudly she said, "Ah, Misella. You were always good at theatrics. Well, now that you are here, I hope you can enjoy yourself." And she gestured to Lord Whittingham who stood by grinning at the show. "Darling, let's move on to the dining boxes, shall we? Would you bring father along?" She clapped her hands as if directing a group of school children. "Come everyone, it is time to dine."

I had to admire her cool and calm performance. This was a new, confident Isobel, in charge, in control. She glowed with authority and self-confidence. She had overcome her clumsiness, so unlike the image of her that Whittingham described for me. I began to wonder if Whittingham would be able to manage her as well as he thought he could. How clever of her to dismiss me in a way that defused the impact I had made. She had never done that before. Perhaps if she had, I might have sought less of Sir Richard's attention and escaped her cruel vengeance.

Left alone as everyone wandered in chattering pairs or groups toward the dining boxes that lined the circular wall, I had to decide whether I would stay for the rest of the evening. It now seemed pointless. There was nothing else for me to do but exit gracefully. But then I noticed a gentleman staring at me from across the room, an odd looking fellow who seemed to feel as out of place as I.

He idled in front of a large buffet table. At first, I thought he had drunk too many spirits and was disoriented. But when he saw me looking at him, he straightened his large frame, his shoulders still hunched as if to deflect my gaze. He flushed and tried to adjust his wig which had slipped to the side of his oversized head. He nodded at me.

Curious, I approached him extending a gloved hand. "We seem to be left without escorts." I smiled. "Nevertheless, I am starving. Would you mind escorting me to a dining box?"

He clutched my hand, crushing it within his lion-sized paw. Squinting, as if short-sighted, he rocked his upper body toward me and growled an introduction. "Ben Turner. At the lady's service if they will make room for the likes of us at their tables. If not, we'll find a pub to fit our higher standards." He grinned and adjusted the wayward wig that had gone askew once again, its left side singed as if held too close to a candle flame.

As I took his arm, a regal-looking gentleman, slender shoulders squared to a military stance, came toward us, a chilly gaze directed at me. Even his linen pocket scarf seemed to stand at attention as he addressed Mr. Turner. "Come on, Benjamin. We have a place for you. We'll have some time to discuss the Society with the others and prepare for tomorrow's meeting."

Benjamin swiveled around to face the intruder. "Have you met Miss Cross, Chaz? Surely not, I suppose." He introduced me with a flourish. "Miss Cross, Mr. Charles Dunning, the renowned barrister of Inns Court." He smacked Dunning on the back and rasped, "We were just on our way to the boxes. We'll make a place for Miss Cross, too. She may be able to advise us. We need a woman's point of view." His pale eyes twinkled as he tucked my hand into the crook of his elbow.

Dunning's face tightened, his delicate nostrils drawing inward as he took a deep breath. I felt soiled by his sneering, dismissive gaze, as if I had muddied his shirtfront or removed his breeches and made lewd advances. He withdrew his linen scarf and held it in front of his mouth as though to protect himself from breathing the air I contaminated by my presence. "You just can't resist the opportunity to embarrass me, can you, Ben? Heaven knows why I put up with you."

He hesitated, seeming unable to decide if he should rush ahead of us or trail behind so that my presence would not appear to be his idea. Turner chuckled and patted his clenched shoulder. "Because you need me, Chaz. I'm your sackcloth and hair shirt. And I win all of the cases you won't touch."

Dunning pushed the hand from his shoulder and stalked towards his dining box, brushing past a liveried servant hovering nearby. With a smile Mr. Turner steered me to the box, bowing slightly to the servant.

CHAPTER 21

A week passed after the wedding, my nights filled with unspeakable humiliation entertaining whatever clients Lady Marian chose to thrust upon me. When I tried to convince her that Whittingham had promised to take care of Lily and me, she laughed heartily. "Still so naïve, my dear," she said. "But, believe me, I will let you know the minute Whittingham shows up on his white horse to rescue you."

Early one evening Whittingham did come to see me, dressed more richly, his arrogance more prominent, than the night I first met him. "I'm severing our relationship," he told me as he stood in the doorway, unwilling to step into my room. "I no longer need you, and besides, Isobel knows everything. She was really quite hysterical when I left her each night after the wedding to thrash about without me in the conjugal bed. She accused me of humping you." He laughed. "That's what she screamed at me—you're humping that whore instead of me. The only way to quiet her was to tell her the truth about us, and how you urged me to pursue her. She was relieved, actually happy, to discover that I desired no part of you in bed either."

He flashed his pig eyes at me and sucked on the end of his unlit cigar. "We managed to reach a compromise. I suggested that she might want to consider rescuing your child–her half-sister, correct?—by taking her out of the whorehouse and into our home, the perfect distraction for her, and the perfect solution for us. She'll leave us alone. We'll both be free of her, and your little bastard will have a decent upbringing."

155

I lunged at him, horrified by his cruel betrayal of me and distraught with myself for trusting him. He knew by now that the one thing I would never give up was Lily. "Liar," I screamed. "You must be mad. And Isobel, too. She will never take Lily away from me. Tell her that, and if she dares to try, I will use every power I have against her."

Whittingham laughed and shook his head. "Ah, Misella, what power? You have none. You are at the mercy here of Lady Marian who will never let you leave. You owe her too much. Far better that Isobel takes Lily off of your hands, because Lady Marian will dispose of her soon. Your little darling will soon become a burden. As she grows older and more demanding, how can you possibly accommodate her while you entertain customers? She'll be sent off to be raised at one of her ladyship's country training schools until she is educated and old enough to join her mother's profession in one of Lady Marian's bordellos."

I attacked him, slapping at him in my disgust and anger. "Get out," I screamed. "You despicable, inhuman. . . ," I sobbed, struggling to catch my breath. "You and Isobel deserve each other. Leave me alone. Leave us alone." I shoved him from the doorway, slammed and locked the door.

I fell panting on my bed, not caring what Sachi had heard, depleted and utterly without hope. Whittingham was right. I had no one to turn to for help, no money of my own, only the clothes and jewels Lady Marian provided. I could no longer even feed Lily without Sachi's help.

A sudden pounding on my door increased the throbbing pain in my head. Sachi glided through the dark room with a candle to answer it. Lady Marian stood vibrating with outrage. "What is going on? Where is she?"

Sachi showed her that I lay in bed, a coverlet thrown over me. I drew myself up halfway and croaked, "Leave me alone. I am ill."

"Well you better recuperate in a hurry, Missy." Lady Marian did not enter the room. "I have a gentleman, Lord Banfrey, waiting to see you. I will send him up in ten minutes."

I raised myself up, bent over the edge of the bed, and vomited. She clucked in disgust and backed away. "Make her clean it up, Sachi," she said. "And you, Miss, better get well very soon. You have bills to pay." She whispered to Sachi, but I could still hear her. "See that she drinks the laudanum-laced tea. Double the dosage if you have to, but I want her better by tomorrow evening." Sachi curtsied and closed the door.

Later, she brought me the tea and gently urged me to drink it before she set about cleaning the rug. I sat up and sipped the strong, pungent tea, reminded of Lady Maltby, feeling as if I were back in her clutches, waiting to do exactly what she demanded.

Early the next morning one of the maids brought me a letter, the Maltby crest gouged into the scarlet wax seal. It was signed by Sir Richard, but was written in a hand I did not recognize:

Misella Cross——

I have decided to acknowledge publicly our sinful relationship and to allow that I may have fathered your child.. As I prepare for my death, my clergyman has convinced me that my confession will help to atone for my weaknesses, for my inability to resist the temptation you placed before me. Perhaps God will forgive me for giving in to your charms and reward me at least for remaining steadfast in my devotion to my dear now deceased wife and our daughter Isobel and for refusing your demands that I leave them to begin a new life with you. At Isobel's insistence. I have given her legal permission to adopt the child you claim is mine so that this innocent child may have a safe and happy home with my true daughter who will give Lily the love and protection she needs and which you in your present circumstances are unable to provide for her.

A Repentant,
Richard Maltby,
Lord of Hawthorn Manor

A calmness descended upon me, unlike any I had felt for a long time, no hatred toward him, no longer any desire for revenge against Isobel, just an unutterable sadness and sense of loss. A resolve that did not seem to belong to me asserted itself. I knew beyond any doubt that I could never leave Lily's future in the hands of Isobel or Lady Marian. Whatever I must do, I would do to keep her out of danger. With a steady hand, I penned a brief note to Isobel——

157

You will <u>never</u> take Lily from me.
Misella

With more thought and care, I wrote a letter to Benjamin Turner.

Dear Mr. Turner:

I desperately need your legal advice in order to protect my infant daughter from those who wish to put her life in jeopardy. I recall the plan you told me about at Isobel Maltby's wedding to find a way to house destitute young women. May I come to see you, at your discretion, as soon as possible? I send this letter to you with my maid Sachi. Would you be so kind as to provide an immediate response?

In gratitude,
Your humble and recent acquaintance
Misella Cross

I gave both notes to Sachi, urging her to rush and deliver them, telling her that Lady Marian wished me to correspond with both parties immediately. I instructed her to deliver Turner's note to Gray's Inn and to wait for a response which she was to bring back to me before she delivered the second note to Isobel only.

With Lily napping in my arms, I paced in my locked room until Sachi's light knock signaled her return. Her voice low, she almost whispered, "Turner will see you at three o'clock this afternoon, Miss, in his office. And I gave the note to Isobel."

"Thank you, Sachi, but I asked you to bring Turner's response to me before delivering the note to Isobel."

Sachi's face reddened. As she lowered her head, I saw tears spring to her eyes. "I am sorry to disobey your orders, Miss," she whispered, "but Lady Bentley saw me leaving without Lily."

Alarmed, I raised my voice without thinking. "You didn't tell her where you were going, did you?"

Sachi seemed about to burst into tears. She shook her head so that the metal rings dangling from her ears swung wildly. "I-I just said I was running an errand—for myself, to pick up some things I needed, at-at the chemist's...." Her voice trailed to a stop. She took a deep breath. "I feared Madam might stop me from leaving again if I returned," she mumbled.

She seemed so distressed, I squeezed her hand. "Please don't be troubled, Sachi. You did the right thing. Did Isobel say anything to you?"

"N-no, Miss. The maid directed me to the drawing room where Isobel was consulting with a heavily whiskered gentleman. I handed her the note and left."

"Thank you for your help, Sachi. You have always been so kind to me and to Lily."

To escape from Swan Court without Lady Marian's knowledge would not be easy. I told Sachi I needed to meet with Turner, a special friend, who would arrange for Lily's care when I could no longer keep her with me. "I have Lady Marian's permission," I lied, "to make this legal arrangement." Sachi nodded, but I could tell she did not believe me. I could only pray that she would honor my request to tell no one where I had gone.

I dismissed her with a smile. After she left, I clung to Lily, covering her sleeping face with kisses. At last, I would have her all to myself.

CHAPTER 22

At two o'clock, I slipped quietly out of my room, with Turner's help never to return, I hoped. My woolen bag, stuffed with extra clothes for Lily, hung from my shoulder. Lily stretched in my arms sucking happily on the sugar tit Sachi had prepared for her. She seemed happy to escape her little prison, kicking her legs and twisting her head to watch the sights around her. The blond fuzz of her hair had grown over our four months at Swan Court into tight ringlets that framed her angelic little face, like one of Raphael's cherubs, I thought. She smiled and threw the sugar treat to the ground as if she no longer needed it to distract her.

With no money to hire a chair for our journey, I walked toward Grays Inn. Although the air was crisp, the sun was sweet on our faces. Lily was an armful, but I cherished the chance to hold her and to giggle with her as she pointed to the horse-drawn carriages, their wheels singing along the cobblestones, the runners with their ornate chairs bumping us as they trundled through the crowded walkways. Lily stared at the people pushing against us, hurrying in and out of the shops lining High Holborn. One finely dressed gentleman, his face a mass of whiskers, almost knocked us over as he shoved his way toward a phaeton for hire that waited by the side of the road.

"Whoops there, Madam," he blurted as my bag fell to the ground. "So sorry." He stopped long enough to grasp Lily as if to secure her in my arms. As I stooped to retrieve my bag, he grabbed Lily again and tried to wrest her from my grasp. "Give her up, Misella," he snarled, "if ya know what's good for ya."

The gravelly voice seemed familiar, reminding me for an instant of Joseph's surly son, Pecky. Lily began to wail, and I feared I might hurt her as I crushed her to me.

I screamed, "Help me, please somebody, help me." At that moment, a chair crashed into us forcing the man to lose his grip. Slipping away from him, I lunged forward toward the street, stumbling on the cobblestones as the kidnapper took after me in pursuit. The crowds were thick, and in the noise and confusion of the street, no one seemed to notice my panic. Lily flopped against me screaming in fright or pain. I could not stop to comfort her.

I crouched behind a milk cart to catch my breath and decide what to do. The kidnapper plunged against the cart tipping over one of the milk cans, a stream of bluish white liquid washing over the stones in front of me and splashing our clothes.

"Make way, make way," shouted a runner forcing a pathway for a coach and four trotting much too fast down the street. Without thinking, I dashed forward hoping to follow the runner and thus escape my pursuer when the coach blocked his way. In my haste, I lost my footing on the wet stones and fell forward. Lily tumbled from my arms.

Before I could utter a cry or rise up from my knees, the coach loomed in front of me, its gold crest flashing in the sun, my vision blurring, my eyes burning with the sudden image of Lily, like a little rag doll, flopping under the hooves of the horses until the carriage wheel ground her to stillness.

I must have screamed her name, though I don't remember. I slumped to the street, my face hitting the stones, and tried to crawl to my baby, but someone held me back. I do remember the feel of the stones against my cheek, rough and hard, the sour smell of milk and sweat and horse manure. A pair of polished boots descended from the carriage and stepped in front of me. A deep voice shouted, "Who is this woman? Help her to her feet." But I wanted to remain where I was, in the dirt and grime, to look at what had happened to Lily because of me.

Rough hands pulled me up. A crowd gathered around me, murmuring, "Oh how awful. You poor thing." A few angry voices shouted out, "This happens too often. Something must be done with these fancy carriages that own the streets."

The man who had pursued me pushed himself forward through the crowd and stood in front of me. The phaeton driver grabbed my arms while the man shouted to the crowd, "Did you see it? This vile woman flung her baby into the street, in front of the carriage. She's a murdering whore. Someone run for the constable." As a few women attempted to retrieve Lily's broken body, he hollered, "No, don't touch the baby. Leave her until the constable arrives and can witness the evil she has committed."

I struggled to free myself from his rigid grip, but other hands imprisoned me as well. I screamed, "No, he tried to kidnap my baby. I ran. I fell. Lily," I sobbed. "My poor Lily. Let me go to her."

The young runner who led the devil's carriage on its frantic ride through the street pushed through the growing crowd to shout, "I saw her, I did. Down on her knees. Hiding behind the cart. Just as the horses approached, she threw the poor babe."

The crowd attacked me, shouting obscenities, pushing and slapping at me. A voice I recognized spoke from the edge of the crowd, Lord Whittingham's voice. "I know who she is. The whore Misella from the Swan Court. I've heard stories about her. Is that her bastard? Poor, innocent baby. Hold her. Where is the constable?"

I swayed in the rough arms of my captors as hands tore at my dress and my hair which fell into my face so I could not see. Blood dripped from my nose; fingernails raked at my face; a hand clutched my throat stifling my breath so I could no longer scream or speak. I welcomed the beating. I deserved to suffer, my pain far less than what Lily must have felt.

The constable arrived amidst shouts of "There she is, Sir. We've got the murderess." The thwarted kidnapper blurted out the runner's eyewitness account, which the boy backed up with his frequent, "That's right, Sir, I saw it all."

"I saw it, too, Sir, with my own eyes," the kidnapper shouted, bruising my arm in his iron grip. "Just as I was about to step into the phaeton. Saw her fall to her knees behind the cart so she couldn't be seen from the carriage or the sidewalk. She throws the little one, Sir, like a bundle of garbage right in front of the horses. I cried out, I did, Sir, but it was too late." The crowd shouted in agreement.

"All right, all right," the constable huffed. "The rest of you can move back." He told the kidnapper, "You there, hang on to her for now." He scanned the death scene, the horses standing still now, bloodied prints on the stones from their hooves. He squatted down to examine my child's crushed body left alone on the stones behind the coach. He stood, eyed the milk cart and, as if I read his mind, I knew he calculated the distance from it to the spot on the street where Lily lay. He walked back to where I slumped in the arms of my captor. Looking upon me with disgust, he spoke to the phaeton driver and the kidnapper. "I'll need you two, and you," he motioned to the runner standing nearby, "to accompany me back to my quarters so I can conduct a proper investigation before we transport her to Newgate." He signalled to his assistant. "You stay, Arthur, and take care of the wee one. We'll have to see who can take responsibility for her burial. Maybe check at the Swan."

The constable approached the carriage whose owner leaned against the side of a wheel. "And you, Sir. No need for you to stay. You may proceed on your journey when the remains are removed."

As my captors dragged me away, I looked back at the bloodied stones that bore the mangled body of my child. "I'm sorry, Lily," I sobbed. "I'm sorry."

PART II

CHAPTER 1
NEWGATE PRISON
1754

Ben Turner approached the massive stone front of the prison, his hawthorn cane bumping along the cobblestones. Grasping one of the iron spikes, he rattled the gate, calling out to the turnkey dozing on the side bench. "Open up."

The frowzy-haired gatekeeper jumped to his feet, a ring of keys hanging from his belt. "Oh, you're back, Turner. Got yourself another pity case?" He pushed a key into the lock and opened the gate. "What's it this time? A starving poacher, a road robber, one of them pitiful pots from the stews?"

Turner lumbered through the opening, pushing the humpback out of his way. "Take me to Misella Cross. Admitted three days ago."

The turnkey grinned, ignoring the insult of the shove, curiosity brightening his pocked face. "The baby killing whore? That's a step down for you, ain't it, mate? She's in the felon's hold, but you can't see her. No visitors. The Ordinary's orders."

Turner grabbed the back of the man's greasy collar in his fist and yanked it tight enough to make him gasp. "I'm her lawyer, and I'll see her right now."

The man shrugged his twisted shoulders and led Turner through the archway where he was confronted once again with the absurd dichotomy between the ornate design of the entrance and the hellhole that festered beyond it.

Tuscan pilasters with their florid cornices invited the eye to examine the four carved niches, the first of which held a marble statue representing Liberty, the word *libertas* inscribed on her cap. At her feet stretched a sleek feline, a reminder of an early prison benefactor, Sir Dick Whittington, whose cat became the emblem of his good fortune. The other three niches contained the figures of Justice, Mercy, and Truth. Turner grimaced at the irony as he passed the gleaming marble fixtures into the dimness of the prison. He had found little of those ideals at work in this dismal place.

They traveled through various noisy chambers into which the interior was divided until the turnkey stopped on the far west side of the prison in front of a thick wooden hatch. "Here we are mate, the women's condemned hold. Better cover your nose." He pulled a dirty kerchief from his pocket and held it over his face before lifting the hatch by its iron ring and step-ping aside. Turner squinted at the row of narrow stone steps that descended into the yawning darkness. A fetid blast of heat and the sounds of clanking chains and shrill voices drove him back.

He confronted the turnkey. "What is she doing down there," he growled. "She hasn't yet been tried. Why isn't she housed in one of the upper wards?"

The turnkey drew back, beyond the reach of Turner's raised cane. "Well, now, you'll have to ask the Ordinary about that. He directed that she be put down there, the cell in the back."

Turner's face darkened. "You send someone for him. I'll see him about this as soon as I return. If she's ironed, he'll pay. You tell him that. Give me the key." He pointed his cane at the turnkey, a threat in his voice. "And you'll leave the hatch open until I return. Understand?"

The turnkey shrugged again and wrenched a key from the heavy ring swinging from his belt. "Don't matter to me none, except the prisoners up here won't like the smell."

Holding his breath, Turner lurched down the steps using his cane to steady himself. He stumbled along the narrow stone walkway past the rusted door of the common hold. A wild-haired hag thrust her grimed hand through the bars as he passed by. Forming a claw, she jerked it up and down. "Save us, won't ye? Lend us your plug tail. We need babes in our bellies to keep us from the gallows. Come in, come in, Mr. Talleywags." The other women in the cell screeched in merriment and hollered obscenities.

He stumbled around the foul-looking puddle forming outside their door and proceeded as best he could to the dark cell at the end.

No sound came from within. He peered through the barred window of the door, the interior illuminated by a lantern glowing on a table in the corner. She sat hunched on a narrow wooden barrack bed, her arms folded in her lap beneath the stained bodice of what once must have been a sumptuous gown. She seemed unaware of the roaches skittering along the damp floor, one clinging to the soiled hem of her gown. Her blond hair drifted in moist strings across her bent shoulders. How different, he thought with disbelief, from the night several days ago when he first met her at the wedding celebration of Lord Whittingham and Isobel Maltby.

The beautiful Misella had dazzled him that night. An intruder in disgrace, standing proud in her shiny gown and jewels, she impressed him with her courage, her bold refusal to let the wealthy hypocrites shame her.

"Misella," he called to her through the cell window, "it's Ben Turner, the barrister from Gray's Inn. May I enter?"

She shook her head, flinging strands of damp hair into her face. With a sob she said, "My daughter is dead, and I am lost. Leave me to rot...to die."

Turner unlocked the door and entered, closing it softly behind him. "My poor Misella. I can help you. I will." He brushed the bug from her gown with his shoe and crushed it. He sat his bulky body upon a nearby stool. "Who gave you the table and the bed and lantern?"

She stared at him, frantically rubbing her ink-stained hands together. Her eyes, dull and lifeless, brightened with a flash of recognition. "I needed them. The minister gave them to me, so I could write. He wants my story, but I don't want him to have it." She scrabbled her hands under the layer of straw on the bed, drawing forth several wrinkled pages of parchment, the writing tiny and cramped as if she feared she would run out of paper. "Will you take it, see that it is printed?" She hesitated. Her voice grew stronger, her eyes bright with passion. "I want young women to read it, to warn them."

Her fingers lighted on his sleeve as if, he thought, one of the sparrows in the square had rested there for a moment seeking a crumb of bread. He caught hold of her arm, as delicate to him in its torn gauze sleeve as a bird's wing.

She did not seem to notice. Her eyes darkened; a slight flush colored her pale cheeks. "I've told the Ordinary he cannot see any of it until I am finished, though he presses me for it. I hoped I could give it to someone before...." She turned her head away from Ben.

He tightened his grip on her arm. "My dear child, let me help you. I can defend you; you will not hang, I promise."

Agitated, she asked him, her eyes shadowed with pain, "How do you know whether or not I am guilty of this crime? I am, I am guilty. I must be. My poor daughter ground to nothing because of my pride, my careless-ness." Tears began to drip down her cheeks. "I do not deserve to live."

"Nonsense!" He took her limp hand in his. "I will see that you are transferred today to better quarters, given some clean clothes and decent food. You do not belong in this filthy hole."

She shook her head. "I have nothing left. I cannot pay for any of those things, and I cannot pay for your services."

He covered her hands with his. "The Society of Artists will pay for everything," he lied. "I need only to ask for funds from our Treasury. Do you remember I told you the night we met that helping destitute women is now part of our mission?"

She nodded, but still seemed troubled. "I have vowed never again to rely on the promises of any man."

His voice gruff, he insisted, "You must trust me, my dear. Give me these pages now and the rest as you write them. Your words will help me as I set about building your defense."

She gripped the pages and whispered, "You may change your mind, Sir, when you discover what I truly am, what I have done."

He pushed his rumpled wig in place and eased the pages from her. Taking her stained hand in his, he warmed it in his large paw. "My dear, I know who you are though we met only briefly. I have sinned too much myself to be shocked by anything you may tell me. Hold on a little longer,

168

and you will see that everything will improve. Now, let us both kneel and say a prayer for your little one who rests in the palm of the Lord."

Sobbing, she slid to her knees on the stone floor. Holding on to the stool with both hands, Turner lay the pages down upon it and slowly lowered himself, the bones of his knees cracking, a sigh of pain escaping his lips. "Oh, Lord," he said, "help us, thy servants, to accept the loss of this precious babe, to overcome our sorrow, and to find with your help, the path to truth and justice for your daughter, Misella Cross. Amen."

He struggled to his feet and reached down to help her up. "I have other news for you," he said, steadying her in his grip. "Sir Richard has succumbed to his illness."

She flinched, a flash of anger in her eyes. "Why should I care? He means nothing to me. He was dead to me long ago." The anger faded as her tears began to flow again. "And now, Lily is dead, too, the most valuable gift he gave me, the daughter that I came to love more than life itself."

CHAPTER 2

Uncomfortable in fancy social settings, detesting the shallow company of the snobbish nobility, Ben Turner had attended the Maltby-Whittingham marriage celebration grudgingly. His law partner, Charles Dunning, who never missed an opportunity to make connections and promote business, had forced him to go. But there he encountered Misella, and she had simply beguiled him, arousing an intense longing in him, a need he had managed to ignore for the past five years—since the painful aftermath of his wife's death when he made a conscience-stricken pledge to remain celibate for the rest of his life.

Plagued by guilty desire after that first encounter, he had, nevertheless, resisted the temptation to visit Misella at the Swan Court. When he received her note begging for a meeting with him, he could not refuse. She needed his help; he wanted to give it. After she failed to show up for the meeting, he waited for hours, hoping she would come. When she didn't, he had a legitimate reason to appear at Swan Court the next morning. On his way to the Swan, news of her arrest reached him when he stopped for coffee at the Covent Garden Coffee House.

He decided to offer her his legal assistance after wrestling with his conscience, examining his motives, collecting as much information as he could. When he found out that Isobel Whittingham hired Sir James Mansfield to prosecute the case in the Old Bailey, and that the Lord Mayor himself would act as judge, his mind was made up. Without counsel, she would not stand a chance even if she were innocent. She would be treated

THE TRIAL OF MISELLA CROSS

as a common felon, accused of a capital crime. The law and the Crown did not allow counselors to defend such cases.

The injustice of that inequity had rankled Ben Turner for years, and he had been working with a few other barristers to change that law. So far, they had met with stony resistance. It would not be easy gaining permission to defend her in court, but he was determined to try.

In the evening stillness of his office, he bent over the parchment pieces of Misella's story, squinting his good eye, too impatient to bother using the clumsy magnifying glass. The loose curls on the left side of his wig smoldered unnoticed as he leaned close to the candle's light. His tea cooling on the desk, his temper flared as scraps of evidence began to come together. "The scoundrel," he muttered.

He didn't hear his partner Charles Dunning enter the law offices or stop outside his open door. "What are you up to, Ben? More of that nonsense about the little trollop?" Ben ignored him and kept on reading. Dunning approached the desk and pushed the candle back. "You'll set your head aflame yet."

Turner looked up. "This dog of a useless eye plagues me. But I'm making progress. I believe the girl is innocent, a victim of that snake Maltby and his ruthless daughter. I can get her off, Chaz. I know it." He tilted back and rested his head against the leather cushion, his heated face aglow. "The Ordinary at the prison is a dangerous man. You should visit with him sometime. It might make you more sympathetic toward some of the poor creatures I try to help."

Dunning snorted in disgust and stepped back as if to avoid a sudden odor. "You've gone too far this time with your charity, Ben. I've been patient enough with some of those minor cases you have helped on our time. You could have spent that time on more lucrative ones. But this one will put you out of business for sure and ruin your reputation. Defending a child-murdering whore! What in the world are you thinking?"

"I do not believe she is a murderess," Turner stated with cool formality. "And a whore by necessity, not by choice."

Dunning laughed and shook his head. "That's what you say about all of them. You believe you can save the whole lot with your sympathy and sermons. In some ways, you are as naïve as a child, willing to be taken in by their sad excuses. Admit it. It's your guilt, Ben, for how you have used them yourself in the past."

Turner exploded from the chair, disregarding the pain in his knees. "No, Sir. I have made restitution for my mistakes, and I have learned from them. We can afford to help the unfortunate; it's our duty. God demands it. I demand it of myself."

Dunning's smooth face tightened in anger, his delicate nostrils drawing inward. "How do you plan to overcome the law and Mansfield on this one? They will never allow you to defend this case. Challenge the Maltby family? A charge of infanticide? You're insane on this one, Ben."

Turner sat back down. Controlling his anger, he stated matter-of-factly, "I know exactly how to do it. With all of the publicity swirling around this case, it's the perfect moment to strike. I'm sending letters of outrage to the members of both Houses, demanding that justice be allowed to work fairly, and listing the arguments against this inhumane tradition in our courts that disallows counsel to the poor souls, like Misella Cross, who need it most. I'll send a copy to all the papers as well. They'll print it. I know they will, to keep this feeding frenzy going. There will be a hue and cry, just wait and see."

Dunning's voice rose, undermining his usually composed demeanor. "As your benefactor here, I demand that you give it up. This is your craziest idea yet. A letter campaign," he snorted. "Bombarding the House of Lords! You'll be the laughingstock of London. She will ruin your reputation for you, and she is not worth that. There is an outcry already in the newspapers, from the pulpits, in the coffee houses, calling for the baby killer's death."

Turner's face darkened, his voice vibrating with indignation. "I will defend this woman no matter what," he barked. "If it takes every quid I have, I'll see justice done here."

Dunning appeared genuinely concerned. "I don't understand you, Ben. You have never been this adamant in dismissing my concerns; my opinion has at least given you some pause in the past. And it is not just your reputation I worry about. I worry about your health, spending time at Newgate with the fever raging. You weave your way through that vast hellhole, mingling with those wretched creatures, breathing in their foul, disease-ridden air." He shuddered and shook his head in disbelief, his face contorted with fear. "They have lost count of how many bodies have been hauled out of there in the last two weeks. You are in danger. Do you even realize that?"

Ben's voice softened. "I am in danger if I ignore the injustice being done to this innocent woman. I cannot do it, Chaz, whatever the consequences. I must try. Would you like to read her story? It might change your mind."

Dunning sighed in exasperation. "This will be the first significant case you will lose, Ben. You will not be able to work your magic on this one. And when you do lose, I will have no other choice but to remove my support and friendship. I cannot let you drag me down with you." With that, he left the office, closing the door decisively behind him.

Turner eased himself back into his chair. His wig slipping sideways, he grabbed it and flung it from him. If nothing else, he knew he could be honest with himself. And perhaps Dunning was right to question his motives on this one. Was he just trying to appease his own conscience once again? "Ah, Tetty," he murmured. "Will I never be able to overcome my guilt, the pain I must have caused you?" He should have insisted that she come to London with him. Then, he might have avoided all of the temptations. But in truth, he wanted to escape from her and the loveless life they led.

He thought of the loneliness he endured for all those years before he met Tetty, years he devoted to books and study and solitude. Orphaned far too young, just a boy when his generous uncle took him in, shared his love of learning and his love of God, and worked himself to death to pay for Ben's education at Oxford.

Even with his degree in hand, he was such a large, awkward boy, clumsy, almost blind in his left eye, speechless in public, prone to blushing furiously around the opposite sex. He experienced the usual boyish crushes, never reciprocated, of course. Eleanor Goodwin with her flowing lava hair and her white skin. Betty Brockman, the laughing, fun-loving milkmaid, who talked to him despite his stuttering responses.

Until Tetty, and their chance meeting at a bookstore in town. She was a widow, twenty years older than he. He was only twenty-three and so innocent about women. She saw him reading *The Aeneid* in an obscure corner where he could not be seen by the clerk who would have insisted that he buy the book. "You must enjoy literature," she said in a low, pleasing voice. "You seem so absorbed in your reading."

He looked up to see a motherly-looking woman, a pleasant smile on her ruddy face, genuine interest in her eyes. "Yes," he mumbled. "But I like to read anything I can get hold of."

She laughed and patted his arm with her gloved hand. "Good for you. I like young people who enjoy learning. I wish I had more patience for it myself, but I guess I have grown too old and my eyes too weak."

"Oh, I don't think you are too old, Madam," he blurted out. "And I have only one good eye myself, but that shouldn't stop me. You might try squinting like I do, or even use a glass which is cumbersome, I know, but sometimes necessary." He surprised himself that he uttered so many words without stopping or stuttering or feeling his face grow hot.

She laughed again, a tinkling sound he liked. "Well, perhaps I should join you in your studies, and you could offer me some encouragement. I have many books at my home that I have yet to open. You might be interested in borrowing some."

He jumped up, the heavy book falling from his lap. He stooped to pick it up, lunging backwards as he righted himself and almost knocked over the table sitting next to him. He set it straight and placed the heavy book upon it. "Oh, I surely would, if I may, if I would not be a bother to you."

"I would be happy for your company, and please, you may call me Elizabeth. I am Elizabeth Masters. How do you do?" She held out her gloved hand.

He encased it in his own and yanked it up and down. "Benjamin Turner, the nephew of Joseph Turner, the bricklayer. I helped him in his work, until he died, that is. Now I work alone." He looked down at his hand still holding on to hers, embarrassed suddenly by the coarseness of his skin and the lines of dark putty under his nails.

She shook her head, her feathered hat jiggling merrily atop her gray-laced auburn pompadour. "I knew Joseph, yes. He did some work for us years ago when my husband was alive." Her wide brown eyes glowed with warmth and approval. "My home is just a few blocks from here, Benjamin. Perhaps you would like to join me now?"

That was how the relationship began. He spent as much time as possible at her home, working his way through her library, eating dinner at her table, enjoying her company. She accepted him. She made him feel welcome and smart, and she laughed often at his shy comments, his warm jokes, thus encouraging him. He blossomed under her attention and approval, and after several months, he asked for her hand in marriage. She offered him so much that he needed. And she had needed him, too. She said yes without hesitation.

Thoughts of their wedding night still brought a blush to his face, pain to his heart after all these years. She tried to instruct him, tried to slow him down, but he was in such a frantic state, so inept, so ignorant of her needs. He entered his own selfish world, disregarding her pleas. "Benjamin, wait. Give me a little time, dear. Oh, stop for just a moment, please." But he forced his way ahead, oblivious to her cries, his crude panting drowning out her gentle voice. He hated to admit it, but things did not improve very much with time and instruction. She seemed unable to enjoy herself. She complained about his size, his rough hands, his hungry mouth, until finally she simply refused him her bed, telling him frankly, "Ben, dear, this kind of intimacy is for youngsters. I am too old for this. Can't we just enjoy one another's company without any of that?"

So he devoted his energy to consuming law books, apprenticing himself to Gerald Plume, the town's lawyer. In time, he knew more than Plume, and he needed wider challenge. Tetty agreed to finance his trip to London to seek better employment and better wages, but she refused to accompany him. "I cannot bear the noise, the filth of that teeming city," she told him. "I'll await you here whenever you can return for a visit. I do wish you well, dear."

She seemed content to read her novels, enjoy her desserts, and her claret, which she drank far more often than she should have. She grew rounder, her face ruddier, her conversation less appealing to him. With a guilty conscience, he accepted her money and escaped, telling himself it was only temporary until he made enough to repay her and keep her comfortable.

He set aside his tea and poured himself a glass of claret from the bottle he kept in the top drawer of his desk. He pulled out his note cards and unstopped the ink bottle. For hours he forgot where he was, his pen scratching across the cards as he read the parchment pages and jotted down his thoughts, his questions, his obscenities when he could not contain his temper.

Had he been no better really than Richard Maltby, taking comfort whenever he could, wherever he could, to assuage the loneliness that often consumed him, the need to be touched, to be held close, to feel the surrender of warm flesh against his own? He understood well the vain longings for affection that a man of strong passion endured.

In those early days he prowled the streets of London, where hot comfort waited on almost every corner, spending Tetty's money to satisfy his lust. He had not given a thought afterwards to the women he used, tossing them coins as if they were the beggars and he the generous one, taking some women home with him when he could to prolong his pleasure. All at Tetty's expense, of course, until she could send him no more money, until she lay dying of apoplexy, and he rushed home to say good-bye, to bury her, and to sell her home to finance his return to London.

In the dark months after her death, he violated her memory in the same desperate way, almost every night. Finally, he found a place to begin as a lowly attorney at Dunning's. With Dunning's help, he achieved his position as a barrister and, in gratitude, made a vow of celibacy and had managed to keep it.

He never used a prostitute's services after that. Instead, he grew in religious fervor. He read Bishop Law's treatise on religion, found comfort, and became a convert to the law of God. He grew in devotion, in wisdom, and in maturity, lonely still, but driven by a sincere need to help others, especially the poor and prostitutes, offering them legal advice when he could. He had never defended one, however, in a court of law, only in arguments with educated friends who chose to dismiss the problems of prostitution, calling it instead a necessary profession, old as Jezebel.

He struggled to his feet. Picking up the twisted wig, he rearranged it and tugged it in place over his own graying curls. He opened the door and headed up the stairs to his living quarters, grasping the banister and hauling himself up one slow step at a time. He needed to retrieve an unspent candle from his dwindling supply, maybe two to keep the office lit until later tonight when he returned from the Society of Arts pre-meeting at the Ye Olde Chesire Cheese, where some lively conversation and a pint or two would dispel the gloom and rekindle his confidence.

His friends would quiz him about the case, but in a kindly way, and he'd wave them off, tell them he still had much work to do, which he did, before the trial began. He would not share with them his worries about the Maltby money and influence nor about the mad determination of the

Ordinary to profit from Misella's story, and certainly not that Dunning had disowned the case, though Dunning would probably be there. But he knew he could count on Dunning to be discreet. The group would find out soon enough. All of London would.

He stopped for a moment on his way out, as he always did, at the little oval painting of Tetty resting on the mantelpiece. "Good night, my dearest. May I with your help find comfort in His divine Mercy and guidance in His Wisdom."

CHAPTER 3

The Society of the Arts devoted its efforts and its money to increasing the country's national riches and improving the arts. Of most concern to the small group who met weekly at the Cheshire Cheese was finding ways to help the poor and better maintain the dismal London workhouses. They formed a committee to share their views, hone their ideas and strengthen their arguments in preparation for the monthly Society of the Arts meetings attended by the entire membership.

On this Thursday evening, the group gathered to discuss the rampant rise in prostitution, an issue of particular concern which they wished to raise at the next meeting of the Society. They planned to craft a proposal to provide some refuge for the prostitutes and their often exposed and deserted children: a Charity House to receive and employ poverty-stricken girls and protect them from the danger of becoming prostitutes. The committee believed this home could also encourage those who had already fallen into prostitution to forsake their profession and become useful members of the community.

Most of the guests at the Cheshire were too busy eating and drinking and chattering to notice Ben Turner's large figure, his rather shabby clothes hanging loosely, as he shambled his way towards the smoke-filled back room. The small knot of gentlemen gathered around the oblong table in the corner ceased speaking as soon as they saw him, looking sheepish as they greeted him and made room for him on the wooden, church-like bench against the wall. When he noticed Dunning at the end of the table, looking peeved, his delicate fingers tapping the rim of his wine glass, Turner assumed they had been discussing his representation of Misella.

He eased himself onto the bench and propped his cane against the wooden half-wall that surrounded the fireplace, the smoke from the coals mingling with the cigar fumes wafting around the table. Straightening his wig, he waved to the bar maid who sidled over and slapped a tankard down in front of him, spilling some of the ale onto the table. "Oops, there you go, love. Don't drip on yourself when you drink," but Turner had already taken a gulp, some of the liquid dripping onto his vest.

The men grinned, except for Dunning who remained dour-faced. Next to him Henry Baker, a fellow barrister and good friend of Ben's, shook his grizzled head. "Easy, Ben. No need to rush. We didn't want to start the discussion without you."

Turner thumped the tankard down. "Well, Henry, it seemed to me when I came in that you were having a serious talk about something."

Saunders Welch, High Constable of Holborn and the group's expert on London's social problems, smiled kindly. "Just some light banter, Benjamin. You know we couldn't have a serious discussion of the proposal without you."

"I'll take you at your word, Sandy." He noticed Bernard Masterson sitting next to Dunning, his spectacles twinkling, his eyes alive with interest. "What are you doing here, Bernie, spying on us?"

Masterson laughed. "I thought I might bring some welcome light into this dark and serious little circle. I'm here to assist, if I can, at Saunders invitation, by the way."

Turner grunted. "You are here to spout the devil's doctrine and make trouble."

"Now, Ben," Saunders warned, "We need Bernie here to remind us of the obstacles we may face in getting this proposal through. We might as well be prepared. Who better to help us sharpen our thinking and our arguments than Bernard who'll raise his objections at the meeting anyway?"

Turner grumbled, "Who better than an immoral scoundrel, you mean."

Saunders overlooked the comment and addressed the group. "Well, gentlemen. Will we be ready to bring the proposal to the meeting tomorrow, or not?"

Henry Baker spoke up, his voice firm. "I think we must. The problem worsens every day. Thousands crowd the streets now—impudent, audacious—they stop respectable men, grab at their coat sleeves, and make obscene suggestions, lewd gestures. Even girls eight, nine years old proffer their sad charms. Where do they all come from anyway?"

"Poor, deserted girls, Henry," said Saunders Welch in a quiet voice, "from the country, the city, left to fend for themselves."

"And Lord knows, they are but a fraction of the problem, Henry." David Wilkes, heavily jowled, mopped his face with his kerchief and added in a raised voice, "Many don't have to walk the streets. Not with all of the wily matrons who provide them with lodging, clothing, protection. Even more notorious are the fashionable houses where the wealthy frolic, those bagnios ornate as palaces." He reddened a bit and coughed into his kerchief. "Not, of course, that I have personal knowledge of such places. Only what I have heard from others."

Masterson chuckled. "Yes, yes, of course, David."

Turner shifted uncomfortably in his chair, wiping another spill from his vest with his bunched up napkin. "We cannot wait. We need to do something now. Legislation lags, and there seems little chance at the moment that stiff laws will be enacted to attack the problem."

Masterson set his wine goblet down with a thud. "You'll never eliminate prostitution by making it a crime, Benjamin, or by trying to enforce laws against it."

"Nonsense, Bernard," said Welch. "We are convinced that strong laws, rigorously enforced, are the only way to rid society of the pernicious stews and the evil they promote. Our proposal is just a pittance when it comes to doing something, but we can forget about Parliament paying attention to anything that's not war-related these days."

"Hear, hear," bellowed Turner, leaning across the table to give Masterson a sharp whack on the shoulder.

Shaking his head, Masterson admonished Welch. "Stop looking at brothels as dens of sin, a social nightmare, and consider the practicality of making them acceptable. Put your money and your influence into that effort."

"Change your tune, Bernie," said Turner, his face reddening. "You've been piping that one too long and it just won't carry."

181

Masterson laughed. "You zealots just can't admit, can you, that pleasure is a driving force of human nature, and copulating is our greatest pleasure. Let society embrace that concept, and let people choose to do what they please as long as it is a choice freely made by both parties." He waved his hand at the others as if to dismiss any further discussion.

Ben Turner lunged forward in his chair, his wig jumping. "No, Sir."

Sighing with clear exasperation, Masterson said, "I know, Benjamin, I know. You would allow no irregular intercourse whatever between the sexes."

Ben rapped the table with his hand causing the silverware to rattle. "To be sure, I would not, Sir. I would punish it much more than is done, and so restrain it.

Masterson chuckled. "A pipe dream, Ben. You'll never restrain it."

Turner half rose from his chair. "In all countries, Sir, there has been fornication, as in all countries there has been theft; but there may be more or less of one, as well as the other, in proportion..." He pounded the table again. "to the force of law."

"Take it easy, Ben," Dunning said, no longer remaining withdrawn and silent. "You are becoming apoplectic. It's only a conversation. We are not in a courtroom. Anyway, the rest of us agree with you—I believe."

As Turner resumed his seat, Masterson edged forward in his chair to say, "You still refuse to believe that private vices can produce socially desirable results. Civil authorities should permit and control prostitution. It cannot and never will be eradicated. Public houses will concentrate a social evil that is otherwise widely dispersed through the city."

Turner wasn't sure if the scoundrel actually believed his own words or was just baiting the group, playing the game of devil's advocate to impress his captive audience.

Masterson continued, "Such houses can be regulated, bringing order to a traffic that often leads to social disruption. Other tangible benefits will result."

The rest shook their heads, Turner and Welch both uttering, "Ridiculous," and raising their hands to stop him from going any further.

Masterson ignored them. "Disease can be controlled." He tapped the table with his index finger. "Valuable time could be saved our law enforcement system, not to mention the outcome for children of such unions, who, spared infanticide, could be properly reared by their mothers. That is, if the mothers could earn a decent living unimpeded by the law or by shifty matrons or patrons who prey on their fears of reprisal. Don't look so horrified, gentlemen." He noticed Turner was ready to pounce, and held up his hand. "Wait, let me finish, Benjamin. Marriage would be strengthened because men would have a greater sense of reality about women. And the debauchery of modest women would cease."

Turner cut in, his voice curling with sarcasm. "Would it indeed, Sir? Would men of power no longer pursue modest women whom they crave to master? Would they no longer wish to overpower on any terms the resolution or surprise the caution of a girl? Would they be content to give up the hunt, those boasters that deck themselves in the spoils of innocence and beauty and prefer to attack only those too weak to resist?"

Masterson seemed taken aback by Turner's outburst. The other men remained silent. Turner had their attention and took advantage of it. "Isn't it true," he went on, "whether they achieve their goal by debauchery or legalized sin, such men are just as content to possess the body without any solicitude to gain the heart?"

"Well said, Ben. Well said." Saunders grabbed Turner's jacket and tried to hold him in his seat, but he pulled away and leaned across to Masterson, grabbing hold of his arm. "Such predators would surely have the least pretensions to triumph if they owe their success solely to a sanctioned business arrangement."

Masterson slapped his hand away. "Relax, Ben. Me thinks thou dost protest too much. Try to remain neutral instead of adopting a spurned woman's point of view here. Are they not, in the end, all financial arrangements, anyway—whether a man takes a mistress, a prostitute, a wife"—he hesitated for a moment—"or a willing surrogate daughter as in the Maltby case which you foolishly believe you can win?" A shocked silence ensued, interrupted by a brutal expletive from Turner.

Saunders Welch stood up. "Hold on, Bernard. That's quite enough. You may leave us. Your role in the discussion is over."

Masterson paid him no heed, further addressing his comments to a livid Turner. "Let's call it what it is, free will, my dear Sir, and there's nothing wrong with those business arrangements, as you label them. I heartily approve of them. They work to prevent the violent effects of appetite from disrupting the social order."

Turner could not contain himself. "Is it free will, Sir, when one of the parties is without other means of survival and has no choice but to comply?"

Masterson smiled, his voice slow and deliberate, as if he were patiently addressing a wayward child. "We always have choices, Ben; you know that, though we can always find reasons to avoid making the unpleasant ones. We convince ourselves that we are trapped with no other outlet. But if we are honest, we have to admit that our choices are driven by our desires, especially those closest to the secret regions of our hearts."

Turner looked down, struck speechless for a moment by the accuracy of Masterson's words, and the sudden intensity of his own guilty conscience.

As Masterson stood and prepared to take his leave, Turner rose, knocking over his tankard. His voice firm, he chided Masterson. "Depend upon it, Sir, severe laws, steadily enforced, would protect us all, especially friendless poor women and children, from the unleashed desires we must learn to control."

Masterson shook his head, waved goodbye, and squeezed his way past a group of noisy revelers gathered around the bar. After his departure, Saunders Welch questioned the others. "Have we changed our minds, gentlemen, about the proposal? Do we need to alter anything in it?"

"No, Sir," Turner barked. "We must improve it. We must make it stronger."

When the meeting ended near midnight, Turner struggled to his feet, refused the last round of drinks, and snatched his cane. "I've still some work to do," he insisted, despite the group's protests, and stomped his way to the front of the pub and out the door. Though the curved alleyway outside was dark, a lone lantern at the end threw off enough light so that he could find his way onto Gough Lane, a short block from his home.

"Hallo, there, Mister." A woman emerged from the shadows as he entered the Lane and grabbed his arm. She leaned toward him into the light, deftly exposing one browned nipple under the ragged gauze of her collar. Blonde matted curls spiraled out of her lace-edged cap. "How's about some company to warm you up tonight?" She slid one foot in front of Turner's and leaned her weight on his arm, making it difficult for him to move on. "For a few quid, I can take you to heaven. You wouldn't be sorry, Sir."

184

Turner saw a flash of desperation in her tired-looking eyes; a deep breath raised the sharp edges of her breastbone. "How long since your last meal?" he asked gently.

Her pale eyes darkened and a flush infused her gaunt cheeks. "I think yesterday, Sir," she mumbled.

Turner took her hand from his sleeve and held it, pretending not to notice its roughness. "If you will accompany me to my home down the street, Miss, I can provide some food for you and a room to yourself for the night."

She seemed relieved for a moment, then wary, uncertain whether to trust him. "You needn't worry, Miss," he said. "I won't use you. I want to help you."

CHAPTER 4

The Ordinary prepared for another nocturnal visit to Misella's new room. Her fresh gown, her dressed curls, the glow in her face, her growing confidence, all rankled him though he hid his anger from her. He had abandoned the daytime sermons, for he did not want to chance another run-in with that blackguard Turner who barred him from entering her quarters. Turner was a stubborn barrier to the Ordinary's holy mission. But righteousness would win. He would convince her with burning selections from the Bible that her salvation rested with him, not with the frumpy barrister and his useless lies. He yearned to get his hands on her confession, to read the rumpled pages she flashed before him, but she held him off, assuring him he would have them when she finished. Of course, the temptress knew how to entice.

Smoke from the candle curled in the misty air, the pewter holder heating his fingers as he headed for the Pressyard and the second floor Castle where she now resided, the best part of the prison. He clutched the Bible to his chest, its smooth leather cool against his hand. Her room was well-supplied with light and nicely furnished, free from ill smells. He wondered how Turner could afford the weekly rent of twenty quid, not to mention the food and the services of the laundress who made the fire and cleaned her room. What licentious acts had the whore promised to perform for him in return? He could well imagine.

He uttered a quick verse to quell such devil-inspired thoughts, one method his guardian aunt had drilled into him that long-ago morning when he awoke with soiled sheets and his night shirt wet between his legs.

She had hovered over him, her metal cross shining in front of his eyes, her voice frigid in the wintry air. "The Devil's at work, William. I could smell his presence the moment I arose. Get up and rid thyself of his poison." She flung his clothes upon the bed. "Get thee to the well and wash thyself clean."

He jumped up shivering and watched in shame as she yanked the sheets from the bed and flung them to the floor. "We must spend this day on our knees in prayer and penance."

He gathered up his clothes and ran barefoot from the little cottage to the back yard. Lowering the bucket into the well, he filled it to the brim and pulled up the rope, the crank screeching like his aunt's voice. He yanked off his night shirt, throwing handfuls of the icy water onto his groin and down his legs.

He still bore the marks of the tattoo she had inscribed that day upon his abdomen, just above the first sprouting hairs. His early manhood covered with a coarse towel, his teeth clenched in agony, she drove the heated needle back and forth from the fire to the bottle of India ink to the replica of the cross she embroidered into his skin.

Each night thereafter they prayed together at bedtime on their knees, her pale lips begging God to protect him from the Devil's visits. Never again did he allow the Devil to tempt him that way until the day He sent this whore Misella into his midst.

The prison chapel, which took up a large portion of the Castle floor, provided a convenient excuse for his nightly visits. He would putter around the altar or lurk about the compartments set aside for the prisoners, pretending to check the printed prayer sheets, until after the gates were locked at nine o'clock, and he could be certain Turner would not show up. On this night he waited until after ten, when the hall was dark and deserted. Shielding the candle flame with the Bible, he tiptoed to her door and slipped the key into the lock.

She sat at the small table in her dressing gown, her profile etched by the fire burning low in the fireplace behind her, outlining the curve of her full bosom, her fingers lifting a half-eaten peach to her lips. Startled by the sound of the door creaking open, she set the peach down upon a china plate and licked her juice-stained fingers "You are later than usual," she said. "I wasn't expecting you tonight."

188

The Ordinary's throat tightened making it difficult for him to swallow. Heat swirled inside him, its moisture escaping through his skin, staining his shirt and the lining of his vest. He struggled to speak, his mouth dry as coal dust, the sudden thirst unbearable. He dropped the key. It bounced and clanked on the floor. He held the Bible up as if to shield his eyes or block his face from her view. The candle wobbling dangerously, he fled, leaving her door wide open.

He escaped into the frosty night air. His breath rasping, he flattened himself against the stone boundary wall in the Pressyard, its narrow walking path deserted. He dropped the Bible and extinguished the candle with his fingertips, the fire scorching his skin. Flinging the holder to the paving stone, he tore at the buttons of his breeches. Its contents sprang into his hand. Gasping, his hoarse cries muted as if coming from a sick child, he sought release. The Devil's milk erupted, webbing his fingers, its wild mushroom scent sending him back to his painful childhood.

He drew his handkerchief from his pocket and scrubbed his hand and the limp traitor that needed to be punished. He slammed himself against the stone wall, the pain erasing any lingering remnant of pleasure and gazed upward. A pale moon scarred the black sky, receding suddenly behind a slash of dark cloud. He fell upon his knees. "Father, forgive me, for I knew not what I was doing. Henceforth, I will without fail honor thy Name and do daily penance for this sin. She, too, must be saved. She must pay for her crimes and seek Your salvation. We must reclaim her soul from the Devil and raise her up to spend eternal glory with You. Thy will be done."

The next morning he entered her room equipped with his Bible and a stronger resolve to work for her soul. She answered his timid knock. "You dropped your key last night," she said, placing it in his hand as he entered the room. Turner was not there, for which he was grateful. Encouraged, he thanked her and placed it in his pocket. "Let us take some time to read the Psalms today."

She shook her head. "I know them. I no longer need to hear them." Moving to the table, her muslin day gown swirling to reveal the toes of her leather slippers, she picked up a gray teapot and poured liquid into one of the matching cups. She set the pot back down on the wooden tray, and juggling the saucer and cup in one hand, with the other she pulled her chair close to the fireplace. She neither offered him tea nor asked him to sit.

He took a few steps toward her. "You need my help, you know."

She waved him away with her hand.

"I can do much more for you than that rascal Turner," he blurted out, his voice rising. "You know you must answer for your crimes. God and the Crown demand it. Turner cannot dismiss the laws of the land, nor can he implore God in your favor to comfort and save you as I, His divine servant, am able to do." The heat from the fire seemed to infuse his voice and redden his face. "Give me your written confession now and let me begin to intercede on your behalf. I must know in detail all the sins of which you are guilty."

"Please, just leave me alone," she whispered. "I have found all the help I need."

"No, I cannot." He lunged forward and grabbed her arm in his fingers, shaking the Bible in front of her. "God in His mercy will help you; let me help you, let me help Him to cleanse your soul."

The door shot open, and Turner plowed into the room, his cane raised in his fist. "Get out of here, you bloodsucking phony. You and your grubby work. Using God as an excuse. Extorting confessions from helpless creatures."

The Ordinary backed away, but raising the Bible aloft in one hand and lifting his chin, he snapped, "And what do you take from her? Spending every minute you can, wheedling her story from her to use in the courtroom." Emboldened, he confronted Turner. "You seek her freedom, oh yes, but not the truth or justice in the eyes of God. You want only to save her earthly life."

Glimpsing a sudden flash of passion in Turner's eyes, the Ordinary experienced a momentary spark of insight, of recognition. "Because you lust after her. You seek her gratitude and admiration; you seek to make her dependent on you and in your wanton dreams, you imagine that you may have her if you can gain her release." His voice rose to a fevered pitch matching the enflamed outrage in his eyes. "So with your fool's passion, you will disregard or try to diminish society's laws, God's laws, in order to achieve your goal." He lowered his voice and appealed to Misella. "I will use your story as an example to help others. I seek only to save your soul from everlasting damnation."

Turner, stunned to silence by the weight of the Ordinary's accusation, said nothing as the minister left the room, slamming the door behind him. He hesitated, straightening his wig, clearing his throat, before limping to Misella. Supporting himself with the cane, he said softly, "You must not trust him, my dear." He took the spilled cup and saucer from her tight grasp. "He will use your confession against you when he testifies at your trial. We cannot let him do so."

She nodded, unable to look at him, refusing to speak. The Ordinary's words churned in her mind, breeding suspicion about Turner's motives, awakening the doubts she had finally put to rest, despoiling the trust in him she had worked so hard to achieve.

He set the saucer on the hearth stone, pulled the other chair close and sat down. "I want you to be prepared, Misella, for how the prosecutor will build his case against you, and what we must do to fight him and the witnesses he will bring forth. He will most certainly use the Ordinary and his experience with similar cases, and the boy who claims himself an eyewitness. He will groom Isobel, his most damaging witness. Right now, given Sir Richard's recent death, her testimony will undoubtedly earn the judge and jury's sympathy."

Misella raised her head and stared into the fire. "I knew that someday Isobel would make me pay for what I did to her," she whispered. Turner tried to take her hand that rested inert on the arm of her chair, but she drew it away and clasped her hands together in her lap.

"We cannot allow that to happen," he asserted. "I must find a way to dilute her testimony, disarm her. That is why I need all of your written confession, my dear. It is the only witness I have to work with. You must trust me. That is all I will ever ask of you."

After a moment, she stood and walked to the table. Pulling open its creaky drawer, she drew forth several crisp pages, setting them down on top of the table. She smoothed them into a neat stack, untied the narrow hair ribbon that held her curls in place, wound it around the bundle of papers, and tied them firmly together. She handed them to Turner. "Here are the rest of the pages. I have to trust you," she said, as if trying to convince herself. "You are my last hope."

CHAPTER 5

Isobel stared into her hand mirror, its tortoise shell handle gripped tightly in her fingers. Tears clouded her vision, smearing the embroidered morning glories along the edge of her dressing gown into a pink smudge. She rubbed lavender-scented goose grease into the lines across her forehead and around her eyes, then dabbed them dry with a linen cloth. She would have to act on her own now that her father was gone. She missed him.

The unfairness of his untimely death had devastated her, just when he had begun to realize how much he needed her, admired her, depended on her as he had never done before. No one needed her now. Certainly not her toad of a husband. He would be no help at all. He didn't care, had never cared about her and even less about her efforts to confiscate the child. He bungled that job miserably. For appearance sake, however, she would keep him around until after the trial and decide later what to do with him.

She would need to be clever, she knew, to outwit Turner. Why he fought so hard for the right to defend that trollop she could not fathom. She supposed that he leered after Misella as most men had, including her father. She just could not understand what drove men—brilliant men, powerful men—to pursue someone so coarse and common. She would never understand. Regardless, Misella would pay for what she had done.

Isobel could not have hoped for a better way to punish Misella than having her child dead and being accused of her murder. Though she had schemed to take the child away from Misella to make her suffer, and then dispose of the little bastard later on, this was perfect justice—two birds with one stone.

Isobel grieved for the loneliness and emptiness of her own life. Her happy plans of beginning a family immediately after her marriage, of having a child of her very own, maybe even two or three, were all destroyed. How she hated Whittingham and Misella for the way they had schemed to betray her, and how she hated herself for being such a fool. She didn't like to dwell on those painful days and nights of what should have been her honeymoon. Whittingham escaping from her as soon as he could with no explanation, refusing her advances, ignoring her demands and tantrums until finally, she screamed at him that she knew all about his relationship with Misella. Her spies, for a price, had revealed his arrangement at the Swan to keep Misella to himself. How that news burned in her breast. When he finally confessed the true nature of their collaboration, she wanted to kill him and Misella, too, and the child, that shameful evidence of her father's weakness.

Thank God she still had her heritance. As Lord Maltby's only legal offspring, she inherited his vast wealth and influence. And she possessed more money than Whittingham could imagine. She blessed her father for his wisdom and foresight in having his lawyers arrange in Ireland a secret marriage contract for her. Whittingham was stunned to discover after the marriage that Sir Richard had made Isobel sole principal of all his land and moveable property. Through a separate estate contract, her father had ensured that her inheritance remained outside of her husband's control.

With nothing but restitution and revenge to fill up her days and lonely nights, Isobel had focused all of her attention on the trial, deliberately converting it into a spectacle. She hired the formidable barrister, James Mansfield, and secured the Lord Mayor himself to judge the proceedings. She aimed to see Misella Cross sway from the gibbet.

Using her money and influence, Isobel planned to appeal to those jury members whose names were whispered to her in confidence in the Queen's own reception chambers. She did have her connections, important ones. She decided to visit each juror in private with an irresistible proposition for each.

She would begin with Angus MacFarland, a man who sought promotion to a judgeship. Smart and highly respected, MacFarland overcame his Scottish heritage, worked unceasingly, and had ambition to rival the King's own. A strict Calvinist prosecutor and minister, conservative and

194

self-righteous, he abhorred the very word *infanticide* and deemed it a crime so heinous that any woman guilty of it deserved the most painful and prolonged death. A tight-lipped bachelor, he disdained not only prostitution, Isobel suspected, but anything to do with the female body.

She donned her most severe black mourning gown with its high stiff collar and starched cuffs. She encased her tightly curled hair in a starched muslin cap trimmed with black ribbon. No need to flaunt her wealth in front of MacFarland. He would respect severity and decorum. At those, she excelled. The hackney coach, normally used by the servants, awaited her. She tucked a small Bible into her reticule along with a hefty linen handkerchief, in case a few tears were needed.

MacFarland rented rooms near Chancery Lane. The housekeeper responded at once to Isobel's knock. "The Reverend will see you now, though he says you are a few minutes early." Isobel almost smiled in return. So, he still wished to be recognized first as a man of the cloth. Fine. That would make her job easier.

She entered a sitting room, sparsely furnished with a large wooden desk in one corner, a narrow fireplace which held a small smoky fire, and two sensible wooden chairs, uncushioned. MacFarland arose from his seat at the desk, withdrew his wire-rimmed spectacles and placed them on top of a single document open on the desk. He walked around the desk to greet her, rather gracefully for such a tall, knobby-boned gentleman.

He stared at her with gleaming, marble-sized eyes from under two of the darkest, fiercest looking eyebrows she had ever seen, giant black caterpillars that rippled as he spoke. "Lady Whittingham, my condolences on the recent loss of your father. May he rest peacefully in the Kingdom of Heaven."

Isobel thanked him in her most demure voice. He directed her to take a seat in front of the fire. She set her bag upon the floor letting it gape open just enough to reveal the Bible. "I am finding it difficult, Sir, to face my life without him. We were so close, especially after Mother died." She drew the handkerchief from her purse and held it in her lap, waiting for a long moment, while he respectfully stayed quiet. Finally, as if she had regained her composure, she pressed the cloth to her lips and spoke. "Reverend MacFarland, I hope I can be frank with you. The trial date has been set, as you know, for the infanticide case against"—she coughed and held the cloth to her lips again–"Misella Cross." He looked startled and a little alarmed.

She continued on before he could comment. "I know, Sir, that you have been appointed to the jury for that trial. It is public knowledge. Of course, I am not here to discuss the case with you, but only to let you know my concerns. The whole sordid story of her influence on my father will come out at the trial. It will be painful for me to hear it, especially now so soon after his death, when he cannot be here to defend himself or deny her lies."

MacFarland drew back, his face closing like a fist, a look of disapproval in his eyes, though his voice held no animosity when he spoke. "Please, Madam, I understand your concern, but I cannot listen to testimony of any kind before the case is proffered."

"Oh, I know, Sir. I know that. I would never want to compromise your position. I am, however, distressed by the news that Benjamin Turner will be defending her. He is such a gull, you know, when it comes to helping prostitutes. I am sure I don't know what he receives from doing so, but I worry that he may turn this trial into a circus to gain attention for the Society of Artists' cause—their mission to build a charity house for prostitutes."

MacFarland nodded, but remained silent. Encouraged, she plunged on. "I fear that if Turner can steer attention away from the crime, the-the *infanticide*...." Isobel smothered a seeming sob in the kerchief and dabbed at her eyes. "He will focus attention on Misella as a poor victim of circumstances and my father's attention." She allowed herself an uncharacteristic burst of passion. "Oh, Sir, how I wanted that child, to raise her as my own. I would have loved her with all my heart."

MacFarland seemed touched in spite of himself. He bent forward in his chair and patted her arm. "A terrible loss, yes. God's innocent babe taken from this world so violently, so senselessly." His face darkened, his brows forming a thick, black line. "So selfishly. Madame, I assure you that the charge of infanticide will be the focus at this trial and will receive my full and absolute attention. I will not be distracted by defensive trickeries, by Turner or anyone else. Nor will I allow my colleagues to be." With a stern look, he arose.

Isobel sprang up and grabbed hold of his hand, shaking it vigorously, tears in her eyes. "I respect your commitment to justice and the law, Sir.

196

Oh, yes. And I do believe that we need judges of your strength and character overseeing our courts. I intend, in fact, to do all in my power to see that you have the opportunity you deserve." She bent down and retrieved her reticule. As she straightened up, she noticed a flash of pleasure lighten MacFarland's dour face.

CHAPTER 6

Deep in thought, Charles Dunning paced the floor of his office. He tried to ignore the thumping of Ben Turner's cane on the hard wooden floor, his mutterings, the rattle of the papers he kept riffling through as he waited. Finally, he lashed out, fed up with Turner's pestering. "Oh, leave me alone, Ben. Please. I can't think with you snuffling and fidgeting over there in the corner. And I don't want to read any of that nonsense. That's your job. You wanted this. I want nothing to do with it. You're on your own. I am out of this entirely."

Turner pulled himself out of the chair. "I won't lose, Chaz. I could use your falcon eyes in the courtroom, but I guess my one good eye will have to do. Anyway, we are ready. I have prepared her well, and she will not falter in the box. I have no doubts about that, my friend."

Dunning refused to acknowledge the hand Turner held out to him. He walked over to the window and stared at the greasy raindrops tunneling down the glass, speckling Turner's reflection, his big drooping head as he thumped through the doorway into his adjoining office.

Dunning could see how obsessed Turner had become with this vile, unclean woman, how the rough edge in his voice disappeared whenever he talked about her, how the light kindled in his eyes, and his face softened. Dunning understood Turner's obsession with Misella's beauty and seeming vulnerability, but he worried about it. He needed to make sure it would end without destroying Turner in the process.

He had read the girl's story without Turner's knowledge, and his defense notes, at first in an effort to figure out how to handle the fallout from the trial when Ben lost, how to control the damage it could do to him, to the law office, and to their reputation. But after reading her story, he thought of a different idea. It required research and travel, money and urgency, but he knew he could manage it. He wasn't arrogant about his skills, never smug, just confident that with his persuasive techniques, he could succeed.

He knew that the new jury system at the Old Bailey provided opportunities for influence, and he assumed that Isobel Maltby realized this and intended to take advantage of it. But if he could not outsmart her and save Ben Turner, he deserved to lose everything. It would take a few days to set all of this in motion and to arrange the late visit with the prisoner. He shuddered at the thought of a healthy man willingly entering that infested hole, but perhaps if doused with herbal potions and carrying a vial of strong vinegar to coat his nostrils, he would be safe enough. A disguise would also be needed, for the risk of being recognized would be too great.

* * *

Dusk settled over the monstrous brick prison as a dark figure drew near the gate, a soiled cloak covering his herb-scented linen shirt. He stood back in the shadows so the acrid odor of the herbs wouldn't overwhelm the doddering gatekeeper. "A delivery," he muttered, rattling the canvas sack he held in one gloved hand, "for a prisoner, Misella Cross, in the Castle." He held out a gold sovereign in his other hand, letting the coin glisten in the light from the man's lantern. "Can you bend the rules a bit, man? I'd have been here earlier, if not set upon by a thug whom I spent some time reprimanding. Broke the crown of my hat in the process." He gestured to the boxy, crooked hat that covered much of his tattered wig. "Better than the crown of my head, I guess."

The gatekeeper reached through the bars to snatch the coin. The cloaked figure pulled his hand back. "Ah ha, my friend, open the gate first and slip me the key." The old man snarled something under his breath and slipped an iron key into the lock. He opened the gate a few inches so the caped man could squeeze through and slammed it behind him.

"Got ten minutes. No more," he wheezed, grabbing the coin before dropping a key into the stranger's hand.

"Another sovereign for you if I'm late. How do I reach the Castle area?" The gatekeeper gave directions, pointing into the gloom with gnarled fingers.

Reaching into the bag and extracting a thick candle, a flint, and the vial of vinegar, the dark figure took off through the arches, He made his way through the Pressyard, past a knot of unsavory-looking thugs gathered in the yard, smoking and mumbling to one another, to the outside stairs leading to the second floor. Having learned which room she inhabited, he dashed up the dark stairway. Before knocking on her door, he whipped off the hat and wig and collapsed them into the canvas bag. He smoothed his mussed hair and knocked softly. Stirring came from within before her quiet voice behind the door asked, "Here again, Reverend?"

"Misella," he whispered. He turned the key in the lock.

At first she did not respond. He waited in silence wondering what he would do if she refused to cooperate with the plan. The door opened a crack, and then she flung it wide open. She gasped when she saw his face. "Jack, oh, Jack, what are you doing here?" She grabbed his hand and pulled him inside.

He blew out the candle, closing the door softly behind him. How different she looked, much older than the last time he had seen her. She wore a simple gown with a high lace collar, her hair swept back under a headband, her face pale and unpainted.

"Misella," he whispered, "we need to be quick. Charles Dunning has arranged for your escape. A carriage is waiting. You need to change into these clothes I am wearing and sneak out of the gate without speaking. The gatekeeper won't stop you. But quick, you have only a minute."

She looked shocked, bewildered. "But what about you? How will you get away?"

He grinned, his dark eyes flashing. Dropping her hand, he bowed with a flourish as he used to do whenever he wanted to lighten her mood. "Remember, Mademoiselle," he murmured, taking her hands in both of his. "I am a skilled Highwayman, and the Escape Prince of Newgate. There is so much you don't know, and I don't have time to tell you. I know how to gain my freedom from this place. I've done it before. Charles Dunning will keep you hidden until I join you. When I do, he'll transport the two of us back to the farm in Ireland where he found me."

"But why, why would he do that?" Misella pulled away from him, her voice rising. "He detests me and has refused to help Ben Turner with my case."

Jack reached out and touched her cheek, moved by the tears and the fear in her eyes. "Hush, please, Misella. It's too long a story, my sweet. He is doing this for Turner's sake. He believes you don't have a chance. You will hang, for sure, and ruin Turner." Jack slipped out of the cloak, pulled the wig and hat from the bag on his wrist. "Put these on and go."

Misella closed her eyes and took a deep, sobbing breath. "Oh, Jack, I cannot put you in such danger. You cannot trust Dunning. He will leave you stranded, or have you picked up, and who knows what he would do with me. Do you really think we would be safe even if we could escape to your sheep-covered hills? Isobel would track me down. She will never give up." She threw the cloak around him and opened the door wide. "You must leave, now."

He grabbed her shoulders and shook her hard, the bag on his wrist rattling. "You wouldn't listen to me before. Now, you must. I will not let you hang."

She shook her head, tears sliding down her cheeks. "Go, Jack. Just go. And don't let Dunning find you. Please." She pushed him as hard as she could through the doorway, and slammed the door.

CHAPTER 7

The public galleries of the Old Bailey's High Court swarmed with well-to-do onlookers eager to witness the most publicized trial of 1754.

Women in fur-trimmed cloaks swished fans in their gloved hands to banish the strong odor of camphor from eucalyptus clusters pinned to their garments. Men in velvet waistcoats chewed garlic bulbs and shuffled their feet as they surveyed the courtroom. Hungry for entertainment, ignoring the unusual April cold, with only garlic and herbs to protect them against the danger of infection, they had queued up before dawn, determined to witness the spectacle of Lord Maltby's adopted daughter reduced to poverty, prostitution, and baby-killing. The trial promised all the dark passion and intrigue of a Shakespearean play. The restless crowd happily paid for their tickets to enter the courtroom.

Guards led Misella Cross and the other shambling prisoners through Dead Man's Walk, an underground passageway connecting Newgate prison to the High Court. The first of the group to be tried, she huddled on the stairs to the courtroom waiting for the judges to arrive. A surly guard blocked her path. "Oh, you're a lucky one, Miss, ain't cha," he snarled. "Something special I guess if the Lord Mayor himself will hear your case. Too bad he don't look kindly on murderers."

Misella raised her vinegar-scented handkerchief to her lips to blunt the poisonous smell of his breath and stared with tear-filled eyes at the Bible, prayer book, and flickering candle chained to the curved stone wall, a last chance to beseech God's favor. She left them untouched. She did not give faith to miracles.

Bending her head, she brushed the tears from her cheeks, refusing to let anyone see her cry, certainly not Isobel or Whittingham or the Ordinary. She would show no sign of weakness, for that is what they wanted, that is what gave them their power. At least, she had learned that much. She knew her last chance for survival had been Jack whose wits might have enabled her escape. But then what? A life hidden away in the fens of Ireland? A shadow life?

Though she pretended to believe the wild-eyed Ben Turner with his passionate promise to save her, she had by now abandoned hope. She did, however, appreciate his fierce devotion, his kindness and generosity. The least she could do for the quaint barrister from Gray's Inn, defender of whores and pickpockets, was to give him this opportunity to perform before the privileged inner circle of the justice system that had long denied him respect and patronage.

Alone at the defense table, Ben Turner, with a discernible grunt, shifted the bulk of his torso sideways to stare with his good eye at the restless gallery mob. They wanted blood, a death sentence. He could feel it. A hanging would prolong the ecstasy.

He wished Dunning were here, but he steadfastly refused to attend the trial. "Say goodbye to your legal career, Ben," he snarled that morning as Ben left for the courthouse.

Ben had fought hard for the right to defend Misella Cross. It had not been easy, challenging the power of the government and the Crown's judges who favored prosecutors and inhumanely denied counsel to common felons accused of capital crimes. Relentless and very persuasive in his fight against injustice, he bombarded the newspapers and every member of both Houses with irate letters, hiring a bevy of scribes to help him. Given the publicity surrounding the case, he knew the government would have to back down in order to appear fair. He'd be penniless soon if not careful, but no matter the cost, he believed Misella innocent and had resolved to prove it.

He retrieved an orange peel from his pocket and slipped it into his mouth for protection. He hoped Misella remembered to chew the citrus scraps and cardamom seeds when she left her quarters and mingled with the other prisoners in the trial holding area. No doubt most of the ragged, chained riff-raff already carried the beginnings of gaol fever in their throats.

The courtroom had been scrubbed with vinegar. Open braziers glowed in the corners emitting the acrid scent of herbs spread across their metal grates but failing to warm the frigid air. Sulphur dusted the circular wooden tiers that housed the judge, the jury, and court officials, providing an additional layer of protection from pestilence.

At 9:15 the bailiff appeared and bellowed into the courtroom, "The Right Honourable Stephen Theodore Janssen, Esquire, Lord Mayor of the City of London."

The Lord Mayor in his crimson velvet robe, hat and chain, entered as all rose to their feet. In his wake followed the Sergeant-at-Arms, the Sword Bearer, and the City Marshal.

The Mayor, who would administer the sentence after hearing the case, took his seat on a raised platform beneath the Sword of Justice, arranging his robe around him and smoothing its ermine-bordered collar. His attendees sat to one side, with the twelve gentlemen of the jury seated together in stalls to the right of the judge.

The Lord Mayor signaled the bailiff who disappeared behind a heavy wooden door. A pall of silence settled over the room. The door thundered open, and Misella appeared in a demure black wool gown. A simple lace cap obscured most of her flaxen hair which had been skinned back into a tight bun at the nape of her neck. Staring straight ahead, her face pale, she trailed the bailiff to the dock. She entered the box and stood erect, her gaze centered on Ben Turner, who smiled at her.

He looked down and began to shuffle his papers, but forced himself to slow his hands and control his breathing He did not want to appear nervous, for her sake and his own. So much did she depend on him, so close had they become, their relationship almost like a marriage. He must succeed. He could not bear the thought of losing this woman who made him feel alive again.

Across from Turner, the prosecutor, Sir James Mansfield, sat at a great slab of a table, his circle of attorneys flapping around him like a clutch of black swans, their dark gowns rustling, their rippled wigs twitching. It was unprecedented for Mansfield to try a case in this lesser court. He worked exclusively in the prestigious King's Bench at Westminster Hall as an advocate for the nobility, prosecuting forgery and inheritance and occasional murder cases against their bastard sons and other greedy, debt-plagued relatives. He was a favorite of the royal judges. But Isobel Maltby's money and influence inspired him to take this case. And more, the publicity had drawn the King's attention and could lead perhaps to a judgeship for Mansfield.

Behind him, on a wooden bench in the witness section, Isobel Maltby Whittingham sat stone-faced next to her husband, her first public appearance since her father's death. Her gloved hands clutched the wooden railing in front of her. A black unornamented headdress framing her face, she resembled an Abbess, the pleated white collar of her gown hugging her neck like a wimple. For now, the grieving daughter had shed the sumptuous gowns and elegant coiffures.

Sir Mansfield stood, took a sheaf of papers from the table in front of him, and walked to the center of the room. Facing the judge, his back to the prisoner, he said, "May it please your Lordship, I am counsel for the Crown against the prisoner at the bar who stands indicted for the pernicious crime of infanticide."

A deadly quiet pervaded the room. "The circumstances of the present case I will open to you as shortly and clearly as I can, but it will be necessary for me to go back a little in time to prove that the crime was committed with intent, that the prisoner did with malice throw her illegitimate babe to its death." He paused, waiting for the murmuring from the gallery to subside. Elevating his voice, he declared, "When we have laid the proof before you, I haven't a shred of doubt that you will find the prisoner guilty of murder."

A flurry of whispers arose from the gallery as Mansfield returned to his table. Twisting sideways, he surveyed the packed gallery. Swirling back around, he addressed the jury again, the sweep of his gown revealing buckled black pumps and a flash of white-stockinged ankles. "Gentlemen," he added, "you must base your decision only upon the words you hear in this courtroom. You must disregard anything whatsoever that has appeared in print or that you may have heard in common conversation."

Ben Turner stared at the black-gowned jury poised like rooks for a game of chess. He tried to decipher any flicker of judgment in the downcast of an eye, the twitch of an eyebrow, or a tightened mouth. But all twelve men appeared steely and attentive, their flinty eyes directed toward Mansfield. Turner knew this jury believed in the rule of law and reason. That knowledge brought him some measure of comfort and hope.

He looked at Misella, her downturned face as colorless as the opaque cap upon her brow, her thin shoulders drawn inward, and her ungloved hands hanging lifeless at her sides. She appeared defeated already. She flinched and raised her head when Mansfield called his first witness, "William Hunter, the Ordinary of Newgate."

Hunter arose from his chair tucked into a corner behind the witnesses' bench. He adjusted his camphor necklace, sliding the dangling loop into the top of his dark vest, and picked up the Bible resting on the broad arm of his chair. Hugging it to his chest, he glided forward, stopping for a moment to glare at Ben Turner before he ascended the small spiral staircase into the witness box. He faced the prisoner and made the sign of the cross. Misella refused to acknowledge him, and he turned back to Mansfield.

"I see that you have brought your own Bible, Reverend," Mansfield began. "We can, if you wish, swear you in with it." The Ordinary nodded in agreement. "That is if Mr. Turner has no objection." He waited a moment, and when Turner remained silent, he proceeded with the oath. In a strong, clear voice the Ordinary swore to tell the truth in the name of God and the Crown.

Mansfield addressed him in a somber tone. "Reverend Hunter, in brief words define your role at the prison."

Hunter scanned the courtroom before he spoke. "I am counsel to all those incarcerated for their crimes. I bring them the Word of God through services I conduct in the prison chapel. And I meet personally with any who request my presence, especially those condemned to death for their crimes." He frowned at Ben Turner. "Though some here may not respect my position as God's surrogate, I willingly expose myself every day to those wretched creatures in their filthy rags, their bodies rotting from veneral ulcers, to encourage their repentance and to urge them to seek salvation."

"A noble endeavor, Reverend, for which the Crown is grateful." Mansfield edged closer to the witness stand. "Were you at any time Confessor to the accused, Misella Cross?"

"I visited her a few days after her arrest. I supplied writing materials and invited her to write down her confession as a means of seeking God's forgiveness and relieving her guilt."

"Her guilt, you say? Did she tell you she was guilty of murdering her child?"

Hunter raised up his eyes as if consulting heaven before he answered. "She did not say so, but she told me that she did not deserve to live. She tried to send me away, telling me that God would not forgive her and that she could not forgive herself for what she had done." He pressed his fingertips together beneath the large silver cross that hung just below his collar. "I have often heard that response from those who, too late, realize the magnitude of their crimes."

"In your many years at Newgate, have you counseled any other women accused of infanticide?"

Hunter bowed his head for a moment and sighed, as if forced to confront painful memories. "Yes, unfortunately, I can recall many such cases, similar situations in which wanton women took the lives of their babes. I am afraid it is an all too common occurrence." He glanced at Misella. "Whoredom is oftentimes attended with the murder of the babe..." He nodded toward Misella. "... begotten on the defiled bed."

Tapping his cane against the leg of his chair, Ben Turner forced himself to remain seated and silent while Mansfield finished his questioning. He straightened his ill-fitting wig and tried to ignore the voices buzzing in the gallery.

Mansfield raised his voice above the noise. "Nothing more, Reverend. Thank you for your service today and your fine prison ministry."

Before Mansfield could call another witness, Turner lunged to his feet. Hooking his cane on the back of his chair, he limped past Mansfield to confront the preacher. "Reverend," he barked, "a few questions, if you please. Who were these women? Can you describe for us any of those cases of infanticide? "

The Ordinary waited several moments before he answered, allowing Mansfield to return to his table and the gallery to quiet down. Clearing his throat, he spoke in a clipped voice. "Two that I can recall immediately were the cases against Nellie Bennet three years ago, I believe, and Margaret Paine, just a few months later."

He coughed and retrieved his handkerchief from inside his coat exposing the cross to full view. "Nellie was a common streetwalker; the other woman, Margaret Paine, was a well-known, upper class courtesan, uh, much like Misella Cross, I believe."

"And did you wheedle written confessions from them as well?"

Hunter drew himself up to his full stature. With a withering look at Turner, he explained to the jury, "Through my efforts, gentlemen, both of these women repented of their sins and embraced their Savior before they died. The example of their repentance and confessions..."

Turner interrupted him. "What did you do with their written confessions?"

Hunter flushed but answered without hesitating. "Copies were printed and distributed amongst the watchful as the women met their Maker at Tyburn."

Turner clamped one paw-like hand on the railing of the witness box as if to balance himself. "How much did you charge for a copy?"

Stepping back, Hunter narrowed his eyes. "A few pence a copy, to pay the printing costs. A small price for a large lesson to be handed down from the gibbet to all who may be tempted to succumb to the Devil."

"How many copies? A thousand? Ten thousand?"

Hunter's voice rose. "Enough! Whatever I needed."

Turner pressed on. "Enough from their penny scribble so that you could bring home a tidy sum. For one hanging, judging from the usual crowds, I guess you could make as much as ten pounds, maybe fifteen, after paying for cheap printing."

Hunter shook his head. Holding up the Bible, he protested, "Those menial sums help finance the work I must do, but I gain a far greater reward in saving souls for God."

Turner pushed closer, pressing both hands against the rough wooden front of the witness box. "Did you tell the prisoners that they would be damned to hell forever if they refused to commit their stories to paper? Did you tell those prisoners that neither prayer nor repentance could save them without written confessions?"

Unintimidated, Hunter held out his arms as if addressing a congregation. "Yes," he proclaimed. "A silent confession is meaningless unless others can learn from it. Repentance must never be easy. It must be difficult and painful and visible, a constant reminder of our weaknesses, of the Devil's power over us, he who invades our every thought, our every dream and plots the defeat of goodness. The Devil speaks to sinners in the depths of their hearts. We must always be vigilant."

He glowered at Turner and pressed on, his sonorous voice echoing through the drafty room. "I am God's servant chosen to do His work in this place. Let not the foot of pride come against me, and let not the hand of the wicked remove me."

Turner interrupted him before he could go any further. "Psalm 36, isn't it, Reverend? What about the one that precedes it? He raised his voice to match the timbre of the reverend's. *'Let not them that are mine enemies wrongfully rejoice over me: neither let them wink with the eye that hate me without a cause. For they speak not peace: but they devise deceitful matters…'*

Narrowing his eyes to slits, the Ordinary cut in. "Are you accusing me of lying about this woman? If so, point out to us those lies."

Turner reacted, a dark flush heating his face. "I'll ask the questions, Reverend," he growled. "I am not in a cell at the mercy of your confessional, and I am not accusing you of lying, only of casting stones unjustly against Misella Cross. There are degrees of sin, are there not? Some much worse than others. Where lies in your judgment book, as God's spokesperson, the sin of prostitution, a woman serving a man's carnal lust? You ordered the defendant to describe in detail, not just the death of her child, but also the things she had done with her customers, didn't you? Turner lunged forward. "Why?"

The Ordinary grimaced as if in pain. Visible beads of moisture collected across his naked brow. His throat appeared to tighten as he tried to swallow. He drew his handkerchief from his pocket and scrubbed at his hand. Struggling to speak as if stricken with a sudden unbearable thirst, he picked up the Bible and cleared his throat, his voice cracking as he spoke. "Prostitution is a sin against chastity that not only blackens the soul of the temptress but that of her victim as well. A sin twice over." Appearing to draw confidence from the jury's solemn nods of agreement, he proceeded, his voice steady, the tensed muscles of his face relaxing. "You may, of course, insist, and I am certain you will, that circumstances often propel a young woman in this direction——poverty, seduction, a child born out of wedlock, and I would agree with you. I commend your efforts to help these fallen women escape such a fate. But they must want to, and many of them do not. That is the greater sin: their refusal to change, or to accept our help."

"Ah, so if help is available and such a woman accepts it, you would consider her to have taken the right path toward salvation?"

The Ordinary held up one hand to stop further questions. "Yes, but that would be a small first step on a very long road for her. She must not lose her footing again and…"

Turner jumped in. "Or her virtue, yes, I understand. So, would you agree that Misella Cross tried to take that first step when she made an appointment with me seeking information about the Arts Society's new home for unwed mothers?" He held up the letter Misella had sent to him. "She was headed to my quarters when the accident happened."

With the aggrieved look of a parent about to counsel a wayward child, Hunter sighed and shook his head. "Well, it might appear that she wanted information, but how can we know if she intended to act on that information? Asking is not doing, Sir. What we do know is that she committed the gravest of sins by taking the life of her innocent child, deliberately tossing her infant like unwanted trash under the wheel of Lord Russell's carriage."

Turner slammed his hand against the witness box. "Wrong, Reverend. And you are not the prosecutor here." He slapped the front of his gown, plunged his hand inside and pulled forth a ragged piece of parchment. "Those two cases of infanticide you mentioned earlier, Nellie Benet and Margaret Paine?"

The Ordinary nodded slowly, his hand stroking the Bible he had laid on the wooden railing. "Yes."

"I have here a copy of the Sessions Papers. Both were accused of murdering their babes, Nellie by slitting the child's throat with the knife she used to cut the umbilical."

The Ordinary shuddered. Cries of disgust vibrated throughout the courtroom. "And Margaret, the courtesan you compared to Misella Cross, smothered her baby immediately after its birth."

Lady Whittingham pulled a linen handkerchief out of her sleeve, dabbing her eyes and sniffling. Lord Whittingham snorted and slapped his gloves against his hand with a resounding whack.

"Both women confessed to their crimes, isn't that correct, Reverend? And no witnesses were brought forward in their defense." Turner waved the parchment in front of the reverend, dropping it on the railing in front of the Bible. "The record confirms that."

The Ordinary remained motionless and silent though his eyes flicked to Lady Whittingham as if he began to suspect where Turner intended to go with his questioning.

"So your linking Misella Cross to Margaret Paine was rather disingenuous when we consider that her case is quite different." Turner raised his voice and ticked off on his broad fingers each point as he made it. "Misella's child was the age of seven months, not a newborn. No one who saw the two of them together will deny that she was a loving mother. She vehemently refused to allow Lady Marian Bentley to send her child away to the country, insisting on keeping the child with her when she was forced into Lady Bentley's employment."

The Ordinary slammed the Bible down, sending the scrap of parchment fluttering to the floor. "And we are to admire her for that? For exposing the child to a den of sin and debauchery?"

"Temporarily, until she could find a way out for them both. Believe it, Sir. I intend to prove it. Yes, Misella Cross was a courtesan, as you so delicately phrased it. But she had little choice as our defense will show. And, Reverend, she did not murder her child. You are finished here, Sir. You may step down."

Compressing his lips into a grim line, the Ordinary picked up his Bible and began to exit the witness box. With a flurry of movement, Turner grabbed another scrap of paper from his pocket. "Wait, Reverend. One more question. You gave the prisoner writing materials and pressed her to write her story. Did she give you her written confession?"

Hunter swung around and glared at him. "You know very well that she did not."

"Yes, I do know that, Reverend. She gave her story to me instead. Let me read you a passage from it so you and the judge may understand why. *"The Ordinary hounds me for my confession, swooping into my room like a black-winged vulture. He looks at me with such loathing while he preaches God's message and sets the conditions for my forgiveness which, he insists, can only come through him. But I have known far better liars than he, and I will not be sold again."*

The Ordinary charged down the stairs, his face crimson, the Bible raised in both hands as if he were about to thrash Turner with it. "You devil," he screeched. "You and the harlot will burn together in hell."

The gallery erupted with startling glee and the stamping of feet. A velvet-coated gentleman leaned over the railing and shouted, "Give him a good drubbing, Reverend!" An ermine-clad woman next to him called out, "Hang them both, the vile sinners."

Turner eased himself around the irate Ordinary and approached the dock. "Just look at me, Misella. Don't acknowledge them."

But Misella could not stop herself from staring in alarm and despair at the heated, hate-filled faces in the gallery. An unkempt vagrant, huddled in the back corner, stared at her with penetrating eyes. He wore a discolored wig that engulfed his cheeks and forehead to the eyebrows, and a battered tri-cornered hat. A stained, pewter-colored cloak encircled his shoulders. When he saw her looking at him, he pressed a finger under his whiskered chin and lifted his eyes to heaven.

Her heart lurched with shock at seeing Jack and with fear at the risk he took. For his protection, she forced herself to look away, though she yearned to keep her eyes on his face. His bravery in coming to this dreaded place to support her strengthened her, and she resolved to remain calm and stoic no matter what happened.

CHAPTER 8

Judge Janssen rose to his feet in outrage, pounding his gavel on the arm of his chair. "Silence from the gallery," he commanded, "or you will exit the courtroom." He ordered Turner and the Ordinary to take their seats and Mansfield to proceed with his witnesses.

Mansfield stood up, moving his torso back and forth, seemingly mocking Turner's convulsive movements as he lumbered back to his chair. With a dismissive wave of his arm in Turner's direction, he told the jury, "Gentlemen, I hope we can restore some measure of civility here with my next witness, Lady Isobel Maltby Whittingham."

Isobel stood and swept forward, marching up the small spiral staircase leading into the witness box. She grabbed hold of the railing with both hands, anxious to erase any lingering effect from Turner's attack on the Ordinary. Her dark eyes darted from Mansfield to Turner to the members of the jury. She did not look at Misella.

The bailiff swore her in. Mansfield stood before her. "Lady Whittingham, if you please, could you tell the court how long you have known the defendant and under what circumstances you came to make her acquaintance?"

Her voice clear and strong, Isobel retorted, "I first met Misella Cross when she came to live with my family six years ago. Her own family was poor. Her useless father could barely feed them. At the mother's request, my dear and generous father agreed to take one of the daughters."

"Why did Sir Richard not just provide Mr. Cross money to carry them through until his situation improved?"

215

Isobel shook her head. "He offered, but Mrs. Cross said her husband would refuse to accept that kind of charity. To lessen his burden, though, she convinced my father to take Misella temporarily as a companion for me." Her voice rose, her face reddened, visible beneath the layer of rice powder. "It was a foolish gesture. I did not need a companion. Mother and I tried in vain to convince Father of that." She patted her eyes with her handkerchief and spoke in a broken voice. "My father was a kind and giving person, eager to help when he could."

Mansfield bowed his head, his voice low, "May he rest in peace, Lady Whittingham. We understand your recent loss makes this trial even more difficult for you."

Isobel gulped. "I must do whatever I can to see justice done." Artfully, she patted her eyes. "And to clear my beloved father's name."

Turner scraped back his chair. He shuffled his papers and dropped a few to the floor. Leaning down to retrieve them, he grunted as his wig fell over his good eye. He pulled himself up and adjusted his wig, seeming only then to become aware that Mansfield glared at him.

Clearing his throat, Mansfield addressed the witness once again. "Please, ma'am, if you could sum up for us why Miss Cross came to leave your home."

"My father secretly installed her in comfortable quarters in London when he discovered she bore the child of Jack Finn, the notorious highwayman. Father dismissed Finn, telling him to leave England or he'd go to prison."

The gallery bustled with movement: fans flapping, gowns rustling, voices whispering. Yet Misella managed to train her eyes straight ahead, resisting the urge to seek out Jack's cherished face in that restless crowd. She wanted to lash out with the truth, to vindicate Jack and herself, to attack Isobel and silence her shrill voice.

Isobel shimmered with self-righteousness. "My father trusted Jack Finn, rescued him from a highwayman's life, and took him into his care. My father was betrayed by both of them." Isobel stared at the prisoner's box for the first time, her eyes drilling into Misella's stoic profile as she stood with her head down, palms joined together. Misella did not look at her.

Isobel resumed her testimony. "Father wanted her to give the child up for adoption, return to our home and live quietly, her reputation intact, until an acceptable marriage could be arranged, but she betrayed him once again. Before he died, father told me what he learned from the lodging house owner—she overheard Misella plotting with Finn to accuse father of violating her and supplying her with abortive powders. Later, when she tried to extort money from him in exchange for her silence, he washed his hands of her. Father was outraged and deeply hurt. We left at once for our estate in Ireland."

Turner rose to his feet, waving a paper. "Hold on, Sir, if you please." He limped to Mansfield and held out the paper. "I have here a signed affidavit from Mrs. Barron, owner of that lodging house, stating that she never saw Jack Finn and never heard anything about him from Miss Cross. The idea, she states here, of Miss Cross's complicity with Finn was suggested to her by Lord Maltby. Mrs. Barron learned those details entirely from him."

Mansfield took the paper and read it while Turner cast a stern eye toward a stunned Isobel, her face ashen above her starched white collar. Mansfield glanced at Isobel, his face grave, his voice somber. "This fiction about Jack Finn appears to be the work of your father, Lady Whittingham. Mrs. Barron swears to this."

"I—I—must have been mistaken, but I was certain father told me he heard this account from Mrs. Barron and, and, well, perhaps she has mixed it up, has forgotten how it truly happened." Her voice tightened. She raised her head in defiance. "Or perhaps Mrs. Barron has chosen to forget. Why isn't she here? Afraid to risk perjury, perhaps."

Turner's voice rang loud in the courtroom. "Madame, the charge of perjury would still apply if she lied in her written affidavit. Mrs. Barron would have appeared willingly, but she has been laid abed with pneumonia." Turner produced another document. "According to this sworn statement from her doctor."

Isobel compressed her lips and regained her composure. "No matter what Mrs. Barron says, we were betrayed. Misella's cruel lies and her attempt to extort money from my father, Lord Maltby, forced us to flee to Ireland."

Turner snorted and retrieved the paper from Mansfield's hand.

Manfield's expression darkened. "Anything else you want to spring on us, Turner?" he muttered so only he could hear. Mansfield glanced toward the gallery and raised his voice. "Any further questions for Lady Whittingham, Sir?"

Turner took his time, folding the paper before answering, "Not at this time, Sir. Later, later." He returned to his chair amid murmurs of surprise from the gallery that he had rattled Lady Whittingham.

Mansfield held up his hand. He waited a moment before he resumed questioning. "Lady Whittingham, can you tell us how and why you came to petition for the adoption of the deceased child, Lily?"

Isobel stood at attention, her head held high. She gazed for a moment at the prisoner's box. The expression of deep sadness on her face did not appear genuine to those few in the gallery who had begun to doubt her. "My husband, Lord Whittingham, told me that Miss Cross gave birth to a daughter and insisted upon housing the innocent babe in her rooms at the...brothel, her residence and place of employment."

She shook her head in disbelief. "When I told Father that the baby lived in a brothel, he wanted to rescue the child.'"

Turner jumped up, his chair sliding against the railing of the witness gallery. "Did he intend to rescue Misella Cross, the poor mother, as well?" he thundered.

Isobel looked startled. Mansfield remained silent, letting Isobel answer the question on her own. "No, of course not." Her voice vibrated with indignation. "The child's mother was beyond saving. She had made her whore's bed. The child deserved a better life, and I yearned to give that to Lily."

Isobel's voice softened. She placed her hand over her bosom. "I am unable to conceive because of a severe childhood illness. I wanted to raise Lily as my very own. To help her, to love her." In the stillness that ensued, she asked Misella, who shook her head back and forth, "Do you not believe that I would have loved your child as my own?"

"No," Misella cried, her voice cracking. "No."

Turner cut in. "Madam, why did you hire a dangerous scoundrel to snatch the frightened child from her mother's arms? Why did you not hire legal counsel to pursue an adoption in a court of law?"

Mansfield whipped around and faced Turner, his expression dark. "Mr. Turner hopes to turn these proceedings into a bawdy, clamorous street brawl with lies and foundationless accusations. Please, your Honor," he asked the Lord Mayor, "can we allow Lady Whittingham the courtesy of telling her story without such theatrical interruptions? Mr. Turner shall have all the time he wishes after I finish."

The gallery tittered. The Lord Mayor spoke firmly. "Yes. Sit down, Mr. Turner. No more questions. Let the honorable Mr. Mansfield finish with this witness."

Laughing louder than most, Lord Whittingham hunched forward in the first row of the witness gallery and slapped his gloves again against his hand with a resounding whack.

The Lord Mayor frowned. "Please go on, Sir Mansfield."

Turner eased into his chair and emitted a long sigh that rippled through the courtroom.

Mansfield stepped closer to the witness box and spoke gently to Isobel. "Lady Whittingham, can you tell us what actually happened after you decided to rescue the babe from life in the brothel?"

Appearing distressed, Isobel batted her tear-dampened eyelashes at the members of the jury, but she spoke calmly. "I wrote a letter to Miss Cross, a friendly letter, in which I made a great effort not to criticize or offend her. I explained that I would be most happy to take the child and relieve Miss Cross of the burden of trying to care for her sweet baby in her present circumstances. I offered Lily a much better life, a chance to be raised in a loving home where all of her needs would be met."

Mansfield asked, "And how did she respond to your letter?"

"I have her response here." Isobel drew a wrinkled sheet of folded parchment from the pocket of her gown.

"Will you read it for us?" Mansfield urged.

Isobel hesitated and looked at Misella who stared at Turner. "The note did not have a greeting," Isobel asserted. "Just these words. 'You will never'——the word is underlined three times——'take Lily from me.'" Isobel waited for the murmuring in the courtroom to subside.

"Is that all?" Mansfield prodded.

Isobel lowered her voice, and members in the gallery strained forward to hear her. "'It is signed 'Misella' and underscored with a dagger."

A gasp erupted from the gallery. Mansfield extracted the letter from Isobel's trembling hand. "We will submit this letter to the jury for their perusal." He studied the letter as he walked toward them. "I believe it is a dagger," he murmured as he handed the paper to Juror Angus MacFarland.

Returning to the witness box he said in a loud voice, "Did you feel threatened by this, Lady Whittingham?"

A few tears brushed her lashes. "Yes," she choked out, "I did. And I was heartbroken. The next day father suffered his fatal stroke. In my grief I almost gave up the thought of doing anything more for that poor baby, but I just couldn't desert her. More than ever, I wanted to do the right thing for the child. A week after Father died, I asked Lord Whittingham to begin legal proceedings to rescue the child." Isobel raised her voice and wailed, "But she was dead, too."

Mansfield coddled Isobel as if she were a child. "My dear Lady Whittingham, we are sorry for your pain and loss. Can you continue?"

Isobel wiped her eyes. "Yes, yes Sir. I would like this trial to be over."

Mansfield reached up and stilled her hands twisting the handkerchief, then faced Turner who sat hunched in his chair. "I have no further questions for Lady Whittingham."

Ben Turner sprang up, papers in hand, taking the room by surprise with his energetic step as he bounded toward the witness box, his cane and his limp forgotten. "Lady Whittingham," he began, his voice as soft and soothing as Mansfield's, "I beg your pardon for subjecting you to more painful and distressing questioning." Isobel remained motionless, her hands folded together.

"When and from whom, Madam, did you learn of the child's death?" Turner asked.

Isobel gaped at him, obviously surprised by his soft tone and concerned expression. Her eyes roamed the courtroom as if she were assessing the mood of the jury and the gallery. Turner rustled the papers in his hands. With a careful smile at him, she began in a monotone to tell the story. "I had just returned from visiting father's gravesite at Hawthorn Manor, and to oversee the placing of his carved stone and statue. Lord Whittingham found me in the drawing room and told me what had happened."

Isobel caught her breath. "My husband was in the area on business and heard a commotion, saw a huge crowd. Normally, he'd have paid no attention. There is always some kind of disturbance in Gray's Lane, but he recognized Lord Russell's coach which seemed to be at the center of things, so he pushed his way through the crowd."

Turner cocked his head. "So Lord Whittingham was there at the time of the accident?"

Isobel eyed him coldly. "Immediately *after* the destruction of the child."

"So he saw Misella Cross being harassed by the crowd. Did he come forward to say that he knew her?"

Isobel shook her head, her voice raised. "He saw the commotion. He—he—saw the little wrapped body being whisked up in the arms of the constable's man. He heard the crowd yelling 'murderous whore'. And the runner from the Russell carriage shouting, 'I saw her do it. Flung the babe right into the street.'"

She paused, as if expecting Turner to interrupt, but he didn't. "The constable cleared the crowd so Lord Russell's coach could be on its way. And before Lord Whittingham could step forward, the constable hustled Misella and a couple of gentlemen away."

Turner bowed his head and quietly asked, "Madame, did you know about your husband's relationship with Misella Cross before you married him?"

Isobel's face reddened, but she did not hesitate. "Yes. And I also know that it ended as soon as we married. Lord Whittingham succumbed to her wicked charms at first, but he soon realized that she had used him to exact revenge on me. She urged him to pursue me. But her little plan backfired when Lord Whittingham fell in love with me and came to realize that what he needed, what he wanted, was a decent Christian woman capable of loving him wholeheartedly and unconditionally."

She peeked over at Lord Whittingham and smiled, her face softening with seeming devotion. He half stood and gave her a crooked bow.

Turner edged closer to the witness box. His sharp voice drew attention back to him. "Why should Misella Cross want to take revenge against you?"

Isobel flushed again and raised her voice to match his. "She resented me because I was high born while she was a lowly fish monger's child. No matter how hard she tried, she could not replace me in my father's or my mother's affections. She was never satisfied. She wanted all of my father's attention. She yearned for a life of privilege, but when, with his generosity, my father gave her that life, she wanted more."

Isobel choked a bit as her voice rose higher and visible beads of moisture collected across her brow. "She not only wanted to replace me; she wanted to take my mother's place as well. She would dress in fancy gowns and jewels my father gave her and force him to take her with him on social and even campaign business when my mother's poor health prevented her from going."

Mansfield appeared alarmed and seemed ready to caution her, to calm her. He stood, but Turner pushed forward. "Did he never ask you to accompany him on these ventures?"

Isobel's face darkened, her mouth twisting as she blurted out, "I could not give him what she offered——the glowing promises of a budding courtesan. She blinded his judgment with her coquetry, and he couldn't see what was happening until it was too late."

"Too late for what?" Turner injected quietly. "Until he had gotten her with child and moved her, unbeknownst to your mother at the time, to Mrs. Barron's boarding house in London? But you knew what was going on. You knew he had made Misella his little courtesan, as you called her, didn't you?"

"No!" Isobel bellowed, her collar limp and crushed with moisture.

Turner whisked another paper from the pile in his hand and held it up so that Isobel could see it. "Do you recognize this letter, Lady Whittingham?"

Isobel gasped, her eyes darting back and forth between Mansfield and her husband. Forcing herself to control her voice, she said, "No, I do not. What nonsense has she given you now?"

Turner shook out the parchment sheet. "Isn't this your father's handwriting, and the Maltby seal broken along the edges of the paper?"

When Isobel shook her head, Turner attacked. "Do not perjure yourself further, Madame. I have confiscated several documents from Lady Marian Bentley's establishment written in his hand. You can hardly deny his ownership of this one to her asking for help in sequestering his 'mistress,' he calls Misella Cross, in secret lodgings in London because, he writes, 'Our liaison has had the usual consequences.' The letter bears his signature. Isn't that so?" Turner's voice was stern, his demeanor no longer sympathetic.

Isobel scanned the letter, the color fading from her face. She seemed, like her father, struck dumb. But when Turner pressed her to respond, she was ready. "I guess," she quivered, "my father did lie about this illicit relationship because the pain of what he had done and his guilt made it too difficult for him to tell us the ugly truth." She raised her head and stared at the jury, her voice gaining strength. "He wanted to protect my mother and me. I am glad Mother did not know about the child before she died. And I am proud of him for keeping the sordid truth from her."

Tears visible on her face, her voice plaintive in the silence of the court-room, she murmured, "And I am ineffably saddened to learn that, if this is true, I have lost not just the child I wanted to adopt, but my own infant sister."

Turner pounced, his face livid. "You knew all along that baby was your sister and that's why you wanted her.'

"No," Isobel screamed. "I did not know."

"You are glad the child is gone, aren't you? Lily was scandalous evidence of your father's betrayal. You wanted to be rid of her."

"No, No," she shouted. "I did nothing wrong." Isobel pointed towards Misella. "She's the one who destroyed our family. My father. My life. Lily's."

Turner waited for Isobel to regain her composure. "You were not surprised by your father's behavior with Miss Cross, were you, Lady Whittingham?" Before Isobel could respond, he plunged on. "You had been through this upheaval earlier. Your father brought another young woman into your home a few years before Misella. A beautiful little Irish lass by the name of Annie Doyle, the motherless daughter of his land stew-ard, whom he sent off to America with a tidy sum of money and a promise to take care of his child."

Isobel reeled back. "Annie has nothing to do with this case. My father helped many people. Her father wanted to leave and didn't want his daughter tagging along with him to America, so my father agreed to help him by taking her in. But Annie became homesick for her own people and returned to Ireland against his wishes."

Turner shot back, "But not against yours or your mother's. You two, in fact, sent her away, didn't you?"

"Yes, we did," Isobel shouted. "She was a back country bog-trotter, a conniving little red-haired trollop. Father couldn't see it, but we did."

"And what happened to her?" Turner asked. "Do you know?"

Isobel snorted. "No, and I don't care to know."

Turner quickly posed another set of questions . "You and your mother were also unhappy about Misella's arrival, weren't you? Why didn't you send her away, too? You allowed her to stay for six years."

Isobel looked uncomfortable. She glanced at Misella who had remained motionless throughout the testimony. "Misella's mother was father's cousin, and we were obligated, he said, to help the family."

Turner nodded, as if satisfied with her responses. "Well, thank you, Madame, for your, ahh, honest testimony. I know it has not been easy for you." He informed the judge, "I have no further questions for this witness."

As Isobel left the witness box, Turner stopped her. "You will find out," he said, his voice ringing through the courtroom, "what happened to Annie Doyle when she appears shortly as a witness."

Isobel recoiled, reeling backwards and bumping her head against the front of the witness box. When Turner tried to steady her, she slapped his hand away and straightened up. She righted her bonnet which had slipped to one side of her head, gave Turner a blistering glance, and stomped back to the witness bench.

For the first time in the courtroom, Misella broke into a smile.

CHAPTER 9

Mansfield arose, looking agitated. He consulted with two of his attorneys before announcing to the courtroom, "We call Robby Blackford to the witness stand."

A youngster of fourteen or so strutted out of the witness section behind the Whittinghams and swaggered towards the witness box. He wore the livery of the Russell household: pressed cambric britches; a snowy lawn shirt, the ruffled cravat encasing his thin neck; a brushed green velvet vest set off with polished bronze buttons, and Lord Russell's insignia glittering in gold stitching along the upper left side of the vest. He sprinted up the stairs, eager to take the stage. His angelic face shone beneath a crown of curly brown hair.

Lord Mansfield waited until the boy was sworn in before he made his way toward the witness. He smiled at him. "Young man, you are the regular runner for Lord Russell, is that correct?"

"Yes, Sir. His only London runner. For two years, Sir. And Lord Russell says I am the best one he's ever employed." The boy gazed around the courtroom as if expecting applause.

"So you accompanied Lord Russell's carriage on the day that the child Lily Cross fell to her death?"

The boy nodded vigorously. "I seen it all, Sir. The whole thing. I was making a path for Lord Russell through Gray's Lane which was very busy that day. I had a hard time pushing through the crowd, and I about lost my voice from screaming at them to make way for the carriage. Had to take a few doses of that cough stuff that night cuz my throat burned."

Mansfield urged him along. "Tell us what you were doing at the time of the accident."

The boy snorted. "Twern't no accident, Sir. I had cleared just enough room for the carriage to move forward. I was yelling at the crowd to stay back when I saw her."

Mansfield interrupted. "Saw whom, young man?"

Robbie Blackford pointed across the wide aisle to the prisoner's box. "Her! She was crouched down out of sight on the side of the road behind a milk wagon holding that baby out in front of her like a big rag doll. The carriage lurched forward gathering speed, and the crowd closed up again. I seen her like this." He stretched himself half way over the railing with his hands out in front of him. "She waited for the horses to thunder past," he grunted, tousled curls falling into his eyes, "and as soon as they did, she just threw her baby onto the stones right in front of the left wheel." He flung his hands forward to create the effect. He seemed pleased with the gasps and the murmurs coming from the gallery as he straightened up, brushing his hair back from his face.

Mansfield signaled for order and proceeded. "Tell us what happened next."

"A lot of screaming, and some men grabbed her and dragged her up off of the ground. And they were shouting, 'Murderer' and 'Whore' and some people were yelling, 'Hold on to her.' 'Get the constable.' And the crowd just got so thick, I couldn't see much else except Lord Russell standing outside the coach."

"What did you do while waiting for the constable to arrive?"

"Well, Sir, I talked with some of the people in front of me, telling 'em what I'd seen, and when the constable came about ten minutes later, he asked if anyone saw exactly what happened. I pushed my way through to him and told him that I'd seen it all, and so he told me to follow him back for the hearing. And Lord Russell, he told me I should go and do my duty, and not worry about him, he'd get home without my help, and the constable told his men to clear the way for Lord Russell so he could leave."

"Thank you, young man." Mansfield gestured to Turner who arose and came forward, using his cane this time and clutching a wrinkled sheaf of papers in his free hand. Mansfield backed grudgingly out of his way.

"Master Blackford," Turner thundered, pointing to the prisoner with the end of his cane. "How many milk cans did Miss Cross upset as she bumped her way behind the cart?"

The boy seemed puzzled. "Milk cans? I-I didn't see any cans upset." He glanced toward the Whittinghams and shrugged his shoulders.

Turner pounced. "Surely, if you saw the milk cart so clearly as she crouched waiting for the right moment, as you suggest, to toss the babe into the flames, so to speak, you must have noticed the milk puddle around her and that her hands and gown, indeed, the child's garment too, were dripping wet, did you not?"

"I don't know." He stared at his hands clenched together now on the railing. "I guess I just looked at what she was doing, not so much at what they were wearing," he mumbled.

"I guess that must be the case," Turner said. "I'd have thought, though, that being the talented runner you are, you might have noticed that a rather large milk can had clanked into the path you cleared." Turner hesitated for a moment looking puzzled himself. "A large can that threatened to trip Lord Russell's oncoming horses," he barked. "You say you didn't even notice it. Yet I have signed statements here," he held up a few of the papers, "from onlookers further back than you were, who swear they saw the can bounce into the street and feared for the safety of the carriage before the accident with the child happened.

The boy scowled and refused to answer. He just shook his head and shrugged his shoulders again, muttering something to himself.

Turner pressed on. "Whom exactly did you talk to?"

The boy looked trapped. His eyes darted to the witness bench and back to Turner. "I don't know. Just some other people standing around. Some shop owners. I didn't pay much attention." He added suddenly, "I was in shock after seeing what happened."

"Was one of those people Lord Whittingham?"

A hush fell over the room, the only sound the faint crackling of herbs twisting over the hot coals. The boy cleared his throat a few times and stammered, "I'm not sure. I never met Lord Whittingham." He paused. "Not 'til today that is."

Turner stepped back as if surprised. "Lord Whittingham is a close friend of Lord Russell. They are often seen in one another's company as many here can attest." Turner waved a hand around the room. "Certainly, the two have ridden together in Lord Russell's carriages on many occasions. And yet, you say you don't know him? Remarkable." Turner glowered at the boy, his voice rising. "You do know that you are sworn to tell the truth, young man, and that you are liable for a charge of perjury if you deny under oath the obvious fact that you knew very well that you had spoken with Lord Whittingham." Turner thumped his cane on the floor, the sound ringing through the silent courtroom. "Several people have verified that fact."

The boy seemed close to tears. He rubbed his eyes, his voice shaking as he spoke. "Yes." His voice came out so low that Turner asked him to repeat his answer. "Yes, I spoke with Lord Whittingham that day. I told him what I saw, and he urged me to go forward and tell the constable the whole story. He said he would make sure that Lord Russell rewarded me for doing my civic duty."

Turner spoke quietly, but his voice traveled throughout the room. "Did Lord Whittingham tell you what to say to the constable?"

"N-no. He asked me questions and helped me to remember all of the details. And told me just to tell what I saw."

"No further questions at this time." Turner walked back to his table, pulled out his chair, and lowered himself slowly into it.

Mansfield arose and questioned the boy. "Did Lord Whittingham add any details to your story that day or prepare you in any way for today's trial?"

Robbie Blackford looked at Whittingham and back at Mansfield. In a firm voice, he asserted, "No, Sir, he did not."

"You may step down, young man. Thank you. The crown calls no further witnesses at this time." He gestured to Turner. "Your witnesses, Sir."

Turner rose up again, his knee cracking in pain. "The defense calls Lord Whittingham."

Whittingham flinched, raising his unruly eyebrows as if surprised by the summons, and murmured something to his wife. She frowned and cast a worried glance at Mansfield who, nodding to her, retained his calm demeanor.

Twisting himself off the bench, Whittingham adjusted the folds of his velvet cape, fluffed the lace ruffles at his neckline, and dropped his gloves into his wife's lap. He snatched his gold-headed cane from her hand as she held it out to him and rapped it on the floor a few times before tapping his way to the witness box. Disregarding Turner, he bowed to the judge, to the gallery, and, with a smirk on his thin lips, to Misella who eyed him with revulsion, color inflaming her face. He sauntered up the steps, the cane held aloft like a torch, the gold knob reflecting the light.

Turner signaled the bailiff to administer the oath and waited for a long minute afterwards, his eyes scanning the sheaf of papers gripped in his hand before he questioned the witness. "Lord Whittingham, what is your relationship to the accused?"

Whittingham sniggered. "I don't have one. I haven't had a relationship with her since the consummation of my marriage to Lady Isobel Maltby Whittingham." He shrugged his narrow shoulders. "I have no need for any other woman." He bowed toward Lady Whittingham and saluted her.

Misella grimaced, shaking her head back and forth in disbelief. Lady Isobel raised her husband's gloves in her hand, shaking them as if in victory, and blew him a kiss. The audience in the gallery tittered.

Turner ignored the display. "You no longer needed Misella Cross because you had gotten what you wanted from her—not illicit coitus but information about the Maltbys. That's the only reason you paid Lady Marian Bentley for exclusive rights to Misella Cross. So that with her help, you could seduce Lady Isobel into marrying you." He pounded his fist against the box. "Isn't that true?"

Mansfield jumped up, but before he could raise an objection, Whittingham motioned him to sit down. "I retained exclusive access to the prostitute because I was captivated by her beauty and her erotic skills. I did discover," he said, his lips curling into a sneer, "that Miss Cross had plotted indeed against the Maltbys, but not with me. I admit that her constant rants about them did raise my curiosity and induced me to find out if they were the monsters she made them out to be. Of course, I found the opposite true, and I fell in love with Isobel Maltby."

"Liar. Fraud," Misella uttered under her breath.

Turner snorted with contempt at Whittingham's deceit. He surveyed the gallery, as if inviting the wealthy onlookers to share his disgust. Many of them, he presumed, knew about Whittingham's sordid pursuit of young boys.

His voice hardened with scorn. "When did you inform Lady Isobel that her baby stepsister Lily lived at Swan Court with Misella Cross?"

"My answer in a moment. Poisonous fumes here, you know." Whittingham flicked his cape aside and reached inside the slit on the right side of his embroidered vest. He withdrew a small jeweled case. Clicking it open, he extracted a pinch of powdered tobacco, snorting some into each wide nostril. With exaggerated slowness he placed the case back inside his vest, withdrew a white linen handkerchief from his pocket and patted his nose.

His face livid, Turner snarled, "Answer the question, Sir."

Fluttering the handkerchief from side to side, Whittingham replied, "I confessed to Lady Isobel before our marriage that I had sinned with the prostitute Misella, but would never stray again. She forgave me." With an exaggerated sniff, he tucked the handkerchief into his pocket and straightened the ruffles spilling out of his vest. "My wife was shocked when I told her the prostitute had a baby that she shamelessly housed in her quarters. Neither Lady Isobel nor I, however, remotely suspected that the child might belong to Sir Richard. We thought Jack Finn was the father. We still do." He gestured to his wife who forcefully nodded her head.

Misella pressed her fist hard against her lips, blocking the shriek of anger and the torrent of oaths that threatened to escape from her throat and jolt the courtroom. She wanted to scream the truth about Whittingham and the Maltbys, how they destroyed her, ripped her heart in two, connived to end her very life. But Turner had warned her not to give in to her emotions. She must let him do the fighting for her.

"Well, you are wrong, Sir." Turner pressed closer to the witness box, his looming bulk a stark contrast to the slight physique of the witness. "Why were you in Gray's Lane at the time of the baby's death?"

Looking annoyed, Whittingham sighed. "As my wife has already testified, I was there on business."

"You, Sir, are widely known as a night owl. Several of your acquaintances have verified that you never go out in the daytime, that you always send your servants to do your business. What business drew you to this location at three o'clock in the afternoon?"

"I had papers to deliver to my lawyer," Whittingham snapped.

Turner attacked, his voice raised almost to a shout. "You were there to oversee the kidnapping of Lily Cross, to deliver her into the arms of your scheming wife waiting anxiously at home. Weren't you?"

Mansfield sprang up, his face scarlet. "This is preposterous. Your Honor, we will not abide such blatant, unsubstantiated lies."

Before the irate barrister could say more, Whittingham addressed the Judge. "Your Honor, I will answer this baseless, ridiculous accusation with the truth." With a scathing glance at Turner, Whittingham focused his attention on the Judge and spoke in a clear, steady voice. "While it is true that I rarely go out in daytime and my servants usually take care of my business, this correspondence was supremely important—the legal papers Lady Isobel and I had completed in hopes of adopting the baby, Lily Cross. That I was nearby when her life ended was a cruel, heartbreaking coincidence." With his hand over his heart, he twisted toward his wife who dabbed at her eyes with her crumpled handkerchief.

Turner expelled a long, loud breath of disgust. "Yes, how convenient that you were there, Sir, at that very moment and managed to talk at length with young Robby Blackford immediately afterwards. Coincidence, indeed. You may step down. I have no further use of you."

As Whittingham strutted down the stairs, his cane tucked under his arm, Turner made a point of stepping back a few feet as if to avoid contamination. In a booming voice he called his next witness, intending to deflect attention away from the swaggering Whittingham. "The defense calls Annie Doyle."

CHAPTER 10

Several people pushed closer to the gallery railing overlooking the courtroom, their necks craned to see the witness bench A slim figure arose unnoticed from the back of the gallery. Turner pointed toward her and asked the bailiff to assist her down the gallery's back stairway and into the courtroom.

As they waited for Annie's entrance onto the courtroom floor, Turner observed Isobel Whittingham. She clasped both hands together and stared straight ahead, the black slashes of her eyebrows and the red streak of her lips a stark contrast to her pasty-looking skin.

The door from the gallery stairway opened and a wisp of a figure floated through. She appeared to be no bigger than a child of ten or so. She wore a modest muslin dress of light gray with long tight sleeves encasing her stick-like arms and a yellowed linen collar that matched the tint of her skin. As she advanced further into the room, her lined face and faded red hair revealed that she was far older than a child, more likely in her twenties.

Turner took her hand and led her to the witness box. She seemed bewildered and unhappy to be the sudden center of attention. He said something to her as he helped her climb the stairs. Her eyes darted once around the room before she lowered her head and gazed at Turner. He explained to her about taking the oath. She cooperated with the bailiff as he swore her in.

Turner began, his voice soft. "Will you tell us your name please, Miss, and tell us how you came to be a witness here today?"

"My name is Ann Margaret Doyle," she stated in a voice surprisingly firm and clear. "Jack Finn found me in Dublin and arranged for me to come here and meet with you in your office."

Turner quietly told her, "You're doing just fine, Miss." In a louder voice he asked, "Why did Jack Finn ask you to meet with me?"

Annie glanced toward the prisoner's box and back at Turner. "He told me that a young woman named Misella Cross was in trouble, just like I was once, and needed our help. He said he would testify, if he could, but he would not be allowed to and would be thrown in an English prison."

"Why?"

"Because a warrant had been issued against him. For robbery and escaping from Newgate."

"Could you tell us how you came to know Jack Finn and the Maltby family?"

Annie looked down, agitated, her hands rubbing back and forth along her arms. She seemed reluctant to answer. Turner waited, giving her time to collect herself.

"I was taken to live with them, the Maltbys, at the age of fourteen. The following year Jack Finn became Sir Richard's coach driver. My mother was dead, and my father wanted to go to America to try his luck, he said, at being a merchant. We lived, he worked, on Sir Richard's Ireland estate. Sir Richard offered to take me in, and he brought me to their home in England." Annie's voice became louder, the words coming faster as if she were afraid she would not be able to finish.

"I was supposed to be a sister, a companion to Isobel, his daughter, but that did not happen. Isobel didn't like me and neither did Lady Sarah. I tried to do everything they told me. Sir Richard was so kind to me, better than a father. He didn't take the drink and did not beat me or pull my hair or kick me as my own father did. And I was so thankful. He talked to me as if I were an adult and taught me many things. He took me through the maze to the secret hermitage. Behind his mansion."

Her voice dropped and wavered. "At first, he made it a game. He'd send me ahead into the maze, but I would get trapped and could never find the center. He would laugh and call to me, 'Where are you little wood sprite? Do I have to rescue you again?' I would run from one row to another each leading to a dead end until I would scream in frustration

234

and panic. At that point, he would find me and take me in his arms and comfort me. After a time, he said I was ready to see the hermitage, and he led me there."

Annie's voice caught in a sob. "And that's when it happened. I thought he loved me. He said he did. And he said it was no sin to show our love and to share my love with him. And I did."

Misella's stoic resolve to remain calm disappeared. Her eyes squeezed shut; her face crumpled with the effort to control her emotions. Tears coursed down her cheeks.

Turner asked gently, "What happened next?"

"Lady Maltby and Isobel attacked me one night when Sir Richard was gone. They called me a little slut and told me to pack my bag, that I was leaving. They made Jack Finn drive me to London. They gave him some money and told him to arrange passage for me to the colonies to find my father. But he didn't do it. He arranged for me to go back to Ireland to stay with some of his relatives in Galway."

Annie took a deep breath and sighed before she went on with her story. "When I got to Dublin, a lovely lady I had met on the boat told me she would arrange a carriage for me to Galway in a few days, and that I could stay with her at her lodging while I waited. But she was a devil, not a lady. She took all of my money and made me work for her. And she made me change my name to Pruitt, I guess so no one would find me."

"What kind of work, Annie?" Turner asked.

With tears in her eyes, she said, "As a prostitute—for the men who visited her lodging house." Her cheeks flamed, and her voice rose. "At first, I refused. She shackled me in a dark room. Beat me daily and refused to feed me until I agreed to cooperate. I finally did. She cleaned me up, dressed me in a lace shift, and sent an elderly, dour-faced gentleman to my room. When he saw my face pale with hunger, and my eyes swelling with tears, he spurned me with contempt and told me to cant and whine to somebody else.

"The next man she sent to me violated me cruelly, despite my cries and my pleas." She hesitated for a moment. "Like the first time with Sir Richard," she murmured.

"I was forced to entertain many others after that. In a few years, she expelled me from her house, as Isobel and Lady Sarah did. She replaced me with a younger, healthier-looking girl." Annie stopped to catch her breath, her thin chest heaving.

"Can you continue?" Turner asked in a subdued tone.

She nodded. "For three years I walked the streets at night, the common prey of lewdness, begging to be relieved from hunger by wickedness. I'd retire from my nightly excursions with other wretches like me in whatever dismal receptacle we could find—lying crowded together, ghastly with hunger. Nauseous with filth. Foul with disease."

A sob broke the uneasy silence of the courtroom. Misella clamped her hand over her mouth to contain her emotions and blotted her eyes with her handkerchief. Ben Turner glanced at her, his eyes dark with anguish.

"I should have listened to Jack Finn," Annie gulped. "He told me not to trust anyone I met until I arrived in Galway."

Turner managed to refocus his attention. "How did Jack Finn find you, Annie?"

"I don't know. He just said he searched and he found me and arranged for me to come here to you. And after I leave here, I will go to Galway to live on a farm."

"You have been very brave today, Annie. Thank you for coming here and telling us your story. You may step down now." Grasping her hand, he helped her down the steps and signaled for the bailiff. "Assist Miss Doyle from the courtroom," he told him.

Though he had remained silent during Annie's testimony, Mansfield, his face crimson, erupted from his chair and addressed the Judge. "I apologize, Your Honor, that you and the Jury have been subjected to such lurid and blatant lies from an admitted prostitute who has little to do with the case before us. It is an unprecedented outrage to bring such rubbish into your courtroom. Mr. Turner should be sanctioned and barred from practicing law."

Turner whirled around to face the Judge, the edge of his robe slapping against his cane. "Mr. Mansfield," he roared, "may remain insensitive and unsympathetic to the ugly consequences of prostitution, but our justice system can not. The courts are content to keep prostitution itself out of the courtroom, but quick to severely punish prostitutes for pilfering a watch or a handkerchief or a few extra coins from their customers to keep themselves from starvation. Yet we pass no laws to address the problems or alleviate the causes of prostitution."

The Judge arose in a flurry of movement, pounding his gavel several times on the railing in front of him. "Mr. Turner," he bawled, "we are here to pass judgement on a case of murder. Stop proselytizing in my courtroom and present your witnesses."

Turner breathed deeply in an effort to control himself. In a quieter voice he answered, "Yes, Your Honor. Give me one moment, please." He shuffled to his table without using his cane, placed the cane on his chair and picked up a sheaf of papers. He approached the prisoner's box. "We call for the testimony of Misella Cross."

CHAPTER 11

Misella dried her eyes, but she could not still the wild pounding of her heart or the wheels of her imagination which carried her back during Annie's testimony to the twisted paths of the maze, the horror of debtors' prison and Swan Court, the familiar feeling that she was about to be devoured. When she heard Ben Turner call out her name, she realized he was standing in front of her and her own testimony must begin.

Turner stood without his cane, both feet spread wide, his hands grasped behind his back, to steady himself and restrict the convulsive twitching that plagued him whenever he became nervous. He did not want to distract his audience or Misella. He needed her to concentrate on his words, on the script they had rehearsed. His billowing black gown hid the trembling in his legs. It was unthinkable to him that she could lose her life if he failed.

He gazed into her troubled eyes with a hard intensity he hoped would bolster her spirits. He intended to bring forth with his questioning the passionate anger he knew simmered beneath her cool repose, the anger that lit up her eyes and infused her voice when he had asked questions about her story. They had not practiced the anger. It must be genuine. She must counter in the minds of the jury the sympathy for Isobel and Sir Richard, the acquiescence that most in the room, unthinking, paid to their class. He wanted to catch Misella off guard and play upon that anger.

"Miss Cross," he began, his voice tender, his tone quiet, "why did you lie to the Ordinary when he asked for your confession?" He raised his voice. "You led him to believe, didn't you, that he would have it when you finished?"

She flinched as visibly as if he had struck her across the shoulders with his cane. A flush spread into her cheeks, and she raised her hand to her mouth. At first her voice was faint, edged with restraint. "I—I needed time to remember all of the details, to put it all down as truthfully as I could." She studied her hands, refusing to meet his gaze. "I guess," she almost whispered, then remembered to speak louder. "I thought that as long as my story stayed in my own hands, I could control my life a little longer."

Turner pressed on. "Did you not intend, though, to give it to him when you finished?"

She hesitated, shaking her head, the color rising hotter in her cheeks. "No, I did not." She raised her eyes, seeking the place where the Ordinary sat. "Though he hounded me for it day and night." She held her head higher, a noble gesture, Turner thought, and spoke with a fierceness in her voice that even surprised him. "I did not trust him. I could not."

His hands now braced against the prisoner's box as if to hold her up, Turner cut into the silence that surrounded the courtroom. "Can you explain why you did not trust him?"

She stared at Turner with pain in her eyes, but she spoke with a strong and steady voice. "I had learned to beware of smooth-talking impostors who interpret God's message to suit their own needs. My downfall began with such a person, but I did not want my life to end with one as well."

"Who began your downfall, Miss Cross?"

Her hands grabbing hold of the spikes in front of her, she glanced at Isobel. "Sir Richard Maltby," she uttered.

Amid the murmurs from the gallery, a snort erupted from Isobel who half rose from the bench, seeming ready to spring forward and leap the railing. Her hat slipped backwards to reveal the gray-laced part of her hair. Lord Whittingham grabbed her arm yanking her back into her seat and muttering something to her.

Turner waited for the restlessness in the courtroom to settle down before he resumed his questioning. "How did this downfall come about at the hands of Sir Richard?"

Misella sighed and raised the fingers of one hand to her forehead as if to shield her eyes from Isobel. "I was a vain, foolish little girl when I entered the Maltby household, and Sir Richard was kind to me. I knew that Isobel and Lady Maltby did not want me there, but at the time I was too young to understand why. Now, of course, I do. When they rejected me, I sought attention and love from Sir Richard. I—I wanted to replace Isobel in his affections, and I did. Did I cause what happened to me later? I cannot claim total innocence. But I entered a world so new and seductive, so different from what I knew. Like Annie Doyle, I was naïve, and I was mesmerized by his charm, and yes, his power and wealth."

Mansfield jumped to his feet and objected. "Miss Cross cannot project her own feelings or failings onto anyone else. She cannot presume to know what anyone else felt."

Turner cautioned Misella to speak only of her own thoughts and feelings.

She agreed. "I admit that I relished Sir Richard's attention, the time I spent with him and the gifts he gave me. I did not realize how much I would have to give back in return." Her face flushed, and she struggled with the words as she went on. "He forced himself on me," she whispered.

"Can the prisoner speak up," Angus MacFarland demanded from the jury box. "We are unable to hear all of her testimony."

Prohibited by law, as the defense attorney, from directly addressing the jury, Turner faced the Judge. "She will speak louder, Your Honor.

Misella spoke louder. "Sir Richard Maltby overpowered me and raped me."

Mansfield stood again, directing his comments to the judge. "Your Honor, I ask what all of this confessing of her weaknesses has to do with the charge of infanticide. She is on trial for that, not for what she did or did not do with Sir Richard Maltby."

Turner ignored Mansfield. "Your Honor, this has a great deal to do with Miss Cross' motivation, and the circumstances leading up to the death of her child. I ask that we be allowed to continue, and counsel can raise his questions about relevance after he has heard her testimony."

The judge arranged his robe and patted his headdress in place before he spoke. "Yes, I agree that we need to hear all of the defendant's testimony."

Turner moved closer to the prisoner box, his eyes drilling into Misella's, willing her to gather strength from him. "Can you tell us, Miss Cross, where and how the attack on you occurred?"

Her face inflamed, she said, "It may shock the court."

Turner again addressed the Judge. "Miss Cross is concerned that the details she is about to reveal may offend you. In fairness, you must hear it all just as she experienced it."

The Judge spoke up. "You must be frank and truthful, Miss Cross." Mansfield grimaced and raised his eyebrows to his group of attorneys.

Taking a ragged breath, Misella raised her voice and began. "It happened in the hermitage at the center of Hawthorn Manor's maze. From the time I first arrived at the Manor, Sir Richard challenged me to find the hermitage. Only he and Joseph, the gardener, knew the way, he told me."

Isobel snorted again, loud enough to create a flurry of exited whispers from the gallery. "Another lie," she scoffed. "I visited the hermitage many times,"

Turner held up his hand, signaling Misella to wait while the excitement died down, then asked, "Why did you want to find the hermitage?

"I-I didn't at first. Not for years. I didn't like the maze. It frightened me. I feared I would lose myself inside it." She hesitated for a moment. "And I did."

"How did you lose yourself?" Turner asked gently.

Tears sprang to her eyes, but she blinked them back. "I-I lost myself before that when I gave in to his—to Sir Richard's—flattery and attention, the loneliness and isolation and humiliation I endured when he traveled away from home. All of that made me want to please him even more, to seek his admiration and his love. And, yes, the diamond and emerald necklace he offered as the prize if I could "master the maze," as he put it.

"Did you also want to show Isobel you could do what she could not?"

Mansfield jumped up. "Stop leading the prisoner, Sir. If we must listen to all of this balderdash, allow her to tell it."

Turner motioned to Misella, and she proceeded, looking only at him and ignoring Mansfield and the others in the room. "I studied the history of labyrinths to learn how to wind my way through the maze. I tied twine to the yew branches and unraveled it on my way, like Ariadne's thread, until I found the center and the hermitage, an enclosed sun-lit room of exotic flowers with a massive statue of a goddess."

She took a deep breath, clutching her hands together as if to stop their trembling. "Sir Richard must have observed me entering the maze, for while I stood in amazement gazing at the wild foliage around me, he breezed through the doorway. 'How do you like my little paradise?' he asked. 'Worth the trouble to reach it, don't you agree?' His shirt was open to his waistline, and he carried a picnic basket for a celebration, he said, because of his re-election to Parliament."

Mansfield stood up again, his voice edged with sarcasm. "Please get to the point, Miss Cross, without painting every petal on the flowers of this romantic rendezvous."

Turner scanned the crowd in the gallery whom he knew wanted to hear every salacious detail. He welcomed their attention and intended to use it to Misella's advantage. "Please continue, Miss Cross, with the details of how you were drugged and overcome."

"Stop leading the prisoner," Mansfield shouted. "Your Honor," he asked, modulating his voice, "could we please request that Mr. Turner stop putting words into the prisoner's mouth."

"Yes, of course, Mr. Mansfield. You are quite right." The judge stood up to command the court's attention. "Mr. Turner, you will abide by the rules of the court and desist from asking leading questions or coaching the prisoner." He remained standing until Turner respectfully agreed to be more careful.

Turner swung back around. "Please continue, Miss Cross."

Her voice shaky but loud, she told the rest of the story: about the mead Sir Richard gave her; how it dulled her senses; how she became disoriented, felt her gown, her stays, her shift ripped apart and his hands and mouth on her, felt him on top of her and inside her, though she struggled to free herself. "All the while," she almost sobbed, "he told me he loved me, needed me, and could not live without me."

She heard cries of disgust from Isobel, the rustling of whispered voices like footsteps through leaves coming from the gallery, the scraping of a chair against the wood-slatted floor, but she stared only at Ben Turner's kind face.

Isobel's reaction seemed to have stirred up the others in the room. The Ordinary rose from his chair, holding up the Bible, his face inflamed with outrage. Choking on his words, he sputtered, "Your Excellency, must we all be exposed to this filth?"

The gallery hummed with voices, the crowd on its feet bending forward over the balcony, eager to hear the rest of the story. Mansfield sat beaming, writing something on a paper and passing it around to his attorneys.

Turner was surprised that, as Misella relayed the details of the attack, Mansfield hadn't raised an objection. But then he realized that Mansfield could claim her complicity in the affair. If she had been at all willing, she was culpable, a participant and not just a victim.

"How did you feel about Sir Richard after that attack? Turner asked, raising his voice above the buzzing in the courtroom.

Pain and embarrassment shadowed Misella's face. She twisted her body sideways away from Isobel and the Ordinary, as if to block them from her view in order to regain her composure. "I felt betrayed. Ashamed. Confused. Horrified—I-I didn't know what to do."

The jury sat grim-faced and silent, Angus MacFarland glowering with aversion at Misella and her scandalous story. Mansfield arose and headed once again toward the prisoner box as the judge called out, "We will proceed without further interruption. If you please, let us move on with the questioning."

Turner retreated as Mansfield bowed to the judge before he confronted Misella, his voice exploding into the courtroom. "Sir Richard, rest his soul, is dead and cannot defend himself against such lies, so we have no one who can rebut this fantastic story. However, I must ask you, Miss Cross, if you so successfully found your way into the maze and the hermitage, what prevented you from leaving it instantly if you found your virtue in such danger?'"

Misella raised her head and her voice. "I did not suspect that I was in danger. And I was accustomed to taking orders from Sir Richard. He wanted me to participate in what I thought would be a celebratory lunch. That was all."

Mansfield crept closer to the box, like a cat toward a tasty morsel. "Were you not surprised to see him in such a state of undress when he entered the hermitage? Had you ever seen him like this, almost bare-chested, his shirt opened to the waistline?"

Misella faltered. "No-no, and I-I was shocked. It did make me uncomfortable, but he-he wanted me to celebrate with him, and I did not want to disappoint him."

Mansfield pounced. "So you were a willing participant?"

"No—Yes, but only when I took the drink, the mead he offered me. Though it made me groggy and confused, I tried to resist his advances. But he overpowered me."

"And from that one incident you ended up with child?" Mansfield's voice curled with sarcasm.

Turner edged in front of Mansfield. "We'll provide all of the details now, Sir, and the consequences that resulted from this attack.

"We cannot wait to hear them." Mansfield smirked as he retreated back to his table.

Facing Misella, Turner whispered, "You're doing just fine. Don't worry." He swayed back and forth, drawing her attention to him and away from the gallery and Mansfield.

"Now, Miss Cross," Turner almost bellowed, "did this attack result in the conception of your child?"

Misella took a deep breath. The stench of smoking herbs that filled the courtroom burned her throat and watered her eyes, a sudden reminder of her long-ago home on Portsea Island. She clenched her hands together, blinking back the tears. "No," she sighed. "That incident began an alliance with Sir Richard that lasted a few months before I found myself with child."

"Why?" Turner demanded in a stern voice. "If you felt so betrayed and shamed by this attack, why did you continue to give in to his wishes?"

Misella raised her head, a look of defiance on her face and in her voice when she answered. "He insisted, and I had no where to turn for help. No family to rely on. No one who cared what happened to me. He told me he loved me, and, in the wake of Lady Sarah's dire illness at the time, he hinted that we could marry after she expired."

A loud guffaw rang out from Isobel. Lord Whittingham and the gallery joined in, laughing out loud. Turner ignored them, raising his voice to drown them out. "To sum up the circumstances, you soon carried his child, and he secured you in secret at Mrs. Barron's lodging house in London. Is that correct?"

"Yes, yes," she murmured.

"Speak up, please," Mansfield called from his table. She winced, and raised her voice, "Yes."

Turner persisted, "And what did you expect would happen next?"

Misella shook her head. "I didn't know, I didn't think about it. He told me he would take care of everything. I-I guess I thought that after the child's birth, I would live at the lodging house and he would support us until Lady Sarah died. I didn't know; I didn't think that far ahead."

"Did you intend to keep the child?"

Misella's expression changed. Her breath and her words came faster. "I didn't think. He tried to convince me that nothing would change between us. That he loved me, and that love, true love such as ours, could not be wrong, not even in God's eyes."

The Ordinary sprang up from his chair, his Bible raised in one hand. "Blasphemy and lies from a harlot," he roared.

"Sit down, Reverend," Turner yelled. "Your testimony is finished. Please go on, Miss Cross."

Misella appeared shaken, but she carried on. "It was not a sin, he said; we were not hurting anyone because no one would find out. 'But it would be living a lie,' I told him. 'It's not a lie,' he corrected me, 'if we have truth between us. If we both agree together to end this problem, our love for one another would endure.'"

The Ordinary rose noisily from his chair, Bible in hand, and joined Isobel, sliding in next to her on the bench. He could be heard muttering to her, "You should not have to listen to such twaddle."

Misella raised her voice. "He gave me the caustic powders to take that would abort our baby. He told me, 'You can return to Hawthorn Manor with your reputation intact and no one will know. This cannot be wrong if we both agree.'"

"And you believed him?"

She shook her head, her eyes misting with tears. "No. I knew it was wrong, and after he left me, I spent the night dwelling on what to do. Am I at fault? I asked God. And I could not avoid His answer: 'You have sinned; go forth and sin no more.' When Sir Richard returned the following evening, I told him I had destroyed the powders, that we must end our illicit relationship, that I would have the child, and with his help, I would live in London and find a way to raise it myself."

Mansfield jumped to his feet. "This is ridiculous!" he retorted. "We have only this woman's word that Sir Richard fathered her child and urged her to abort it. And we know how adept she is at lying. Madame, where is your proof?"

Slowly, Ben Turner pulled another document from inside his robe. He studied Isobel's outraged face and felt a moment of sympathy for her and regret for what he must do. She had been a devoted daughter, and he knew she wanted to protect her father and his reputation.

He addressed Mansfield directly. "We have here, Sir, indisputable evidence from Sir Richard Maltby himself, in his own hand, that he fathered this child. "Would you care to see it first before I read it for the court?"

Gasps and excited cries arose from the gallery and from the witness bench where Isobel had risen to her feet and stood swaying. Mansfield grabbed the paper out of his hand and squinted at the writing. After a moment he donned his eyeglasses and began to read in earnest. His ruddy face lost some of its color. He thrust the document into the hands of the attorney sitting near him and confided with him in a low voice.

Turner waited, enjoying the tension that infused the room, the rustling and murmuring, the startled looks on the faces of the jury, Angus MacFarland's dour frown.

"Well, Sir?" Turner grunted.

Mansfield handed the folded letter back to him without a word. Turner flashed it open in one hand, holding it close to his good eye. Like a scroll reader on the steps of a cathedral he called out in a loud voice:

Misella Cross——

>   *I have decided to acknowledge publicly our sinful relationship and to allow that I may have fathered your child. As I prepare for my death, my clergyman has convinced me that my confession will help to atone for my weaknesses, for my inability to resist the temptation you placed before me. Perhaps, God will forgive me for giving in to your charms and reward me at least for remaining steadfast in my devotion to my dear now deceased wife and our daughter Isobel and for refusing your demands that I leave them*

to begin a new life with you. At Isobel's insistence, I have given
her legal permission to adopt the child you claim is mine, so that
this innocent child may have a safe and happy home with my true
daughter, Isobel, who will give Lily the love and protection she
needs and which you in your present circumstances are unable to
provide for her.

> *A Loving and Repentant,*
> *Richard Maltby,*
> *Lord of Hawthorn Manor*

Amidst the commotion in the courtroom, Mansfield drew himself up to his most forbidding stance. "On his death bed, in the presence of his clergyman, Sir Richard questions the veracity of Miss Cross's claim that the child is his. Why would he do that, Miss Cross, if he believed you had been honest with him?"

Shaking with anger, Misella lashed out. "For the same reason he avoided taking responsibility for Lily from the day of her birth. To punish me for disobeying him. To discredit me for giving birth to our child. To ruin my reputation."

Mansfield called out in a stentorian voice. "It seems, Miss Cross, you have ruined your reputation well enough on your own. Do you deny that you were at the time of Sir Richard's death a prostitute plying your trade nightly at the Swan Court brothel?"

Misella drew in her breath and answered in a clear voice. "No I do not deny it, but I did not ..."

Mansfield cut her off. "Whatever the circumstances surrounding the conception and birth of this child, this letter provides uncontestable evidence that in his concern for the child's welfare, Sir Richard sought to do the right thing. The child should have been handed over without question to Lady Whittingham."

Turner exploded. "No, Sir. The child should have been acknowledged from the beginning and supported by its father, which it was not. Acknowledgement would have prevented the sad lengths to which Miss Cross was driven in order to provide for her child, whom she loved deeply."

"Loved? The same child she tossed like flotsam to its death in a final act of revenge against Sir Richard and Lady Whittingham?" Mansfield's voice had risen to a shout, unlike his usual demeanor in a courtroom.

"That, Sir," Turner bellowed, "is what you needed to prove but have failed."

The Judge rose to his feet. The gavel in his hand, he pounded the wooden railing again. "Enough, gentlemen. Enough of this outrage. You will both act with decorum in this courtroom. If you have witnesses to rebut the prosecution's charge, Mr. Turner, than bring them forward without further theatrics."

"Yes, your Honor, I shall." Turner straightened his gown, twisted and gaping open from his clawing for documents inside his pockets. He adjusted his disheveled wig. "I will proceed first with my questions for Miss Cross, with her side of the events that took place on the afternoon of the child, Lily's, tragic death. We do not deny that Miss Cross engaged in prostitution for Lady Marian Bentley at her establishment in Swan Court, but the charge that she willfully caused the death of the child we will absolutely refute."

He positioned himself once again in front of the prisoner and raised the fingers of his left hand to her in a kind of greeting to indicate that she was doing well. "First of all, Miss Cross, I must ask you to swear that you never had intimate relations with the coachman Jack Finn. Will you swear to that?"

Anger inflamed Misella's eyes; her cheeks bloomed with sudden color. "I swear upon my poor child's soul that I have never known Jack Finn in that way." She forced herself to stare at Turner, resisting the temptation to let her eyes seek the comfort of Jack's in the gallery. She would not endanger him. "And the work as a prostitute I was forced to engage in at Swan Court for Lady Marian shames me to the core of my soul. She placed me in her debt and then sent me to debtor's prison. To save my child from that nightmarish place, I had to go into her employ. I had no other means of support. Sir Richard refused to help me and his infant daughter."

"Thank you. Now, Miss Cross, you were on your way to my office on the day of the accident. Will you explain why you made an appointment?"

Fatigue evident in her face and in the slumping of her body against her hands that gripped the spikes in front of her as if lifelines, she explained.

"I knew about the Home your group raised money to support, the home for wayward girls and their children. Prostitutes, or—or any others who needed help." She paused, flicked her eyes toward Isobel. "I had received that note from Lady Whittingham…"

"Yes. The note about her intentions to pursue adoption proceedings?"

Misella nodded, remembered about answering the questions, and stated, "Yes." Pain darkening her eyes, she cried, "I could not give up my daughter. I had struggled to keep her with me, to protect her from harm. I could not bear to give her up. I hoped to find a way to save her. And myself."

Turner's voice softened. "So tell us what happened as you made your way to my offices?"

"I held Lily in my arms. She had been cooped up in her little room with her nurse far too much since our arrival at the Swan four months earlier, so she loved being outside for a change and experiencing the movement of the crowds and the carriages and the noise. She clapped her hands and pointed at the people near us, especially the women with their high pompadours and gaudy hats. She laughed at the horses clopping by." Misella's voice broke, and she waited a moment to gain control.

"We were being jostled and bumped by the crowd, but she did not mind, though I did. They slowed me down, and I did not want to be late for my appointment. A nicely dressed gentleman bumped against me quite hard, and my bag slipped from my fingers. He apologized, and as I stooped down to retrieve the bag, he grabbed hold of Lily and tried to wrench her from my arms. "Give her up, Misella, " he said. I was surprised he knew my name.

I might have screamed; I can't recall, but I know I clutched Lily to me as tight as I could, pushing to get away from him. I darted through the crowd trying to run. Lily started crying because I held her so tight, but I was frightened. The street was too crowded to cross, but I spied a milk cart standing still on the side of the road. The milk driver lounged against the cart waiting, and I rushed toward it thinking I could hide behind it. One of the cans had toppled onto the stones spilling milk in my path. The stones became slippery, and I fell against the cart just as the horses from the carriage drew level with me. And Lily," she added with a sob, "I lost my hold on Lily. She tumbled from my arms into the path of the carriage. The wheels..." She broke down, unable speak.

Turner tried to soothe her with his voice. "From your arms to the hand of God whose will we cannot understand. You loved your daughter and you grieve that you have lost her, but you did not kill her. It was an accident precipitated by the actions of the would-be kidnapper. Do you have any idea who he was?"

She shook her head, gulping and patting her eyes with the kerchief she had drawn from her pocket. "His voice sounded familiar, and I thought I might have heard it at Hawthorn Manor. But I could not say for sure."

"Therefore, you can only speculate about who he was and where he came from. But we will prove with our next witness that the event with the milk cart happened as you described it." He shuffled over to the witness box. "We call Martin Gibbons."

A wrinkled face leprechaun of a man skipped forward from the bench, holding his peaked cap in both hands. He bounded up the stairs and balanced his cap carefully on the ledge of the witness box, his black curly head barely visible above the railing. He raised one hand and saluted Turner. "At your service, Sir." A few chuckles could be heard from the gallery.

After the swearing in, Turner asked him to state his occupation and why he appeared as a witness.

"Well, Sir, I'm the owner of Gibbs Milk, tis what me customers call me: Gibbs. Three sturdy cows and the finest milk cart ye'll find on the Strand or just about anywhere. Gibb's milk ain't thinned with river water and thickened with chalk dust like other milks are. No, Sir, I'm an honest tradesman. Trustworthy." He peered up at the gallery. "And I give a fair price, too."

Turner thanked him for his good business practices and asked him to state his case as a witness.

He dipped his head, the curls bouncing up and down. "Well, twas my milk cart that the young lady, ah, Miss Cross, stooped behind. I felt me a jolt as I watched the crowd, waitin' for my usual customers, and I heard a milk can hit the stones. It was the biggest can on me cart. I yelped plenty loud as all that fine milk of mine gushed onto the stones. But before I could see the culprit, I heard screams and people crying out. When I dashed around to the back of the cart I saw her," he gestured toward the prisoner, "lying on the stones dripping with milk, crying out for her young un and trying to crawl towards that little bundle under the wheel. A couple of chaps pulled her up, yelling that they had the murderess. They told others to run for the constable. A sad scene, Sir. Horrible to see."

"But you didn't actually see it happen?" Turner asked. "You only saw what happened after the accident."

"Yes, that's right, Sir. I couldn't rightly speak up when the constable came, cause I hadn't seen the whole thing as some others said they had. But I couldn't think that the young lady was faking that grief. I didn't believe for a minute that she threw the baby on purpose, Sir."

"Pure speculation, counselor," Mansfield bellowed from his chair, not bothering to stand up.

Turner disregarded the outburst but asked Mr. Gibbons if he could explain why Misella's grief seemed genuine.

"Well, Sir, those milky stones were very slippery. I almost slid to me knees myself when I dashed to the back of the cart. Grabbed on to the side to keep myself upright. The young lady's explanation makes sense to me. With a babe in her arms, how could she stop herself from falling?"

"Thank you for your testimony, Mr. Gibbons."

"You are welcome, Sir." Gibbs snapped up his cap and placed it on his head. After descending the stairs, he tipped his cap to Turner and resumed his place on the witness bench.

Turner declared to the judge, "I have no further witnesses, Your Honor. Unless Lord Mansfield has more to bring forth, perhaps he would proceed with a summary of the prosecution's case."

Mansfield rose and approached the jury. "Gentlemen, we contend, and our witnesses have made clear, that the prisoner had motive to do away with her child and thus created the opportunity to do so. Furthermore, an eye-witness has testified here that he saw her commit the crime. Miss Cross herself has admitted that she has harbored revenge, even hatred, for the Maltby family, especially Sir Richard and his daughter, Lady Whittingham. Why? Because they possessed what she did not—wealth, nobility, class, sophistication. That is what she wanted, and that is what Lady Sarah Maltby and Isobel refused to give her."

Isobel sat up straighter and stared at Misella, her lips set in a grim line.

"We have only the defendant's word," Mansfield declared, "the word of an admitted prostitute, that Sir Richard supposedly provided her with abortive powders, urged her to take them, and abandoned her when she refused. Gentlemen, this is one of the oldest subterfuges known to man. Did he have an illicit relationship with her? Yes, he comes close to admitting as much in his letter. But it is also evident that he suspected his coachman Jack Finn might have been the father of her child."

Mansfield hesitated, taking the time to look up at the gallery where Annie Doyle sat, no longer hidden from view, as if to suggest a similar connection between her and Jack Finn. "Lady Whittingham has indicated to me that the defendant did have a close relationship with Finn. Sir Richard believed he had been tricked by her, mesmerized by her beauty and her charm to the point that he did whatever she asked of him, gave her whatever she wanted—expensive gowns, jewels, a secret hideaway where she could give birth to her bastard and use it to manipulate him even more, to secure his loyalty and snatch him away from his true family. Or as a last resort, to use the child to extort money from Sir Richard for her silence."

"It didn't work. In the end, Sir Richard was not fooled. He washed his hands of her, leaving her to the likes of Jack Finn, a common crook, whom Sir Richard, in his generosity, had also tried to help. With the highwayman Finn, as with Miss Cross, Sir Richard became a victim of their trickery. Yet so great was his love for his daughter, Isobel, that on his deathbed, he took responsibility for a child, possibly not his so that his childless daughter could rescue this poor brothel baby and give her a loving and decent home."

Isobel emitted a loud sob, stood up, and riffled through her pocket, drawing the eyes of everyone in the room. Pulling forth an embroidered handkerchief, she clamped it to her mouth. Lord Whittingham stood up, put his arm around her, and drew her down to the bench. The Ordinary patted her arm, whispering something to her.

Mansfield observed the scene, sadly shaking his head in apparent sympathy for Isobel, before directing his attention back to the jury. "Gentlemen, Miss Cross testified that she sought help from Benjamin Turner. She insists she was, in fact, on her way to meet him the day of the so-called accident, to arrange a better life for herself and her child. But I ask you, if she sincerely cared about the welfare of her child, why did she not seek this kind of help sooner? Why did she wait until she received Lady Whittingham's letter proposing adoption before she sought counsel? You heard the stark and angry contents of the letter she sent in response to Lady Whittingham—"You will never take Lily from me!" The word "never" underlined with a dagger. What else does that suggest except murderous rage?

"The phantom kidnapper, who the defendant claimed in her testimony tried to wrest the child from her arms and precipitated her panic and rush to escape, has not been named. Where is he?" Mansfield scanned the entire courtroom. "Has the defense produced him or anyone in the crowd that day who witnessed his attack?"

"And finally, the witness Robby Blackford, the runner for Lord Russell's carriage, who has testified here under oath that he saw the defendant throw her child under the wheel. True, he may not have seen the milk can that had tumbled into the street, but his eyes at the time were riveted on the horses and the carriage. It is his job to make sure they are proceeding forward without trouble. And that focused attention was only distracted by the movement he saw when the defendant flung her child forward—that is what he testified, that she *flung* the bundle into the path of the wheel."

Mansfield glared at the prisoner. "Murder of her own innocent child was Misella Cross's final act of revenge against the Maltby family." Shaking his head, his face hardened with disgust as if he were being forced to look upon something rotten, he swung back toward the jury, his voice now somber. "Gentlemen, based upon this evidence, you must find the defendant, Misella Cross, guilty of the terrible crime of infanticide."

Ben Turner rose frowning at Mansfield who swaggered, a little too much he thought, back to his place where the rest of his counselors sat beaming. He debated about using his cane, whether it would add a dash of style or would make him appear weak. He decided to forego it. He walked ponderously toward the Judge, hoping his slow step would look measured and deliberate rather than handicapped. He hadn't looked at Misella at all during Mansfield's summary. He did not want her melancholic attitude to inhibit him, to make him fearful or make him second guess himself.

"Your Honor," he began with a reasonable, measured tone. "Misella Cross is not guilty of this crime of which she has been falsely accused. Let us begin with the so-called eyewitness, Robbie Blackford. The only things he could have witnessed on that day, in the place where he stood, at the moment of the accident, were the heads and upper bodies of the horses and the swaying carriage itself. He could not remember or describe the milk can, because he could not see it. And if he could not see the milk can, he could not have seen the defendant as she fell and lost her grip on her child. Nor could he have seen Miss Cross lay prostrate with horror on the stones, with the body of the child she loved bleeding under the wheel of the carriage."

Misella bowed her head. Though she tried, she could not stop the tears. She stood silent and motionless while they dripped from her chin, wetting the linen bodice of her dress.

Raising his voice, Turner asked, "Did Robbie Blackford lie? No, I don't believe so. I do believe that he was easily influenced that day—by the turmoil of the crowd, the voices yelling 'Murder,' and the accusations put forth by the would-be kidnapper himself. Above all, Robbie Blackford was encouraged by Lord Whittingham to believe that he saw a crime that did not take place. Young Blackford saw the whirl of horses shaking their manes and the on-coming carriage; he heard the commotion, felt the electric vibrations of mass hysteria, and sought the excitement of impressing the crowd and the constable, for he wanted to be an important part of an investigation. He is a decent lad, young and ambitious, a good employee by all accounts, but he is not a reliable eyewitness." Turner waited for a moment and then repeated his claim. "Robbie Blackford is not a reliable eyewitness."

"The kidnapper? No, we cannot produce him. Miss Cross would probably be unable to identify him because he was quick, no doubt disguised, and in the crush of the crowd and in her shock and fear and her instinctive need to escape from danger, she focused on fleeing as fast as she could. Whoever hired him, we could not say. While we have our suspicions, they are only speculation and cannot be admitted here where facts and reason must reign."

Angus MacFarland shook his head, a scowl darkening his face, his dark eyebrows drawing together in a frown. The rest of the jurymen listened with closed faces as well. Turner heard a *Humph* from Mansfield, and a spatter of whispering from the gallery or the witness bench, he could not be sure. He discounted them all and plunged ahead.

"The Prosecutor asks you to consider why Miss Cross did not seek my help sooner to save herself and her child from the devilish environment of which she was a victim. Let me explain why. At the time and given her desperate situation, the Swan establishment offered her the best choice for the safety of her child."

"She was penniless after the birth of her child. Sir Richard abandoned her, refusing to accept any responsibility for his actions. She pawned all of the gifts he showered upon her. How could she find respectable work as an unmarried penniless woman with a child? Why not murder the child at that time? It would have made her situation much easier. But she didn't. In innocence and naiveté she sought the help of the only other person she could think of in London, Lady Marian Bentley, whom she did not know and had never met. But she knew Lady Marian was a friend of Sir Richard's. Misella Cross thought perhaps Lady Marian could intercede on her behalf with Sir Richard and convince him to provide for the child."

Mansfield had the audacity to laugh out loud and his attorneys to titter in accompaniment. The gallery joined in. Exasperated, Turner implored the Judge, "Your Honor, if you please, may we have some decorum here?"

Mansfield jumped to his feet with an exaggerated apology for not controlling his reaction. "Your Honor, you have my solemn promise I will observe the dignity of the court no matter what Mr. Turner tries to assert." The Judge agreed and signaled Turner to proceed.

Turner glared at Mansfield, then resumed addressing the Judge. "We cannot prove to you beyond a doubt that Sir Richard fathered her child. We have only the defendant's sworn testimony that he did, and that she never engaged in intimate relations with the coachman Jack Finn. But does it seem likely to you that Isobel Whittingham would have wanted to adopt, or for Sir Richard to urge her to, if this were the offspring of Jack Finn, a notorious highwayman?

"You must understand that Misella Cross was duped, manipulated, no doubt drugged in the hermitage, and corrupted at the hands of Sir Richard, her surrogate father, who should have protected her. Instead, he groomed her, from her very first days at the Maltby estate, to depend on him for the attention and affection she in her loneliness could find nowhere else. Certainly not from Lady Maltby or Isobel, who had been through this experience earlier with Annie Doyle. Yet Miss Cross posed a more difficult situation for them because she was a relative of Sir Richard's and all were aware of that connection. Sir Richard used that fact to his advantage."

Behind Turner's back, Isobel squirmed with outrage on the witness bench, flapping her fan and shaking her head. She whipped her head around to face the gallery and mouthed, "He lies. He lies."

"You have heard Annie Doyle's story," Turner noted solemnly. "All that separates her story from Misella Cross's is that Sir Richard did not impregnate her, by the grace of God it seems. But she suffered a similar fate."

Turner extended his hand and counted on his fingers each of the similarities: "Taken in by his seeming affection, devotion and fatherly concern. Left in his care with no one to intervene on her behalf or to protect her from his silver-tongued promises before he raped her in the hermitage and afterwards. Thrown away when she became too attached, too much of a burden. Left destitute to survive on the streets."

"We are not here, however, to decide the question of Sir Richard's guilt, but only if Misella Cross is guilty of murdering their child." Looking intently at the Judge, Turner raised his voice. "Nothing, Your Honor, that you have heard in this courtroom today, *nothing*, can convince you that Miss Cross is guilty of such a diabolical crime."

He hesitated for a moment, allowing the stillness in the courtroom to linger for a few moments. "Was she guilty of youthful vanity, of naiveté, of being awed by such wealth as she had never encountered, of being desperate for affection and acceptance? Yes. Of being grateful to her mentor? Yes. Of being swayed by the passion and the desire to please him, to do whatever he asked of her? Yes. But that gratitude stopped at the door of his last request of her—to abort their child. That she would not do. She devoted her being to protecting that child, no matter what she had to do. Accepting Lady Marian's ultimatum in order to save her child from the dregs of Fleet Street Prison. Keeping the child with her in that den of iniquity until she could find a safe alternative. And she finally did when she learned from me at the Whittingham wedding of a new charity house for women. That is what she intended to arrange at our meeting on that final day of her child's life.

"Why would she give up the child she fiercely loved and desperately fought to keep at the very moment when a solution was within her grasp? And why would she give her beloved child to the family that had participated in her downfall? She made that point clear in her terse response to Lady Whittingham's letter. But in that incident let us not, Your Honor, confuse justifiable malice with murderous rage.

"Is Misella Cross guilty of prostitution? Yes, she had no choice. Is she guilty of murdering her child? Absolutely not!"

In the breathless silence of the courtroom, Turner bowed to the Judge. He offered Misella a wistful smile of hope. Sadness shone through her tears, but she responded with a faint smile that curved her lips for a moment. Returning to his seat with a heavy, deliberate pace, he felt the burn of Isobel's gaze. He twisted around in his chair to stare, unmoved, at the deathly pallor of her face.

The Judge rose magnificently from his throne, his robes flaring in crimson folds around him, drawing all eyes to himself as his voice boomed through the room. "Gentlemen of the jury, your function now is to weigh the explanations and the evidence you have heard, allowing all due force to the reputations of those who offered them, and to decide to the best of your abilities the outcome of this case. Go forth; convene with all due honor, and return with your decision."

With Angus MacFarland in the lead, the jury, their faces set in stone, rose as one, a straight line of black robes, to file through the door on their left,.

His eyes focused on Misella, Turner tried to assess her state of mind. She had listened to the judge with a steady and stoic attention, but now she seemed to be making a great effort to appear calm. She shifted her handkerchief back and forth in her hands, and then grasped the spiked ledge of the box tightly, leaning forward with the stance of a school boy about to vault over a fence.

The wild look in her eyes frightened him. He struggled to remain in his chair wanting to go and comfort her, to take her restless hands in his and tell her how he felt. He yearned to bring her some peace of mind, to take care of her. In his old, foolish heart he wanted to ask for her hand in marriage.

He would not allow himself to think that she might be found guilty. The possibility terrified him, he who had always believed in the beauty of his profession, the wondrous ability of the law that, when applied fairly, could allow both sides to dispute any human assertion made under any circumstances. Now, however, he despised the freedom it granted its practitioners to manipulate the truth. He feared for the first time that Socrates was right in calling the law an illusionist game of trickery.

258

The courtroom room hummed with muted voices, the scraping of chairs, the rustling of silks, and the flapping of fans. Mansfield stood within the closed circle of his helpers, their heads nodding, their muffled voices drifting across to Turner who sat slouched gloomily in his chair. He supposed he should try to look more confident. But the effort seemed too much for him at that moment. He could no longer bear to look at the Whittinghams consulting in the corner with the Ordinary, their smug faces glowing with anticipation.

He turned to gaze at the gallery, the greedy onlookers bustling like a hive of swarming bees, the women bending to their neighbors, their fans furiously stirring the lace on their collars, their hat feathers flopping in rhythm with their bobbing heads and yapping jaws. Some of the men raised glowing cigars to their pursed lips, ignoring the ban intended to protect the ancient wooden beams that could flare in an instant with the drift of a live ash. A few dandies sported silver flasks that flashed in the glow of the hooded candle sconces. An intermission at the Globe, he thought, "a damn party."

The Judge remained in his chair conversing with his colleagues until the jury room door reopened and the bailiff approached. He entered the aisle leading to the Judge and whispered to him. The Judge stood and addressed the courtroom. "Gentlemen, the jury will come forward. Please rise." Murmurings of surprise reverberated through the chamber. The jury had been out less than fifteen minutes.

A hush descended over the room as the jurymen entered. Only the steel-capped heels of their shoes could be heard clicking against the stone floor as they entered one by one and took their places. The foreman, Angus MacFarland, his dark face impassive, spoke quietly to the Judge who told him to announce the verdict.

"Your Honor and Gentlemen of the Court, we have reached a partial verdict. In the case of the Court of her Royal Majesty versus Misella Cross, accused forthwith of murdering her infant daughter on the tenth day of April in the year 1754, we find the defendant Not Guilty."

An uproar of shouts and cries burst from all corners of the room. Mansfield and his men stood, stunned into silence. Turner, too, was struck speechless. He grabbed the table in front of him and braced himself against it, his heart pounding with relief and exhilaration. He could hear hoarse, gasping sobs behind him which he assumed came from Isobel.

The Judge pounded his gavel on the wooden ledge in front of him. "Silence," he bellowed. "Allow the Foreman to speak."

MacFarland raised his voice so that his brogue rang out over the heads of the councilmen and lawyers. "On a second count we find the defendant, Misella Cross, guilty of the willful and deplorable crime of prostitution."

Turner flew out of his chair, his cane clattering to the floor. He caught himself just in time from releasing the string of obscenities that burned in his throat. He forced himself to suppress his outrage at this trumped-up charge.

The Judge arose and pronounced, "The defendant will return to Newgate gaol to await sentencing which will take place tomorrow at the end of the Spring Sessions. This concludes our Session in this courtroom today."

Turner shambled as fast as he could without his cane to reach Misella in the prisoner's box. Edging the bailiff out of the way, he grasped her hand to help her descend the stairs, her face blank as a sleep-walker's. He spoke softly to her so as not to startle her. "My dear, at least you have your life back. Leave things to me. All will be well, I promise."

She shivered as if consumed by a sudden blast of wintry air. Her eyes dull, she whispered, "It is over." The bailiff grabbed her arm and led her to the door through which she had entered just a few hours earlier. She seemed not to notice the flurry of activity around her, the chattering voices, the leering faces in the gallery, Isobel's outraged cries bleating from the witness area, the stern face of the Ordinary who made his way to the front of the room, his merciless eyes following her as the bailiff led her away.

Turner slumped back into his chair, his brief moment of elation replaced by despair and guilt. The jury had found a way to chastise Misella by making prostitution itself, for the first time, a punishable crime. And through her, they punished him for bringing the issue and consequences of prostitution so visibly into the courtroom. He believed the Judge's sentence would be harsh. No doubt, Misella would be transported to the New World. He had saved her life, but because of him, she would lose her freedom.

CHAPTER 12

The bailiff's grip on Misella's arm tightened as he dragged her through the opening and slammed the door shut behind them. He released her arm but grabbed her collar in his fist and shoved her down the damp stairway in front of him. "Back where you came from for now," he snarled. She stumbled down the steps and along the dark passageway now emptied of prisoners.

"If only I could," she thought, "go back to the shore with Father's boat bobbing in the waves, the water lapping against my shoes, gulls diving from the sky." She knew she should be grateful that her life had been spared, and she had not even thanked Benjamin Turner for the miracle of that. In her growing despair, with the debris of her life strewn before the court, she almost wished she had been made to pay for Lily's life with her own.

When she stared into her own heart, could she truly claim that she was not guilty?

In her hatred against the Maltbys and her all-consuming desire for revenge, had she used the kidnapper as an excuse, a momentary opportunity, to get rid of the constant reminder of her sins, and the burden that Lily had become? No, no. That could not be. She had loved her daughter. Loved her still.

The bailiff marched her to her rooms, threw open the door, and pushed her inside. "With the Sessions over, you'll be outta here in a day or so when your sentence is handed down," he snarled. He lounged in the doorway, his pocked face twisted with contempt. "But don't think you've escaped the

261

hangman. You could swing at Tyburn yet." He backed out, slammed the door, and locked it.

She dropped onto her bed without removing her shoes or cap. She felt hollow, gutted like one of her father's codfish. She curled her knees up to her chin, unable to close her eyes, afraid to sleep or to think about the future, staring at nothing but a stone wall. She no longer cared what might happen.

She awoke shivering, her teeth chattering in the damp chill of the dark room. A soft tapping on her door ceased for a few moments and began again a little louder. Stiff from the cold, she struggled to her feet and waited to hear a key in the lock. *The Ordinary*, she thought at first, *come to gloat and thrust his heartless God at me once again.*

Like a blind woman, she shuffled through the dark, her arms stretched out until she reached the door. She placed her hands against it and listened. "Misella." She heard Ben Turner's gruff whisper. "I need to talk to you. Will you let me in?"

She tried to speak, her voice hoarse with sleep or an oncoming illness. She coughed and rasped, "I cannot. I do not have a key."

In the silence that followed she thought perhaps he had gone away, but then he spoke, his voice strong and reassuring. "I'll be right back with a key. It may take me a few minutes, but we have a little time. Don't worry."

What did he mean? she wondered. Why so little time? He must know her fate already and came to prepare her before the bailiff reappeared in the morning to take her to the Judge for sentencing. Shivering from the cold, from fear, she stumbled to the desk and groped for the flint to light the candle, her stiff fingers clumsy as she tried to strike a spark. She was about to give up and crawl back to her bed when a spark jumped and the tallow caught. She lit two of the other candles in the room and worked at the kindling in the fireplace until a weak flame traveled sluggishly along the logs and grabbed hold. She emptied freezing water into the blackened teapot, some of it dribbling across her hands, and set it on top of the weak fire. It would take time to heat, but she could wait, if there were time, she reflected, remembering Ben's words. She lifted the wool coverlet from the bed and wrapped it tightly around her shoulders.

She nudged a chair close to the fire unconcerned about stray sparks and sat on the edge, her hands stretched toward the warmth. Her mind wandered back to her childhood as it often seemed to do these days. She imagined she heard her father's fish cart rolling to a stop outside the hut, his boots scraping against the wooden plank in front of the door in a useless effort to remove the mud. She heard again the push of the door as he tried to open it against its rusted groans of protest. When he entered, she turned to greet him, to tell him that the tea would soon be ready on this chilly night.

But it wasn't her father. Ben Turner heaved his body into the room, his bulky shadow looming across the stone floor. He rested his cane against the brick corner of the fireplace and pulled her chair back a little. "Too close, my dear. You'll ignite your gown if you're not careful." He picked up another log from the box, and, stirring the glowing embers with it, he placed it carefully next to the tea kettle. "No steam. Not ready yet." He retrieved the three-legged wooden stool from the corner and placed it next to her. Then he inched himself down until the bend of his knees allowed him to sit.

She stared at him for a moment as if trying to recall his name. She swallowed a few times, hoping to relieve the dryness of her throat. "Why are you here? It must be late. What time is it?"

He took her hand, engulfing it in one of his. With his free hand, he loosened his scarf, unwinding it impatiently and knocking his wig askew. He unbuttoned his great coat and slipped it off letting it fall in a heap behind the stool. "It is very late. I should not be here. I bribed the turnkey. He'll blackmail me for weeks, I expect."

The hiss of the tea kettle interrupted him. He picked up his scarf and struggled to his feet. "Let me fix us a cup of tea first, and I'll tell you why I came." With the scarf wrapped around his hand he plucked the kettle from the logs. He shambled to the small desk and placed it next to the guttering candle. "I'm an expert at this," he chuckled. "I used to do this every night for Tetty during our marriage." He hesitated for a moment. "When I was at home." He drew the teapot from the corner of the desk and pulled the tea canister from the drawer where she kept it. "Often she would tell me, 'Ah, Benjamin, you have become a tea master.'"

He measured the tea leaves with care, dumped them into the pot, and slowly poured the steaming water. "The trick is in the slow steeping of the leaves and knowing the precise moment when they are ready. It took some time for me to learn that. I used to be too impatient to wait." He set the cups next to the pot and tapped the lid with his fingers as if he were counting time. He did not look at her.

She watched his large rumpled form in the shadowed light, his head down, his gaze focused intently on his task as if a perfect cup of tea would make everything fine. With the growing warmth coursing through her, she felt calmer, almost hopeful again as if his sheer size and gruff affection could shelter her from any harm. He poured the tea, and balancing both cups on the palm of his wrapped hand, the other hand curved gingerly around them, he shuffled back to the fire. "Here we are, my dear. Take care not to scald yourself."

She took the cup, grateful for the heat against her fingers. Not wanting to stare at his clumsiness as he resumed his place next to her, she gazed into the fire. They did not speak, but sat blowing into their cups. When she heard his vigorous slurping, she began to sip her tea. He lurched up once more. "More tea, my dear?"

She shook her head. He went to the desk for more for himself and came back but did not sit. He stood behind her, clearing his throat, tapping one foot upon the floor as he blew into his cup. She waited for him to speak, his nervousness slipping into her and disrupting the little calm she had achieved.

"Misella," he began, "I received notice of the Judge's ridiculous sentence. You will be transported to the colonies as an indentured slave." His voice wavered. "For a term of seven years on the charge of prostitution. Once again, you'll be sold to the highest bidder for who knows what kind of work.

"Pah." His voice curled with contempt. "It is a trumped-up, superficial charge, a punishment never before administered for prostitution, a situation all have conveniently ignored until now, and the Judge knows it. Oh yes, many prostitutes have suffered this same fate but never for prostitution, always for some kind of thievery charged by their customers. The self-righteous hypocrites in that courtroom did not have the evidence to charge you with infanticide, and so they found another way to punish you." He threw his cup into the fireplace, the tea sizzling as the cup shattered.

She jumped, and he reached out, slipping the blanket from her shoulders and cupping them with his large, warm hands. "I am sorry, my dear."

His voice softened as he nudged her from her chair and whirled her around to face him. "For everything that has happened to you." He shoved the chair out of the way with a kick and drew her close.

"I have spent these hours since I heard doing everything I could to change this sentence." His voice cracked, and she saw tears shining in his eyes. "And my dear, I have succeeded with the help of the Archbishop who has admired the charity work I have done."

A surge of happiness altered his blunt features, lighting his face with a youthful glow. His grip tightened almost making her gasp as he clutched her to his chest. "Oh, Misella, there is hope ahead for you, for us. The Archbishop has convinced the Mayor to change your sentence to the marking of your hand and, and...," his voice faltered into a breathless whisper, "allowing you to marry me."

Her throat closed with shock, and she could not speak, her words trapped within her chest. She knew she could never accept his proposal, but she did not want to hurt him.

"That will satisfy the Mayor that your life of prostitution is over." He began to caress her hair, running his hand over her curls, his other hand spanning her waist, holding her close. She felt his lips brush her forehead. The stiff curls of his wig scraped her cheekbone, and she inhaled some drifting specks of powder. She held her breath to prevent a sneeze, not wanting to cheapen this moment for him.

He misunderstood her silent shudder. He let go of her, his face infused with pain and embarrassment. "Of course, I would not want you to accept this offer if it offends you." He limped away from her, his body slumping like a deflated sail, and said with quiet dignity, "If I have offended you in any way, I am deeply sorry. Please forgive me." He seized his cane. Leaning heavily upon it, he bent down as best he could and retrieved his discarded coat and scarf.

With both hands, she caught hold of his arm. "Please, Benjamin. I am not offended. I am honored and grateful that you care so much for me that you would do anything to help me. I cannot thank you enough for all you have done. You saved my life. I know that. So much has happened. I need some time to absorb all of this. I did not think I would have a future." She bowed her head. "Will you give me some time to think this through?"

He sighed, thumping his cane against the stone floor in a slow rhythm of despair. His voice when he finally answered was gruff. "Of course." He set the cane down on the chair and struggled into his coat. He slipped the rumpled scarf around his neck where it hung forlorn and uneven. "You will have to give the Mayor's messenger your decision when he appears early in the morning to take you to the courtroom for the last session so that the sentence can be carried out immediately."

He did not look at her as he retrieved his cane and clumped to the door. He opened it, drew the key from his pocket and turned to her. "The marking sounds grim, but it is done swiftly, one thrust of the smoldering iron against your thumb. It seems cruel, but banishment would be far more painful for you, I believe—perhaps even more painful than marriage to me. I'll await your answer."

She watched him lumber through the doorway, heard the key turn in the lock, and remained standing where she was. Turner was a good man; he would protect her and take care of her. This she knew with certainty now. He would always, she thought, look at her with that soft shine of love and devotion in his eyes. He would be tender with her, obsequious to her every need. His oddities no longer frightened her. They had become a comfort rather than an embarrassment. She did not love him, but she respected him and trusted him.

She thought about this opportunity to escape from her miseries through the benign comfort of marriage to a respected barrister, but here in this place of her downfall, she could never escape from her infamy. The outward mark upon her hand would forever remind her, and others, of her past, but far worse would be the invisible mark upon her soul if she allowed him to hope, and he would, that she might someday come to love him. She knew better. She could not even love herself. It would be dishonest to deceive him. She could not live with such a mark upon her conscience.

Banishment to the New World seemed to her almost a privilege now, a rare chance to find some hope of happiness in a far off region that might restore her once again to honesty and peace. She would find the strength to survive for seven years while awaiting her freedom. Before she weakened, she hastened to the desk and drew forth her writing materials, setting the tea things aside. She pulled the chair over and sat down, drawing the stopper from the squat little bottle of ink and taking up the quill with shaky fingers.

Kind Sir:

Your proposal this evening brought me what I never thought to have, proof that I am loved at the hour in which I most needed it. You think better of me than I deserve, though I hope to be in time what you wish me to be, what I wish to be, and what I have hitherto satisfied myself too readily with only wishing——a strong and honest woman with her head held high, able, once again, to return love.

If I am to have any chance of achieving the serenity and salvation I so desperately seek, I must accept my original sentence. Perhaps, in that wild and unknown region across the seas, I may yet find that young woman I dream of being.

Continue, Dearest Sir, your prayers for me that my good resolution may not be in vain. I hope, despite the long distance that must now come between us, our friendship may endure longer than life.

With most sincere affection and gratitude, I remain your humble servant.

Misella C.

Brushing the tears from her eyes, she folded the parchment in half and inscribed across the back in her best handwriting: *The Honorable Mr. Benjamin Turner, Gray's Inn.*

CHAPTER 13

Late that evening, Turner let himself into the office, his face raw from the rare April snowstorm and the wind. He unwound the soaked scarf muffled around his neck and removed his damp outer coat. Not bothering to shake off the encrusted snow, he tossed them to the floor along with his cane. Stumbling to his desk in the bone-chilling darkness, he fumbled for the flint and struck vigorously several times until the tallow dish caught and his tumbled papers flared into view. He fell into his chair, his breath rasping, his knees aching. "Midnight," he muttered into the stillness, "and I am again alone in this hour of darkness and vacuity."

He could not prevent the thought that reared up, as it so often did, that he was naught but a poor helpless fool reduced by a blast of wind, and by the fallaciousness of hope, to weakness and misery. No woman would want him. He knew by instinct, nay by long and painful experience, that Misella would refuse him with kindness, with humility, with the tired arguments he had heard from other women— except Tetty—that he was too good for her, that she could not besmirch his reputation, that she considered him a dear friend whom she did not want to lose within the petty snarls of marriage.

In exhaustion and despair, he rested his head upon the pile of parchment on his desk, the pieces of her story that he would keep, no matter what happened. At least, these would remind him of what he had won and what he had lost.

He awoke to the sound of fists pounding upon his door, as if to break it down. The candle had gone out, leaving a congealed pool of grease that had spilled from the holder and invaded several of the parchment pages. He raised his head, his neck stiff and throbbing worse than his poor knees. He doubted if his knees would allow him to rise from the chair.

The pounding increased and then ceased. He sat up and discovered faint daylight escaping into the room as Charles entered his office. "What in the world have you been doing, Ben? Aha, out celebrating from the pasty looks of you. Too much port, I'd gather, and all without me. I waited for you at the Cheshire Cheese for hours. Where did you go, you sly, old dog? I had planned to grovel when I saw you, to eat crow and take back every negative thing I said about you and this trial."

Dunning picked up Turner's discarded, damp coat and scarf and hung them on the hook. He snatched up the cane and twirled it between his delicate fingers. "I'll admit it to the world, Ben. I'll put it in writing. Your performance was magnificent. To get that poor whore off the way you did. You are the master."

He tossed a folded sheet of parchment onto the desk. "A thank you note, I gather, from the merry maid on her way to the boat at Blackfriars. The boy who delivered it said she insisted that he give it to no one but Benjamin Turner. But he happily let me have it for a guinea and my solemn promise that I would place it into the hands of the great barrister himself."

Turner said nothing. Pushing himself up from the desk, he grabbed the flint and went to work on the limp wick withered within the mass of tallow on the metal plate. Dunning strolled to the bookshelf across the room and drew down a fresh candle in its holder. "Here, here, Ben, let me do it. You'll never get anywhere with that dismal mess." He grabbed the flint from Turner's trembling fingers and struck it against the stone. A spark flashed and caught hold, the candle igniting.

Turner pulled it forward and opened the letter. Leaning into the candle as close as he dared, he squinted his good eye and scanned the single page. He threw it onto the other piled papers. Pulling a set of keys from his vest pocket, he jingled through them until he found the one he wanted, jammed it into the lock, and opened the top drawer of his desk. He pulled out a slim bag of coins, slid back his chair, and attempted to stand. Seizing his cane from the desk where Dunning had propped it, he used it to raise himself upright, leaving the drawer gaping open, the keys swinging from the lock. He stumped over to the coat rack, flung his damp wig to the floor and yanked his coat down, thrusting first one arm in a sleeve and then the other, transferring the cane back and forth until he managed to heave the coat in place around him.

Dunning picked up the note and read it. "Look here, Ben, where are you going? Not to see the girl off, I hope. You'll freeze out there, and you'll not be able to go aboard anyway. And you certainly don't want to mingle with that scurvy bunch of prisoners milling onto the ship."

He walked over and grabbed hold of Turner's cane. "Just let her go. You've done enough for her already."

Turner wrenched the cane from Dunning's grasp, fury enflaming his face. "I want the name of the merchant contractor who funds the prisoners' passage on the *Seaflower*," he demanded. "Have it for me when I return." He fled through the doorway and out into the swirling snow. Blindly, he humped down the stairs into the deserted street, determined to find a carriage or a chair or if not, he would walk to the river, but he had to see her once more before she left.

CHAPTER 14

Misella squatted inside the packed cart, her lace cap layered with snow, her face buried inside the collar of her thin cape to avoid the dead eyes and wracking coughs of the other ragged women shivering around her. Her knees screamed for release, her back bruising from the crush of the wooden slats that slammed against her with every rut in the street. She could hear the whistles in the distance from the coal barges floundering their way along the river so she hoped the driver must soon reach the wharf.

Theirs was the last group taken from the prison, delayed because of last-minute reprieves from the Bishop for a few women who had earned the benefit of clergy but been mistakenly included in their group. To assure that the prisoners arrived at the ship on time, the guards removed the women's shackles and herded the group into a horse-drawn cart rather than parade them through the streets as usual to the quay.

Misella almost changed her mind while she waited in the prison yard, almost sent the bread boy to bring Ben Turner to her. Instead, she slipped the boy the note and the last half-crown Turner had given her. Now, how she longed to see Turner's kind, craggy face, hear his gruff voice, feel his bear-like hands warming her own.

When the cart lurched to a stop, the driver shouted, "Make way for the last load of doxies here." The quay resounded with commotion: planks groaning under the thumping hooves of bawling cattle; dock men crying, "heave," "pull it up, ya addle pate;" wet ropes creaking; half-furled sails whipping against the wind.

The chains securing the rear of the cart clanged as the driver freed the lock and dropped the heavy panel to the stones. "Be quick," he growled, "if you don't want a basting to take with you." He raised his crop and stepped back allowing just enough room for the prisoners to stumble one by one onto the street. "Line up on the dock in front of that shack over there."

Waiting while all of the women staggered forward, Misella stretched her aching legs. She hugged her cape around her, holding tight to the small cloth bag that held her belongings, and tried to get her bearings as she lurched down onto the wet stones. The driver gave her a shove that sent one foot slipping into a crevice in the stone pathway leading up to the quay. "Get your bob tail movin and catch up."

She cried out at the sharp twist to her ankle, but hobbled as fast as she could so as not to call any more attention to herself. The wharf and surrounding street teemed with a great bustle of people at this early hour. She could see in the distance old men and small children peering through the rails on London Bridge at the barges and boats passing through with the tide. Young men swung their way down to the pilings on rope ladders to lay baits and lines. She had lost track of time, but realized it must be Sunday, church bells tolling loud and long.

She pictured the church tower at Portsmouth, the peal of its bells resounding for miles, and her father hauling in his catch on Sunday mornings, ignoring the Sabbath in order to feed his family. For a moment hope fluttered within her, a sudden yearning, however foolish, that perhaps she might see him again someday in Boston. But he would not recognize her now, and she would not want him to know what she had become.

A ship's mate stood at the front of the sorry line of prisoners, flicking open the women's tattered capes or shawls and running his hands slowly along the front of their bodices. "Got to search for contraband," he grinned, "and fleas," he added, as he pulled down their stays and fondled their breasts, though he knew the women had been washed down with vinegar before they left the prison yard. When he finished with each one, he pushed her forward to his co-worker standing behind him who ogled their gaping gowns, yanked off their caps, and doused their heads with a camphorated liquid. "Up the gangplank," he hollered to the dripping, freezing women.

Misella felt her anger rising, the blood rushing through her sluggish veins as she watched. Like a mannequin, she had endured the cleansing in

274

the prison yard while the leering guards eyed her nakedness with relish, but this public humiliation she would not allow. When the mate pulled her forward, she clutched her cape closed in her frozen hands. "Don't you dare touch me," she warned. "You know we are clean."

The mate flung his head back, startled by her boldness. A sneer crossed his carbuncled face. With a guttural laugh he said to his companion, "Listen to this, Flinty, this dirty little bunter says she's clean, don't need no dousin. I think we're gonna have ta douse both ends of this one." Flinty leapt forward to help as the leader grabbed hold of Misella's rigid fingers and began to pry them open. Flinty yanked off her cap and grabbed hold of her hair, pulling her head back with one hand and imprisoning her arms.

She felt her cape rip open and next, her bodice, a rough hand tearing at her stays.

"No," she screamed, unable to resist. "No," she whimpered as the cold air snatched the last warmth from her skin.

She heard a yelp, and Flinty's hand released her hair, a whack, and he dropped his hold on her arms. From the corner of her eye, she saw the arc of a cane as it whistled through the air and cracked across the ship mate's busy fingers. He cried out and reeled back to face the livid rage of Ben Turner towering over them.

"I'll have your bloody heads on a spike," Turner howled, slicing at both men with the cane, knocking first one head and then the other, drawing welts and opening skin with its metal tip. His breath swirled up in misty clouds and his chest heaved as he ranted, "I'll have the King's promise to string you up and your Captain, too, for this." The men covered their heads with their arms and backed away to the end of the gangplank, happy to see the ship's first mate running down the plank, his sword drawn.

"Hold on, there. What's the meaning of this? You can't interfere with our business here." The uniformed mate stuck the point of the sword menacingly against Turner's heaving chest. "Who the devil do you think you are?"

Turner lowered his cane and caught his breath, his reddened face steaming above his disheveled scarf. "Benjamin Turner," he gasped, "Member of the King's Counsel for the city and this young woman's lawyer." He put his arm around Misella, who held her torn cape together with shaking fingers, and gathered her into his embrace. He rested his moist cheek against the tousled top of her head for a moment. Straightening to his full stature, he warned, "This unwarranted, licentious attack against my client is an outrage. You'd best fetch your Captain if you know what's good for all of you."

The first mate hesitated and then replaced his sword in the scabbard. "These men were just doing their job, Sir. Preparing the prisoners to come aboard and insuring that they bring no vermin or diseases with them."

Turner's face flamed a darker red. "You know and they know that the prisoners are washed and cleared before they arrive here. This shameful mauling, this public humiliation will not stand in a court of law. These women remain within the jurisdiction of the Crown—on this dock, on the ship, in the colonies. "

The first mate looked surprised and puzzled. "You're worried about the modesty of prostitutes and thieves?" He grunted in disbelief. "They need to be controlled, Sir, to understand who is in charge. Believe me; we have plenty of experience dealing with their kind on board the *Seaflower*. We know how to handle them."

With a menacing look, his cane raised once again, Turner barked, "Bring your captain to me. Tell him I come here at the behest of Admiral Dunning. He'll know what I mean." He would risk Charles' fury by using his estranged father's notorious influence in the slave shipping industry. He didn't care; he'd employ whatever bribery he could to protect Misella.

The bewildered mate shrugged his shoulders. "Wait here, Sir. But I must take this last prisoner on board."

Almost calm, Misella eased herself out of Turner's embrace and stood alone, inhaling her last taste of English air. She knew, as this crew did, that Turner was bluffing. The Crown cared little about what happened to prostitutes, on British soil or beyond the seas. The country was glad to be rid of the convicts, who faced a death sentence if they tried to return. And the King and his countrymen knew that plenty of young, innocent flesh remained to take their places.

She drew a deep breath and placed her hand on Turner's rumpled sleeve. "Please, Ben," she pleaded, "let me go quietly. I am ready. Thank you for helping me." She gathered the folds of her cape around her and clutched her small bag in both hands. "I won't forget you. I promise."

As she reached the gangplank, a drunken vagrant staggered out of the crowd of onlookers milling around the dock and bumped into her, almost knocking her over. Misella cried out at the wrenching pain in her sore ankle. Ignoring her, Flinty and his companion grabbed hold of the drunk. "Watch out, you knobhead, or you'll join the rest of these vermin on board," the first mate roared.

The drunk wobbled, his battered hat slipping forward over his yellowed wig. "Beg pardon, Gentlemen," he slurred. "In fact, I set sail for the New World in a few days—as a free-willer, not a prisoner. Allow me to wish you fair travels." He hiccupped and grinned. "We have an old saying where I come from that may help you on your journey. 'Chin up, eyes to Heaven.'"

Misella gazed into the lively blue eyes she knew so well and smiled at him before the shipmates flung him aside and shoved her forward. She refused to acknowledge the trio of crew members who stomped up the gangplank behind her. But as she ascended the warped boards, she could feel Jack's eyes on her, and she trusted he would know that his words filled her heart with courage and joy and hope that she would see him again.

Through the blur of his good eye, Ben Turner watched her disappear into the wooden jaws of the ship as he waited for the captain to appear. After a time, the first mate reappeared at the top of the gangplank. Behind him towered a commanding figure wearing a dark, tri-cornered hat trimmed with gold lace.

As the first mate pointed to Turner, the captain brushed past him and sped down the gangplank, the gold embroidered edges of his collarless frock coat flapping against his white breeches. A frown tightened his swarthy face. "Well, what is it? We are about to set sail. I don't have time for chitchat."

Turner drew the bag of coins from his pocket. "Fifty pounds here, Sir, with more to come at the end of your journey if you ensure that one of the prisoners in your midst, Misella Cross, is well taken care of and arrives, unmolested, in good health. I give you Admiral Dunning's word on it."

The captain glanced around and edged closer to Turner. "How much more?"

"One hundred pounds sterling." Turner didn't know how he'd get that much money together in a few months, but somehow he'd manage.

"Whew," the captain whistled through pursed lips. "That's ten times what she'd bring on the market in Maryland. What's in it for you?"

"Never mind why. And she becomes a free-willer as soon as you land. I'll take care of your merchant contractor here."

The captain fingered the flat, brass button at the top of his vest. "I'll need a guarantee, a promissory note."

"As will I," Turner asserted.

The captain approved. Signaling the first mate who stood watch at the top of the gangplank, he mimicked writing across the palm of his hand. The first mate vanished and soon came running down the gangplank, a carved box clutched to his chest. The captain opened it, whisked two pieces of parchment, a small bottle of ink, and a quill from within. Laying them down on the lid, his back to the wind while the mate held the box steady, he pushed up his white-laced cuff and dashed off his promise. With a flourish, he handed the paper to Turner. Turner wrote his note and held out his hand to seal the bargain. "Thank you, Captain Barclay. We will meet again." The two seamen returned to the ship.

Reaching one hand into his pocket, Turner withdrew a small portrait of Misella he had excised and framed from an advertising booklet made available to a closed circuit of the Swan's distinguished clientele. He had acquired the copy from a wealthy acquaintance without her knowledge.

The portrait was somewhat disappointing. In faded umber, it lacked the warmth of color, the animation of her living presence. But it would have to serve for now. Her face, solemn beneath the busy pompadour, was lovely, its form resembling the heart-shaped locket she wore around her neck: a proud neck, uplifting her head, her serious eyes gazing forward, her lips parted as if to speak, as if to promise him again that she would never forget him.

Unaware of the crowds bumping around him, or the icy wind that whipped tears into his eyes, Turner braced himself with one hand on his cane, watching as the ship began to grind away from the dock.

He imagined himself following Misella Cross to the New World, aboard a ship like the *Seaflower*, standing at the rail as he sailed away, the shores of England melting into the sea. "Soon," he muttered into the wind, "One day, soon."

AUTHOR'S NOTE

"Where the devil do all these bitches come from?" was a common question in eighteenth-century London where the heart of the city swarmed with prostitutes. *The Trial of Misella Cross*, inspired by two Samuel Johnson essays (1751), provides one prostitute's answer to that question.

Between 1750 and 1752, Samuel Johnson (poet, essayist, moralist, and compiler of the first English dictionary) published a series of essays called *The Rambler* on all kinds of subjects—character studies, allegories, criticism. Their object was to instruct the reader in wisdom or piety. In two of these essays Johnson takes on the persona of a prostitute, Misella, and tells her story of poverty, seduction, betrayal, and descent into prostitution. At this time, prostitution in London was rampant. Poor women, unmarried women, women who gave birth out of wedlock had very little means of survival, so many were forced into prostitution. And, of course, were blamed for the situation they were in.

Born poor himself, Samuel Johnson had great compassion for the downtrodden and for the plight of prostitutes. That he "loaned" his pen to one to tell her compelling story is remarkable since most men at that time cared little about these women whom they so willingly used and abused.

The novel re-imagines Johnson's brief essays, exploring not only Misella's descent into prostitution as he did, but also the inner workings of the prison and legal systems in eighteenth-century London. The character of the barrister Benjamin Turner is modeled after Johnson himself, although Johnson was a writer, not a lawyer. Copies of Johnson's original essays are provided in the Appendix.

In Part II of the novel, I have used some of Johnson's own words from his Misella essays: in Chapter 4 when he argues against the legalization of prostitution, and in Chapter 10 when Annie Doyle describes her days as a streetwalker.

To provide a more dramatic trial proceeding, I have taken some liberties in depicting the eighteenth-century English courtroom. At this time in England, defendants were typically denied the benefit of legal assistance, had to defend themselves in court, and had to prove their own innocence. Though some defense lawyers fought against this injustice and were in time permitted to raise points of law on behalf of the accused, they were not allowed to provide full legal representation (as Ben Turner does for Misella), nor could they address the jury directly or summarize the case before them until the nineteenth century.

I adapted Johnson's captivating essays into a novel because I wanted to tell Misella's story from a twenty-first century perspective, in a woman's voice, in a postmodern world that mirrors in many ways the eighteenth-century world in which she lived: a time of growing materialism and acquisitiveness, when the poor, the weak, the powerless—especially women—were exploited or abused, and compassion was rare.

ACKNOWLEDGEMENTS

I am grateful for the friends and family who read the manuscript in various stages and provided valuable feedback: Karen Bushaw, Debbie Carlson, Gail Duberchin, Laura Durnell, Nancy Harless, Karen Hildebrandt, Rita Mahoney, Jennifer and Caley Scott, and Patricia Whitney. I am especially indebted to Dr. Vesna Neskow and Dr. Carol Poston for their careful reading, keen insight, and helpful suggestions. With immense gratitude, I thank Maureen Stack Sappéy, editor and writing coach, for her patience, encouragement and guidance through several drafts of the manuscript.

My sincere thanks to the Norcroft Writers Retreat for Women, the Ragdale Foundation, and Our Lady of the Mississippi Abbey for providing sustenance, time and space for me to write.

Several works informed my research—first and foremost, James Boswell's *Life of Johnson* which initially sparked my interest in and love for the "Great Sage," Samuel Johnson. I have borrowed generously from Boswell's portrayal of Johnson in creating the character of Benjamin Turner. I am also indebted to Liza Picard's *Dr. Johnson's London;* M. Dorothy George's *London Life in the Eighteenth Century;* Arthur Griffiths' *The Chronicles of Newgate;* Francis Grose's *Dictionary of the Vulgar Tongue;* Anne Laurence's *Women and the Transmission of Property: Inheritance in the British Isles in the 17th Century;* Thomas Legg's *Low-Life:* David Lemmings' *Professors of the Law;* James Peller Malcolm's *Anecdotes of the Manners and Customs of London during the 18th-Century;* Robert Robson's *The Attorney in the 18th-Century;* T.

Rodenhurst's *Portsmouth Guide—1800*; G. L. Simons' *A Place for Pleasure*; and the Old Bailey's *Sessions Papers 1740-1760*. I also appreciated the kind assistance from the staff at the British Library and from Lynda Wix at the Carrow House Textile Museum in Norwich, England.

Above all, thanks to my beloved family for their unwavering support and encouragement, and especially to my husband, Hank, whose love sustains me, always.

APPENDIX

THE

RAMBLER

No. 170   Price 2d.

To be continued on Tuesdays *and* Saturdays.

Saturday, *November 2, 1751*

Confiteor; fi quid prodest delicta fateri.
Ovid.

I grant the charge; forgive the fault confess'd.

To the RAMBLER

SIR,

I A M one of those unhappy beings, from whom many, that melt with pity at the sight of all other misery, think it meritorious to withhold relief; whom the rigour of virtuous indignation dooms, often without a sufficient knowledge of their case, to suffer without complaint, and to perish without regard; and whom I myself have formerly insulted in the pride of reputation and security of innocence.

I am of a good family, but my father was burthened with more children then he could decently support. A wealthy relation condescending to make him a visit in a journey from London to his country seat, was touched with compassion of his narrow fortune, and resolved to ease him of part of his charge by taking the care of one of his children upon himself. Distress on one side and ambition on the other, were too powerful for parental fondness, and the little family passed in review before him that he might take his choice. I was then ten years old, and without knowing for what purpose I was called to my great cousin, endeavoured to recommend myself by my best courtesy, sung him my prettiest song, told the last story that I had read, and so much endeared myself by my innocence, that he immediately declared his resolution to adopt me, and to educate me with his own daughters

My parents felt the common struggles at the thought of parting, and *some natural tears they dropped, but wiped them soon.* They considered, not without that false estimation of the value of wealth which poverty long continued always produces, that I was raised to higher rank than they could give me, and to hopes of more ample fortune than they could bequeath. My mother sold some of her ornaments to dress me in such a manner as might secure me from contempt, at my first arrival, and when she dismissed me, pressed me to her bosom with an embrace which I yet feel, gave me some precepts of piety, which, however neglected, I have not forgotten, and uttered prayers for my final happiness, of which I have not yet ceased to hope, that they will at last be granted.

My sisters envied my new finery, and seemed not much to regret our separation; my father conducted me to the stage-coach with a kind of cheerful tenderness, and in a very short time, I was transported to splendid apartments, and a luxurious table, and grew familiar to show, and noise, and gaiety.

In three years my mother died, having implored a blessing on her family with her last breath. I had little opportunity to indulge a sorrow, which there was none to partake with me, and therefore, soon ceased to reflect much upon my loss. My father turned all his care upon his other children, whom some fortunate adventures and unexpected legacies enable him, when he died four years after my mother, to leave in a condition above their expectations.

I should have shared the increase of his fortune, and had a portion assigned me in his will, but my cousin assured him, that all care for me was needless, since he had resolved to place me happily in the world, and directed him to divide my share amongst my sisters.

Thus I was thrown upon dependence without any resource. Being now at an age in which young women are initiated in the world, I was no longer to be supported in my former character without considerable expence, and therefore, partly that I might not waste money, and partly, that my appearance might not draw too many compliments and assiduities, I was insensibly degraded from my equality, and enjoyed few privileges above the head servant, but that of receiving no wages.

I felt every indignity, but knew that resentment would precipitate my fall. I therefore, endeavoured to continue my importance by little services and active officiousness and for a time preserved myself from neglect, by withdrawing all pretences to competition, and studying to please rather than to shine. But my interest notwithstanding hourly declined, and my cousin's favourite maid began to exchange repartees with me, and consult me about the alterations of a cast gown.

I was now completely depressed, and though I had seen mankind enough to know the necessity of outward chearfulness, I often withdrew to my chamber to vent my grief, or turn my condition in my mind, and examine by what means I might escape from perpetual mortification. At last, my schemes and sorrows were interrupted by a sudden change of my relation's behavior, who one day took an occasion when we were left together in a room, to bid me suffer myself no longer to be depressed, but to assure the place which he always intended me to hold in the family. He assured me, that his wife's preference of her own daughters, should never hurt me; and, accompanying his professions with a purse of gold, ordered me to bespeak a rich suit at the mercer's, and to apply privately to him for money when I wanted it, and insinuate that my other friends supplied me, which he would take care to confirm.

By this stratagem, which I did not then understand he filled me with tenderness and gratitude, compelled me to repose on him as my only support, and produced a necessity of private conversation. He often appointed interviews at the house of an acquaintance, and sometimes called on me with a coach, and carried me abroad. My sense of his favour, and the desire of retaining it, disposed me to unlimited complaisance, and though I saw his kindness grow every day more fond, I did not suffer any suspicion to enter my thoughts. At last the wretch took advantage of the familiarity which he enjoyed as my relation, and the submission which he exacted as my benefactor, to complete the ruin of an orphan whom his own promises had made indigent, whom his indulgence had melted, and his authority subdued.

I know not why it should afford subject of exultation, to overpower on any terms the resolution, or surprise the caution of a girl; but of all the boasters that deck themselves in the spoils of innocence and beauty, they surely have the least pretensions to triumph, who submit to owe their success to some casual influence. They neither employ the graces of fancy, nor the force of understanding, in their attempts. They cannot please themselves with the art of their approaches, the delicacy of their adulations, the elegance of their address, or the efficacy of their eloquence, nor applaud themselves as possessed of any qualities, by which affection is attracted. They surmount no obstacles, they defeat no rivals, but attack only those who cannot resist, and are often content to possess the body without any solicitude to gain the heart.

Many of these despicable wretches does my present acquaintance with infamy and wickedness enable me to number among the heroes of debauchery. Reptiles whom their own servants would have despised, had they not been their servants, and with whom beggary would have disdained intercourse had she not been allured by the hopes of relief. Many of the beings which are now rioting in taverns or shivering in the streets, have been corrupted not by arts of gallantry which stole gradually upon the affections and laid prudence asleep, but by the fear of losing benefits which were never intended, or of incurring resentments which they could not escape; some have been frighted by masters, and some awed by guardians into ruin.

Our crime had its usual consequence, and he soon perceived that I could not long continue in his family. I was distracted at the thought of the reproach which I now believed inevitable. He comforted me however with the hope of eluding all discovery, and often upbraided me with the anxiety, which perhaps none but himself saw in my countenance, but at last mingled his assurances of protection and maintenance, with menaces of total desertion, if in the moments of perturbation I should suffer his secret to escape, or endeavor to throw on him any part of my infamy.

Thus passed my dismal hours till my retreat could no longer be delayed. It was pretended that my relations had sent for me to a distant county, and I entered upon a state which shall be described in my next letter.

I am,

SIR, &c

MISELLA

LONDON:

Printed for J. PAYNE, and J. BOUQUET, in Paternoster row, where letters for the RAMBLER are received, and the preceding numbers may be had.

Samuel Johnson

THE

RAMBLER

No. 171   Price 2d.

To be continued on Tuesdays *and* Saturdays.

Tuesday, *November 5, 1751*

Taedet coeli convexa tueri.
VIRG.

Dark is the sun, and loathsome is the day.

To the RAMBLER

SIR,

I N O W sit down to continue my narrative. I am convinced that nothing would more powerfully preserve youth from irregularity, or guard inexperience from seduction, than a just description of the condition into which the wanton plunges herself, and therefore hope that my letter may be a sufficient antidote to my example.

After the scruples, hesitation and delays which the timidity of guilt naturally produces, I was at length removed to a lodging in a distant part of the town under one of the characters which are commonly assumed upon such occasions. Here being by my circumstances condemned to solitude, I passed most of my hours in bitterness and anguish. The conversation of the people with whom I was placed, was not at all capable of engaging my attention or dispossessing the reigning ideas. The books which I carried to my retreat were such as heightened my abhorrence of myself, for I was not so far abandoned as to sink voluntarily into corruption, or endeavor to conceal from my own mind the enormity of my crime.

My relation remitted none of his fondness, but visited me so often that I was sometimes afraid lest his assiduity should expose him to suspicion. Whenever he came he found me weeping, and was therefore less delight-fully entertained than he expected. After frequent expostulations upon the unreasonableness of my sorrow, and innumerable protestations of everlast-ing regard, he at last found that I was more affected with the loss of my innocence, than the danger of my fame, and that he might not be disturbed by my remorse, began to lull my conscience with the opiates of irreligion. His arguments were, such as my course of life has since exposed me often to the necessity of hearing, vulgar, empty and fallacious, yet they at first dazzled me with their novelty, filled me with doubt and perplexity, and interrupted that peace which I began to feel from the sincerity of my repen-tance without substituting any other support. I listened a while to his impious gabble, but its influence was soon overpowered by natural reason, and early education, and the conviction which this new attempt gave me of his baseness completed my abhorrence. I have heard of barbarians, who when tempests drive ships upon their coast, decoy them to the rocks that they may plunder their lading, and have always thought that wretches thus merciless in their depredations, ought to be destroyed by a general insur-rection of all social beings; yet how light is this guilt to the crime of him, who in the agitations of remorse cuts away the anchor of piety, and when he has drawn aside credulity from the paths of virtue, hides the light of heaven which would direct her to return. I had hitherto considered him as a man equally betrayed with myself by the concurrence of temptation and opportunity; but I now saw with horror that he was contriving to perpetuate his gratification, and was desirous to fit me to his purpose by complete and radical corruption.

To escape, however, was not yet in my power. I could support the expences of my condition, only by the continuance of his favour. He provided all that was necessary, and in a few weeks congratulated me upon my escape from the danger which we had both expected with so much anxiety. I then began to remind him of his promise to restore me with my fame uninjured to the world. He promised me in general terms, that nothing should be wanting which his power could add to my happiness, but forbore to release me from my confinement. I knew how much my reception in the world, depended upon my speedy return, and was therefore outrageously impatient of his delays, which I now perceived to be only artifices of lewdness. He told me at last, with an appearance of sorrow, that all hopes of restoration to my former state, were forever precluded; that chance had discovered my secret and malice divulged it, and that nothing now remained, but to seek a retreat more private, where curiosity or hatred would never discover us.

The rage, anguish, and resentment which I felt at this account, are not to be expressed. I was in so much dread of reproach and infamy which he represented as pursuing me with full cry, that I yielded myself implicitly to his disposal, and was removed with a thousand studied precautions through by ways and dark passages, to another house, where I harassed him with perpetual solicitations for a small annuity, which might enable me to live in the country with obscurity and innocence.

This demand he for a while evaded with ardent professions, but in time, appeared offended at my importunity and distrust, and having one day endeavoured to soothe me with uncommon expressions of tenderness, when he found my discontent immoveable, left me with some inarticulate murmurs of anger. I was pleased, that he was last roused to sensibility, and expected that at his next visit, he could comply with my request. I lived with great tranquility upon the money in my hands, and was so much pleased with this pause of persecution, that I did not reflect how much his absence had exceeded the usual intervals, till I was alarmed with the danger of wanting subsistence. I then suddenly contracted my expences, but was unwilling to supplicate for assistance. Necessity, however, soon overcame my modesty, or my pride, and I applied to him by a letter, but had no answer. I writ in terms more pressing, but without effect. I then sent an agent to enquire after him, who informed me, that he had quitted his house, and was gone with his family to reside for some time upon his estate in Ireland.

However, shocked at this abrupt departure, I was yet unwilling to believe that I was wholly abandoned, and therefore, by the sale of my cloaths, I supported myself, expecting that every post would bring me relief. Thus I passed seven months, between hope and dejection, in a gradual approach to poverty and distress, emaciated with anxiety and bewildered with uncertainty. At last, my landlady, after many hints of the necessity of a new lover, took the opportunity in my absence, of searching my boxes, and missing some of my apparel, seized the remainder for rent, and led me to the door.

To remonstrate against legal cruelty was vain; to supplicate obdurate brutality was hopeless. I went away I knew not whether, and wandered about without any settled purpose, unacquainted with the usual expedients of misery, unqualified for cabinet offices, afraid to meet an eye that had ever seen me before, and hopeless of relief from those who were strangers to my former condition. Night at last came on in the mist of my distraction, and I still continued to wander till the menaces of the watch obliged me to shelter myself in a covered passage.

Next day, I procured a lodging in the backward garret of a mean house, and employed my landlady to enquire for a service. My applications were generally rejected for want of a character. At length, I was received at a drapier's, but when it was known to my mistress that I had only one gown, and that of silk, she was of opinion, that I looked like a thief, and without warning, hurried me away. I then tried to support myself by my needle, and by my landlady's recommendation, obtained a little work from a shop, and for three weeks, lived without repining; but when my punctuality had gained me so much reputation, that I was trusted to make up a head of some value, one of my fellow lodgers stole the lace, and I was obliged to fly from a prosecution.

Thus driven again into the streets, I lived upon the least that could support me, and at night, accommodated myself under penthouses as well as I could. At length, I became absolutely pennyless, and having strolled all day without sustenance, was at the close of evening accosted by an elderly man, with an invitation to a tavern. I refused him with hesitation; he seized me by the hand, and drew me into a neighbouring house, where when he saw my face pale with hunger, and my eyes swelling with tears, he spurned me with hatred and contempt, and bad me cant and whine in some other place, for his part, he would take care of his pockets.

I still continued to stand in the way, having scarcely strength to walk farther, when another soon addressed me in the same manner. When he saw the same tokens of calamity, he considered that I might be obtained at a cheap rate, and therefore, quickly made overtures, which I had no longer firmness to reject. By this man I was maintained four months in penurious wickedness, and then abandoned to my former condition from which I was delivered by another keeper.

In this abject state, I have now passed four years the drudge of extortion and the sport of drunkenness; sometimes the property of one man, and sometimes the common prey of accidental lewdness; at one time tricked up for sale by the mistress of a brothel, at another time begging in the streets to be relieved from hunger by wickedness; without any hope in the day but of finding some whom folly or excess may expose to my allurements, and without any reflections at night but those which guilt and terror impress upon me.

If those who pass their days in plenty and security, could visit, for an hour, the dismal receptacles to which the prostitute retires from her nocturnal excursions, and see the wretches that lie crowded together, mad with intemperance, ghastly with famine, nauseous with filth, and noisome with disease, it would not be easy for any degree of abhorrence to harden them against compassion, or to repress the desire which they must immediately feel to rescue such numbers of human beings from a state so dreadful.

It is said that in France they annually evacuate their streets, and ship their prostitutes and vagabonds to their colonies. If the women that infest this city had the same opportunity of escaping from their miseries, I believe very little force would be necessary; for who among them can dread any change? Many of them indeed are wholly unqualified for any but the most servile employments, and those perhaps would require the care of a magistrate to hinder them from following the same practices in another country; but others are only precluded by infamy from reformation, and would gladly be delivered on any terms from the tyranny of chance. No place but a populous city can afford opportunities for open prostitution, and where the eye of justice can attend to individuals those who cannot be made good may be restrained from mischief. For my part I should exult at the privilege of banishment, and think myself happy in any region that should restore me once again to honesty and peace.

I am,

S I R, &c

M I S E L L A